Harness the Fire

Jeffrey Poole

Jeffrey Poole's Epic Fantasy Books
Bakkian Chronicles:
The Prophecy
Insurrection
Amulet of Aria
Disneyland Debacle (short story)
Winter Wonderland (short story)

Tales of Lentari
Lost City
Something Wyverian This Way Comes
A Portal for Your Thoughts
Thoughts for a Portal
Wizard in the Woods
Close Encounters of the Magical Kind
The Hunt for Red Oskorlisk (short story)
May the Fang be With You (Pirates trilogy #1)
The Hammer is Strong with This One (Pirates #2)
These are Not the Stones You're Looking For (Pirates #3)
Blast from the Past

Dragons of Andela
Harness the Fire
Strike the Spark
Crash the Thunder

Mysteries by J.M. Poole
The Corgi Case Files Series
19 delightful cozy mystery novels featuring corgi
sleuths, Sherlock and Watson

HARNESS THE FIRE

Dragons of Andela, Book 1

JEFFREY POOLE

Secret Staircase Books

Harness the Fire
Published by Secret Staircase Books, an imprint of
Columbine Publishing Group, LLC
PO Box 416, Angel Fire, NM 87710

This book is a work of fiction. Names, characters, places and
incidents are either the product of the author's imagination or
are used fictitiously. Any resemblance to actual events or locales
or persons, living or dead, is entirely coincidental. Although the
author and publisher have made every effort to ensure the accuracy
and completeness of information contained in this book we
assume no responsibility for errors, inaccuracies, omissions, or any
inconsistency herein. Any slights of people, places or organizations
are unintentional.

Book layout and design by Secret Staircase Books
First Secret Staircase paperback edition: February, 2025
First Secret Staircase e-book edition: February, 2025

* * *

Publisher's Cataloging-in-Publication Data

Poole, Jeffrey
Harness the Fire / by Jeffrey Poole.
p. cm.
ISBN 978-1649142030 (paperback)
ISBN 978-1649142047 (e-book)

1. Andela (Fictitious location)—Fiction. 2. Epic fantasy fiction 3.
Dragons and mythical creatures—Fiction. I. Title

Dragons of Andela : Book 1.
Harness the Fire
Poole, Jeffrey, Dragons of Andela epic fantasy series.

BISAC : FICTION / Fantasy/Epic.
813/.54

For Giliane —

You are the hardest working person I have ever met. I'm so very lucky to have you by my side. Love you, babe!

Acknowledgements

It's a lot of work to create a brand-new fantasy world. New characters, new rules, new magic, and so on. What I had envisioned taking only a few months ended up taking nearly two years. But, now that the world has been created, sequels should be considerably easier! As for this book, I have a lot of people to thank. Let's get to it.

First and foremost, my wife, Giliane. She allows me to run crazy story ideas by her and she even does the same for me. Nothing beats having my wife come up to me and say, 'Grab a notebook, I have an idea!'

I'd also like to thank all my Posse members who beta read for me. I appreciate you guys taking time out of your busy schedules to help this author *not* make an ass of himself. Posse members for this book include: Jason, Elizabeth, Sharon, Wendy, Michelle, John, Diane, Caryl, Hellen, and Yuliya. Also, for our Secret Staircase Books beta readers—Sandra Anderson, Paula Webb, and Susan Gross—thank you for your amazing attention to detail. You are the best!

And, of course, I'd like to thank you, the reader. Thanks for giving this book a chance when I know there are hundreds of thousands to choose from out there. I hope you enjoy reading it as much as I did writing it. Happy reading!

J.

Table of Contents

Prologue

"What'd I miss? Anything? It figures. I step out for a bite to eat and look what happens: two destroyed mechanics. How did that happen, anyway? The least they could have done was wait for me to return."

"No one forced you to leave."

"I was hungry!"

"So was I, but you didn't see me leave, did you?

The first speaker pointed at the flurry of activity in the valley, far below.

"Catch me up. How did Thunder destroy Terra's mechanics in such a short amount of time?"

"Short?" the second speaker snorted. "You were gone for nearly an hour. I'm honestly surprised the battle isn't over."

"I wasn't gone that long, was I?"

"You were. Now shush. Something is happening. I think Terra may be trying to regroup. What do you think?"

"If Thunder tries anything, then I'd say Terra will be able to stave off this attack."

"You're mistaken. Thunder has the advantage. Terra's flank is open, unprotected. It's only a matter of time."

"Says who? Look. Terra still has their full army."

"As does Thunder, if you hadn't noticed. Plus, Thunder has their mechanics."

"You mustn't forget, Terra had mechanics, too."

"True, but they have all been destroyed, haven't they?"

The two dragons were perched high up a snowy mountainside, well out of visual range of either combatant. Having watched the fighting for the last several hours, the two companions sat, mesmerized, by the sheer brutality happening hundreds of feet below. The first speaker pointed a curved, heavily-scarred talon.

"Look, there they go again. Hey, get a load of that. Terra managed to repair one of their mechanics. It appears to be fully functional. They may lose the battle, but it certainly won't be for a lack of trying."

"Fat load of good one mechanic will do them," came the gruff response. "Terra has just the one, whereas Thunder has four."

"Five," the first speaker corrected. "I think you missed that one over there. But, it matters not. Terra will prevail."

"Will not."

"Will so. Terra is a much mightier force than Thunder."

The second speaker snorted with exasperation. "Tell that to the Terran King. He's retreating."

"Blast it all to... he's a kai, isn't he? Where's his counterpart?"

A few moments of silence passed as each observer tried valiantly to locate the Terran King's trusted companion.

"He must.have fled. How disgraceful."

"He must be there, *somewhere*," the first speaker insisted. "No one would've abandoned their kai. It's unheard of."

Just then, a huge pillar of stone shot skyward, splitting the green turf as easily as a dirk going through a sheaf of parchment. Combatants scrambled for cover as the ground trembled with anger.

"Ah. There he is. I knew he wouldn't flee."

"Liar. You just accused him of that very notion."

"Did not."

The black-clad warriors, allegiant to the Thunder King, quickly retreated from the giant earthen spike as it disappeared into the ground. After a few moments, the jagged pillar was back, appearing nearly a hundred feet away, and closer still to the Thunder King's retreating army.

"I told you Terra couldn't be defeated," the first dragon said, with a smug smile on his face.

"This battle isn't over. Behold. The Thunder King has called for his own counterpart."

Sure enough, a shadow quickly flitted over the two observers as the sleek, reptilian form of the Thunder King's dragon put in an appearance.

"What do you think? Wind? Water?"

"Smoke."

"Pah. The Thunder King would never bond with such a dragon."

"He would if he shared the same region, wouldn't he? It's not as if he has many choices, is it?"

"It'll be smoke, just you wait and see."

"Do you even know where a smoker would reside?" First Speaker asked. "Not to mention what a 'smoke' region would look like?"

"It doesn't matter," Second argued. "Smoke dragons exist, whether you believe in them or not. I've seen one."

"You have not."

"I have so."

A bolt of jagged blue electricity suddenly arced through the air and exploded at the feet of the blue-clad Terran warriors. Those who weren't flung to the ground scattered. The two observers shared a quick look with one another.

"Spark. I wouldn't have called that one."

"Nor would I," Second agreed. "We were both wrong. I didn't even know there was a human settlement on that peninsula."

"That's because there isn't."

"Obviously, there is."

"You're mistaken, as usual."

"We've never established I've been wrong in the first place."

A second bolt of lightning lit up the sky as it slammed into the valley. As before, the humans scurried to safety. The second observer nudged his companion and pointed a heavily-muscled, dark-brown foreleg at the Thunder King's black-clad army.

"What did I tell you? Thunder King, with the forces of lightning at his disposal, has turned the tide of the battle. Terra King is retreating."

The first viewer scratched at the base of one of his two spiraled horns, seemingly deep in thought. After a few moments, his bright red skull swung back and forth.

"Terra King can still pull this off."

"He hasn't got a chance, Vanze."

"Fancy a wager, Brakis?"

It was Brakis' turn to scratch an errant itch on the side of his great skull. He silently observed the battle for a few more moments before he grunted and turned to his friend. The large Fire dragon studied his comrade for a few more moments before sighing.

"Very well, Vanze. What are the stakes?"

"If Thunder prevails," Vanze began, "then … hmm. Very well. If Thunder prevails, then I will take over your hunting duties."

"For how long?" Brakis asked curiously.

"Shall we say a week?"

"Make it a fortnight."

Vanze finally nodded. "Very well. Two weeks."

"And if Terra triumphs?" Brakis suspiciously asked.

"If Terra triumphs, then you will spend an entire day…"

"I'm waiting," Brakis urged, after Vanze had trailed off.

"…on the Ice Plains."

"Terra and Ice don't mix," Brakis reminded his friend.

"Aha! You're saying you won't do it? Then I win by default."

"You did *not* win," Brakis growled. "Very well. The wager has been set. Should Terra prevail in this skirmish, then I will spend a day on the Ice Plains. In fact, I'll spend *two* days on the ice."

For the first time, Vanze frowned. "What makes you so confident all of a sudden?"

Brakis pointed at the valley. "Because Terra King is currently surrounded by Thunder King's forces."

"He doesn't look pleased," Vanze mused. "Look at all that gesturing. Do you think they're too far away to hear what they're saying?"

"If you stop your prattling, we might be able to find out."

"When's the last time you feasted?"

"If you're insinuating I'm irritable because I'm hungry," Brakis angrily snapped, "then I'll push you off this mountain myself."

Vanze clicked his fangs with amusement and promptly fell silent. Together, after the ambient noise had quieted, they were able to hear the conversation taking place between the two biped leaders far below.

"I told you," Terra King was saying, "I know nothing of what you speak."

"You're lying," Thunder King accused. "You *must* be. You have it hidden somewhere. I know it must be nearby. I'm not leaving until you tell me where I can find it."

"You're mad! I have no idea what you're talking about! I've never laid eyes on it!"

Vanze nudged Brakis on his shoulder. "He's going to do it!"

"Hush," Brakis scolded.

Thunder King promptly pulled his sword and plunged it deep into Terra King's chest.

"Telling me you don't have the one thing I've been keeping you alive for wasn't the wisest of moves, old friend. Very well. I'll find it myself."

"What's Thunder looking for?" Brakis wondered aloud.

"Who knows?" Vanze grumped. "Whatever it is, the fun is over."

"Don't you have something to be doing?"

"Like what?"

"I'm hungry."

Vanze groaned. Realizing he had indeed lost the bet, he sighed, and spread his great reptilian wings. "Fine. What are you in the mood for?"

With that, Vanze launched himself off the mountain and banked north, in search of some hapless prey.

1 – Zeira

For what felt like eons, the lone figure flew, gliding on the backs of the strongest currents high above the thick layer of cirrus clouds. These particular winds, she knew, were how most of her brethren could get from one side of their region to the other, all with minimal effort. Of course, the currents were so strong that only her kind would ever dare to use them, and that suited her just fine.

Detecting that her altitude had dropped several dozen feet, she beat her wings a few times to restore her position. The tips of her maroon-colored wings entered her peripheral vision. Automatically glancing to her right, and then quickly to her left, she verified both wings were undamaged, a habit which had been drilled into her ever since she hatched. When one relied on one's wings as their primary method of locomotion, it was prudent to ascertain they were undamaged periodically throughout the day.

A bank of fluffy white clouds appeared suddenly in her

path, giving her no time to swerve away. Bracing herself, she ended up punching her way through the billowy mists so hard that the cloud practically exploded. Tucking her wings close to her body, she gave herself a little shake, dropping like a stone. Now, several hundred feet below the currents, the flyer decided this was as good a time as any to take a look around and see if she should alter her course.

She emerged from the swirling vapors and gazed upon the landscape far below. This was nothing like her region. There was no smoke, no fires, and certainly no lava anywhere. All the scents she was accustomed to were also notably absent: hot, molten stone and oftentimes sulfur. Out here? The only thing she could smell was vegetation, and it was something she really didn't care for.

Yes, it was time to change directions. *Head north until you see grass*, her king had instructed. *Then, turn west. There, it is said, you'll find their tribes.*

Growling irritably, she noted the rich, green grasslands extending in all directions as far as the eye could see. Also visible was a fast-moving river, flowing east, which looped up and around the plain's fairly flat topography. Tiny tributaries snaked off in all directions, although they didn't extend far.

Her tired gaze shifted south. Oh, what she would do to gaze upon the comforting magma fields of her home. Her scales would shield her from the intense heat, of course, but not before thoroughly warming her. Not like the blasted cool winds in this region. How did the vegetation not freeze solid? How could anything survive out here?

Grunting, she dipped her left wing and gracefully turned to the west. The sun was still overhead, and thankfully not in her eyes. It wasn't that late in the day. Yet. How far would she have to go? When could she expect to find a tribe of *them*, the bipeds? What if … what if another of her kind had already beat her there? What she needed, she thought crossly, was to find a tribe isolated from all the others. That should make them easier to approach.

Making a decision, she dipped her right wing and turned north once more. Yes, this would do. The king had instructed everyone to turn at the first appearance of vegetation, signifying the arrival of the grasslands. But, if she were to venture farther north, then the odds were in her favor that no others would have followed. There, she decided, as she congratulated herself, was her best chance at success.

She continued north for several more hours, but then, much to her surprise, a vast blue expanse of water opened up before her. She groaned. She had reached the sea, had obviously gone too far. No tribes had ever been discovered living on that barren wasteland, so she immediately turned left. Flying high above the shore, but well within her visual abilities, she began her search again.

Was she fooling herself? Wasn't this type of mission better left for those who were more experienced? More motivated?

She snorted, sending a jet of dark smoke from each nostril. Motivation? Of that, she was certain there could be no argument. No one could be more properly motivated than she. Let any of her kind try to challenge her on *that* particular subject.

Even alone, flying by herself high in the sky, she felt the pang of embarrassment. She had been mocked for so long, by so many, that she had learned to hide her ... *condition*. It wasn't something she was proud of, nor was it anything she wanted others to know about. That, and that alone, was the primary reason she was on this quest.

Quest, Zeira repeated, giving herself a chuckle. She had never quested for anything in her life. Her mother, she had realized, had inadvertently sheltered her more than any of her siblings. Why? Because her mother knew how mercilessly her siblings had tormented her, how cruel her fellow dragons could be once they learned she ...

Zeira shuddered. Even alone, she avoided thoughts of her ailment. She could only hope that finding a suitable rider would elevate her standing among her peers. Maybe then she'd feel as though she was worthy of belonging to the highly esteemed Phoenix caste. Maybe then she would make her mother proud.

So, when Zeira had heard the urgency in her king's voice, coming from within her own mind, she knew her time had come. Her king was calling for help. Two facts stood out:

there was something wrong with the land, and it was getting worse. Somehow, and she didn't know how, there was a chance that she, Zeira, might be able to do something that could help. The king, it would seem, was summoning the kai, and since the last surviving few were so old and feeble that they could barely pick up a sword, let alone wield it, more had to be found.

Dragon riders, Zeira had excitedly thought. What could have happened which warranted a request for eligible dragons? Everyone knew how rare eligibility was, yet the king had implored his subjects to try. And the only way was to present yourself to one of the tribesmen. Only then could you tell if dragon and rider could bond with one another.

What *had* attracted her interest were the king's constant references to past deeds. Dragons and their kai, working together, were strong! They were formidable! Surely, if someone such as she were eligible for a kai, then her condition would be overlooked. *That* was worth making the journey. *That* was worth leaving the comfort of her cave for an unknown amount of time.

The Dragon King's heavily scarred visage appeared in her mind, but not telepathically—a memory. A very important, life-changing announcement. Bemused, she allowed the memory to play.

Greetings. Your attention! This news is critical to our survival.

Throughout Andela there is a disturbance, an imbalance. Humans are battling humans. Dragons are fighting other dragons. This warlike behavior threatens the very fabric of our world. If we do not act, if we choose to look the other way, we are sealing our fate and our world is doomed.

Beginning tomorrow, all available dragons will determine their eligibility to carry a kai. If you're old enough to fly, you're old enough to try. That will be all.

With the words of the Fire King fresh in her mind, Zeira scanned the passing landscape far beneath her. There were still no signs of the tribesmen, nor was there any indication they were living in the area. And to the north, only open sea. Everyone knew the tribesmen were incompatible with water, so where were they? A quick check in all directions confirmed that which she dreaded most:

I think I made a wrong turn somewhere.

She growled with frustration. Some dragon she was turning out to be. She had been given simple, basic instructions on where to go. Now, however, it was clear she was nowhere close to that destination. Should she turn around and retrace her course? Or, perhaps, she should try turning south for a while?

I have no business being here, she irritably thought. Let's recap, shall we? Sense of direction—terrible. Ability to defend myself—even worse. Chance of discovering eligibility—next to nothing. Probability of success—zero.

That one thought alone almost had her turning about, until she remembered the Fire King's face. He was worried. What in this great world could possibly trouble their fearless leader? What could intimidate a dragon of his immense size?

Movement from below caught her attention. Hopeful that she had finally located a band of the elusive tribesmen, the red dragon banked left, keeping her wing dipped low. Spiraling overhead as she slowly dropped in altitude, she grunted with surprise as the source of the commotion was revealed: a centaur.

She had never seen a live being that was not a dragon but had heard tales of these half-horse, half-tribesman creatures that ran on four legs. This one was wounded; blood flowed freely down one of the hind legs and it bellowed in pain. Dragons always came to the aid of one another, regardless of caste, and Zeira's training came back to her.

She tucked her wings and dropped like a rock, slamming into the soft grass so hard that her legs sank halfway into the ground. It must have recently rained in this place. Thankfully, there was no one here to laugh at her.

"I always thought dragons were more graceful," the centaur chuckled. His smile faded as a grimace of pain appeared on his face. "If you're here to eat me, then all I ask is that you make it quick. I'd rather be dragon fodder than dinner for *them*."

With a great effort, Zeira pulled herself free from the ground and turned to face the oncoming threat. She bared her teeth and growled a warning. The centaur hobbled forward while reaching for a bow strapped across his back. However, he was holding it like a club.

"I'm completely out of arrows," the centaur admitted. "That's never happened to me before, I'm afraid. Can you … er, *will* you do something about *that*?"

Zeira's eyes narrowed as she studied the small, unfamiliar creatures which were returning her frank stare. It was almost as if they were wondering if their larger numbers could possibly take them both on.

"What are they?" Zeira asked.

"You've never encountered slags before?"

"No. There's nothing like them back home."

The pack of snarling creatures, reassured by their greater number, advanced. Like the centaur, they were quadrupeds, but with opposable thumbs on all four legs. Most were hairless, but a few had splotchy black fur. The slags had short, snub-nosed faces which, unfortunately, had mouths full of sharp, pointed teeth. Many of the creatures had retreated into the safety of the trees after Zeira's arrival, proving themselves to be nimble climbers. Now, however, since the much larger predator hadn't attacked, they were regrouping.

"You are from Fire, are you not?" the centaur asked. "You have wings and are red. Wonderful. Be ready with your flames. If they attack again, hit them with everything you've got. Let's show these detestable creatures what it feels like to be on the receiving end of an attack."

Zeira groaned. "It's not that simple. My, er, flames are not … reliable."

The centaur studied her face for a few moments.

"Please pardon my ignorance. My knowledge of dragons is more severely limited than I had thought. I was under the impression red dragons, such as yourself, are from Fire. Dragons from Fire are supposed to be able to produce fire in some fashion. Is that not so?"

"Not this one," Zeira reluctantly admitted.

"Well, if you can't breathe or spit fire, could you at least bite them in half?"

"If you want it bitten in half, then I suggest *you* do the biting. Those slag things look like they'd taste terrible."

"Balderdash. You're easily four times the size I am. You are a threat. I, on the other hand, am nothing more than lunch, I'm afraid."

At that moment, one of the slags bunched its muscles and sprang forward. Expecting just such an attack, Zeira easily caught the monster in mid-air with one claw. She studied the snarling beast for a minute before looking north. The gentle lapping of the sea was less than fifty feet away, on her right. She bared her fangs as she brought the creature up close to her face. Thinking it was about to be eaten, the slag, which resembled nothing more than a hairy hobgoblin, whined piteously. Growing angry, Zeira tossed the slag into the air, and when the timing was right, lashed out with her tail, knocking the slag nearly a hundred feet into the water. The surface of the sea began frothing angrily. Curious, she and her new centaur friend studied the choppy waves. Of the slag, nothing remained.

Zeira turned to her strange friend and pointed back at the water. "I assume there's something in the sea?"

"What *isn't* in the sea?" the centaur dryly returned.

Zeira pointed at the water and faced the rest of the pack. "Come after me again and, so help me, the rest of you will join him."

"The slags do not understand speech," the centaur quipped, as he sidled closer to Zeira's side. "They are never … "

A few members of the pack howled, and fled in different directions.

"…going to do what you ask. Hmm. I clearly need to return to my studies."

"Are you going to be all right?"

"I could ask the same about you," the centaur returned. After a few moments, he bowed. "Agrius, at your service."

"Oh. Uh, Zeira."

"Well, Zeira, may I ask you a personal question?"

Zeira held her breath, knowing full well what was coming.

"If you must."

"What would prevent a Fire dragon from using her own fire, especially when their very life is threatened? You may be the first Fire dragon I have ever met, but some things are still assumed to be correct."

"And what if I'm keeping it to myself because it is a sensitive topic?" Zeira challenged.

Agrius' face fell. "My humblest of apologies. I should have known something was amiss. I do hope you can forgive me."

"It isn't something I like talking about," Zeira began. "I would need to eat something ... displeasing. It's part of the reason I'm here. I'm searching for tribesmen. Do you know where I can find some?"

Agrius gasped. "You seek a kai!"

"Is it that obvious?"

"You're no warrior," Agrius began, as though he had been tasked with determining her motivations. "Your talons are shiny and blemish-free, which suggests you have not participated in any battles."

Zeira was silent as she studied her own claws, as if seeing them for the first time.

"In addition, you claim you are seeking tribesmen, yet there are none to be found in these parts. That suggests you are more than likely lost, and that's a trait I have never applied to a dragon before."

Zeira harrumphed angrily to herself.

"Therefore, it becomes obvious to me that you have an ulterior motive," Agrius cheerfully continued. "Everyone knows two heads are better than one. You obviously seek a kai. How am I doing?"

"Painfully well," the dragon reluctantly admitted. "Why are you ... no, wait. *What* are you?"

"My dear fellow, have you never encountered a centaur before?"

"I beg your pardon! I am no *drakken*!"

"Drakkaina! Oh, my sincerest apologies once again, dear lady! Yes, I hear it now." Agrius gave a mighty sigh. He glanced back at his wounded leg and then up at her. "As you have no doubt deduced for yourself, you're not catching me at my best."

"You're injured."

"A bite on the leg," Agrius acknowledged.

"What will happen now?"

"I will implore you to be on your way. I don't want you to be here when it happens."

"When *what* happens?" Zeira curiously asked.

"I'm done for. I acknowledge and accept that. I'm the one who ventured off, following some silly insect because I thought it might have been rare. Before I knew it, I was miles away from my herd, alone, and confronted by slags. They have been driven away, yes, but it's only a matter of time before something else takes their place. I am wounded. There will be no escape for me."

Zeira frowned. "I will not abandon you. Surely, we can get word to others of your kind. They will help."

"They would if they knew of my predicament. If you go to tell them, I will be unprotected and therefore attacked. If you don't go, then my leg will become infected, and I will still die. So, I will choose the nature of my passing. I choose the quicker death."

Zeira smiled as an idea formed. "Then, allow me!"

She lunged forward, eliciting a squawk of surprise from Agrius.

* * *

"This is not what I had in mind."

"I know."

"Will you just fly me over the water and let go? That'll be the quickest yet, unless you expect me to expire from fright. Let's face it, I'm not that far off."

"You don't sound like you're afraid," Zeira exclaimed, as she struggled to stay aloft. Holding Agrius in her claws was easily the heaviest weight she had ever carried while flying. Perhaps this wasn't her wisest decision? "And if you don't stop squirming, I may end up doing exactly that."

"Centaurs were never meant to fly!" Agrius protested, as

he peeked through his hands. "Oh, mages be damned, go higher! Can you not see that? Go higher!"

"It's just a tree. I can avoid hitting a tree."

"Then prove it!" Agrius practically screamed. "You're headed right for it!"

Deliberately waiting until the last moment, Zeira sharply banked right and, flying almost vertically, with one wing pointed toward the ground and the other straight up in the sky, she easily avoided the tree.

"Do that again and I'll personally soil your scales," Agrius vowed. "That is, if I haven't already."

"That's gratitude for you. Now, where are we going?"

"Sunset was an hour ago. It's too dark to see anything."

"Not for me. We're headed southwest. In the distance, there are two grassy knolls. The one on the left is slightly smaller than the one on the right. Does that help?"

"The Mounds of Isabeau! Thank the gods! My home is close. The herd typically grazes on the southern side of the right mound."

"Grazes? You feed like pack animals?"

"You can see that we centaurs are derived from tribesmen and horses, can you not?"

"Horses? What are those?"

"My, my, you *have* led a sheltered life, haven't you?"

"Well, I've never dropped a centaur from this height before," Zeira was quick to point out. "I'm always eager to try new things."

"Your point is taken. Can you see my herd yet?"

"I don't see any centaurs," Zeira admitted.

"Blast. They wouldn't have moved the …"

"They're here," Zeira interrupted. "I just don't see them."

"Then, how do you know?"

"I can smell more of your kind."

"What's that supposed to mean?"

"You have a very distinctive scent," the dragon calmly explained, as she drifted lower to the ground. "That same scent is heavily saturated in this area."

"Well, if you don't see my herd, then what *can* you see?"

"More knolls, but smaller, rounded."

"Our lodges! No wonder you haven't been able to see anyone. It's probably the middle of the night. We centaurs are *not* nocturnal beings. Do you see a, er, knoll larger than the rest, but more rounded?"

"I see a circular hill much larger than the others, but nowhere near the size of the two we just flew by."

"That's our infirmary. You can place me there. I only hope our healer, Barrus, is awake."

"Well, *someone* is awake."

"How can you tell?"

"I'm being shot at."

"What?"

"Arrows are being fired at me."

"But … can't they see that I'm here?"

"Evidently not."

"Are you injured?"

"No mere arrow can pierce a dragon's scale."

"Thank the fates."

"They're your people, Agrius. Can't you make them stop?"

"Set me down. Hurry!"

Zeira touched down just outside the enormous, domed lodge. She could see another centaur peering angrily out at her from within the darkened interior. An arrow pinged loudly as it made contact with the back of her head.

"Would you all stop that?" Agrius bellowed. "Mages be damned! Zeira here saved my life! Is this any way to repay her?"

The pinging arrows immediately ceased. After a few moments, a figure materialized in front of her, looking up at her with an amazed expression.

"A dragon! What … Agrius? Explain yourself! Why would there be … are you injured? Did the dragon attack you? I knew it! Sound the alarm! I always said …"

There was an audible *clang*, as if something metallic struck something *else* that was metallic.

"Did you just do what I think you did?"

"The *dragon* carried *me* here, Barrus!" Agrius snapped. "What else do you think she's doing here?"

"Attacking us, what else?" Barrus hotly returned. He stepped out from within the infirmary and scratched his graying head. "Of all that's good and sacred, that's a big one."

"Big?" Zeira snorted, overhearing. "I am the smallest Phoenix I know."

"You do *not* look like a phoenix," another centaur argued, appearing from behind Barrus. This one, Zeira noted, was much younger and his skin was darker. An apprentice to the healer? "The phoenix is feathered. You're scaled."

"This is a drakkaina," Agrius slowly explained. "She came to my aid when an entire pack of slags were ready to tear me apart."

"I see blood," Barrus announced, pointing at Agrius' injured leg. "You've been bitten?"

Agrius pointed at the large dragon sitting companionably on her haunches. "That's why she carried me back. I couldn't have made the journey home on my own."

Half a dozen centaurs approached, each holding a torch. Several of Agrius' kinsmen held their torches aloft and gawked at Zeira.

"She's not Terran!" one of them protested.

"Your powers of observation do you credit," Agrius dryly observed. "Nay, she is not from Terra. This is Zeira, and she's a Phoenix drakkaina, from Fire."

"Blaze," Zeira corrected. "It's what we call our home."

"How long have you been away from your home region?" Barrus asked, concerned. "As you no doubt know, no living thing can exist outside their home region longer than a fortnight. Have you felt any effects of the Fade yet?"

"I've only been gone one day," Zeira assured her new friends. "It shouldn't affect me that quickly, should it?"

Barrus shrugged. "Well, possibly. How often have you made these journeys? I only ask because Fire, er, Blaze, is far to the south, among the Durkham Mountains. You have been traveling for only a day and yet you originated in these mountains?"

Zeira shrugged. "Traveling velocity increases when you're not concerned with topography."

"What are you doing here?" one centaur asked.

"She's searching for tribesmen," Agrius cheerfully answered.

"Tribesmen?" Barrus incredulously repeated. "There are none in these parts, I assure you. The closest village would be ... hmm, at least thirty leagues south of here."

"Southwest," Agrius softly corrected.

"Whatever. However you look at it, you would seem to be in the wrong place, dragon."

Agrius frowned. "Her name is Zeira, Barrus. She has a name, just like you."

Barrus bowed low. "My apologies, Zeira. You are the first dragon I have ever met and conversed with."

"Are Terran dragons that, er, unfriendly?" Zeira hesitantly asked.

"Have you met many?" Barrus challenged.

"I've never seen a Terran," Zeira admitted.

An older centaur appeared, flanked by four others holding bows notched with arrows. The newcomer looked at Agrius and then down at his leg. He then turned to Zeira and scowled.

"Did you do that, dragon?"

"If I bit his leg," Zeira haughtily informed them, "then he wouldn't *have* that leg. My jaws are much too large to make that bite. And, just to let you know, those arrows would be ineffective against me."

Agrius approached the lead centaur and bowed. "Korem. Listen to me when I tell you Zeira did not do this to me. We were attacked by a pack of slags."

"Since when is a dragon threatened by mere slags?" Korem wanted to know. "She could have dispatched them all without trying that hard."

Agrius raised a hand. "Umm, hello? My new friend wasn't worried about herself, but about me. And did you hear what she said? Someone was shooting at her. Someone was shooting at *me*! I can only assume it was you lot. You should be ashamed of yourselves."

"It is *you two* who should be counting themselves lucky," one of Korem's four guards countered. "Had we wanted to inflict damage, then we would have."

A low growl appeared in Zeira's throat which was loud enough to cause everyone, including Agrius, to take a few steps back. Zeira turned angrily to her new friend.

"These are your people, but they aren't mine. By your leave, I will go. To stay any longer will put *their* health at risk."

A commotion began somewhere behind them. Turning to see what was headed their way this time, Zeira was startled to see that everyone, including Korem, had suddenly dropped to one knee. Angrily pushing his way through the onlookers, the newcomer turned to face the dragon. This centaur, Zeira noted, was younger than Agrius.

"Please, allow me to extend my apologies," the young centaur began, throwing a dark look at Korem and his entourage. "You have saved the life of one of our own. For that, I am ... er, I mean, *we* are grateful. Aren't we, Korem."

Zeira blinked with amusement. It may have sounded like a question, but this newcomer wasn't expecting an answer. Looking over at Korem, the dragon could see that the elder centaur was properly chastened, refusing to take his eyes off the ground.

"Lord Aldebrand," Agrius exclaimed, bowing low. "My eternal thanks for your swift intervention. I'm afraid we have yet to extend any amount of kindness to Zeira here and it shames me."

Royalty. Zeira was impressed. This one was young, so more than likely not a king. Perhaps a prince?

"I have never been this close to a dragon before," Lord Aldebrand confessed, as he looked up at her with wide, wondering eyes. "What are you doing here?"

Zeira pointed at Agrius. "For your information, I was returning ..."

"Oh, I don't mean him," the young prince interrupted, with a smile. "I mean, what are you doing so far away from your home region? You are red, which makes you a Fire dragon. You're from Fire, aren't you?"

"Blaze," Zeira corrected, "and yes, I am."

"What are you doing here?" Lord Aldebrand pressed. "Are you searching for someone?"

"I am on a mission," Zeira answered, "by order of the

King. Er, *my* king."

"Wonderful!" Lord Aldebrand exclaimed, clapping his hands. "I pledge my assistance. I'm so tired of hearing about how we shoot first and ask questions later. I'd much rather be helping people. But first, I must know. How quickly did you dispatch those malodorous slags? It was an entire pack, was it not?"

Zeira suppressed a chuckle. It sounded as though the centaur prince was disappointed; he hadn't been there to confront the vicious creatures himself. Putting his eagerness aside, Zeira decided he was probably just as inexperienced with the real world as she.

"It was an entire pack, aye," Agrius confirmed.

"The nearest pack of slags is nearly four hours away," Korem pointed out. "What were you following this time, Agrius? A cloud? Bird?"

"Butterfly," Agrius sheepishly admitted. "If not for my new dragon friend, I would have been done for. I was hoping we could show her some kindness."

"How can we help?" Lord Aldebrand asked, throwing a frown in Korem's direction.

"Tribesmen."

"Bipeds? There are none around here."

"I know this, Your Highness," Agrius began. "You know this. However, as you can see, she's not from around here, which means *she* doesn't know this. I know those infernal bipeds are prone to wandering, and I'm hoping one of our scouts might have picked up a trail or two?"

"There's been some activity to the west," Lord Aldebrand admitted. "Perhaps that is what the fuss is over?"

"Do we know the nature of this activity?" Agrius asked.

"No. We have dispatched scouts, but we don't expect them back any time soon."

"How far is it?" Zeira sounded eager. "Distances are no matter for a dragon."

"At least a hundred leagues," the young centaur reported. "You will rest here for the night."

Muted conversations immediately erupted from all sides. Lord Aldebrand's frown returned and he stomped his front hooves several times.

"Zeira, get some rest. You have a long way to go tomorrow. And don't worry, nothing will bother you as you rest. In fact, Korem and his followers will make certain of it."

* * *

"You'll want to keep the coastline in sight as you head west."

"They'll be near the water?"

Agrius nodded. "Oh, yes. Tribesmen are seldom found away from a source of water. Many of the inlets are freshwater, so the number of suitable locales are many."

"Thank you for your help."

"No, Zeira, it is *I* who should be thankful. Go. Be safe."

"How will I know if I've found the right area?" Zeira wondered. "What if I go too far? What am I looking for?"

"Just follow the coast. When the sea becomes a narrow channel separating land from ice, you'll know you're there."

Agrius reverently placed a hand on her foreleg.

"Thank you, my friend. Safe journeys. I am in your debt."

Nodding, Zeira spread her wings and leapt into the air. Airborne, she pointed her nose west and ascended until she felt the currents take hold, adjusting her wings until she was flying due west. She focused on the horizon and hoped the centaurs had given her accurate information.

Nearly two hours later, Zeira's senses came fully awake. Puzzled, she checked the skies, fully expecting to see another dragon, but there was nothing else in the air for many leagues in any direction. What, then, had tripped her senses?

Her eyes were drawn down to the water. There, in the distance, she saw the great ice sheets of the north venturing closer and closer to land. Her eyes widened as she recalled what Agrius had said: 'When the sea becomes a narrow channel separating land from ice, you'll know you're there.' Did this mean her search was finally over?

Tucking her wings, she descended. Once the ground was only a few hundred feet away, her senses pinged again. There was something nearby, something that heightened her draconian senses. Were tribesmen in the area? Could she have lucked out and found a kai already? In all the history of her kind, a dragon and her rider had never found each other as quickly as this. Where was the meditation to see if she was compatible? If a suitable biped was nearby, why couldn't she sense their presence?

Her nostrils flared. A strange, unknown scent materialized, but not from below. It came from somewhere close by. Her gaze shifted to the massive sheet of ice less than half a league away. Was frozen water capable of smelling like that?

Opening her senses, she waited for her coursing thoughts to settle. Maintaining an altitude of several hundred feet, she slowly circled as she tried to pinpoint where her senses were pulling her. *There!* Zeira could see a disturbance in the water. Another dragon? An unknown water creature? Perhaps … perhaps it was the tribesmen she had been so desperately seeking?

Flying overhead, Zeira studied the scene. An object had broken the surface of the water and was now zig-zagging across the sea, creating huge ripples of water that eventually washed up on shore. Try as she might, Zeira couldn't identify the object. Her senses were tingling like crazy, so that could only mean whatever *it* was, she was able to bond with it. But, what could it be?

Zeira landed on the closest shore and approached the water's edge. Whatever the nature of the creature, it apparently wasn't as fascinated with her as she was with it. Perhaps it was some type of predator, trying to lure her into the water?

Zeira snorted with disgust. She didn't care *what* kind of creature it was. Nothing in the great realm of Andela could possibly persuade her to enter the water. Hadn't her mother warned her against this very thing? Hadn't she explained that several of her fellow Phoenix dragons had lost their lives when coming into contact with the forbidden region?

It simply wasn't worth it.

Right about then, the noises in the water stopped. Zeira scanned the surface of the sea, alarmed. The object was back, and this time, it appeared to be angling straight toward her!

A hundred feet from shore, the disturbance paused, as

if it was undecided. Then, as the waves and ripples subsided, Zeira got her first look at what was making waves in the water. It was a live creature after all!

A dark blue neck, topped with a sleek, narrow skull, rose gracefully out of the water. Two jet-black eyes stared at her for a few moments before the neck was withdrawn. A small circle of rapidly dissipating bubbles was the only sign the strange creature had ever been there.

A few moments later, the head reappeared farther away. The head rotated until it was looking straight at Zeira. Those black eyes blinked a few times before disappearing underwater yet again. Zeira waited. Sure enough, the neck was back, and it was farther, still.

Realization dawned. It wanted her to follow!

Chapter 2 – Andela

For once in her life, she didn't think about the consequences. Pushing aside her mother's warnings about the open water, she leapt up and snapped her wings open, heading away from shore in an attempt to overtake the strange creature. However, try as she might, the creature was pulling away, swimming faster than she was flying. How was that even possible?

She beat her wings and tucked her legs close to her body to increase her velocity. Even so, the only thing she could see in the water was a trail of bubbles and an ever-increasing wave of ripples. Growling with frustration, she found she was still no match for the being in the water. What was it? How could it swim so fast?

Suddenly, Zeira noticed she was gaining on her adversary. Yes! She *knew* something had to be amiss. A swimmer just couldn't possibly move faster than … no. No! It couldn't be!

It would appear that the swimmer had deliberately slowed, to allow her to catch up. Once Zeira passed overhead, however, she was surprised to see that her *prey* hadn't moved. In fact, the head was still there, in the sea, bobbing up and down.

Flying overhead, and maintaining an altitude of several hundred feet, Zeira curiously looked down at the aquatic creature and tilted her head. Had it injured itself? Was it in distress?

"Are you well?" Zeira called down. "If you're all right, I'll be on my way."

The head rose, neck bent backward so that it was staring straight up at her. Then, the creature wriggled with delight, looking out, at the open sea, then back at Zeira.

"Can you understand me? Do you *want* me to chase you?"

It continued to stare, imploring. As Zeira debated what to do, a second head appeared, and then a third. As one, all three stared up at her with wide, unblinking eyes. What harm could come of another round? Yes, she might have detested the water, but as long as she kept her distance from the surface, what danger could befall her?

"Very well. After you."

Just like that, all three heads dipped below the surface and now-wider trail of bubbles took off. Zeira tucked her wings and allowed her much larger mass to propel her downward. Fifty feet above the surface, her wings opened and she zipped forward. Remembering a trick her mother had taught her when she was a hatchling, she regulated her breathing and concentrated on the sound of her wings.

She was gaining!

Her mother had been right! If you were able to ... what's this? Now *she* was falling behind. How? Why?

Growling, she channeled more power into her wings and ordered herself to keep her head and tail level with the horizon, with only minor adjustments here and there as needed. However, her concentration had broken, and she watched with dismay as her playmates increased their lead.

Growing frustrated, she was about to give up and rise back above the solitude in the clouds, when it dawned on her: the creatures in the water were probably just as curious about her as she was with them! So, how could she use that to her advantage?

The answer to that was easy enough. She might not have been the fastest flyer, but she could hold her own with her feats of aerobatics. Tucking a wing, she immediately rolled until she was on her back, flying upside down. Looking up (down), she glanced at the water's surface and saw that one of the swimmers was now watching her.

Executing a double-barrel roll, she kept an eye on the water. Now, all three were there, interested in her movements.

Deciding to show-off a little, she folded both wings flat against her back, dropped her tail low, and opened her tail wing, which she typically used as a rudder. It flipped her, head over tail, until she was flying right-side up again.

All three swimmers were staring straight up.

She had their attention now.

Zeira dropped her tail and extended her tail wing, not realizing she'd dropped much closer to the surface. Her tail wing dipped into the water, snapping her to a sudden stop, and she executed a spectacular belly flop.

Sputtering wildly, eyes wide with fright, Zeira tried to launch herself but her wings couldn't find purchase. She let out a panicked roar and tried again. Now, her water-logged wings flapped impotently against her back.

Just then, something wrapped around one of her hind legs. It was thick, incredibly strong, and powerful. Nearing panic, she tried to pry the thing off her, but it held on. A second *tentacle* attached itself to her left forearm. Another appeared on her right. One of the sleek narrow heads popped up next to her shoulder.

With a start, she realized her three admirers must be helping her. As if they'd attached a tether to her, she began to glide purposefully through the water. Exhausted, Zeira went slack and allowed herself to be guided back to shore. Once she felt solid ground beneath her feet, she shakily pulled herself from the water and collapsed on the shore.

Nearly fifteen minutes passed while she tried valiantly to regain her breath. Once the wheezing stopped, Zeira finally looked at the water, half-expecting to find several sets of eyes staring back at her. But her rescuers had long departed. What they were, and why they had come to her aid, she'd probably never know.

"That's too bad," Zeira softly muttered. "I think I was winning."

Before you started showing off, you mean.

Zeira froze, mid-step. Her head angled up and she checked the sky. No, she was still alone.

Who's there?

Really, Z? Has it been that long?

Rizzen?

Who else?

What do you want, Rizzen?

Am I not allowed to talk to my friend?

You know full well I'm on a mission. You are, too.

I was.

You found one? You found tribesmen? Do you have your kai?

I found some tribesmen, aye.

And?

I'm not eligible, Z. Apparently, I lack the ability to bond with another living creature. No Kai for me.

I'm sorry, Rizzen. I know how much you wanted to help.

As much as you, Z. Have you had any luck?

I, er, …

You're not eligible, either?

I … don't know. I haven't found any tribesmen, so I don't know if I can make the bond.

What do you mean? You headed north, didn't you? North of the valley?

No game, no water, and certainly no trace of any tribesmen. Wait, north of the what?

I told you to head north, for no more than three or four hours. You'll find a huge basin, with a large lake to the west. There are no fewer than three tribes there right now. I flew over them less than two hours ago.

Hmm.

You didn't follow directions, did you? Where are you now?

Umm …

You don't know, do you? I've always said you have the worst sense of direction. How could you have missed it? All you had to do was head north.

I did fly north.

Sure you did. For how long?
Z, for how long?
Perhaps six or seven hours.
Six or seven hours? You made it all the way to the sea, didn't you?
I did, only …
Out with it. What happened? Where are you?

She explained to Rizzen and once her exasperated friend's presence faded from her mind, Zeira groaned, rose to her feet, and shook herself off. She basked in the bright sunshine for a while to finish drying her wings. Once airborne, she circled the area in widening loops, just to verify there weren't any of the small bipeds nearby. Sighing, she pumped her wings and returned to the safety of the clouds.

Flying west for nearly three hours straight brought her significantly closer to the great ice sheets of the north than she had ever been. What had Agrius said? When the sea narrows so much that the land and the ice are within walking distance of one another? Did that mean she had finally arrived?

Emerging through the thin, wispy clouds, Zeira's vision cleared. Yes, this *had* to be what Agrius had been talking about, but much to her chagrin, there were no traces of the elusive tribesmen on the open steppe below. Her eyes drifted to the nearby ice fields and she grimaced. Tribesmen wouldn't willingly live out on the ice, would they? If that was the reason she couldn't find them, she may as well turn about now. Tribesmen, like dragons, couldn't live on more than one region. And one couldn't get more opposite of Fire than Ice. No tribesmen, living on Ice, would be able to bond with a dragon from Fire. Er, Blaze.

Sighing, she returned her attention to the land below her. This *had* to be where Agrius wanted her to search. Landing in the soft grass, Zeira inspected the surrounding environment. A gentle breeze was blowing from the west, causing the grass to gently sway in the wind. She sniffed the air, but it only confirmed what her eyes were telling her: there was nothing here.

Turning about, she was about ready to cast her wings and take off when she hesitated. Something had just tickled her wyverian senses in the same way a powerful aromatic could tickle her nose. Zeira looked around the open grassland a second time. Ripples of waving grass ahead, lapping water behind her, and the shores of the huge northern ice floes, nearly two leagues away.

However, she felt a gentle pull to her left, to the east. Glancing that way, she gasped with surprise as the strange, tickling sensation returned. Something was out there!

Folding her wings flat against her back, Zeira headed back the way she had originally come, except this time, she was on land. She hadn't made it more than twenty steps before the tingling intensified, and her nose flared. Her supposition about the lack of tribesmen was correct. The distinct scent was dragon! The question was, *where*? She spotted nothing in the sky, nothing on the vast grassland.

If there was a dragon out there, he — or she — was doing a very commendable job of hiding. Closing her eyes, Zeira allowed herself to be directed by her senses. She took tentative steps in each direction, but the sensation vanished, as if someone had turned off a light.

Sighing, and still puzzled about what had pinged her senses, Zeira took a step backward, intent on retracing her steps to see if she could make the curious sensations return. She only made it a few feet before something bit the underside of her right foreleg. She snatched the leg upward and checked. No bites. And the pain had vanished. What was going on?

She placed her leg back on the ground, but almost immediately yanked it back up. The sensation returned, more powerful than before. There was something definitely amiss.

Then, her vision wavered. Zeira blinked and shook her head. No, it wasn't her vision, but the very air itself, as if giant heat waves, which she was quite familiar with back on Blaze, were rising up from the ground. After a few moments, a large section of the gently rolling grass winked out, replaced with a concave scar on the ground. Zeira used a talon to scratch at the surface. Bits of stone flaked off and tumbled down the sloping sides of this scar.

Zeira's eyes widened. It was a crater. What was the purpose of concealing it? Her home region of Blaze had plenty of craters formed by magma eruptions. This one, though, was nowhere close to the size of those. Whatever caused this one must have been small, Zeira decided.

Still, it was at least a hundred feet across. Something had slammed into the ground to create this crater.

Carefully picking her way down the rim of the crater, she paused as she stepped into the direct center of the depression. There was no vegetation here. No grass, no trees, and no signs of life anywhere, especially that of tribesmen. As she stared at the ground beneath her feet, she sensed a difference in the texture of the stones. Sinking a talon into the loose pebbles, she idly toyed with the rocks for a few moments until she hit something that didn't move; something large.

Compelled in a way she couldn't explain, she began to dig frantically. The object was a huge slab of ice. This chunk of frozen seawater must have somehow broken off from the nearby glacier and flown through the air to …

Flown through the air? That couldn't be right. How could a piece of ice, easily three times the size she was, have created a crater as small as this one? Based on the object she had unearthed, this crater should have been ten times the size it was now. Besides, why hadn't the block of ice shattered upon impact?

Unknown forces must be at work here, Zeira decided as she continued to work.

A few moments later, after sweeping a final layer of stones off the top of the ice, her eyes widened with shock. There was something there, entombed within the ice. It almost looked as if …

Zeira stifled a curse and snapped her head back. A pair of green reptilian eyes were staring—unblinking—back at her. She had found a dragon —frozen in the ice!

Curious to see if the dragon might be from Blaze, she fervently cleared the dirt and stones from around the slab of ice. Wait, was that her imagination or had she detected movement from the dragon? Could it possibly be alive? From the looks of things, this particular dragon had either fallen asleep, with his wings extended, as though he needed to beat a hasty retreat, or else … or else, *someone* had done that to him. Or her. She couldn't tell if the poor dragon was male or female. The only thing on her mind was what she could do to help the poor imprisoned dragon.

The first, obvious response was to melt the ice. However, all she had to do was think about producing flames and her breath would come in gasps and she'd inevitably start hyperventilating. It wasn't a pleasant sensation. Besides, even if she wanted to … to … help in that manner, her digestive system would most certainly not cooperate. Perhaps, if she found a bug or two, she might … what in the world was she thinking? Was she actually considering putting her insides through that turmoil again?

Shuddering, Zeira returned to her work. It took nearly a full hour of relentless digging to completely uncover the huge slab. Plus … she broke a talon. Not bad, mind you, but enough to make her growl every time she looked at her left claw. Phoenix dragons were never designed to dig, that was for certain. Now that the chunk of ice was uncovered, Zeira got her first look at the dragon it concealed.

It was a pale color, although distorted by the ice. It wasn't Terran, and it certainly wasn't from Blaze. Water, perhaps? After all, it *was* frozen.

She picked at the slab of ice and briefly wondered if she could find a large boulder with which to help free the strange dragon. Granted, there was nothing but grass in all areas, crater excluded, of course. Then again, the shoreline was literally a leap away. The chances of finding a suitable tool were definitely in her favor.

The moment Zeira returned to the top of the crater, she paused. A new scent had manifested, and unfortunately, there was accompanying audio: the sounds of scurrying, from hundreds of tiny feet. Zeira held her breath and became as still as a statue. After all, the best method to determine where a sound was coming from was to eliminate as many other noises as she could.

Her head swiveled right. Whatever was approaching was doing so from the south. Her eyes opened and she scanned the horizon. There! She could see stalks of grass moving from side to side, as though something was marching through them. Whatever was headed her way was small. Incredibly small, if it was no taller than the blades of grass, which barely reached past the first knuckle of her claws. Another look south had her frowning. Yes, they may be small, but there must be hundreds of them; thousands! The entire meadow was crawling with them, seeing how the gentle breeze was now gone, and every blade of grass was swaying.

Her instincts were warning her that the situation had turned bleak. Whatever these things were, they clearly didn't fear dragons, so it was time to depart. However, her eyes fell on the exposed chunk of ice, and the helpless dragon trapped within, and she hesitated. Could whatever was headed their way have the ability to chew through ice and potentially put that dragon in danger?

Zeira sighed. She couldn't risk it. There was only one way she was going to be able to successfully deal with these things, and that was with fire. Zeira immediately turned tail and ran to the water's edge. There *had* to be something here she could eat which would upset her stomach, but what?

Rocks, Zeira decided. Stones. Insects typically lived under them, so the sooner she found some larger boulders, the better. However, after turning over the fifth stone on shore, she reluctantly had to admit that perhaps living next to water wasn't in the insects best interest? There was nothing to be found.

The crater! Of course! Beneath the grass was layers of dirt and stone. All she had to do was dig. Zeira hurried back up to the crater's rim, eyed the swaying movement in the grass that was edging ever closer, and hurried down to stand next to the immobile dragon. Eyeing her chipped talon and letting out an exasperated growl, she began to dig again. This time, there was no finesse involved. Zeira tore into the earth, looking for something, *anything*, she could eat that would, unfortunately, upset her stomach.

A boulder half the size of her head was uncovered. Noticing the clicks and chitters of whatever was approaching was growing steadily louder, Zeira groaned, hooked a talon under the stone, and gave it an expert flip. The boulder flew out of the crater and rolled noisily away. So, had there been anything living under the rock which might be used to help her out of this predicament?

No worms, no worms, no worms.

A wriggling mass of green, crawling over a large, pulsating white lump, caught her eye. A nest of pleaters had been disturbed, and they were now headed in all directions. They might not have been her most disliked type of bug, but they were close enough. Just the sight of those fat, slimy larvae writhing on the ground was enough to make her insides revolt. And, just like that, her stomach recoiled in disgust. If she wanted fire, all she had to do was put a few of those things in her mouth.

Before she could talk herself out of it, Zeira snatched the white, papery egg sac, dripping with some yet-to-be-identified goo, and popped it in her mouth. Almost immediately, she could feel the dozen or so pleaters that had been crawling around the egg sac start dropping onto her tongue. Closing her eyes, and ordering herself *not* to be sick, she chewed.

Her digestive system, as expected, immediately balked at the contents. Loud rumblings began and her abdomen rippled with unease. Zeira eyed the approaching horde and, just as the first wave of small red insects emerged from the thick grass, faced the opposite direction. A sharp pain swept through her abdomen and she gasped at the unexpected pain. Unfortunately, it was now only a matter of time.

Zeira heard the gurgling her body was making, felt her abdomen growing as gas was produced, and closed her eyes. She whipped her tail out of the way and then made sure she was *pointed* in the right direction. She didn't have long to wait.

The blast decimated everything behind her, extending backwards for nearly a hundred feet while simultaneously shoving her forward. Such was the force of the blast that she was pushed over the rim of the crater and down onto the center, coming nose-to-nose with the prone form of the strange dragon encased in ice. Once she was sure the flames were gone, she risked a look behind her.

For once, she was pleased the strength of her ... *digestive system* was as powerful as it was. The tiny red insects, whatever they were, had been obliterated. Then again, so had a huge swath of grass. The scorched formerly-green blades crumbled to ash and fluttered away.

With the threat eliminated, Zeira returned to the chunk of ice. How, then, should she go about rescuing her fellow dragon? Could she risk another blast from her ... posterior? Would it melt only the ice and not the dragon who lay within?

The green eyes seemed to follow her as she slowly paced around the ice. Without having to worry about whatever damage those red bugs could make, perhaps she could take the time to carefully chisel him out of his ice prison? Perhaps she could find a suitable boulder and smash her way through the ice. That would work, wouldn't it?

Zeira reversed direction and resumed pacing. What if ... why did it look as though the eyes were still following her? Could it be that the dragon was conscious within the ice? Could it actually be alive?

Wanting to test her supposition, she dropped to the ground, making herself as flat as possible. Yes! Those eyes were watching her! They had swiveled in their sockets and tracked her down to the ground. The dragon was most definitely alive. However, that could only mean it was trapped. She had to help!

"How do I get you out of there?" Zeira mused, as she resumed her pacing. "I don't suppose you have any ideas, do you?"

The green eyes shifted up, looking above and behind her. Turning, Zeira inspected the damage her ... *incident* had inflicted on the environment. Had the strange dragon witnessed the attack? Was he wanting her to use her flames to escape his icy prison?

"That really isn't a good idea. I don't like to think about that unless I absolutely have to."

The green eyes flicked upward and stayed there. Curious, Zeira turned to look. She didn't see anything out of the ordinary, but unfortunately, her curiosity got the better of her, so she returned to the top of the crater. The chittering was back, only it was fainter this time. The red insects were on their way back. If she was going to free this other dragon, then now was the time to do it.

Zeira hurried back to the slab of ice.

"Do you hear those things coming?"

The green eyes looked up, and then down, and then back at her. The yellow dragon was giving her the equivalent of a head nod!

"Can you get yourself out of that?"

Now the eyes looked left, and then right. That would be a 'no'. Obviously, or else it would have done so by now.

"Oh, don't ask me to do that," Zeira pleaded.

Those two green eyes stared straight at her, as if seeing into her very soul.

"You saw what happened earlier, didn't you? You saw what I have to do in order to produce fire? It was embarrassing enough, and that was when I thought there was no one watching. I'd really prefer *not* to do it again. Couldn't I just use something, like a stone, to chip away the ice?"

The yellow dragon's eyes narrowed, and the corners of his mouth curved upwards in the beginning of a smile. The eyes shifted back to the top of the crater, and even though the pale reptilian face didn't change expression, Zeira couldn't help but feel a look of concern had appeared on his features.

"Fine. Why not? What could be more embarrassing that producing fire from your backside? Why, having to do it *twice*, of course."

Already on questionable ground with her stomach, her thoughts drifted back to the moment she had placed the moist nest inside her mouth and had felt the pleaters wriggling about. Right on cue, her stomach gurgled. Zeira sighed as she felt the next blast ready itself.

After the second burst had dissipated, Zeira turned to inspect the slab of ice. The last thing she wanted to see was her new friend still trapped in his prison, which meant another blast of fire would be necessary. Thankfully, that wouldn't be the case.

Small pieces of ice tumbled off the newcomer as it slowly stood. Heavens above, she had no idea he was so big! He must have been curled into a tight ball. Higher and higher the freed dragon rose, as it stretched out its neck, then wings, and finally its back and tail. As the strange dragon moved, Zeira couldn't help but notice the odd dragon's coloring: yellow, with jagged black stripes visible on the chest and torso, and black wings.

Noticing movement, the much larger dragon looked down and met Zeira's gaze.

"Thank you, young one. You have no idea how long I've had that kink in my neck. It feels *soooo* good to be able to finally move about."

"How did you get in there?" Zeira asked, as she looked up at the much larger dragon. "How long have you been a prisoner?"

Before the stranger could answer, both dragons suddenly lifted their noses and inhaled at the same time. Alarmed, Zeira turned to look up at the rim of the crater when she noticed her new friend doing the same.

"Can you smell it, too?" Zeira nervously asked. "It's the insects again, isn't it? They've returned."

"More than that, I'm afraid," the yellow dragon returned. "They're already here."

"Blast," Zeira grumbled, as she rose to her feet. "Well, since there's no need to hide my secret from you, seeing how …"

A large, friendly claw was placed on Zeira's shoulder and gently pushed her down. "Don't worry. I've got this."

At that exact moment, the newly freed dragon stretched out both of his wings to their fullest potential. A low rumbling began, and as her companion lifted his neck, as if to maximize the distance from the ground to his head, Zeira thought she noticed glowing eyes. An ear-splitting roar followed, and before she could react, bolts of pure energy exploded from both of the yellow dragon's wing talons. Jagged arcs of energy lanced through the air and landed unerringly on the rim of the crater.

One after the other, bolts of white fire slammed into the earth, causing multiple explosions as the rim of the crater vanished beneath a thick cloud of dust. After what felt like an eternity, the dust cleared. That section of the rim was gone. More of the grass and earth had disappeared, and in its place were huge gouges in the earth. As for the horde of red insects, there was no trace.

Amazed and impressed, Zeira turned to her companion.

"I don't think we've met. I am Zeira, of the Phoenix caste. Er, from Blaze. And you are?"

Black wings were folded flat and the great yellow neck eventually lowered until the newcomer's head was less than a dozen feet from the ground.

"I am Skellig."

"Where are you from, Skellig? I've never seen anyone like you before. Are you Terran?"

"Terran? Do I look like one of those lumbering wingless quadrupeds to you? Zeira, you really should get out more. My species is Spark, and I call Gale my home."

Chapter 3 — Skellig

Where is Gale? Is it nearby? How exciting! I've never heard of your home region. Mine is Blaze. My kind live in the mountains. Do you live in the mountains, too?"

"I do not," Skellig answered, when Zeira hesitated long enough to take a breath. "There are only a few mountains in Gale, and those are reserved for His Lordship."

"His Lordship?" Zeira repeated, puzzled. It had been over an hour since she had freed the Spark dragon from his prison, and thus far, their course had taken them due west. They had been flying in silence until Zeira's curiosity got the better of her. "Is that another name for your king?"

"King? You infer there is one who rules us all? There isn't. It isn't possible, due to our being unable to survive on foreign lands. Each region rules its own. It's the way it's been ever since time began."

"Tell that to the Dragon King," Zeira murmured. "No one talks back to him. If he calls, you answer."

"The Dragon King, eh? Well, that'd be one way to refer to oneself. As I understand it, each region has its own leader. I believe the Terran leader calls himself Overlord. Water is Imperator. Yours just happens to call himself *king*."

"Have you been to all those regions?" Zeira asked, amazed. "How can you be away from Gale for so long? Don't you worry about the Fade?"

"Of course, I worry about it," Skellig returned. "Every dragon who ventures out of his home region does. That's why you limit the length of your journey, young one."

"Why do you keep calling me 'young one'? You're not that much older than me, are you?"

"You've yet to pass your first century, haven't you?"

"Maybe. What about you? Have you passed your first?"

"I've passed my *twelfth*, young Zeira."

The magnitude of that statement sank in. This was someone who clearly has had more experience. Perhaps Skellig would be able to help her on her mission? A dragon who has been alive for over twelve-hundred years would certainly know where to find tribesmen, wouldn't he?

"Ask."

"What was that?"

"You want to ask me something. Go ahead."

"How did you know I want to ask you a question? Are you picking up my thoughts?"

Skellig shrugged. "I told you I had places to be, and you offered to accompany me. We're now over two dozen leagues from where we had originally met. You clearly need me to do something for you, and you're struggling to find a way to approach the subject. Let me put your mind at rest. You have done me a favor, young Zeira, by freeing me from the ice. I can certainly do one for you. What is it you require?"

"Tribesmen."

"You want tribesmen? Whatever for? They are small, skinny, and taste terrible. Trust me when I say they aren't worth the effort. Surely, you can find other things to eat."

"I don't want to eat them," Zeira insisted. "I, er, need just one."

"Ah. I believe I have deduced why you are here, Zeira.

You seek a rider, don't you? You want a kai?"

"Is it that obvious?"

"You've lived a sheltered life. You have, shall we say, an *unusual* situation with regards to the source of your flames. You're old enough to establish your honor. Is that why you underwent this journey?"

"I undertook this journey because my king asked for help," Zeira explained.

"So, Blaze knows as well," Skellig softly murmured.

"Blaze knows *what*?"

"It would seem my Lord Myrdaynth has issued directives similar to your king."

"Your Lord *who*? Is that the leader of your region?"

"The reason you haven't met anyone who looks like me isn't too surprising. The journey to Gale takes many days of flying. I doubt you'd be able to make it, young one."

"Do you have to keep calling me young? I'm old enough."

"Old enough to *what*?" Skellig dryly asked. "Old enough to fly? Sure. Old enough to defend yourself? Barely. Old enough to fly *nonstop* over a sea so immense that it would take days and days of flying without setting foot on land during that time?"

Zeira's eyes widened. "The Endless Sea?"

"It would take seven days of solid flying before I'd reach my home," Skellig stated.

"Fading sets in after a fortnight," Zeira softly recalled. "If you've already traveled seven days to get here, and ... the ice prison. How long were you trapped?"

"Five days."

"But, that only leaves ..."

"There's no time for me to make it home, I know."

"What are you going to do?"

"My fate has been sealed, so do not trouble yourself. I came in search of something that could have been used against our adversaries, but alas, it was for naught."

"You were looking for something? Can you tell me what?"

"It doesn't matter anymore. I found something that I thought could help, but was mistaken. It was only a piece."

"What was it?"

"It doesn't matter. I ran out of time."

"This item you're looking for, was it to help your king?"

"Lordship," Skellig corrected, "but yes."

"Does Gale need help, too?"

"Haven't you figured it out yet? What threatens Blaze, threatens us all. *All* of Andela needs help. If we who live here do not stand together to face this foe, then we will soon no longer have a region to call home."

The pair of dragons soared high over a long, narrow valley. To the north, the frigid waters of the Persen Sea were visible. Massive chunks of ice, so large that the two of them could have easily landed on them, were serenely floating on the surface. Further to the north, Zeira could see the pale blue edges of the huge glaciers, source of the giant icebergs. Her mother's warning sounded in her head once more.

What is ice but frozen water? What does water do to fire? No, Zeira, it is too dangerous. You must avoid the ice at all times.

Her mother would have a conniption if she knew the ice region was now within visual range. Well, what she didn't know couldn't hurt her.

As they flew, in companionable silence, something Skellig had said troubled her. He wouldn't be able to make it back to his home before he faded. The Spark dragon seemed nice enough. There had to be something she could do, but what?

"There's nothing you can do, young one," Skellig's gentle voice suddenly announced, startling her. "I knew this was a possibility even before I started on my journey. I have no regrets."

"You said you were also looking for something. If you'd found it, would it have saved your life?"

"In a manner of speaking. I wanted to save time, so I thought if I could have found an oron, then I would simply ask it where I could find my future kai."

"Oron?"

"It's an ancient artifact. You might know them as seeing stones. I don't think there are many left."

"And you knew where to find a seeing stone?"

"I thought I did, but I found only a fragment."

"What happened then?"

"I cleared away the ice from the oron piece, and when I went to claim it, there was a flash of light. When I woke, I was encased in ice, unable to move."

"How horrible."

Skellig snorted. "I can confirm it *wasn't* my best day."

"We need to figure out how to save your life," Zeira declared, matter-of-factly.

"I told you, there's …"

"Don't interrupt. I simply do not accept there's nothing that can be done. We must think about it. We have a few days to figure it out, right?"

"Definitely no more than two."

"All right. Let's assume we find some tribesmen, and one of them becomes your kai. Does having a kai affect the rate of the Fade?"

"That's one way to look at it," Skellig said, nodding.

"How would *you* look at it?" Zeira inquired.

"Having a kai will stave off the effects of the Fade for nearly two months, thus allowing …"

"…thus allowing dragon and rider to travel greater distances?" Zeira exclaimed, delighted.

"Exactly," Skellig said. "If I find a suitable kai, then I could return to Gale in plenty of time."

"Then *that* is what we must do," Zeira decided, nodding her head.

"A comforting thought, if a touch unrealistic."

"Why do you say that? It's not impossible."

"I respect your courage, young … apologies. Zeira. I respect your courage; however, your expectations are unrealistic. I am a lost cause. Instead, we'll focus on you. Now, tell me. How much time do you have? Be specific."

"I've only been on this particular journey for three days, so that means I have eleven days left."

Skellig nodded. "Perfect. You still have plenty of time. You'll be fine."

"If we find some tribesmen," Zeira began, "then you get to have first dibs. You're more in need than I am."

"Let's not fool ourselves," Skellig sighed. "We both know that the chances of finding a suitable kai, so far away from our regions, is highly unlikely. You are a Fire dragon, Zeira. I am Spark. We are clearly nowhere near either of those regions. We are not going to find suitable tribesmen in the middle of Terra."

"Then, how are we supposed to help fight this growing evil if we don't have riders?" Zeira protested. "My king said if we were going to combat this threat head on, then we must have the power of the kais."

"Mine said something similar," Skellig admitted.

"And, since you told me you were seeking some stone, I'm guessing you've had no more luck finding a nest of tribesmen than I have?"

"Correct."

"I was told the only compatible tribesmen would be those living in the same region as I, only ..."

"...you didn't find any, did you?" Skellig guessed. "I am in the same predicament. Gale is a very small region. There haven't been tribesmen living around us for many hundreds of years. So, either we are doomed to failure, or else ...?"

"...or else *what?*" Zeira wanted to know.

"Or else we were possibly misinformed."

"About what?"

"About the limitations of compatible kai."

Even though they were alone, and flying hundreds of feet up in the air, Zeira lowered her voice, as if she thought there was a chance she could be overheard.

"Are you suggesting tribesmen are more compatible than they think?"

"I will admit what I'm suggesting goes against everything we've ever been taught. But, look at the facts. Look how scarce the bipeds are. Have you seen any since commencing this trip?"

"This trip with you, or my ... right. My trip. I will agree with you. I've been told over and over where the tribesmen should be, but have yet to find a single specimen."

"That goes for both of us," Skellig confided, "and I've been traveling a lot longer, and a lot farther, than you. So, I have to ask myself: are we missing something?"

"Wait. You've come all the way from Gale to … where *is* Gale again? How far away and in what direction?"

Skellig extended his front left foreleg and pointed southwest of their current position. "That way. Blink, and you'll probably pass right over it."

"It's that small?"

"It's that small," Skellig confirmed.

"And all dragons there are Spark?"

"Are all dragons from Blaze a part of your Phoenix caste?"

"Well, no. There are four castes: Phoenix, Spurt, Magma, and Scoria."

"Spurt? Did you actually just tell me there are spurt dragons?"

"Well, yes. Their flames are limited. They only have so much fuel before they have to wait and regenerate their strength. To make matters worse, their blasts aren't that strong."

"Tell me about the Phoenix caste," Skellig requested, as they crested a rolling plain and, for the first time, several pine trees appeared in the distance. "What are their characteristics?"

Zeira shrugged. "Smaller, greater intelligence, and they have …"

"…unique methods of expelling fire?" Skellig interrupted, giving her a toothy grin.

"No. That's just me, unfortunately. What I was going to say was, Phoenix dragons have respected positions in our community. Scholars, advisors, and leaders. That's the caste I belong to."

"Were you being trained for something?" Skellig wanted to know, as they both pumped their wings in order to clear the tops of the pine trees that were rapidly approaching.

"No. Why do you ask?"

"No reason. I find that unusual, young Zeira."

"You do? Why?"

"Don't you want to help your fellow dragons? Don't you want your existence to mean something? I mean … what are your aspirations?"

"To make my mother proud," Zeira said, becoming glum.

"Is she not now?"

Zeira shrugged. "She says one thing, but her actions speak differently."

"And is that why you are on this mission?" Skellig asked.

"You're nosey."

Skellig grunted once before turning to give her a friendly smile. "I've been called worse. Prithee, answer the question. Are you here on behalf of your ... caste? Or on behalf of yourself?"

"Both, I guess. I wanted to prove to my king that I was old enough to fight. I wanted to do something to make my mother proud. She warned me this was a foolish idea. Thus far, she's right. I've been lost, attacked, and haven't found my kai, let alone a tribesman to test."

"Well, I have a backup plan. I like you, young Zeira. I will help you with what time I have left."

Zeira turned to her much larger friend and studied his face. Backup plan? Did it have something to do with what he said earlier, something about a special stone?

Skellig flew close and held out a claw. In it was something small, which true to his word, resembled a rock. However, that's where the similarities ended. This particular rock, which was no larger than one of her fangs, was emitting its own light! The stone was bathed in an eerie green glow. Was this the seeing stone Skellig had been talking about? Hadn't he said he couldn't find it?

"Behold: a piece of an oron. *This* is what drew me to the northern glaciers. And, *this* is what was responsible for trapping me in the ice."

"It's just a rock," Zeira observed, "except it's glowing."

"Do you see the green glow? This is a Terran fragment."

"I don't follow."

"Place the three different fragments together, and they'll form an oron stone. Terra, water, and fire."

"You thought you had enough time to locate three separate pieces to assemble this seeing stone?"

Skellig shook his head. "I had forgotten that intact stones would separate into their basic elements if left alone for a

long enough period of time. As soon as I spotted this in the
ice, I knew I had found what I was looking for."

"How did you know that was buried in the ice?"

"Let's just say I had some help."

Zeira shrugged. "If you say so."

Skellig stretched out his foreleg and held the fragment out
to her. "This is yours now. You'll have a much better chance
of using it than I will."

"Me? What am I supposed to do with that?"

"What else? Find the other pieces. If you can do that, you
can use the power of the oron to find what you're looking
for: a suitable kai."

"And you hoped to use the stone to do the same thing?"

"I was going to ask it to show me some way to save my
region."

"By finding a kai. I get it."

Skellig shrugged. "A kai, or a weapon, it didn't matter.
That was my plan."

Noticing the much larger Spark dragon was still holding
out his leg, expecting her to take the fragment, Zeira sighed.
She tucked her wings and glided in, under Skellig's body.
The yellow and black dragon allowed his foreleg to dangle
beneath him and then waited for Zeira to take the glowing
green stone. Once she had it, the two of them drifted apart.

"How does having one piece of it help me?"

"No clue. I had hoped to try it out, but time is not on my
side. The longer you have it, the more I'm hoping you'll be
able to determine what to do next."

Zeira stared at the glowing shard in her claw. Just then,
she was buffeted by a gust of wind, which threatened to tip
her over. Closing her claw around the fragment, she righted
herself and was about to ask about the feasibility of flying
lower when she paused. Her entire foreleg was tingling, and it
was no surprise that it was the same one holding the fragment.

"What is it?" Skellig asked.

"Hmm?"

"You're feeling anxious. Your heartbeat has elevated.
What's wrong?"

"You can tell that all the way from over there?"

"Yes."

Zeira sighed. She really needed to figure out how to do that.

"You will soon enough, young Zeira."

"Stop that. I don't like knowing you can pick up my thoughts when I can't pick up yours."

"Then don't make it so easy to do."

"What? Are you saying I think too loud?"

Skellig smiled. "That was a joke. Now, what happened?"

"A gust of wind …"

"No, not the wind. I'm talking about the fragment. You felt something, didn't you?"

"Oh. Yes, I did. I thought I was going to drop your fragment, so I clutched it tightly in my hand. Once I did, though, my claws started tingling."

"I knew it!" Skellig happily exclaimed. "It's leading you to the next piece, I'm sure of it!"

"The next piece of the seeing stone?"

"Yes. Can you tell where you're supposed to go?"

"From feeling some tingling in my talons? No."

"Do try," her much larger companion insisted.

"I have no idea what I'm supposed to do."

"Hear me out. This is just a thought. Perhaps, just *perhaps* you could start by being silent and opening your senses. My guess is that you'll be able to sense the location of the next piece."

Zeira regarded Skellig's impassive face for a few moments. "If you know how to work it, then why don't you keep it? If it's as simple as allowing yourself to be drawn to the location of the next piece, then don't you think you should keep it?"

"You're assuming the next fragment is nearby," Skellig corrected. "For all we know, the next suitable fragment could be at the bottom of the sea, or on the other side of the world."

"Oh."

"Do you feel anything?"

Zeira took several deep breaths in an effort to steady her rampaging thoughts. "I'll try."

Clutching the fragment tightly, Zeira opened her senses and waited for the tingles to return. This time, though, they didn't. Instead, what she felt was an immediate sensation of wrongness. In this case, it felt as though she was heading in the wrong direction.

"We …" Zeira falteringly began. She cleared her throat. "I think I have something."

"Let's hear it," Skellig eagerly said.

"I get the immediate sensation of flying in the wrong direction."

"I'll hang back and watch. See if you can find the direction that feels right to you."

Zeira immediately pointed right. "That way."

"That was quick. Are you sure?"

"You should've told me it was the same feeling as when I found you."

Her much larger companion was taken aback. "What?"

"How do you think I found you?" Zeira countered. "I don't know how I knew, but I just *knew* another dragon was in the area."

The Spark dragon fell silent.

"And right now it feels like we need to be going *that way*."

"Then, by all means, lead the way, Zeira."

The two dragons banked right, and headed toward the open sea. As they neared the coastline, however, Zeira was surprised when the sensation lessened. Just like that, she was headed in the wrong direction. Again.

"Would you give me some notice?" she grumbled.

"Did you say something?" Skellig asked, flying close.

"We're going the wrong way again."

As if this had happened before, Skellig shrugged. "Very well. Which way now?"

Zeira held her right foreleg out and pointed where she felt she had to go. Much to her surprise, her claw dropped until she was pointing straight down.

"You want us to land?" Skellig skeptically asked.

"It's not me," Zeira insisted. "But … yes, I'm being pulled to something down there."

Once on the ground, both dragons inspected the area. Tall vibrant evergreens stretched up over a hundred feet in places. Others weren't quite so big.

"We're approaching the border of Timber. Now, where to?" Skellig wanted to know.

Zeira closed her eyes and waited for the tingling sensations to return. Her head moved, and she automatically repositioned her body. Raising a claw, she pointed west.

"That way. It's not far."

"There's nothing out here but grass," the Spark dragon observed.

"Grass, a few trees, and there, half a league to the north, is the sea. I'm not sure this is right. I don't know what I'm ... wait. Here. It's here!"

Both dragons paused.

Skellig chuckled. "If you say we're here, then I'll believe you. What now?"

Zeira kept her eyes closed and pointed another claw. When she opened them, she was dismayed at where she was pointing. "We have to dig? Have I not broken enough talons on this trip?"

"You dug me out of that crater," Skellig said, as he idly picked his teeth with one of his talons. "I guess it's my turn. Step aside."

Turf, dirt, and small pebbles began to fly as Skellig dug. Within moments, a hole appeared and then widened. Skellig leaned forward and sank his talons into the soft soil, uprooting huge chunks of dirt and boulders, tossing them aside. In a few moments, Zeira heard Skellig grunt with surprise. The digging stopped, and the yellow dragon climbed out of the hole.

"What is it?" Zeira asked. "Did you find something?"

"I did, yes. See for yourself."

Zeira stretched her neck over to see into the hole. Skellig had dug deep enough to draw water! She straightened, scratched a claw on the side of her head, and moved off as a thought occurred.

"Now what?" Skellig wanted to know, as he fell into step beside her.

"Is there water everywhere, or just there?"

Skellig looked back at the hole he had dug. "That's a good question. I would think so, with the sea nearby."

"Let's find out. It's my turn to dig. How deep did you go?"

"About a dozen feet, I'd say."

Zeira began to dig as quickly as possible. Ten minutes later, she stepped back and motioned to Skellig.

"Is this the same depth?"

"Did you find water?"

"No."

"Then, you're probably not deep enough."

Zeira pointed at her hole. "Are you sure? It looks like it is."

Skellig's long neck appeared beside her. "I stand corrected. I think you may have gone deeper."

"Then, why didn't I encounter water?"

Skellig pointed back at his hole. "Because the water is only there, where you indicated?"

"Was there something *in* the water?"

Skellig shrugged. "I never bothered to check. I will do so now."

Zeira followed her new friend back to the first hole and watched as the Spark dragon reached into the hole. After a minute or so, Skellig gave up.

"There's nothing there, I'm afraid."

Zeira looked at the fragment she was holding and shook her head. "Why send me here? If it wanted water, then why not take me over there, to the sea?"

Skellig suddenly turned back to the hole, dipped one of his forelegs into the water, and then carefully licked the tip of his talons.

"It's freshwater," Zeira guessed.

Skellig shook his head. "No. It's seawater."

"There's more to this than it would seem."

"Where are you going?" Zeira inquired, as she tucked the oron fragment under a loose chest scale.

"Let's see if you are led anywhere else."

Both dragons spread their wings and took to the air. Once they were airborne, Skellig nodded his head at Zeira and let her take the lead. Closing her eyes, Zeira placed a hand on her chest and wondered where she should head next. Right on cue, the tingles returned. This time, it felt as though she was being pulled away from the hole. It also appeared the oron fragment was leading her on a course parallel to the sea.

Less than fifteen minutes later, both dragons were back on the ground.

"Again?" Skellig wryly asked.

Zeira shrugged. She pointed at a spot beneath their feet.

"There. There's something down there."

"More water," Skellig guessed.

"Probably. This is my quest. I'll do it."

Skellig extended one of his muscular forelegs and prevented her from taking a single step.

"And I can dig this thing faster than you can. Plus, I'm not worried about breaking a talon."

"Breaking a … you *were* eavesdropping on me!"

"I said it before, if you want to keep your thoughts to yourself, then you'll need to think quieter."

"How?"

Skellig snorted with amusement before turning his attention on the ground before them. Less than five minutes later, a hole large enough to accommodate Zeira, and easily a dozen feet deep, had appeared. Sure enough, water had appeared at the bottom of the hole, and was slowly filling it.

"More water," Zeira observed. "Seawater again?"

Skellig tasted another sample. "Yes. What does that tell us?"

Zeira turned to look at the shoreline, visible in the distance, and sighed. She didn't know what it meant, and certainly didn't know why seawater would be found this far inland. Wanting a closer look, she slowly climbed down, into the hole.

"Be careful," Skellig's voice warned, from above her.

But, before she could say anything, the ground began to tremble. A large, three-foot long talon hooked itself under her right foreleg and, before she knew what was happening, Zeira found herself being *lifted* out of the hole. Skellig placed her on the ground and moved the bulk of his body between her and the hole. Impressed with the speed in which the Spark dragon moved, and the simple fact that he was trying to protect her, Zeira fell silent.

"What was that?" Skellig quietly asked. "You felt it, too, didn't you? There was a temblor."

"A terra temblor," Zeira agreed, nodding.

The ground trembled again, but before either of them could do anything, a section of grass behind the hole swelled upward, as though something was trying to push its way up, through the earth. A jet of water splashed up, out of the hole, and soaked the two of them. Moments later, the trembling lessened and stopped.

"Did we awaken something?" Zeira quietly asked.

"Stay there. I think …"

The trembling began anew, only this time, it was centralized to an area behind them, as though whatever was responsible for the tremors was moving east. Skellig held a talon to his mouth, signaling quiet, and pointed toward the distant hole they had dug earlier. Even from their distance, they could see a second spout of water erupt from the ground.

"That's from our first hole, isn't it?" Zeira excitedly whispered. "What does it mean?"

"It means we were being followed, and from the looks of it, we've been discovered. Come! I want to know what has been spying on us!"

Both dragons, Fire and Spark, leapt into the air and angled themselves east retracing their route as quickly as possible. As they neared the location of the first hole, Skellig snorted with surprise as a huge jet of water blasted up from below. The Spark dragon pointed at the water, but immediately noticed Zeira wasn't looking. In fact, she was looking down, at the ground, and was pointing at something in the grass.

"Look! Do you see that?"

Skellig looked down at the rolling fields of grass and sucked in a breath. Something was there! Something *under* the grass was racing along, like a giant mole at work. What was it? How was it able to dig so fast?

"It looks as though it is headed to the sea," Skellig announced, from somewhere on her right.

"You've never seen the like before?"

"No."

"What would *you* do?"

"The oron fragment singled it out. Now, it would appear that, whatever it is, it is fleeing from us. I say we pursue. I, for one, would like to know what creature we are dealing with."

Zeira nodded, tucked her wings close to her body, and allowed gravity to do its work. She and Skellig fell from the sky, in tandem. The two of them snapped their wings open less than a hundred feet from the ground and silently glided toward the water. Below them, not only matching their speed but *pulling away*, was the subterranean anomaly.

Faster and faster the two dragons flew, yet no matter how hard they tried, they could not overtake their strange adversary. Zeira's eyes opened wide. She pointed again at the rapidly moving phenomenon down below and looked at her companion.

"What if you were right? What if this fragment *did* lead us to another fragment, but whatever is down there found it first?"

Skellig scratched his chin. "Well, that would explain why we were led to it and why this other entity wants to elude capture."

"It's heading for the sea!" Zeira exclaimed, as she watched the line of disturbed earth and grass. "What's it planning on doing? Tunneling under the water?"

Skellig narrowed his eyes. "I don't …"

Detecting a note of alarm coming from the much larger Spark dragon, Zeira risked a quick glance at Skellig. He had trailed off, as if a thought had occurred, and now he appeared unsure of himself.

"I think we should stop," Skellig decided.

"What? Why?"

"First, we aren't going to make it to the sea before it does."

"Maybe if we …"

"No, young Zeira. Observe. No matter how fast we fly, whatever *it* is moves even faster. I think that's their intent: reaching the sea."

"Do you really think they'll tunnel their way under it?"

"Most likely. Think about it. We won't be able to follow once it does."

"Blast. What else?"

"Hmm?"

"You said *first*."

"Ah. You are correct. I was going to say, second, we don't need to. I think I know what's below us."

"You know what we're chasing?" Zeira asked, anxious.

"I do. And if I'm right, that'll mean … yes. There it goes. Can you see it?"

Zeira looked north just in time to see the water turn frothy at the shoreline, followed immediately by an explosion of bubbles and turbulent water. By the time she blinked and tried to figure out what had happened, the only thing left to see was a rapidly dissipating trail of disturbed water, heading northwest. Whatever they had been chasing was now long gone.

"What just happened?" Zeira cried. "It reached the water and it exploded?"

"No. Look to your left. Do you see the ripples of water? That's the wake of the creature we have been following."

"But … that would mean it moves faster *in* the water than out!"

Skellig nodded knowingly. "As well it should. That, young Zeira, was a valthan."

"A *what*?"

"A water dragon, Zeira. We were chasing a water dragon!"

Chapter 4 — Nuri

That makes no sense whatsoever. If we were pursuing over water, then sure, I could believe that. You keep calling me young, and I guess I *am* naïve about a great many things. However, you are *never* going to convince me that we were pursuing a ... a ... what was the word again?"

"A valthan."

"Right. You will never convince me we were pursuing a valthan *over land*. That just isn't possible."

"And we're now pursuing over water. What's your point?"

"My point?" Zeira blinked her eyes a few times before pointing down, at the surface of the water hundreds of feet below them. "How can you say we're pursuing over water when we can't even see what we're pursuing?"

"We don't need to be able to see the valthan," Skellig mysteriously said. He twisted his long, serpentine neck until he was staring straight at her. "We have *you*."

"Me? What's that supposed to mean?"

"You were able to follow the valthan over land. We should be able to …"

"How, exactly, *did* the valthan pull that off?" Zeira interrupted. "We followed a water dragon over land. That shouldn't be … wait. We didn't, did we?"

Skellig grinned and shook his head. "We most certainly did not."

"We followed, but they were underground. The valthan must have dug tunnels."

"Which explains the geyser of water over the two holes we dug," Skellig added.

"A valthan can tunnel that fast?" Zeira asked, amazed.

"Or else we interrupted the valthan while they were preoccupied doing something else."

Zeira nodded. "So, *that* is why they were fleeing. The valthan was upset we were able to follow them, even though we couldn't see them."

"That's my guess," Skellig confirmed.

"Have you seen a valthan in the flesh before?"

"Not up close," Skellig admitted. "They live their entire lives underwater. As a result, their contact with other species is extremely limited."

"How many regions have you visited?" Zeira asked.

"Why the sudden interest in my travels?"

"You admit to traveling?"

"As much as I can, aye. There's a whole world out there, Zeira. It deserves to be explored."

"But … but how can you? Travel, I mean. Don't you worry about the Fade?"

"Not typically, no, and *that* is because I'm a Spark dragon. I still have high hopes that I'll manage to find a piece of Gale."

"What is that supposed to mean?"

"Oh, I apologize. I keep forgetting not everyone has learned the same things we have."

"What do you mean by that?" Zeira wanted to know.

"Gale is my home. It's where I'm safe, just as you are safe on Blaze, correct?"

"Correct."

"Gale is not just in one location."

"Now you've lost me."

"Gale doesn't occur just in one spot. It's a … a … convergence, if you will, of several specific regions, or elements. Do you follow me?"

"No."

"All right. Let's try it this way. The base elements of my home region are terra, obviously, and water. That means Gale has much of its borders on the sea. With me so far?"

"Sure," Zeira confirmed, although she had no clue where Skellig was going with this.

"Look around you, Zeira. Do you see any land bordering the water?"

"Of course. We're flying over a coastline. Wait. You're telling me we're flying over Gale right now?"

"Not quite. I'm trying to make you understand that, whenever *I* see land and water unite, then I will usually investigate, to see if it's Gale."

"What sets Gale apart from *all* areas where terra meets water?" Zeira curiously asked.

"The presence of a third base element. If the third is present, then by definition, it becomes Gale. Our very world is defined by these characteristics."

"Well? This third element? What is it?"

"Metal."

"Metal? You're telling me there's a region called *Metal?*"

"I have no idea what it's called by the inhabitants," Skellig admitted. "I just know the land exists, although to be honest, I've never met any dragons from there."

"Wait. Just wait a moment. You're suggesting that, should you find an area that happens to have all three … what did you call it? Elements? If you find a location that has all three of your elements, then that qualifies as your home and you're able to stave off the Fade?"

"I'm not suggesting anything," Skellig argued. "I'm *telling* you that's how it works. Well, that's how it works for me. I can only assume it works for others, too. You just have to discover where else your home region might be."

"I'm having trouble understanding this. You're telling

me you just fly around until you find a spot that qualifies as Gale?"

"In essence, yes."

"What happens if you can't find a safe spot in time?"

"Then I'd cease to be, wouldn't I?"

Zeira was amazed. Her new friend sounded so blasé about the possibility of dying. Did he really care that little about whether or not he faded?

"Of course I don't," Skellig said, giving her a concerned look. "I have no intention of fading, Zeira, and will actively avoid it all costs. Again, if you don't want me picking up your thoughts, then don't shout them at me."

"But, you're taking risks every single day!"

"I don't think you understand how big this world is," Skellig began, as he angled his head to scrutinize the passing scenery far below them, "and how frequently those three elements can be found together."

"How do you know if they do?" Zeira curiously asked.

"How do you know when you're back in Blaze?" Skellig countered. "I'm guessing your body will know immediately if the elements it needs are nearby. Let me ask you this: how often have you left Blaze?"

"To venture to another region? Never."

"I knew you were inexperienced, Zeira, but I had no idea you were *so* inexperienced."

Zeira automatically lifted her nose higher in the air. "There's no need to be rude."

"I apologize. I meant no offense. The reason I ask is, once you leave your region, and spend any amount of time away from it, the moment you return, you'll know it. You'll *feel* it. It's the same for me. Whenever I touch down in an area that I suspect to be Gale, I'll instantly know whether I'm right or not. And, the more you're away from your region, the more you'll be able to fine-tune your senses to seek out what I call *havens*, or isles."

"Havens?"

"Think of them as a small portion of your home surrounded by foreign regions on all sides, hence the name *isle*. By definition, an isle is a piece of terra, surrounded by water. In this case, a *haven* is a piece of your home region, where you are able to hold off the Fade."

"Are you telling me that there could be additional regions of Blaze somewhere down there?"

"We'd have to know more about Blaze and which elements it contains, but aye, I'm guessing Gale is not the only region that has been misrepresented."

"Incredible," Zeira breathed.

Unnoticed by either dragon, the land hundreds of feet below them suddenly vanished as they began crossing a wide inlet. Also of note was the almost immediate appearance of a trail of bubbles, which fell in line behind them.

"Wondering what your home region's elements are?" Skellig asked, after another couple of minutes had passed.

"Yes. I'm wondering if you could be right."

"I'm still here, aren't I?" Skellig countered. "By rights, I should have faded long ago, yet I'm still here."

"What do you think my elements are?" Zeira asked.

"I don't know anything about Blaze, so it's hard to say. Terra and fire come to mind. I have no idea what the third element could be. There could even be a fourth, you never know."

"Wow. Four elements? My home has four elements?"

"I was just making a point. We have no idea how many Blaze has."

"How many elements are there?"

Skellig held out a foreleg, as though he was going to use his claws to keep track of the count. "Well, I know of terra, water …"

"But those aren't elements," Zeira interrupted. "Those are regions."

"And the regions are based on the elements," Skellig reminded her. "Our whole world is limited by geography, but, as I mentioned before, we Spark dragons have determined that it isn't geography restricting our movements, as everyone believes, but these base elements. Now, as I was saying, there's terra, water, fire, ice, metal, jewel …"

"Jewel? There are jewel dragons?"

"So young," Skellig lamented. "Stop interrupting. Hmm.

Where was I?'

"Jewel."

"Ah, right. Jewel. I met a ruby dragon once. Prettiest dragon I have ever seen. Then again, it didn't help matters he was a male, and didn't take kindly to my staring."

"When did you visit the jewel region?" Zeira asked, envious.

"Let's see. Three years ago, if memory serves. I called it *Bounty*."

"Bounty? That doesn't make any sense."

"As in *bountiful*," Skellig added.

"Oh. Renaming regions, regions appearing when none should, and regions I've never known to exist. What is this world coming to?"

"For someone who has never traveled before? It must be mind-blowing. For those of us who do want to travel? It's a game-changer. Ah, he's back."

"Who's back?"

Skellig pointed down. "Our friend from before."

Zeira stared at the distant ground and waited for her eyes to focus. Movement in her peripheral vision had her shifting her gaze to the sea. It was the valthan. Not only was it back, it was now pacing them.

"I wonder how long he's been down there."

Skellig grunted once. "He's never left. For some reason, we have attracted his interest. I say we confront this challenge head-on."

"I don't know if that's wise," Zeira hesitantly began. "I've never encountered a valthan before, so I have no idea what we'd be up against. Do you?"

"No. However, life is too short to spend time speculating. Come. We'll take him together."

Zeira watched her new friend spiral down and land on the coast. What was she doing? How did she end up traveling with someone who was so keen to pick fights with a stranger? She didn't have anything against this valthan. The water dragon was probably just curious. Should she fly away?

I wouldn't fault you for doing just that, young Zeira, Skellig's gentle thought came. *I shouldn't forget just how inexperienced you*

are. I apologize. I will let no harm befall you. But, if you'd like to leave,
I won't stop you, nor will I hold it against you.

Sighing, Zeira adjusted her wings and allowed herself to land beside her much larger companion. Together, the two of them stepped onto the beach and faced the open sea. There, approaching fast, was the valthan, who had swerved and was now on a direct intercept for their exact location.

Preparing for the worst, Skellig stretched his wings out and extended his wing talons, a sure sign he was about to summon — or expel, since she hadn't determined where the bolts of lightning had come from — his unique abilities. Forgetting that it was a subject of embarrassment, Zeira dug through the sandy soil and unearthed several types of aquatic invertebrates. Scooping up the wriggling, scaly creatures and holding them firmly in her hand, Zeira turned to face the sea.

Just before the trail of bubbles would have struck land, the momentum came to an abrupt stop. Waves of water washed over their legs as the wake of their pursuer's chase caught up with them. After a few moments, the water receded, and they were staring at an open, calm sea.

"What now?" Zeira quietly whispered.

"Hush. The valthan is still there."

"You can see him?"

"No, but I can smell him. You can't?"

"Of course I can. I was just wondering if you could."

Zeira couldn't see his face, but somehow she *knew* Skellig was smiling. Before she could say anything, a heavily scaled blue head—much narrower than either hers or Skellig's—perched on a long sleek neck, rose gracefully out of the water. The valthan's skull had two spiraled horns angled back, away from its nose. The body was long, sinewy, with a thin, light-blue ridge—perhaps a fin—running down the center of its neck.

The valthan stared first at Skellig, the more imposing figure, and once it was decided that no aggressive moves were being made, both Zeira and Skellig were given a surprise. A thin set of small front legs, which had been tucked so tightly against the valthan's body that they had been practically invisible, appeared. The valthan swam closer still, and then took a few hesitant steps out of the water, onto the beach.

Much longer than either of them, the valthan cautiously inched closer until it was less than twenty feet away, with the bulk of the water dragon's body safely in the sea. The water dragon looked again at Skellig, and then at her, only when Zeira and the valthan locked eyes, the water dragon cocked its head, as though questioning.

"Who are you?" Skellig demanded. The Spark dragon had yet to stand down his defensive posture, and with both wing talons extended, Zeira knew he was moments away from summoning his power. "Why are you following us?"

"I'm not following you," a cool, *feminine* voice answered, as the blue head turned to face Skellig. "I'm following *her*."

Surprised, Skellig turned to look down at Zeira, who had to fight the urge to hide behind her companion's much larger form.

"Me? Why? I don't know you. I've never met you. In fact, I've never met one of your kind before."

"I know you haven't, and never have I ever encountered a Fire dragon. However, I heard you were making this journey."

Skellig turned incredulously to Zeira.

Zeira nodded. "We've never met."

"Then how does he …"

A low, throaty growl emanated from the valthan

"…*she* know about you?" Skellig hastily amended. "Wait, forget about that. Who are you, anyway?"

The valthan flicked her eyes over to Skellig's. "You may call me Nuri."

Zeira nervously cleared her throat. "I am Zeira, and this is Skellig. We're, uh, pleased to meet you."

"How did you know about her?" Skellig demanded. "I only met her earlier today."

"When she freed you from your ice prison, I was there."

"*How?*" Zeira wanted to know. "Were you the one who dug those tunnels?"

Nuri slowly nodded. "That was me, aye."

"Why?' Skellig asked, gentler this time. "That must have been a lot of work."

"Not for one who's adept at digging," Nuri idly commented.

"You must really enjoy digging," Skellig decided. "Somehow, and I don't know how, you have powers of premonition."

"I do not, no," Nuri finally admitted. "But my queen does."

At this, the bulk of Nuri's body became visible. The valthan's form might be slender and sinewy, but what she lacked in mass she made up in length. A handful of coils were slowly twisting and turning in the water behind Nuri's torso, which had to extend an additional twenty feet into the water. That made the valthan at least forty feet long!

Catching sight of their amazed expressions, the water dragon spoke. "Yes, that's just me."

"Why don't you come out of the water?" Zeira asked, in an open invitation to join them.

"Maybe she can't," Skellig quietly told her.

Zeira's eyes widened. "Oh. I hadn't thought of that."

"To address both of you, since neither of you seem to realize that the subject of your conversation is standing before you *and* can overhear you, yes, I can move about on terra, only ..."

"It's not as efficient," Skellig guessed.

"Correct. I will match my abilities in water to anyone with wings. But, out of water I'm vulnerable. In the water, unmatched."

"What are you doing here?" Zeira asked. "You were told about me? Well, here I am. Make that, here *we* are. What do you want?"

"I ... I ... want to join you."

Surprised, Zeira shared a look with Skellig. "Can I ask why?"

"I know about the threat Andela is facing," Nuri began. Her long coils began fidgeting about in the water. "I know about the call for dragons to find their kai. As you can imagine, the valthan are excluded from this endeavor."

"Why?" Zeira asked.

Skellig finally decided Nuri was not going to attack them and folded his wings against his back. Lowering the bulk of his body so that he was resting on the ground, he looked at

Zeira and tsked her.

"What?" Zeira demanded. "Do you know why?"

"I do, yes. It might have something to do with the simple fact that tribesmen cannot breathe underwater."

"I … oh."

Hearing a snort of laughter, both Fire and Spark dragons glanced over at their new friend, who was valiantly trying to keep a neutral look on her face.

"You were saying?" Skellig prompted.

Nuri nodded. "Yes. As I was saying, we valthan will never be able to say we had a kai. However, I refuse to sit on my coils and do nothing. Nearly four dozen of us volunteered to search the seas, to see if there might be something that could help us. My queen wouldn't have it, I'm sorry to say."

"Er, why not?" Skellig hesitantly asked.

Nuri scowled irritably. "I can only guess she knew something we did not, that perhaps there *isn't* anything in the sea that can address this enemy, so why bother?"

"Yet, you came anyway," Zeira pointed out.

Nuri nodded again. "Correct. I wanted to try. There had to be something I could do to be useful. That's when I was pulled aside and informed about you, Zeira. I was told a Fire dragon was currently undergoing a quest to find a kai, and it would behoove me to become part of that mission."

"Did you find out why?" Skellig curiously asked.

"I was simply told that, in order for this cousin from Fire to succeed, they were going to need some help. I was being given a chance to do something, so I took it."

"So, there are no others?" Zeira asked, as she stretched her neck to the left and right, looking back at the sea.

"I came alone," Nuri announced. "I would imagine it has something to do with me being the swiftest and fiercest of my kind. Again, I didn't argue. Somewhere out there was a chance to right the wrong, to fix the imbalance. I'm pleased to say that I finally found you."

"Your speed in the water is amazing," Skellig admitted.

Nuri lifted her head high into the air. "I am unmatched."

"How are you supposed to help us if we have to fly inland?" Zeira wanted to know.

"The only thing I can do is get myself as close as possible," Nuri informed them. "There must be something I can do."

"Maybe it's you," Skellig proposed. "Did you know we were tracking you, too?"

The valthan gave a visible jerk of surprise.

"You were following me, too? How?"

Zeira looked over at Skellig and gave him an imploring look.

This is your mission, Zeira, Skellig thought to her. *It's up to you how much you want to tell her.*

If you're about to reveal secrets, a new voice announced, which could only belong to the valthan, *then I should inform you that I can hear the two of you, too.*

Zeira shrugged, retrieved the oron fragment she had been given from beneath her loose scale, and held out a claw. After a few moments, Nuri leaned forward, and catching sight of the green glow, the valthan lowered her head until her nose was less than a dozen feet from the broken stone. She blinked a few times and then looked up, at Zeira.

"What's this?"

Zeira's hopes fell. "I was hoping you'd recognize it. This is what I was using to follow you."

"That piece of rock allowed you to follow me? I doubt it."

"She doesn't mean physically," Skellig interjected. "She was pulled in the direction you were traveling. That's how we were able to follow you to the sea."

Nuri was silent as she studied the object in Zeira's hand.

"Have you seen one of these before?" Zeira wanted to know.

Nuri shook her head, sending droplets of water in all directions. "I have not, I'm afraid."

"Blast," Skellig grumbled. "We were hoping you might have another piece."

"You want another one?" the valthan asked. "Why?"

"Three pieces make up a whole," Zeira explained. "Once you have three, then you can make an oron stone."

"Ah. *That* I've heard of. You wish to use the stone to show you your heart's desire, is that it?"

Zeira scratched an errant itch on the side of her face.

"I guess. I do want to find a kai, but I wouldn't call that my heart's desire."

"And you, Skellig?" Nuri asked, turning to the Spark dragon. "Do you wish to use this stone, too?"

"Only long enough to find the closest piece of Gale."

Zeira turned to her enormous companion. "What? I thought you said it was everywhere."

"Little pieces of my home can be found in many places," Skellig confirmed, "but thus far, it doesn't seem to be *here*. I fear my traveling days have finally caught up with me."

"You seek something?" Nuri asked, concerned. "Perhaps if you tell me what you seek, then I might be able to help? I know these waters very well."

"I doubt it," Skellig argued. "What I search for is an area of land that has a vein of a very specific metal running through it."

"What kind of metal?" Nuri asked, as if the Spark dragon's request was the most logical thing to ask for.

When Skellig fell silent, Zeira glanced his way.

"She asked what kind of metal. Do you know?"

"I do not," Skellig confirmed. "For all I know, it could be gold. I promised myself that, if I happened to find a haven before I fade, that I wouldn't leave it until I knew for certain what the third element was."

"I have to admit I was secretly hoping you were joking," Zeira sighed. "Locating one of your havens has become my top priority."

Skellig looked pointedly at the fragment she was still clutching.

"And *that* is why you now have the fragment. I won't be able to finish searching for the two other pieces. That now falls to you."

Nuri stared at Skellig in silence for a few moments before shaking her head. "You're grim. I wouldn't be giving up just yet. You said you had two days left? Let's make the best of them, shall we?"

"Look, I appreciate the offer," Skellig slowly began, "but unless you're me, there's no way to verify you've found what I need."

Zeira groaned. "Don't give up on us yet, Skellig. We have two days. Your luck may hold."

"Only by finding a haven, and we both know there's none nearby, so no."

"There's nothing else to be done?" Nuri asked. "There's nothing else you can think of which could stave off your fade?"

"*My* fade?" Skellig repeated, frowning. "All the dragons of Andela face the threat of fading should they wander away from their home region. It isn't *my* fading, but *everyone's*."

"Not mine," Nuri clarified. The valthan turned to look back at the open sea behind her. "If your region just so happens to be the largest, then you're practically free to travel whenever and wherever you'd like."

Zeira looked down at the fragment of stone in her hand and her eyes widened. She held the shard of oron aloft and waggled it in front of Skellig's face.

"What about this? What were you going to use this for, had you been successful in finding all three pieces?"

"I told you, a kai, what else? Or a weapon. Anything that could guarantee victory."

Nuri perked up. "You seek a rider? How will that help you?" Skellig and Zeira both stared at the valthan as though she had just sprouted wings. "What? Did I say something wrong?"

"A kai," Skellig slowly explained, "will mix his—or her—power with your own."

"I know this," Nuri pointed out.

"Dragon and rider will each complement the other," Zeira added.

"I know this, too," Nuri added.

"The presence of a suitable, fully bonded kai extends the amount of time it takes to Fade."

Nuri blinked a few times. "I did not know that."

"That's why so many dragons are hesitant to start journeys," Zeira told the valthan. "A high percentage of those who leave never come back."

"Yet you chose to go," Nuri reminded her.

Zeira nodded. "I did, aye. The risks are high, but the

stakes are higher."

Nuri was silent for a few moments before she nodded once, as if she had just made up her mind.

"Well, there's no time like the present. Skellig, let's find you a kai."

"We cannot find the tribesmen," Zeira sadly reported. "I've looked everywhere for them. Skellig has looked, too. They're nowhere to be seen."

"Tribesmen?" Nuri slowly repeated, clearly unfamiliar with the word. "I thought you were looking for a kai."

"We *are* looking for a kai," Skellig clarified. "A tribesman is what you call the kai before they become a, er, kai. Does that make sense?"

Nuri held up one of her thin forelegs and wiggled two of her claws.

"Just to be certain we're talking about the same thing, you're looking for the bipeds? The ones who move around on two appendages, are small, make an inordinate amount of noise, and taste terrible?"

Skellig chuckled and nodded. "Those are the ones."

"I know where some are," Nuri excitedly announced.

Zeira and Skellig shared a look.

"Where?" Zeira eagerly asked.

"Will you show me?" Skellig added, at the same time.

"I stumbled across one of their nests ..." Nuri began.

"Villages," Skellig softly interrupted.

"What?"

"It's what I heard tribesmen call each other when there's more than one."

"Ah. Very well. As I was saying, I came across one of their villages a fortnight ago as I was hunting sturgeon."

Both Zeira and Skellig nodded, comprehending. Since Blaze was nowhere near the sea, and since seafood was not readily available, sturgeon was considered a delicacy to the Fire dragons. Zeira drooled accordingly.

"Where are they?" Skellig wanted to know.

Nuri looked east. "That way, at least a hundred leagues away."

"How did I miss them?" Zeira moaned. "That's the way I came, and I didn't see anything."

"Perhaps you were flying too high?" Nuri suggested. "Or perhaps flying too fast? Maybe you weren't far enough north? Or perhaps …"

"I get it," Zeira angrily interrupted. "I have no one to blame but myself."

"It's not important," Nuri assured her. The valthan looked at Skellig with concern evident on her features. "If you're too weak to make the flight, I could make my way there, find one of your tribesmen, and bring them back here to you."

"Too weak?" Skellig scoffed. He huffed out his chest and tried to look imposing. "I may only have two days left, but I'm not an invalid. I can make the flight. Besides, the chances of finding an eligible tribesman on your first attempt are slim."

About ready to push herself back into the sea, Nuri hesitated. "Eligible? What do you mean?"

"How can you not know about eligibility?" Skellig asked, dumbfounded. "Not all dragons can bond with a kai, and not all tribesmen can be a kai. It's very specific."

"On top of which," Zeira hastily added, "only tribesmen from our home regions are eligible to us."

Nuri hesitated a few moments as she digested this bit of news. "This village I found? It's on Gale?"

Skellig shrugged. "I don't know. I won't know until I get there."

Nuri turned to Zeira. "What about you? Could this be your home region? Wait. It occurs to me that I haven't asked you where you're from. You're a Fire dragon, aren't you?"

"Phoenix," Zeira confirmed. "I come from Blaze."

"Blaze," Nuri repeated. "I do not know where that is."

Zeira pointed southeast. "Back that way."

"Near the water?" Nuri hopefully asked.

"I'm sorry, no."

Fully in the sea now, Nuri dipped below the surface, only to appear nearly two hundred feet away a second or two later. "Very well. Time is wasting. Are you two ready to fly?"

Skellig spread his massive wings. "Always."

Zeira did the same.

Nuri flashed them each a devilish grin. "Do try and keep up."

* * *

"I don't understand how she can swim so fast."

"Finding it difficult to keep up?"

Zeira eyed her companion. After a few seconds, she groaned. "Yes."

"Did you know she's not swimming as fast as she could?"

"How do you know that?"

"She told me."

Zeira stared at Skellig with undisguised confusion written all over her face. "How? Is she talking to you like the two of us can talk? Without speaking, that is?"

"Yes. If you quell your thoughts, you'd be able to pick up hers, too."

"Next you'll be telling me that she can already pick up mine."

Skellig fell silent.

Zeira turned suspiciously to the only other dragon sharing the sky with her and frowned. "She has, hasn't she?"

"She has," Skellig confirmed, chuckling. "But, don't hold that against her. She says you …"

"Think too loud," Zeira interrupted. "I get it."

Nuri? Can you hear me?

Of course.

Zeira started to apologize but stopped herself. *Are we close?*

We are nearly there.

This place you're taking us … this village … are there many tribesmen there? Will there be enough candidates for everyone?

I'm not looking for a rider. Bipeds are troublesome, always fighting, and they care little about anything but themselves.

"Tell us how you really feel," Skellig softly murmured, which earned him a snort of amusement from Zeira.

We don't have a choice. My king needs every eligible dragon to find a kai. That's the only way we can address whatever is threatening us.

What do you know about this threat?

Honestly? Not much, Zeira admitted. *Our king spoke of great battles, fought when there shouldn't have been anything to fight about. Tribesmen with tribesmen, dragons against dragons, and so on. It's being blamed on the fact that we always seem to be picking fights with the Terran dragons.*

Do you typically quarrel with the Terran dragons? Skellig asked.
No.

This imbalance has affected Gale just as much as it has Blaze. We have started three skirmishes with neighboring regions, and there aren't even that many of us.

We feel it, too.

Detecting a wave of curiosity, and a brief flash of shock, both aerial dragons automatically glanced down. Flying much lower than they typically did, at a height of three hundred feet off the ground, the two companions immediately looked left, toward the sea. Had something spooked Nuri?

Not spooked. But I haven't seen this for many years. In fact, I didn't know they still did this.

Did what? Skellig wanted to know. *Where are you?*

I'm to the east; I see you. See the larger of the two peninsulas jutting north?

Yes.

I'll lead you; you need to see this.

By the time Zeira and Skellig had joined their valthan companion, what they saw drew them both up short. Nuri was still mostly in the water, but at least a dozen feet of her front half, including her front forelegs, was out of the water and resting on the ground. Directly before them was a wooden structure in the shape of a pyramid. On the side facing the water was a small platform. On this platform was a wide dais, and strapped to it was something that was struggling to free itself of the bonds keeping it there.

"Would you get a load of that?" Skellig remarked, snorting with amusement.

"What is it?" Zeira asked, genuinely confused. "What are we looking at?"

Skellig settled himself to the ground and turned to look at Zeira. He then pointed back at the wooden structure.

"There's something you don't see every day."

"I don't know what I'm looking at," Zeira reluctantly admitted.

Skellig stepped out of the way and then pointed at the

platform.

"You wanted to find one of the tribesmen, young Zeira. Well, there you go. I give you one … I don't know, Nuri. I can't tell if it's a male or female. Can you?"

Nuri moved closer and looked down at the tiny, struggling biped. "I don't know, either. I've never been this close to one."

The trussed-up being emitted a high-pitched squeal as the three of them leaned down for a closer look. After a few moments, Skellig straightened and looked at Zeira.

"It's a female, I'm sure of it. You can have this one. I'm sure there will be others." Skellig turned expectantly to Nuri, who nodded.

The gag that had been stuffed into the biped's mouth suddenly fell away as evidently the female tribesman had bit through the cords holding the gag in place. She took one look at the three dragons, all looking expectantly down at her, and let out a blood-curdling scream. Then she passed out.

Chapter 5 — Biped

It's rather anti-climactic, don't you think? We travel all this way, seeking out one of their kind, and when we find one? None of us want anything to do with it."

"I never said that," Zeira complained.

"I don't see you helping it off that platform," Skellig pointed out.

"I still don't understand," Zeira protested. "What's it doing here? Why has it been immobilized?"

Skellig and Nuri shared a quick look. Zeira knew that only a few seconds elapsed, yet the two of them seemed to be locked into some type of silent conversation. After a few more moments had passed, the valthan finally nodded.

"Zeira," Nuri patiently began, "do you see this structure before you? I'm talking about this pyramidal wooden creation. Well, it's called an *altar* and it's used to hold sacrifices."

Zeira looked down at the unresponsive creature still trussed up on the offering table, and frowned.

"A sacrifice? For what?"

"I think you'll discover that it's more for a *who* than a *what*," Skellig added.

"I'm still lost," Zeira admitted.

Skellig made a sweeping motion with his claw, indicating the three of them. "If I'm not mistaken, then I do believe that *she* is an offering to *us*."

The three dragons stared at the unconscious biped in collective silence. After a few moments, Skellig nudged the figure as gently as he could with one of his talons. When the female tribesman didn't respond, he shared a helpless look at his two companions before shrugging.

"What do we do now?"

"We need to wake it up," Nuri decided. "Tribesmen don't like water. I propose we give it a good splashing. That ought to wake it back up."

Skellig nodded. "Do it."

Nuri shook her head. "Your arms are longer than mine. It'd be easier if you do it."

"Fine. Here, give it to me."

Nuri passed the unresponsive tribesman to Skellig, but not before slicing the biped's bonds away with a swipe of one of her talons. Nuri retreated into the water to watch as Skellig, with the female tribesman splayed out in his palm, unceremoniously thrust his claw into the water. Horrified, Zeira used her tail to swat Skellig's arm.

"You can't just do that to a tribesman. They don't breathe underwater. You have to be gentle about it."

Skellig grunted by way of acknowledgment. He pulled his claw out of the water and was rewarded with some angry squawks coming from the tiny creature, who was now very clearly awake. Setting the small being on the ground, the three of them crowded close once more.

"Oh, please don't eat me," the creature implored, using a soft, high-pitched voice. "Whatever you think I did, I didn't do it. Please, humans taste terrible. We're not worth the effort."

"You speak?" Zeira asked.

"What? Of course I speak, as do you. What of it?"

Skellig lowered his head so he could study the small

biped up close. After several seconds of silence had passed, the Spark dragon straightened, smiled at his companions, and held up a claw, with a single talon extended.

"I do believe we may have discovered the first intelligent example of this species. Did anyone know these things could talk?"

"We've been looking for you," Zeira formally began. This caused the biped to squeal with alarm. "Well, not for you, but for others of your kind. You're the first we've encountered, so you'll have to do."

As agitated as the female tribesman had been, it was now silent as it stared up at the three of them. Zeira felt a pang of pity for the creature, having been abandoned by its kind, and for what? So that someone like them would happen along and consume it? What purpose could that possibly serve?

"You're not going to eat me?" the small biped nervously asked.

"I, for one," Skellig began, as if he was giving a speech, "do not care for the taste. Besides, I got a bone stuck in my fangs once and it took me nearly a fortnight to get the blasted thing out."

The small creature blinked its fearful eyes up at the towering Spark dragon, emitted another high-pitched shriek, and bolted. Almost immediately, it collided with Zeira's tail, which she had at the ready since she was fairly certain the tiny creature would try to pull off a foolish stunt like this. She hadn't wasted this much time searching for one of the elusive bipeds only to let it escape now.

"Please let me go!" the creature wailed.

"Do be quiet," Zeira scolded. "None of us are going to eat you. The reason we wanted to find a … if you try to run again, you won't like … and, it's running again. Nuri, would you?"

"With what?" the valthan demanded. "My arms aren't long enough to snatch the crazy thing as it goes by!"

"Then grab it with your tail!" Skellig ordered. "Don't let it get away!"

The tribesman managed to elude Nuri's many coils, but anyone could see that it was only a matter of time before it was apprehended again. Once it was, all three dragons were actively scowling at it, which caused the poor thing to break down in tears. Zeira looked up at her companions and saw both of them were staring, waiting for her to make the first move.

"Can you understand me?" Zeira began slowly.

"Of course I can," the biped insisted, between sniffles.

"Good. Listen carefully. If you try to escape, then you'll just be caught. The three of us are looking for ..."

"... two," Nuri gently corrected.

"Right. The two of us are looking for kais. We want riders, only we can't seem to find many of your tribesmen. You are the first we've come across, so perhaps you could kindly ..."

"Tribesmen? Why do you keep calling me by that name?"

Zeira shrugged. "It's just what we have always called you creatures. Your kind typically travel in packs, er, *tribes*."

"For the record, we call ourselves *humans*," the female insisted. "And are you sure you're not going to hurt me?"

"You're more valuable to us alive than dead," Skellig nonchalantly announced.

The human's eyes widened with alarm once again.

"Don't pay any attention to him," Zeira told the human. "You don't want us to call you a tribesman? That's fine. What was that word you said earlier?"

"Human."

"Ah. Very well. Human, if you ..."

"You can call me by my name. It's Jerica."

"Your name?" Skellig interjected, surprised. "You're telling us that tribe ... er, humans, have names?"

"You have a name, don't you?" Jerica challenged, as she looked up at the imposing yellow dragon. "I assume you all do. Well, so do we."

Skellig looked at Nuri. "Did you know that?"

"I did not," Nuri confirmed.

"Are all dragons like you?" Jerica suddenly asked.

All three looked down at the human.

"Why do you ask?" Zeira wanted to know.

"You aren't the bloodthirsty, always-hungry reptiles that we've been led to believe."

"Always hungry?" Nuri snorted. "Well, there may be some dragons who fit that description, but not us. At least, I don't think that's us."

Zeira pointed at the altar. "Who put you on that thing? Was someone trying to get you killed?"

Jerica's face fell. "My village held a lottery. I was the unfortunate winner."

Skellig held up a claw. "Wait a moment. Let me see if I have this straight. You were chosen to be an offering, to some ... how did you put it? Bloodthirsty, always-hungry reptile? What was that supposed to have accomplished?"

"The baron thought that perhaps a sacrifice would help appease you dragons."

"Us dragons?" Zeira repeated. She glanced at Skellig, who shrugged and looked at Nuri, who also shrugged. "And what's barren? Never mind. Do you tr... er, humans, not get along with dragons?"

"We get along just fine!" Jerica practically cried. "As long as we don't get eaten, you'll find that most humans are very amenable to a wide variety of situations."

"Something must've happened," Skellig decided. "Why else have this altar, and then strap you to it?"

"You're not the first, are you?" Zeira softly asked, appalled.

Jerica hung her head. "I was not. It started three weeks ago. One of our hunting parties was attacked by a dragon. Then, one of our boats disappeared, never to return. What else were we supposed to think? So, the baron decided that reparations should be made."

"Reparations for what, exactly?" Nuri asked.

"Well, for whatever you think we did to anger you," Jerica answered.

Skellig held up a hand and signaled the human to wait. Then, motioned for Zeira and the valthan to huddle close. Turning back to look at Jerica, he pointed straight down.

"Wait right there. Please. I need to confer with my associates."

"You certainly don't sound like any dragons I've heard of," the human admitted.

"Hold that thought. What do you two think? Zeira, you've been wanting to find one of these things, er, humans, and we have found one. I say we test it. Um, that is to say, *her*. Go ahead and see if this particular one is eligible."

"I've always wanted to see this," Nuri admitted, excitedly. "Perhaps ... perhaps if we choose to simply swim on the surface, then maybe we valthan can find kais, too?"

Skellig shrugged. "It couldn't hurt to try. Zeira?"

Zeira lowered her head until she was looking at the human eye-to-eye. This, understandably, did not sit well with the much smaller human, who began to tremble and back away.

"I'm not going to hurt you," Zeira assured her. "I'd like to find out if you're eligible."

"To be a dragon rider?" Jerica asked. "Hardly. The only people in my village who can do magic are the mages, and that'd be Doolan. However, he's so old that I'm sure he'd fall off if ever given a chance."

"Nevertheless, may I try?"

Jerica stared silently at her for a few moments before dropping down into a cross-legged sitting position.

"You asked politely, and I appreciate that. Go ahead. Do whatever it is you're going to do."

"Thank you."

"What's she going to do?" Zeira heard Nuri ask Skellig.

"We must be quiet. Zeira is going to attempt to sense the human's presence with only her mind. If they can connect, then each will be able to sense the other's thoughts. Zeira will be able to use Jerica's senses, as Jerica will be able to share Zeira's."

Closing her eyes, Zeira quieted her mind — as much as she was able — and opened her senses. She was immediately drawn to her right, which wasn't surprising, since that was where Skellig and Nuri were quietly waiting. As with all dragons, she was able to pick up their thoughts, but since she wasn't the most experienced at reading other dragons' minds, it took a few minutes before it happened. Nuri, it would seem, was hungry, and was wondering if she or Skellig would find it offensive if she were to dip back into the water for a quick bite to eat. Skellig, picking up the valthan's thought, too, told her to go ahead.

Then, just as she started to think that she'd have to keep searching for other tribesmen, er, humans, a new presence appeared in her mind. As the seconds ticked away, and the new mental connection strengthened, she was surprised to hear Jerica's voice. She was eligible! This human was capable of being her rider!

That's just great. Now I'm hearing voices in my head. What would my father think?

Taking a breath, Zeira sent her first thought to a non-dragon being.

I'd say he'd congratulate you on becoming a kai.

What? Who is this? Are you one of those dragons?

Zeira looked over at the human girl and saw that she was shifting her gaze between her and Skellig. She thumped her tail on the ground a few times and offered the girl a smile.

"Of course it's me. Did that voice sound like Skellig's?"

"Well, no. Wait, I heard your voice inside my head! Does that make us telepathic?"

"It makes dragon and rider telepathic," Zeira corrected.

"But ... I don't *want* to be a rider!"

"This unease your tribe has been feeling," Skellig said, drawing the girl's attention, "the source of it is the same which drives us to seek kais. Do you want to help your fellow ... humans in addressing this issue?"

"Why did you hesitate to say humans?"

"It just doesn't sound right," Skellig decided. "Say it with me, only slower: *hee-yoo muns*. Tribesmen makes you sound so much better, more dignified. I'm just saying."

"You can take it up with the baron," Jerica laughed. "What happened to the other one? The long, skinny one?"

Zeira turned to look out at the water. "Nuri? She was hungry, so she went looking for something to eat."

"How do you know that?" Jerica curiously asked. "Can you pick up their thoughts like you could mine?"

Zeira nodded. "That's right. All dragons have the ability to communicate in such a fashion. It's a little harder for me, just because I haven't done it much."

Skellig tapped the side of his head. "She has too many thoughts bouncing around in there."

Jerica giggled, then turned to Skellig. "What about you? You're looking for a rider, too?"

"I am, but it'll have to be another person. We cannot bond with someone who has already bonded with another."

"Oh. Zeira, you're saying you and I are bonded?"

"I can sense your thoughts, and you can sense mine," Zeira explained. "To tell you the truth, I don't know what else we have to do. Skellig, do you?"

"I just assumed it wouldn't ... apologies. I do mean you, Jerica. I simply assume that you would be unable to share anything with other dragons once you bond with your first."

Jerica turned her full attention on Skellig, sat on the closest rock, and smiled at the Spark dragon. "Would you care to try?"

Skellig turned to Zeira, who shrugged. "It'd be harmless, right?"

"I'm not worried about you stealing her, if that's what you mean," Zeira replied. She nodded at the human girl. "Go ahead and try. His need is greater than my own."

"What does that mean?" Jerica wanted to know.

"I'll explain it later," Skellig assured her. "Very well. Close your eyes and try to clear your mind."

The human girl's eyes closed. "I'm ready when you are."

Zeira watched as Skellig settled himself to the ground and lowered his head until it was just a few feet away from the girl's. Then, after only a few seconds had passed, Skellig's eyes snapped open.

"You can sense her," Zeira guessed.

"How is this possible? Perhaps she hasn't fully bonded with you yet?"

"Don't worry about me just yet," Zeira scolded. "I'm more concerned about you. Do you feel anything?"

"It's as I thought. I cannot ... just a moment."

Curiosity piqued, Zeira watched Skellig closely for some type of sign he was able to sense their new human friend. After a few moments, Skellig's eyes opened and instantly sought out hers.

I can sense her, too. We have spoken and shared thoughts! It's ... I have ...

What? Tell me!

Zeira, it feels like I've found a haven! Do you know what this means?

Are you suggesting you're no longer in danger of fading?

Yes!

Skellig, that's wonderful news!

It is, and it isn't.

How so?

"What's going on?" Jerica asked. "Why have you two fallen silent? Are you speaking telepathically?"

She deserves to know, Zeira silently told Skellig.

"She deserves to know *what?*" Nuri suddenly asked, as her head rose out of the water. A few moments later, their valthan friend was standing next to them. "Did you try bonding? Were you able to sense her?"

"Yes," both Zeira and Skellig said, in unison.

Nuri stared at the two of them for a moment before shaking her head.

"Well, which is it? Who has found their kai?"

"He has," Zeira said, pointing at Skellig.

"Have not," Skellig argued, pointing back at Zeira. "She bonded with the human first."

"Clearly not, since you just told me that you're now no longer in danger of fading," Zeira pointed out. "That supersedes any claim I may have."

"Oh, no you don't," Skellig said, as a low growl began emanating from deep within his chest. "I ..."

"Excuse me? I think the subject of this particular argument should be allowed to say a few words."

The dragons fell silent and—as one—all dropped their gazes down to the human. Jerica rose to her feet and approached Skellig.

"So, I could sense your thoughts just like I could sense Zeira's. What does that mean?"

"That's not supposed to be possible," Nuri insisted.

Jerica turned to the valthan. "Why? Can't I choose which dragon I want to bond with?"

"I thought you didn't want to be a kai," Zeira reminded her.

"Wait, you're right. I … forget about that for now. For the sake of argument, let's say I did. Wouldn't I get to choose?"

Zeira shrugged. "Well, ordinarily I'd say yes, but in this case, Skellig's need is the strongest."

"What is that supposed to mean?" Jerica asked.

"For him, it's a matter of life or death," Nuri added.

Jerica stared at the largest of the three dragons. "What does she mean by that?"

"I have only two days left before the Fade."

"Fade?" Jerica sputtered, as she leapt to her feet. "You're talking about dissipating, aren't you? But … I thought only humans were limited by geography. It affects dragons, too? That must mean that everything, and every creature, must have the same limitations. That, well, that is to say, er…"

"… stinks," Nuri finished, drawing nods from the other two.

Zeira pointed at Skellig. "But, the moment you bonded with him, then the threat of fading, well, faded. It's as though he returned to his home region of Gale."

Surprised, Nuri looked at Skellig for confirmation. When the Spark dragon nodded, Nuri hissed with surprise.

"You've already bonded with the human? I thought she was Zeira's?"

"I don't belong to anyone," Jerica clarified, as she crossed her arms over her chest. "Do you really consider your precious riders as objects?"

The same look of sheepishness appeared on the faces of all three dragons. Nuri held up one of her comically tiny forelegs.

"Now, no offense was intended, Jerica. I simply meant to say that, of the three of us, Skellig's need is strongest, since he was due to fade in a few days. Now, it would seem, since he has bonded with you, then you …"

"Except I haven't," Skellig interrupted.

Nuri looked helplessly at Zeira. "But I thought you said that he had? How would he have stemmed off fading if he hadn't?"

Zeira rounded on Skellig. "Is that true? You haven't bonded with the human?"

"Granted, I've never bonded with a human before," Skellig admitted, shrugging, "so how would I know?"

"Try to do some magic together," Nuri suggested.

"M-magic?" Jerica stammered. "I can't do magic. I'm not a mage, I'm sorry."

"One of my kin had a kai," Skellig announced. "He told me that, once a bond has been created with a kai, both dragon and rider would be able to sense each other's thoughts. Each of them could also share their other senses. What one sees, so does the other."

"Well, that doesn't work," Jerica decided. "I sensed Zeira's thoughts before, and I've also sensed Skellig's. If what you're saying is true, then I've bonded with both of them."

"That isn't possible," Nuri repeated, frowning.

"Right, so if I've bonded with one of you two dragons, then I'd like to find out which one, all right? I'm just not sure how to do it. I've never been able to do magic."

"That you know of," Zeira quietly added.

Jerica shrugged. "That's a fair point. Very well, what do I need to do?"

"Physical contact," Skellig said. He lowered his neck until his head was resting on the ground. *I truly hope that I haven't bonded yet. I'd hate to take Zeira's kai from her.*

"I heard that," Jerica accused, as she tapped the side of her head, "up here. And, for the record, I'm not in physical contact. Does that mean Nuri's right? Are you and I a bonded pair?"

Skellig shook his head at the same time Nuri nodded. Catching sight of each other, the two largest dragons shared a smile.

"We need to test this," Zeira decided. "Skellig, you're a Spark dragon. I've seen you emit bolts of lightning from your wing talons Try to do something now."

"It's going to be the same," Skellig insisted. "I don't feel any different."

"Physical contact," Nuri said. "Jerica, would you please humor us? Place yourself into physical contact with Skellig."

Jerica looked up at the sinewy valthan and smiled. "You asked politely, and you said *please*. I'll do it for you."

Zeira watched the human stride fearlessly up to Skellig's head and place a soft hand on one of the Spark dragon's exposed lower fangs. After a few moments, Jerica looked up at Nuri.

"Now what?"

Nuri turned to Skellig. "Do it. Summon lightning."

"This is a waste of time," Skellig muttered. "Zeira, Nuri, step away from me, if you please."

"What about me?" Jerica timidly asked.

"If you are my kai," Skellig began, as his great wings unfolded and he stretched them out to their fullest potential, "then you, as a rider, would be immune to anything I can do."

"And if I'm not?" Jerica nervously asked.

"We'll worry about that when and if the time comes," Skellig decided. "Now, don't move!"

Skellig's torso began to glow. It swelled ominously, as though the Spark dragon was gulping large amounts of air, even though he wasn't. After a few moments, the visible glow on Skellig's torso shot upward, toward his wings. Briefly illuminating the wing's skeletal structure, as if lit from within, the glow quickly worked its way to the wing talons where, after another few moments had elapsed, a massive flash of light erupted out of each wing talon. The two flashes merged into one giant pulse of energy, which exploded outward in all directions.

"That's never happened before," Skellig said, surprised. "I don't know if that's a misfire of …"

The Spark dragon trailed off as he turned to look at his two dragon companions. Nuri was resting in the water with her head on the beach and her eyes closed. Similarly, Zeira lay on the ground, breathing quietly. Remembering that a fourth person was there, albeit human in nature, Skellig lowered his head and inspected the area.

"Jerica, are you there?"

"Yes. I'm by your left front foot."

"Ah. There you are."

"What happened to the others?"

"I'm not sure. I've never seen my abilities behave that way before."

"You haven't? Not ever?"

"Never. You, human, had something to do with it, I'm sure. Before we get into that, we need to be sure our companions are all right."

Nuri was the first to regain consciousness, and that was only when Skellig gently nudged the side of her head.

"What happened?" the valthan asked, as she lifted her head and gave it a shake. Her eyes fixed on Jerica and they widened. "Something happened with her, didn't it? You two *have* bonded, haven't you?"

Skellig nodded. "It would appear so. Or else my abilities have misfired."

"Have you ever misfired before?"

"That's a rather personal question, don't you think?"

It was the valthan's turn to flush with embarrassment. "I'm sorry. I didn't mean anything by that. What I meant was, have you ever lost control like that before?"

"Oh. Then … no."

"Jerica, do you still maintain you don't use magic?"

"It's not that I don't want to," Jerica clarified, "but that I can't. Magic has never run in my family."

"Ooooo, what happened?"

Everyone turned to Zeira, who was shakily regaining her feet. "What'd I miss?"

"You were knocked out," Jerica reported.

"I was? How?"

Jerica and Nuri both pointed at Skellig.

"You knocked me out? Why?"

"Well, I didn't mean to," Skellig responded, growing defensive. "I've never generated a blast like that."

Zeira's eyes widened. "So, it's true. You've bonded with her."

"I swear I haven't," Skellig insisted, "but, I will admit that I can hear her thoughts. I presume you can hear mine?"

"I did earlier."

A loud splash sounded from Nuri's direction. The valthan had slapped the water with her tail in a practiced move to get everyone's attention. She pointed at Jerica and then at Zeira.

"All right, it's your turn now."

"There's no point," Zeira argued. "If the two of them have already ..."

"Just humor me and try, will you?"

"Fine," Zeira grumped. *What do you have to worry about? You're a valthan. You'll never have to worry about finding a kai.*

"True, but she wants to."

Zeira turned to the small human. "You heard my thoughts? But, that's ..."

"... impossible?" Nuri dryly finished for her. "I know, I keep saying the same thing. Zeira, lower your head. Let's have Jerica do the exact same thing she did with Skellig."

"This isn't going to work," Zeira murmured, as she lowered her head.

Jerica approached and laid a tentative hand on Zeira's nose. "There. Now what?"

"Zeira, it's your turn to try and do something," Skellig urged.

"But ... you *know* what has to happen in order for that to, er, happen."

"What is she talking about?" Nuri wanted to know. "She's a Fire dragon. She spits fire. What's the problem?"

Skellig made a shushing motion with his hand at Nuri while trying to offer the small fire dragon a supportive smile.

"We're all friends here, Zeira. You told me this is why you were seeking a kai. Well, let's find out, shall we?"

"But ..."

"It's nothing to be ashamed of," Skellig continued.

"But ..."

"I have no idea what's going on here," Nuri interjected. "Is there something wrong with Zeira's fire?"

"It's why she's seeking a kai in the first place," Skellig answered. "I will not tell them, Zeira. That responsibility is reserved for you."

Zeira sighed heavily and groaned. Keeping her eyes firmly fixed on the ground, she explained why she couldn't summon fire like all other Fire dragons. Much to Nuri's credit, she didn't blink an eye at the unusual circumstances necessary to properly invoke Zeira's fires.

"Can you become nauseous at will?" Nuri curiously asked.

"I have to eat something first," Zeira miserably answered.

"And if I could produce something that would give the intended results, all without having to consume it? Would you be interested?"

Zeira perked up. "You're suggesting you can make me nauseous just on sight alone?"

Nuri nodded. "I can. I have just the thing. I'll be right back."

Zeira shook her head in disbelief. Where had this knowledge been her entire life? If she could avoid eating nasty insects, she'd be all for it!

Five minutes later, Nuri was back. She promptly swam up to the beach, reared her front torso out of the water, and spat something at Zeira's feet. It was several feet long, pale, and writhing on the ground in copious amounts of slime. The sight of the creature wriggling about in a pool of its own slime, along with the wet squelching noise it made, was the most disgusting thing Zeira had ever seen. Imagining that creature in her mouth had her digestive system rumbling its protest.

"Is it working?" Nuri asked.

"Yes. I need everyone in front of me. Now!"

Skellig hurried over to stand next to Nuri at the water's edge. Since Jerica was still in contact with her nose, Zeira now knew that she was free to ... how did she want to describe it? Let it rip? Fire away? Whatever. It was time to show everyone the power she had at her disposal. Too bad such obvious extremes had to take place before she was able to wield her ...

A cloud of super-heated steam erupted from her hind end and struck a nearby copse of trees. Leaves and pine needles fell from the sky as the affected trees wilted, and every living thing fell silent.

"Judging by the expression on your face," Skellig began, "I'm guessing that has never happened to you before, either?"

Zeira could only nod.

"She shot out steam from her tail end," Jerica softly

muttered. "There's something you don't see every day."

Zeira's head fell. Surprisingly, Jerica was by her side in a flash. "Oh, no, I'm so sorry! I didn't mean anything by it!"

"Do you have any idea," Zeira slowly began, "of what it's like to be a Fire dragon and the only way I can line anyone up in my sights is to use my tail as a pointer? Imagine, if you will, what my life was like, hiding my abnormality and simply pretending I didn't have any flames."

"But you do," Skellig argued. "Front end, back end, it doesn't make any difference."

"It does to me," Zeira insisted. "You cannot possibly understand how embarrassing it is."

"And *that* was why you wanted to find a kai," Nuri said, nodding. "It makes perfect sense now. You were hoping that, with the addition of a rider, your combined abilities will overcome your … weakness."

Zeira reluctantly nodded. "That was my thinking, aye."

"Was that steam?" Jerica asked, as she joined the others at the shore. "You said you're a Fire dragon. Did the two of us produce something different, the way Skellig and I did?"

Zeira could only nod. She was reeling with several new revelations. First, she wouldn't have to eat disgusting insects, ever again. Thanks to Nuri's … wait. What *was* that thing she had dropped on the beach, anyway? Without making eye contact with the pool of slime, and the strange fish writhing about in its own goo, Zeira gestured in that direction. She detected movement in the pool and had to take several long gulps of air in order to combat the queasiness. Thankfully, her digestive system returned to normal.

"If I ever ask, don't tell me what it is," she began, which drew chuckles from her companions, dragon and human alike. "I can't thank you enough. I'm quite certain I'll never have to consume another insect again."

"You're welcome," Nuri said, nodding. "It's called a hagfish. Or slime eel, whichever you prefer."

"Blech. I didn't know fish could look like that."

"Or sound like that," Skellig agreed. "I was right there with you, Zeira. One more second of having to look at Nuri's present would have made me sick, too."

Zeira refused to look back at the slime pool. "Is it gone? Tell me you got rid of it."

Nuri nodded. "In a matter of speaking, aye."

"Do *not* tell us what you did with it," Skellig ordered. "Ever."

Nuri smiled. "Deal. Now, seeing how both of you have had similar reactions to Jerica's touch, namely producing some type of ability you've never seen before, what does that tell you? She hasn't bonded with anyone, has she?"

Both Skellig and Zeira shook their heads no.

"Does that mean I could bond with either of you?" Jerica curiously asked.

As one, Fire and Spark turned to the valthan.

"Don't look at me," Nuri said. "I can't have a kai."

"Because you can swim and breathe underwater," Skellig said, nodding. "What if you didn't? What if you just swam along the surface? That way, you could have a rider on your back."

Nuri's mouth closed with an audible snap. The valthan turned to look down at Jerica and cocked her head.

"What are you suggesting?" Jerica asked, as she slowly backed up. "I can't breathe underwater!"

"As Skellig pointed out, what if I don't duck below the surface?" Nuri curiously asked. "I'm wondering if I could bond with you, too."

Jerica smiled up at the water dragon. "Sure, why not? I've never ridden a dragon before."

Zeira watched as the small human approached Nuri's still form and contemplated how to scale her back. Placing an open claw next to the girl, Zeira waited for Jerica to climb on before lifting her high enough to clamber onto the valthan's long, sinewy back.

"Keep her safe," Zeira ordered.

"On the open sea, there's no one safer than me," Nuri assured them. "Don't go anywhere. We'll be right back."

In the blink of an eye, the valthan was gone, leaving a trail of ripples and bubbles.

"I confess I had no idea anything could move that fast in the water," Skellig observed.

"She can swim faster than I can fly," Zeira reminded her friend.

"You, perhaps, but me? I'm eager to try my luck. I'm joking, of course. I know she's faster than either of us."

A few minutes of silence passed.

"Do you think she'll be able to bond with the human?" Skellig eventually asked.

"There's something amiss here," Zeira decided. "She can pick up my thoughts. I know she was picking up yours. You generated some type of electrical blast which rendered Nuri and me unconscious. You said it has never happened before?"

"Correct."

"And as for me? Well, you've seen my flames at work before. I shot water out of my rear end, Skellig. Water! People are going to think I'm peeing myself."

Skellig snorted with amusement. "Highly unlikely, young Zeira. Everyone will be more focused on the simple fact that you have a kai."

"Well, so do you," Zeira reminded him.

"Aye, that's true. I wonder how the human is able to bond with both of us?"

"Or give the appearance she's bonded with us, yet she hasn't?" Zeira added.

"A fair point. Do you know of anyone who has ever had a kai?"

"Not for centuries. I ... of course! Now I remember!"

"You remember what, exactly?" Skellig asked, interested.

"The kais! We wanted to know if there was any way to tell whether or not Jerica had bonded with anyone?"

Skellig grunted once by way of acknowledgment.

"Any tribesman who becomes a kai will be given a mark. How on Andela did I forget that?"

"What kind of mark?" Skellig asked.

Zeira shrugged. "I don't remember where the mark will be, only that she will have one. The marks denote the home region. If you're a kai, and your home is Blaze, then your mark will be a fang. If you are Spark, and from Gale, that's lightning, and I believe that will be a ..."

"... scale," Skellig interjected. "I've heard this before,

too. Can't imagine why I've forgotten it, either."

"Jerica says she's Terran," Zeira said. "If she bears the mark of terra, then that is, er, wait. I know this. Terra, terra, terra. That's … horns! Yes, horns."

"And if she doesn't bear the mark?" Skellig slowly asked.

"We'll worry about that when we find out."

Skellig shrugged and, detecting movement from the north, looked over in time to see Nuri practically materialize out of thin air. A few seconds later, her high-speed wake caught up with them. Before Zeira could duck out of the way, a wave washed ashore and suddenly, she was up to her knees in water.

"Sorry 'bout that," Nuri apologized. "I typically outrace the waves, and only rarely do I venture to shore."

Zeira rose up on her hind legs and stretched her neck out. "How's Jerica? Were you able to pick up her thoughts?"

"You could just ask me, you know," came Jerica's voice. "Lie down, would you, Nuri? I'd like to get off."

"Of course."

Once the human was back on solid ground, Zeira and Skellig crowded close to the water dragon.

"Well?" Skellig pressed. "Were you successful?"

"I don't even know where to begin," Nuri admitted.

"From the beginning?" Skellig suggested.

"You weren't gone that long," Zeira pointed out. "What happened out there?"

"Well, first and foremost, yes, the two of us were able to sense each other's thoughts."

"All three of us," Skellig breathed. "I don't know how that's possible."

"That makes all of us," Nuri agreed. "Now, not only could we sense what the other was thinking, the bond between us protected her when she was underwater."

"What?" Skellig snapped, growing angry. "You said you wouldn't dive underwater. What happened?"

"I slipped up and forgot she was there," Nuri admitted. "A particularly nasty wave was approaching and I reflexively did what I always do in those situations: dip below the surface. How long were we under, Jerica?"

"Not long," the human answered. "For a few seconds, I'd say. Once Nuri realized what she did, she rushed to the surface and immediately checked to make sure I was all right. When I told her that not only was I fine, but was able to breathe underwater, we did a few tests. That's what took so long. We wanted to find out how I could survive underwater while Nuri swam."

"You can breathe underwater," Skellig repeated, amazed. "Something is definitely amiss here."

"What did you figure out?" Zeira asked, at the same time.

Nuri shrugged. "Not much. I can only assume that there's protective magic involved when physical contact is made. What the nature of that magic is, I cannot say."

Skellig eyed the tiny human and looked thoughtful. "Didn't you say that you are unable to perform magic?"

Jerica nodded. "I did, and that's because I can't."

"The pulse of energy which knocked out my two dragon companions says otherwise," Skellig argued.

Zeira held up a claw. "Hello! I shot out steam from my rear end. I've never done that before."

"And for a brief time," Nuri continued, "I had a kai. It makes me wonder if all kai behave the same, or is it just with this one?"

"I am no kai!" Jerica insisted. "Wouldn't I know it if I was?"

"I think we're getting ahead of ourselves," Zeira said. She faced Skellig. "I don't know about Gale, but in my region, we were told that only tribesmen living on Blaze could bond with us. Is that not so in Gale?"

Skellig nodded. "You are correct."

"But … she's not from either of those regions!" Nuri argued. "How can she bond with dragons from a different land?"

"What about you?" Skellig countered. "You said that you valthan have accepted the fact that you can never have a kai. What would you say to that now?"

"The reason I said it is because it's true," Nuri insisted. "For obvious reasons, we valthan cannot have a rider on our back. Why it worked for this human, I do not know."

"Ergo," Skellig continued, "this particular human has demonstrated she has magic of some sort."

"When you say it like that, it makes me want to believe you," Jerica said.

"Believe it," Skellig told her. "Based on what we've seen, I'd say it's safe to say your magic has something to do with water, am I right?"

Jerica held up her hands. "If it is, it's news to me. I'm the youngest of three sisters. None of us have magic in our blood, and that goes for my parents, too."

"Have you heard of kais bearing special marks?" Zeira asked, hoping to change the subject.

The human girl shook her head. "No, why?"

"It's a final test for us to see if you have bonded — willingly or unwillingly — with one of us," Skellig explained. "The marks are based on your home region."

Zeira watched the human girl stiffen with surprise, as if she had just been told an insect had landed somewhere on her skin.

"Where?"

"It's behind your ear, I think," Zeira said.

"No, it should be on your right shoulder," Nuri argued.

"You're both wrong," Skellig said. He tapped the inside of his right foreleg. "It'd be right here. One of my ancestors had a kai, and that's where he always said his rider was branded."

"Branded?" Jerica blurted, outraged. "I am *not* going to let any of you think I am your property. Do you hear me?"

"Poor choice of words," Skellig apologized. "His mark was a scale, and it was on the inside of his wrist."

Jerica immediately slapped a hand over the leather bracer she wore on her right wrist and whirled around. Very slowly, when she was sure she wasn't being watched, she removed the bracer and inspected the area for herself. After a few moments of silence, Zeira's curiosity couldn't be contained any longer.

"Well, Jerica, what do you see?"

The human slowly rotated until she was facing the three of them. Each of her fellow dragons, Zeira noticed, had the same expression on their face: anxiety. Each of them clearly wanted Jerica for themselves, but who would be lucky enough to be selected by the human?

"What symbol do you see?" Skellig gently asked. "Is it a scale?"

"No."

"A fang?" Zeira hopefully asked.

"No."

Skellig and Zeira turned to Nuri, who shrugged.

"How about a tail?"

Jerica shook her head. "I'm sorry, no."

"Do you have a mark of some sort?" Zeira finally asked. Jerica nodded. "I, er, do, yes."

"You do?" Skellig sputtered. "Oh, of course. You have the Terran mark, I should have thought to ask. Does anyone know the symbol for Terra? Zeira, Blaze is a neighbor. Do you know?"

Zeira tapped the top of her skull. "Horns, I believe."

The three dragons stared at the girl in silence, waiting for her to confirm or deny the nature of the mark on her arm.

"It's not horns, no."

"Well, then, what do you see?" Skellig asked.

Jerica uncovered her arm and held it up for everyone to see.

"It's a dragon. An entire dragon. Horns, fangs, scales, tail … everything. So, is that significant?"

Chapter 6 — First Task

You need to slow down. Rizzen, please. You're speaking too fast. Yes, I said the mark was a full dragon. No, I'm certain I haven't misidentified the mark. I'm looking at it now. What? It makes her a *what*? I'm not familiar with that term. Is it … no, you're going too fast again."

"What's going on?" Jerica quietly wanted to know.

"Zeira has initiated a mental connection to a friend of hers," Skellig explained softly. "She's speaking aloud for your benefit, so that you can follow along with the conversation."

"It's for your benefit, too, isn't it?" the girl asked.

Skellig tapped the side of his head. "Not for dragons. I'm able to hear both sides of this conversation. It would seem *you* have started a very lively debate."

Jerica looked at her arm. "You're referring to this infernal mark, aren't you?"

"Aye."

"Dragons are the best," Jerica praised. "Is there anything

your species can't do? You can fly, spit fire, and talk to each other without really talking. I'll be honest. I'm jealous."

"Look at Nuri," Skellig urged. "She doesn't have any wings, which means she cannot fly."

The valthan looked up. "What was that?"

"Miss Jerica was just telling me how much she envies us dragons."

"I may be a bit biased," Nuri agreed, nodding, "but I can agree with that."

"She may not fly in the air," Jerica began, "but she certainly can fly in the water. I never knew anyone could swim so fast. Are all you water dragons capable of swimming at such extreme speeds?"

Nuri shrugged. "I have yet to encounter anyone who could outperform me in the water."

"Even other valthans?" Skellig asked, interested.

"Aye, even among my own kind. I've always been an adept swimmer."

"No, Rizzen," Zeira stated, shaking her head. Her eyes were closed and she was resting on the ground. "I'm not going to do that. What do you mean, why? For starters, you don't treat a companion like a possession. Would you want someone to do that to you? No? What a surprise. I ... what's that? No, I'm not being difficult."

"What are they arguing about?" Jerica whispered, as she sidled closer to Skellig. "Do you know?"

"I do," the large Spark dragon confirmed. "Zeira's acquaintance is suggesting your mark is nothing more than a fluke and should be removed."

Jerica looked at the inside of her right wrist and nodded. "This friend of hers might be on to something."

"You should know that Zeira's friend suggested burning it off ..."

"I don't think so!" Jerica cried, as she whipped her arm behind her back.

"... or biting it off," Skellig continued.

"I'm liking her friend less and less," Jerica muttered.

"I will not let any harm befall you," Skellig promised.

Before the human girl could say anything, they heard a

loud, disgruntled snort. Zeira's eyes had opened and she was slowly rising to her feet.

"And she thinks she's the level-headed one. Pssht. Skellig and Nuri, you heard?"

"We did," Skellig confirmed.

Nuri nodded.

Zeira looked at the tiny biped and her features softened. "Did they tell you what happened?"

Jerica pointed at Skellig. "He did. And, I'd like to point out that he said he won't let anything happen to me."

Zeira stared at her much larger companion, surprised. A sense of gratefulness washed over her. "Thank you."

"Was your friend able to identify the mark?" Nuri anxiously asked.

Zeira took a deep breath and nodded. But, before she could speak, Jerica nervously cleared her throat.

"Is this mark really that special?"

Zeira nodded. "More than you can possibly imagine. Before I tell you what it means, let's review what we know. For starters, we know you're eligible to be a kai. No, Jerica, don't argue with me. I see that you want to, but all three of us were able to sense your thoughts, and you, in turn, could sense ours. That, by definition, makes you a natural kai."

Jerica sighed. "Fine. Go on."

"Did you catch what I just said? All three of us were able to share your thoughts and senses. A typical kai will only bond with one dragon, yet you are able to bond with each one of us."

"Is that a bad thing?" Jerica slowly asked.

"Far from it. Not only could you pick up our thoughts, but we could pick up yours. On top of which, you seem to be able to bond with any of us without permanent effects. And before you ask, I'm talking about sharing a second dragon's senses after sharing the first."

"Not to mention bringing in a third," Skellig added, as he gave Nuri a friendly nudge on her shoulder.

"Rizzen correctly identified what kind of kai you are," Zeira continued.

"There's more than one type?" Nuri asked softly.

Skellig shrugged. "If there is, then this is the first I've heard of it."

"No, you haven't," Zeira countered.

"You're suggesting I have heard of different kais? I assure you, I have not. I ..."

"Merrik the Daring."

"Merrik the Daring?" Jerica curiously repeated. "Who's that?"

"Merrik," Skellig breathed. "Of course."

"The greatest of all the dragons," Nuri reverently added.

"Why didn't I think of that?" Skellig complained.

"Would someone kindly tell me who Merrik is?" Jerica requested, raising a hand.

"Merrik was from Blaze," Zeira answered, in a hushed tone. "He was from the magma caste and is the most famous dragon from my home region."

"A magma dragon?" Jerica repeated. "What did he do? Spit lava?"

"He *lived* in the lava," Zeira clarified. "His physical prowess was unmatched, he was a great flyer, and he could go wherever he wanted, whenever he wanted."

Nuri perked up. "That's right. He could spend weeks on whatever region he wanted! I had forgotten about that."

"That makes two of us," Skellig confessed.

"And how could he do all that?" Zeira continued. "With the help of his kai, of course. His rider was from Gale, but they were still able to bond. Don't you get it? Merrik was great because his kai was a *kairie*."

"I don't know what that means."

"You're a kairie, Jerica," Zeira told the human. "You can bond with any dragon, and step foot onto any region, for any duration."

"No, I can't."

"Actually, you can," Zeira argued. "The three of us are proof."

"I can't be. None of my family can do magic."

"Until now," Skellig smugly announced. "You saved my life, human. For that, you have my eternal gratitude. I had given up days ago."

"I did *wh-what*?" Jerica sputtered. "How? When? I didn't do anything. I swear!"

"I would have succumbed to the Fade. I am a very long way from Gale, but have found ways to stay alive. I'm sure you're familiar with the process?"

Jerica nodded. "Go on."

"Now, I was in danger of Fading. I had less than two days, but was fully prepared to accept the inevitable. Yet, *you* happened along and just like that, I felt the effects of fading recede. Now it makes perfect sense. You're a kairie, the first Andela has seen in a hundred of your lifetimes."

"She's a kairie!" Nuri was saying. "I should have trusted my instincts. I *knew* something was different the moment I realized I could bond with her."

Zeira approached and sank to the ground. Once she was reclining comfortably, she looked at the small human and sighed. "I feel you should know that you can have your pick of dragons, from anywhere, and at any time. Once word of this gets out, you're going to be the most sought-after, highly desirable human in all of Andela!"

"I'm going to need you to explain how this *kairie* thing works," Jerica said, looking at the tiny dragon figure on the inside of her wrist. "What do I have to do to make it work? That's provided I believe all of this, by the way."

Skellig excitedly explained it all again. "Zeira, myself, and Nuri: Fire, Spark, and Water. Three different regions … well, make that *four* if we include you. You can have your pick of dragons."

"I don't want to have my pick of dragons," Jerica returned. "I'd much rather stick with you three, thank you very much. I know and trust all of you. Can you say the same about other dragons?"

"No," Zeira decided. "Nuri's right. There'd be a mad free-for-all if word got out you were available. In fact, the three of us would probably end up embroiled in fights in order to keep you safe."

"I don't want anyone getting into a fight on my behalf," Jerica said, growing both sad and angry at the same time. "Couldn't I just go back to what I was?"

"You were a sacrificial offering when we met you," Nuri pointed out.

"All right, that's a fair point. So, I'm this all-powerful dragon rider. Now what?"

Zeira looked at her companions. "I say we stick together as we try to figure out what to do next."

"You mean we should travel together?" Skellig hesitantly asked. He looked over at the valthan, who offered him a nod in return.

Zeira looked at the large Spark dragon. "She saved your life. The least you can do is repay the favor."

"I wasn't suggesting I abandon you three," Skellig insisted. "Besides, you'd make it less than a league without me."

Zeira and Nuri shared a brief look before they each grinned and looked away.

"Whatever you'd like to tell yourself," the valthan decided. "Wait, are you inviting me to accompany you on your quest?"

"We all want the same thing, don't we?" Zeira stated, as she looked at each of her companions in turn, finishing with the water dragon. "All of us in Blaze were tasked with finding kais, should we prove to be eligible. Skellig has said the same. Nuri, you've alluded you want to help, isn't that right? However, you've admitted that you weren't sure how to do that. Well, I think this is how. Come with us."

"Have the humans been impacted by this threat, too?" Nuri wanted to know.

As one, all three dragons turned to look down at the small biped. Jerica, in turn, sighed and nodded gravely.

"Cael might not be the biggest village," Jerica began, "but we still get news. We know there's something wrong. Doolan, our mage, won't say, but then again, that really isn't too surprising. He isn't the sharpest tool in the shed. But we've been getting random attacks on our hunting parties, and ..."

"By dragons?" Zeira anxiously asked.

Jerica shrugged. "I don't know, and honestly, I'm glad I don't. I probably don't want to know what the baron and his soldiers found last week." After seeing the blank looks worn by her dragon companions, Jerica sighed. "Our village is known for our steady supply of sturgeon. Smoked sturgeon is the

Thunder King's favorite dish. Therefore, much of our village relies on the sea for its livelihood. Last week, we, uh … lost one of our larger ships. My father says there were no survivors, but I get the impression he wasn't telling me everything."

"What did he leave out?" Zeira asked.

"If it was, indeed, a dragon attack," Nuri began, "and let's assume for the sake of argument that valthans were to blame …"

"Who else would it be?" Skellig demanded. "She said her village borders the sea."

"We already know something isn't right," Zeira said. "In Blaze, our king was starting to suspect neighboring tribesmen of attacking our game."

"Were they out of food?" Nuri curiously asked.

"There's plenty of food for everyone," Skellig angrily responded. "How could your king be so quick to judge?"

"Because there were witnesses," Zeira replied.

Jerica stepped into the huddle the three dragons were having and cleared her throat. "Excuse me, but I was the one speaking. May I finish?"

Skellig looked over at Zeira and snorted with amusement. "Your human, your problem."

"No, she's not. She's yours. I gave her to you."

Exasperated, Jerica let out a sigh. "Well, I, for one, would like to hear the end of your story, Nuri. Would you continue? I'd like to know what you suspect happened to my people."

Nuri nodded. "Of course. Jerica, what you have to understand is that, if we valthans were responsible for the, er, disappearance of your vessel, then that would mean the attack happened on the open sea. Believe me when I say that nothing outperforms us in the water. You've witnessed how fast we can swim, isn't that so?"

Jerica nodded.

"Traveling at those speeds … perhaps to best illustrate my point, I can demonstrate what I mean. Stay right there. Skellig, prepare to deflect. Are you picking up my thoughts?"

The Spark dragon nodded. "I am. I'll be ready."

"Good. Jerica, observe."

With considerable effort, the valthan pushed herself back

into the water. After a few moments, she simply vanished, but not before kicking up a wall of water nearly twenty feet high. It would have slammed into Jerica and swept her away had Skellig not spread his wings and deliberately stepped in front of everyone's favorite human. Zeira hastily approached Jerica and spread her own wings around her, although it wasn't necessary. After a few moments, the water drained back into the sea and the three of them were left speechless, staring at one another and all thinking the same thing: how could anything swim that fast?

"Had one of the valthans attacked your vessel," Nuri's voice explained, from inside Jerica's mind, "there wouldn't have been anything left but debris from a wrecked hull. Your *ships*, they're made of wood?"

Jerica gulped nervously and nodded.

"A valthan swimming at full-speed would have punched through your ship as easily as fangs through flesh."

"That is a horrible analogy," Skellig's voice scolded.

"Oh. My apologies. Needless to say, it wouldn't have had a chance."

Another wave of water appeared in the distance.

"From Nuri?" Jerica asked.

Zeira nodded. "Indubitably."

"Where is she?" Jerica wanted to know.

"I'm already here," Nuri's voice answered. "I deliberately accelerated so that I could neutralize the wave before it breeches the shore."

"Neutralize the wave?" Skellig repeated, confused. "What does that mean?"

"Observe," Nuri's voice said. "The wave approaches. As it does, a quick strike of the tail at the base of the wave, which is obviously below the surface, will effectively break it apart, rendering it completely harmless."

Sure enough, the rushing wall of water collapsed in on itself just as it reached the beach's tiny inlet. A few meandering waves eventually reached shore, but were only strong enough to lap at their feet. The valthan's head rose gracefully out of the water and winked at Jerica.

"As I said, if your vessel was attacked by the valthans, then

I'm truly sorry to say there wouldn't be much of anything left."

"I'm beginning to see that," Jerica admitted. "What do the water dragons have against us, anyway?"

Nuri sadly shook her head. "Nothing. I'm not aware of any skirmishes with the tribesmen, nor any other species."

"How long has it been happening?" Zeira asked. "In Blaze, we share a mountain with a roc flock. They ..."

Both Skellig and Nuri turned to look at Zeira with disbelief all over their features. Skellig held up a claw.

"Excuse me, but did you say *rock flock*?"

Zeira nodded. "That's right. Don't you have rocs in Gale?"

"Plenty," Skellig said, nodding, "only our rocks don't travel in flocks."

"What do they travel in?" Zeira wanted to know, clearly missing the fact that both of them were talking about different things.

"Ours don't travel," Skellig said. "Wait. Could a rock flock be another name for a landslide?"

Zeira tilted her head as she stared at her large companion. Exasperated, she turned to Nuri, but discovered the valthan was just as lost as she was. Finally, Zeira looked down at Jerica, who helplessly spread her arms.

"I'm sorry, I don't know what a rock flock is, either."

"Giant birds," Zeira explained, "almost as big as we are. You really don't know what I'm talking about?"

"Giant birds," Skellig breathed, relieved. "You call them rocks?"

"R-O-C," Zeira spelled. "I think I understand your confusion. So, what do you call them?"

"Birds," Skellig answered, eliciting a snort of amusement from Nuri.

"They're so much bigger than your normal birds," Zeira pointed out.

"Big ones, little ones, green ones, red ones, it doesn't matter," Skellig argued.

"Fine. Do you have big birds in Gale?"

"No. Not many birds live in my region, but then again,

that probably has something to do with the simple fact that it's always gloriously windy there. Birds tend to favor calmer weather."

"He's got a point," Nuri decided.

"Speaking of Gale," Zeira said, "what about you, Skellig? What's going on with your home?"

"Are you asking if there are any problems to speak of?" Skellig wanted to know. After seeing Zeira nod her head, the Spark dragon shrugged. "Other dragons, mostly. By definition, Gale is the convergence of several different elements, each of which …"

"Elements?" Nuri interrupted.

"I'll explain later. Every neighbor we have, it would seem, is finding reasons to quarrel with us. As far as I'm aware, we haven't done anything, either."

"It's affecting everyone," Jerica guessed.

Zeira nodded. "Exactly. Therefore, since we all want the same thing, we should stick together. With you, Jerica, we have a fighting chance of accomplishing our mission."

"I want to help," Jerica admitted. "I'm in."

Zeira turned to Skellig, who nodded. "Count me in."

Together, the group turned to Nuri.

"I'm limited by the availability of water, obviously," Nuri announced. "As long as I'm able to render assistance, you have my skills."

"Who's the leader of our group?" Jerica asked.

Skellig and Nuri automatically pointed at Zeira.

"Me? I have no leadership experience. Perhaps Skellig? Or maybe …?"

"This is your mission, young one," Skellig told her. "I'm just along for the ride. Besides, you saved my life, remember? I hereby pledge mine to help yours."

"I don't know what to say to that. What if I don't know what I'm doing?"

Nuri swam as close as she could and offered Zeira a smile. "Then just fake it. Chances are, we'll never be able to tell."

"All right, Zeira," Skellig began, after everyone had a good laugh, "this is your mission. How do you want to proceed?"

Zeira reached under her loose chest scale and retrieved the

oron fragment. Admiring it in her open claw, she reluctantly held it out and let her three companions see it.

"Ooo, how pretty!" Jerica exclaimed. "How do you get it to glow like that?"

"It's a fragment of an oron stone," Skellig explained. "Get three fragments together and you'll have yourself the ability to seek out whatever your heart desires."

"Where'd you get it?" Nuri reverently asked.

Zeira pointed at Skellig. "He gave it to me."

"Why'd you do that?" the valthan wanted to know. "Is there something we need to know about that piece of stone?"

"I gave it to her when I thought I was going to fade," Skellig explained.

Zeira held out the piece of oron. "Since you're not in any danger of Fading, do you want it back?"

"You hold onto it for me. Perhaps the stone will speak to you, seeing how it refused to talk to me."

"Talk? You're telling me this thing is intelligent?"

Zeira's claw sprang open and allowed the fragment to fall to the ground, as though she had just discovered she was holding a live gromp. When nothing happened, she sheepishly retrieved the stone and then stepped closer to the shore's edge so that Nuri could have a better look at the glowing green piece of stone. Holding it low, Zeira watched Jerica approach and gingerly poke a finger at it.

"Well, I think it's very pretty," the human decided.

"Zeira, you've used the fragment to track Nuri," Skellig began, "and I'm pretty sure it's how you found me in the first place. I say you should use it again. Perhaps it'll send us to the location of the next piece?"

"And it could very well send us in the wrong direction," Nuri argued. "How much do you trust that thing?"

Zeira shrugged. "It found him, and it allowed us to follow you, so I'm with Skellig. Let's see if we can figure out …"

"What is it?" Skellig asked, growing concerned. "Do you feel something already?"

Zeira stared at the object in her hand and finally nodded. She turned to the left, then the right, and finally, spun in place. After a few moments, she pointed northwest.

"That way."

"That was quick," Nuri decided. The valthan turned to look in the direction Zeira was pointing. "Nothing that way but water. That's my element. Shall I go look?"

"I say we should all go look," Skellig decided. Then, catching sight of the disapproving looks from his companions, he nodded. "But, that's a decision for Zeira to make, isn't it?"

"We will all go," Zeira announced. "Jerica, I don't want you to do anything you ordinarily wouldn't. Would you like to come with us? Personally, I hope you do."

"I'd be honored. My father would be proud of me. I just wish he knew I was safe."

"I promise we'll find a way to let your sire know you're fine," Zeira promised. "Therefore, there's but one question remaining: would you prefer to fly or ride?"

"I don't think my stomach can handle flying just yet. If it's all the same to you two, I'd rather go with Nuri."

The valthan took a few hesitant steps out of the water, and then lowered her body until it was resting on the ground. "Shall we?"

An hour later, they were well on their way. The two aerial dragons, in deference to their aquatic companion, chose to fly over open water. Land was to their left, while nothing but the open sea was visible on the right, with the occasional glimpse of a distant ice sheet visible far to the north. Flying companionably side-by-side, several hundred feet above the sea, both dragons glided comfortably on the backs of the northerly air currents, having to flap their wings only once every ten minutes or so. Visible directly beneath them was Nuri, who had told both aerial dragons that she was deliberately keeping her pace slow so that the two of them could keep up. Their smallest companion, so it would seem, had been complaining of seasickness, and had expressed a strong desire to *not* soil anyone's scales.

"Any idea where we're going yet?" Nuri's voice asked, from inside their heads.

"Not yet," Zeira sadly admitted. "I'm constantly checking to make sure we're heading in the right direction, and as soon as I bank left or right, I get an immediate sense of unease."

"That explains the constant weaving back and forth," Nuri said. "I started to follow each time you did that, but I keep forgetting that I have a kai at the moment. She's warned me that too much weaving makes her nauseous."

Jerica's voice interjected, "It's easy to see the two of you are still on the same course, so all we have to do is maintain a direct course and keep an eye on you two."

"We've been flying for over an hour now," Skellig reported. "I think we ... Zeira, what is it? I can sense the alarm spreading through you."

"We're going the wrong way," Zeira reported. "I don't get it. Just a few moments ago, we were headed west, and that was in the right direction. Now I need to turn around."

"There's nothing down there," Skellig insisted.

"Except for that small island we just passed," Nuri pointed out. "I think what we're looking for must be on it. Jerica and I will arrive first and ensure it's safe to land."

"We are?" Jerica softly squeaked.

"No harm will befall you," Nuri promised.

Skellig, however, had different plans. He tucked his wings close to his body and fell from the sky like a stone. Just before he was due to make landfall, his wings snapped open and he landed on the shore with such force that he ended up creating a large crater.

"Well, that's one way to do it," Nuri mused.

The valthan arrived at the water's edge and carefully walked her front end out of the water. Once Jerica was on solid land, Nuri retreated to the safety of the sea and watched as Zeira executed a graceful landing next to the Spark dragon. Skellig automatically turned to Zeira.

"Here? Are you sure? Aside from a few trees, and small field of grass, nothing seems to be here."

"There must be *something* here," Zeira insisted. "It's just the same as it was when I found you frozen in that chunk of ice."

"Look around," Skellig implored. "There's nothing here for us."

It was Nuri's turn to be surprised. The valthan's nose lifted and swung around until it was squarely facing Jerica. A few moments of silence passed. When it became clear Nuri wasn't offering any further explanations for her actions, both Zeira and Skellig gave a low cough.

"Ahem, ahem."

Nuri's gaze shifted to the Spark dragon. "Yes?"

"You're staring at Jerica. What's the matter?"

Nuri looked back at Jerica and held out a hand, encouraging her to continue. A few more seconds of silence passed. Jerica slowly approached the grass and squatted near a small section that had turned brown, as if that particular area hadn't been getting enough water.

"Does this stand out to anyone else besides me?" the girl asked, raising her voice.

"It's dead grass, what of it?" Skellig inquired.

Jerica began singling out various details.

"The rest of the grass is soft, green, and luxurious. The trees seem fine. Only this area is affected."

Three dragon heads shifted to look at the surrounding countryside.

"She has a point," Zeira conceded. "What is wrong with that patch of grass?"

"Does it matter?" Skellig demanded. "We're wasting time."

"We were led here," Nuri reminded their large companion. "Something about this island bears investigation. Thus far, the only thing worth noting is this one patch of grass."

"We're here because of dead grass?" Skellig skeptically asked.

"Perhaps we need to *fix* the grass?" Zeira idly suggested.

Skellig turned to regard her with a neutral expression.

"What? What'd I say? I think Jerica is on to something. Everything else here looks perfectly healthy. *That* doesn't."

"You're suggesting you want us to water the grass?" Skellig skeptically asked.

"It couldn't hurt to try," Nuri added.

Skellig sighed. "Fine. What do you want to water it with? I have an idea, but I don't think you're going to like it."

Zeira stared at the Spark dragon and waited for what she knew was coming.

"No, not like that. We should find some water."

"There's water everywhere," Nuri helpfully pointed out.

"You can't water plants with seawater," Skellig argued. His long neck inspected the confines of the small island. "I don't smell freshwater anywhere. I don't think this is possible."

Zeira's eyes widened. "This is a test! It's an obstacle!"

Skellig eyed the brittle patch of grass. "Strange obstacle. If we are to overcome this … dilemma, then that would mean we would need to locate freshwater."

"On an island where none exists," Nuri added.

Zeira caught the large Spark dragon giving her a sidelong glance.

"What?"

"Well, when we experimented with Jerica earlier, did you not produce steam? Is that not a form of water?"

"Are you asking me to … to … on the grass? In front of everyone?"

"True," Skellig admitted. "That wouldn't be much of a challenge."

Zeira breathed a sigh of relief. "Oh, good."

"However …"

Zeira's relief evaporated in an instant. "What? What now?"

"We'll never know until we try. It will also be a good example for you to see if you can activate your abilities without having to consume a rather loathsome-looking insect. For the record, I sure wouldn't want to."

"Fine," Zeira grumped. "I do so under protest."

"So noted," Skellig quipped, doing a remarkable job of keeping a neutral expression on his face. "After you."

"I may not be producing fire at the moment," Zeira slowly began, as she turned about so that her tail end was facing the grass, "but I do know contact with steam will hurt. I would advise you all to stay in front of me. Jerica, if you would?"

Once the rest of the group were standing directly in front of their Fire dragon companion, and Jerica had placed her hand on Zeira's foreleg, everyone fell silent. Zeira closed her eyes and brought up the image of Nuri's hagfish, swimming in its disgusting pool of … She trailed off as her stomach immediately recoiled. Feeling her abdomen swell with gas, Zeira sighed, lowered her head, and lifted her tail.

SSSSsssssssssssssssss!

Zeira felt a cloud of super-heated steam erupt from her hind end. Cringing, she turned to watch it drift lazily out across the small clearing. The cloud didn't make it far; at the first gust of wind, the tiny droplets of water almost immediately sank into the earth. The grass, however, remained unaffected.

"It didn't work," Skellig observed. "May we leave now?"

Zeira shook her head. "No. There must be something else we can try. What about you?"

"What about me?" Skellig wanted to know. "I cannot produce water."

"But you can produce lightning," Zeira reminded him. "Perhaps you could shock the grass?"

"The grass is already dying," Skellig pointed out. "A bolt of electricity is not going to make it better."

"Could we at least try?" Zeira urged.

Skellig sighed. "Fine. This time, you all will want to stay as far away from me as possible."

"Can he really summon lightning?" Zeira heard Jerica quietly ask, to which she nodded her head.

"He can, aye," Zeira confirmed. "I've seen him do it."

By the time Zeira made it to the other side of the tiny island, Nuri was already waiting at the water's edge. Jerica sat astride Nuri's back.

Skellig extended his wings and stretched his neck skyward. "Is everyone clear?"

"We are," Zeira confirmed. "How accurate are your lightning bolts?"

"I could knock a pebble off your head," Skellig returned. "Why do you ask?"

"Because you're facing the wrong way. The grass we're trying to restore is behind you."

"Is it? Well, I'll be. Umm, thanks? All right, here we go."

Sparks emitted from Skellig's wing talons. After a few moments, the thin, spidery lines of electricity had encompassed his entire body. Just then, twin jagged bolts of lightning erupted from his wing talons and arced downward, striking the grass, sending a large cloud of dirt and debris skyward. Skellig allowed the bolts of energy to slam into the ground for a full ten seconds before refolding his wings and ceasing the rampant electrical crackling. He moved forward for a closer inspection.

The air cleared and the three of them whistled with amazement.

Nuri demanded. "Did it work?"

Skellig sighed. "Er, the grass was not restored."

"It didn't work? It's all right, Skellig. You tried. We'll just have to …"

"You didn't let me finish," Skellig interrupted. "The grass hasn't been restored, but then again, that might be because there *isn't* any more grass."

Curiosity getting the better of her, Nuri pulled herself out of the sea and slowly walked the thirty feet across dry land to join her companions. What she saw drew her up short. Skellig had been, indeed, telling the truth when he had said the grass hadn't been restored. That was because the dead grass was now gone. In its place was a dark, narrow tunnel!

"What do we have here?" Nuri asked, more to herself than to anyone.

"It's a tunnel," Skellig matter-of-factly announced.

Nuri sighed. "I can see that. I meant … never mind."

"What I want to know," Zeira began, causing the others to fall silent, "is if the grass was hiding the mouth of the tunnel, or if Skellig's lightning blasts are so strong that this tunnel formed as a result?"

Two dragons and one human turned to the Spark dragon.

"If you're wondering whether or not I know my own strength, the answer is no."

"Someone needs to go down there and check things out," Jerica decided.

Heads were nodding.

"I agree," Zeira said. Then she looked at Nuri. "Would you?"

"You're the only choice to go down there," Skellig said. "None of the rest of us would fit. Aside from Jerica, that is. Do you really want her venturing down there on her own?"

"No," Nuri sulked.

"No," Jerica quietly added.

"Fine. I'll go. If I get stuck, I'm counting on you two to pull me out."

Nuri slowly moved into the tunnel and eventually disappeared down into the depths of the earth.

"What do you think she'll find down there?" Jerica anxiously asked.

Zeira shrugged. "Unknown. It might be nothing. It might be water. It might be ... well, I don't know."

"Treasure?" Skellig hopefully asked. "Jewels? Maybe it's a clutch of diamonds so big that ..."

"I'm hoping it's another fragment of the oron stone," Zeira interrupted, once Skellig had taken a breath.

Skellig nodded. "I had forgotten about that. You were led here, after all."

Zeira stared at the hole in the ground. As leader of this expedition, it really should have been her venturing inside, only Skellig had been right. Their aquatic companion was the only one who could fit. Perhaps she should have suggested enlarging the tunnel?

"Here she comes," Skellig reported, as faint tremors could now be felt. "I wager there's nothing down there."

Zeira looked at the much larger lightning dragon. "You wish to place a wager?"

"Why not?" Skellig challenged. "Let's see who is right."

"What are you wagering?" Zeira asked, intrigued.

"Hmm. I have a bright blue sapphire that I could stake, only it's back in Gale, so that doesn't really help us. Oh, I know. Loser has to hunt for the winner's food."

"For how long?" Zeira cautiously asked.

"My appetite is second to none, so let's just say it'll be for tonight only."

"Very well, you have a deal."

Nuri's head appeared.

"I heard the stakes of the wager," the valthan began, as she extricated herself from the tunnel. "Skellig, you lost. You'll never believe what I found down there!"

"Drat," Skellig growled.

"What is it?" Jerica excitedly asked. "What's down there?"
"It's another dragon!"

Chapter 7 — Gocri

You're kidding. There's another dragon?" Exasperated, Zeira turned to Skellig, who shrugged. "What in the world was it doing buried in the ground? Then again, I found you much the same way. I'll bet whoever imprisoned this one was also responsible for imprisoning you, too."

"What else can you tell us?" Skellig asked Nuri.

"Well, whoever it is looks to be bigger than all of us. The tunnel dead-ends about twenty feet in. Before you know it, you're snout-to-snout with the imprisoned dragon."

"Frozen in ice, as before?" Zeira quietly asked.

"I do not know how Skellig was found before," Nuri pointed out. "Whereas at first glance, it looked as though the poor fellow was encased in a solid block of ice, a closer inspection proved otherwise. If I were to venture a guess, I'd say that, somehow, he has been imprisoned in a solid block of crystal."

"You said *he*," Jerica said, raising a hand. "Are you certain it, er, he is a male dragon?"

"Males are much larger than females," Nuri helpfully supplied.

"What kind of dragon is he?" Skellig wanted to know.

"I don't know," Nuri admitted. "I haven't encountered many other species."

"What color is he?" Zeira asked.

"White."

Zeira shook her head. "I'm with Nuri. I have no idea what that could be. Skellig, what do you think?"

"Frost."

Everyone turned to the Spark dragon.

"Frost?" Nuri repeated, shaking her head. "As in, the ice sheets of the north? Nothing can live out there in the wastelands."

Skellig pointed a heavily muscled arm at the tunnel. "Yet, *he* does. Haven't you figured this out yet? No one really knows much about anyone else! Why is that? Because none of us can survive outside of our home regions. You, Nuri, would seem to be the luckiest, since your region is the vastest."

"I am the fastest," Nuri said, nodding.

"Vastest," Skellig clarified. "*V*, not *f*."

"Vastest. Aye, I will agree to that. What should we do about him?" Nuri wanted to know, as she turned to look back at the tunnel.

"That's easy," Zeira said. "We free him."

"What if he's dangerous?" Jerica argued. "What if he decides I'm nothing more than a snack?"

"Then he'd have to go through the three of us," Zeira told her. "Together, we are stronger." When no one else had any objections, Zeira turned to her companions. "We need to figure out how to free the frost dragon from his prison. Any thoughts?"

"This isn't ice, but crystal," Skellig reminded her. "This won't be easy."

"What breaks crystal?" Jerica wanted to know.

"Ordinarily, I'd say a blunt object," Skellig decided. "Thrown with significant force, that is."

"There isn't enough leverage in the tunnel to launch

an object large enough to generate the force you're talking about," Nuri pointed out. "It's way too narrow, and it curves about quite a bit."

"Could you somehow enlarge the tunnel so that others would fit?" Zeira asked.

Nuri held up one of her short, almost vestigial forelegs. "Not with these, I'm sorry to say. I can barely scratch my nose with these things."

Skellig snorted with laughter and looked away.

"You each have an ability," Jerica began, as she started singling out the three dragons towering over her head. She faced Zeira. "You can spit fire. Well, kinda. With my help, it turns to steam."

"I don't think that's going to help us here," Zeira quipped, eliciting a few chuckles from Skellig.

"And you," Jerica continued, looking at the Spark dragon, "can produce very powerful blasts of lightning. Would that shatter a large chunk of crystal?"

"I would think not," Skellig answered, shaking his head.

"Then there's you," Jerica finished, as she turned to the valthan. "You have proven yourself unmatched in the water, but on land? I'm not sure how you could help."

"That makes two of us," Nuri dryly added.

"Where does that leave us?" Zeira asked.

Jerica held up a hand. "I think this is yet another obstacle, and one that we have to overcome. Together."

"I don't see how," Skellig said.

"First, we need to determine what will free him," Zeira decided. "Then, we figure out how to make it happen."

"My father accidentally broke one of my mother's crystal goblets once," Jerica reported.

"A goblet is a utensil for tribesm ... human use, is it not?" Zeira slowly asked.

"That's right, yes."

"Therefore, it's much smaller. I don't see how that's helpful."

"Zeira, if you let me finish, I'll explain."

Zeira smiled and offered the human a nod. "Go ahead."

"My father broke my mother's goblet, all without laying

a finger on it."

The three dragons perked up.

"How?" Skellig demanded.

"My father is a blacksmith," Jerica explained. "Hallis is the best blacksmith in all of Cael. He was hammering out dents on a sword when he struck the blade in such a way that it caused a loud reverberating tone. Mother was outside, waiting for him to finish, and was holding a cup of wine. The glass shattered in her hand, cutting her in several places."

"I'm not sure how that is going to help us," Zeira admitted.

Nuri, on the other hand, looked thoughtful. "Tones. The crystal responded to tonal frequencies!"

"You know about things like that?" Zeira asked.

The valthan tapped the side of her head. "As a matter of fact, I'm an expert. I use echolocation to navigate underwater."

"Echo-*what*?" Skellig asked, curious.

"Echolocation. I send out various tones, through the top of my head, between my horns. The tones will bounce back to me and essentially tell me what obstacles lie in that direction."

"You can emit these tones?" Skellig asked.

"For me, it's like humming," Nuri explained. "I hum to myself, and I instantly know what's ahead of me."

Skellig then looked at Jerica. "I think you may be the key to solving this."

"Why do you say that?" Zeira asked, puzzled.

"Because of this mark?" Jerica asked, as she frowned at her wrist. "Very well. Let's hear your idea."

Skellig pointed at Nuri. "Her tones, my power. I think that might be enough to break this poor fellow free from his prison."

"You're not going to fit down there!" Nuri protested. "And I certainly don't want to be in the way when you let one of your lightning bolts go."

Skellig then pointed at Jerica. "Our human has demonstrated the ability to bond with any of us whenever she comes into physical contact. With me so far?"

Nuri nodded. "I am."

"I am, too," Zeira added.

"What if ..." Skellig began, "what if Jerica is touching the two of us when that happens?"

Zeira watched the human turn to stare at the tunnel before returning her gaze to the Spark dragon. "You're suggesting a human can bond with two dragons *at the same time*? I don't think that's ever been attempted before."

Jerica shrugged. "There's a first time for everything. I'm game."

"I believe the resulting hybrid blast of power would be sufficient to defeat the crystal prison," Skellig explained.

"Seeing how you can't fit down there," Nuri began, "that would mean I'd be the one in the tunnel. If you're suggesting Jerica needs to be in physical contact with me, then what are you suggesting she touch? My tail? That's the only part of me she'd be able to reach."

"Sounds about right," Skellig mused.

"And ..." Nuri continued, becoming more agitated as she talked, "that would mean Skellig's bolt of lightning would have to go through Jerica and then into my ... oh, that is *so* not happening! I am *not* going to let you two shoot a jet of lightning up my rear end!"

"It'll be perfectly safe," Skellig tried to assure her.

Nuri rounded on the much larger Spark dragon. "How can you know? Have you ever shot a bolt of lightning up your ... your ... *butt*?"

"Er, no."

"I didn't think so. What makes you think that I'm going to allow that?"

"Because," Zeira softly answered, "it'll help a fellow dragon. You don't strike me as being someone who could willingly turn away from a creature who needs help."

"Blast," Nuri grumbled. "Skellig, if I get shocked, then I'm personally dragging you out to sea and drowning you."

The corners of the Spark dragon's mouth curved upward in a smile. "Deal."

Nuri returned to the foreboding hole, gave Skellig a withering look, and then slowly, almost reluctantly, proceeded down the tunnel. The rest of the group could still see the tip of her dark blue tail, swaying back and forth. Zeira watched Jerica take a breath and then reached out a hand to grab Nuri's tail. Then, Skellig approached and gently held out a wing talon. Using her other hand, Jerica grasped the talon and nodded her readiness.

"Go ahead, Nuri," Skellig's voice said, in Zeira's mind. "We're connected."

"You want me to do something?" Nuri's voice returned. "But I thought ... I thought you were going to send a bolt of lightning through Jerica, and then through me."

"No. We just need to be connected. I honestly don't know if this will even work, but I am willing to try, too. Therefore, it's in your claws now."

"What do I do?" Nuri stammered.

"Pretend you're swimming," Zeira suggested. "Pretend you're just swimming along and, all of a sudden, something appears in your path and you need to see what's behind it. So, use your echolocation skills and find out what's on the other side of that block of ice."

"Oh, of course. I can do that. Just a moment."

"Now, before you do," Zeira continued, relaying instructions through their shared telepathic link, "count it down from ten. That way, Skellig will know when to call forth one of his lightning bolts."

With both signaling their readiness, Zeira started the countdown. "Ten ... nine ... eight ..."

"I can't believe I'm willingly allowing someone to shoot a lightning bolt up my ..." Nuri's thought came.

"... five ... four ... three ..."

"I hope this works," Zeira heard Jerica softly exclaim.

"... two ... one ... now!"

A few seconds of silence passed.

"Zeira, did it work?" Jerica anxiously asked. "I didn't feel anything. Has that poor dragon been freed?"

Zeira shrugged. "I'll ask. Has ..."

"I heard, and the answer is no. Skellig, let's go again. In three, two, one ... now!"

Zeira watched Skellig's wing talon sparkle with energy as bolts of electricity snaked out from him, traveled through

Jerica, and on down the length of Nuri's body. Zeira approached the small human and crouched low.

"Are you all right? You're not injured, are you?"

"Can't feel a thing," Jerica confirmed. "I saw the energy blast this time. Thank goodness, I seem to be immune to it."

"One more!" Nuri's excited thought came. "It's working! There are cracks throughout the crystal! Come on, Skellig! Send us your best!"

Skellig grunted once. "As you wish. I'll count it down this time. Jerica, brace yourself. Firing in three, two, one, go!"

All of a sudden, the entire island began to tremble. Jerica immediately dropped the tip of Nuri's tail and looked worriedly up at Skellig.

"I have a bad feeling about this."

Zeira scooped up the tiny human and followed Skellig to the other side of the small island.

"Nuri? Are you there? Can you hear us? We're clear! We've moved as far as we could from the tunnel."

"Which doesn't do me any good," Nuri grumped.

"Are you all right?" Skellig asked, concerned. "I'm heading back to you. Something isn't …"

"No!" Nuri's sharp command brought Skellig to an immediate standstill. "The tunnel has collapsed. I don't want anyone else to become trapped!"

Alarmed, Zeira shared a look with Skellig, who immediately hurried off. Zeira glanced at the small human and held up a single claw.

"Stay."

Hurrying back to the mouth of the tunnel, Zeira looked with dismay at what was left of the entrance to the white dragon's prison: a mound of dirt and stone. Of their valthan friend, nothing could be seen. Skellig, much to his credit, brushed past Zeira and immediately started digging.

"Help is on the way, Nuri. Don't panic."

"You have my eternal thanks, Skellig," came Nuri's frightened thought.

It took nearly five minutes of digging to unearth the tip of Nuri's tail. Once enough had been uncovered, Skellig grasped the tail with his hand and prepared to pull.

"I'm sorry for what I'm about to do."

"No apologies necessary," Nuri's voice assured him. "If you can get me out of here, you won't hear any complaints from me."

"Zeira, help me. Grab hold."

Ever so slowly, the valthan was pulled from the collapsed tunnel. Zeira felt the terra tremors happening beneath her feet and briefly wondered just how unstable the ground really was.

"The answer to that is incredibly so. Step aside, Fire. I've got this."

Zeira turned at the voice, but before she could react, a heavily muscled arm gently, but firmly, pushed her aside as though she were nothing more than an irksome insect. The huge hand clamped onto Nuri's tail just a few feet from Skellig's and, together with the Spark dragon, they pulled the struggling valthan from what was left of the tunnel. Only when Nuri was standing beside them once more did the color of the newcomer's scales dawn on her: they were white! Seeing Zeira's eyes widen with surprise, Skellig turned to see what had captured her attention.

It was the imprisoned dragon! It was not only free, but was now standing before them. The biggest surprise, however, came with size. He was easily twice as large as Skellig, which meant Zeira was dwarfed by their new friend. What kind of dragon was he?

"Glacier."

Zeira blinked a few times and fought the urge to cock her head. "A glacier dragon? I figured you'd be Ice."

"You're young, Fire. I'll let that slide for now."

"Who are you?" Skellig demanded. "What were you doing under the ground?"

"You're one to talk," the huge white dragon returned. It gave Skellig a speculative look before resuming. "Were you not discovered in much the same fashion?"

"How could you possibly know that?" Zeira whispered.

"You *are* young, aren't you?" the glacier dragon said, shaking his head. "There is much that can be learned simply by opening one's senses, Fire."

"My name is Zeira. I'm not Fire, but Phoenix."

"I wouldn't have called that one," the white dragon returned. "I am Gocri."

Skellig approached and gave a small bow. "Skellig. I'm a Spark, from Gale."

"I've been to your region," Gocri said, as he straightened so that he could see over the treetops and out to sea. "Not very hospitable, if you ask me."

"It suits me fine. What about you?" Skellig challenged. "I would think a little wind would be more preferable than living on a sheet of ice."

"Under," Gocri corrected.

Skellig cocked his head. "What's that?"

"I live below the ice. Peace, comfort, and isolation. Three qualities you can't get anywhere other than Bliss."

Skellig's head jerked up. "Bliss? Did you just call your region *Bliss*?"

"That's its name, aye."

"Bliss?" Skellig repeated, for a third time.

"It is where we are the happiest," Gocri shrugged. "Bliss seemed to be the most apt name."

The three other dragons shared a look, and Skellig appeared ready to say something derogatory, but a subtle shake of Zeira's head managed to stave off the Spark dragon's verbal assault.

"If you like your den so much," Nuri said, after giving herself a thorough shaking to dislodge the clumps of dirt still clinging to her scales, "what are you doing here? How did you end up in a block of crystal?"

"Crystal? Is that what it was? I thought it was ice at first, but when it resisted my attempts to free myself, I suspected something was wrong. As for what I was doing there, I would imagine the same as you: I was looking for something, *anything* which might help me get the spear out of that fool's hands."

Zeira looked at Nuri, who looked at Skellig, who then stared blankly back at Gocri.

"You're not looking for a way to successfully confront that troublesome biped?"

Jerica appeared by Skellig's front foreleg. Before she could say anything, Gocri's two silver eyes fixated on hers. A growl sounded, and if Skellig hadn't stepped in Gocri's path, Zeira was certain the huge glacier dragon would have attacked poor Jerica.

"What is *that* doing here?" Gocri demanded. "It's a human! You can't trust humans, no matter how small they are. They're devious, malicious, deceitful …"

"And yet this one saved your life," Zeira interjected, perhaps a tad harsher than she had intended. "If it wasn't for her, you'd still be encased in that slab of crystal."

"She had nothing to do with my escape," Gocri scoffed. "I felt the crystal weaken in strength. I, alone, was able to break free. It was no thanks to a human, I assure you."

Nuri shared a look with Zeira. Moments later, the three of them positioned themselves behind Jerica and they all glared at their much larger friend. Gocri found himself taking a few steps in the opposite direction, shaking his head in disbelief.

"No. Say it isn't so."

"I don't know what you have against humans," Zeira coldly began, "but it ends now. Not only did Jerica help free you, but she did so by splicing together Nuri and Skellig's power."

Gocri's eyes widened with surprise. "Next, you'll tell me she was in physical contact with both of you at the time I was able to finally break free of my prison."

"Yes, she was," Skellig confirmed. "She's a kairie, the first in … in … you know, I really don't know how long it's been. Nearly a hundred years, I would imagine."

"Try four hundred nineteen years," Gocri softly muttered. His silver eyes jumped back to Jerica's. "Human. You're a kairie? Show me the mark."

While Jerica bared her inner wrist to the dragon, Zeira nudged Nuri on her shoulder.

"He's heard of a kairie!"

"He also identified each of us," Nuri pointed out. "He knew you are Fire, Skellig is Spark, and I am Water."

"That's a good point," Zeira conceded. She turned to face the newcomer. "Gocri, how is it you've heard of the kairie? None of us had any idea what it was."

"That's because you're young," Gocri returned. "None of you three have ever had a kai, have you?"

Zeira shook her head, followed immediately by Skellig and Nuri.

"Well, my mother has. Three times, the first of which was a kairie."

"What?" Zeira sputtered. "Your mother carried a kairie? But I thought those special riders hadn't been seen in hundreds of years?"

"They haven't," Gocri confirmed. "My mother was one of the last few who could freely visit the regions. Any region."

"Were they all before your time?" Jerica asked.

Gocri shook his head. "No. I remember each of them well."

"Did they do something to contribute to your distrust of all humans?" Skellig wanted to know.

"You could say that," Gocri said, nodding. "My mother's last kai betrayed her, which resulted in her death. So, you might be able to see why I don't trust tribesmen."

Jerica slapped a hand over her mouth. "Oh, how horrible! I'm so sorry! Gocri, I would never do such a thing to you. You can trust me."

"Trust is earned, not bestowed, human," Gocri coolly responded. "We shall see."

Jerica pointed at the three other dragons towering over her. "I've bonded with each of those three, and will count it as an honor when I'm able to bond with you."

"If," Gocri returned. "*If* I allow it."

"You should consider it," Skellig said. "She bonded with me and Nuri at the same time. I never would have thought it possible, but there you have it. You are standing here, in front of us, because of her."

"Could you tell us about this Thunder King person?" Zeira asked. "This is the first I've heard about him. Is he the one responsible for setting us against each other?"

"My species has been attacking the humans' boats," Nuri said, hanging her head.

"We've been fighting with the Terrans," Zeira reported.

"We've noticed," Gocri said, nodding. "My king has

been worked up to a frenzy. He wants to attack anything that moves. Thus far, he hasn't acted on his word, but it's only a matter of time. Our most skilled warriors were sent out, looking for some means to end Thunder's maniacal reign of tyranny once and for all."

"Thunder," Skellig repeated. "He isn't Spark, is he?"

"I hope not," Jerica softly told Skellig, as she laid a hand on his side.

"Me, too," Skellig quietly admitted.

Gocri stared at the Spark dragon for so long, in utter silence, that Skellig actually became nervous and took a few steps back.

"Was it something I said?"

Gocri immediately pointed down at Jerica.

"I'm not talking about a fellow dragon. I'm talking about a human."

Jerica perked up. "There's no human Thunder King. I'm certain of it."

"Who do you think governs you?" Gocri returned.

"I don't think, I *know*. Our king, of course."

"And what region are you from?" the Ice dragon inquired.

"Terra."

"The Terran King bows to Thunder, just like every other human king I've seen," Gocri reported.

"I've never heard of our king bowing to anyone," Jerica protested.

"*All* kings are allegiant to the Thunder King, ever since the decisive battle," Gocri added, growling his displeasure. "The last king to oppose Thunder's rule died after a sword was plunged through his heart."

"That's terrible!" Jerica exclaimed. "And, why haven't I heard of this? When did this happen?"

The enormous Ice dragon shrugged. "Early this year, I believe. Thunder thought for certain he had found the final resting place, and when it proved to be a false lead, Thunder took the news … poorly."

"What final resting place?" Zeira wanted to know. "What is Thunder looking for?"

"He searches for the Rastan Spear."

"He's looking for *what*?" Zeira curiously asked.

"The Rastan Spear," Gocri repeated.

"Can you tell us what's so special about that spear?" Jerica timidly asked.

"It's made from a special metal," Gocri explained. "The wielder of the spear has undreamed of powers."

"Could you give us an example?" Nuri asked.

Gocri shrugged. "One of the most common benefits of these types of weapons is the increase of your own unique ability."

"These *types* of weapons?" Zeira repeated. "Are there more?"

Gocri nodded. "A few. Whatever metal they're made from is highly coveted. They're all imbued with unusual powers. So, what do you get when you have implements with strange powers and you introduce the bipeds into the equation?"

"You get tribesmen acting even crazier than they typically do," Skellig muttered. Then, stifling a curse, he looked down at Jerica and offered her a smile. "Oh. Er, sorry. I meant no offense."

Jerica waved off the Spark dragon's concerns. "None taken. What a sheltered life I must have led. I have no knowledge of any of this. I wonder if my parents know?"

"That is a detail to worry about at a later date," Zeira decided. She looked at Gocri's imposing form and sighed. "You seem to know more about what's going on than we do. We were all tasked with finding a way to stop our home regions from going to war with the neighboring ones. Could this Thunder King you speak of ... could he be the one who's responsible for creating this threat?"

"Let's put it this way," Gocri said, as he began to draw symbols and diagrams in the dirt. "This human king was a nobody for years. Then, on a day no different from any other, he appeared at the head of a large army, complete with a dragon companion in tow. He engages—and defeats—a rival king in an epic battle. Now, I may not be the best person to ask about human history. So, Jerica, is it? Correct me if I'm wrong, but how long has it been since one human kingdom has battled another?"

The lone human let out a breath of relief. "Finally, a question I know the answer to: at least fifty years. We used to wage wars against ourselves all the time, but lately it seems to be a thing in the past."

"Yet, this particular battle happened at the beginning of the year," Gocri insisted. "Tell me, all of you, when did these *problems* arise with each of your regions? By any chance, could it be around the same time? Early this year?"

Jerica was already nodding. "My village is on a remote, northern peninsula. We're a quiet, peaceful people, yet our boats were attacked. You're right. The first instance was just after Farrow's Festival."

"I'm not familiar with that term," Gocri admitted.

"It's a festival celebrating the arrival of the winter storms." Jerica eyed her dragon companions and smiled. "Our village relies on the sea for a living. When the seas ice over, it means we have nothing else to do but go home and wait for the ice to melt. Most of us look forward to the rest."

Zeira cleared her throat. "The first skirmish we had with our Terran neighbors also coincides with the same time frame. Even the centaurs I met earlier told me a few of them had openly attacked anyone caught by themselves."

"Centaurs," Skellig grumbled. "Don't get me started about them."

"We can all agree," Nuri said, drawing everyone's attention, "that bad things started occurring just as Gocri said they would. So, although it's hard to believe, that could only mean that this one human is responsible for causing all these problems. What, then, can be done? Can't we simply just find this biped and chomp this fool in two?"

"If he wields the Rastan Spear," Gocri said, "he will be nigh unapproachable. No, we would need to find a way to neutralize the power he wields."

Zeira felt her hopes crumble. Just when she thought there might be a way to help bring an end to the building tension between the various dragons, now she finds out a magic-infused weapon is at play? How could they possibly neutralize that?

"This Thunder King," Zeira slowly began, "is using

a magic-enhanced weapon. Is there some type of magical device we could procure that would level the playing field?"

Everyone turned to Gocri, who shrugged. "Now you know why I'm here, young one."

"Why does everyone keep calling me young?" Zeira protested. "I'm no youngling. I'm old enough to fly, to hunt, to …"

"… take on forces you have no hopes of defeating?" Gocri dryly asked.

"Leave her be," Skellig ordered. "I owe her my life. There's a reason why she's the leader of our group."

"You all answer to her?" Gocri sputtered, incredulous.

"We do," Nuri confirmed, nodding. "Since we all want the same thing, will you be joining us?"

"We could use your help," Zeira added. "We're all looking for the same thing."

"You speak of the oron stones?" Gocri asked. "How do you know I, too, have been searching for one?"

"You have?" Zeira repeated.

Gocri nodded. "What about you? Have you been successful? Have you found one?"

"We have one fragment," Skellig replied, "and it led us to you. Do you have another fragment?"

"I do not," Gocri said, shaking his head. "Wait. Your fragment of oron stone led you to me? Whatever for?"

"Oh, I don't know," Skellig began, as he idly scratched a few designs in the dirt, "perhaps it has something to do with your being locked in a crystal prison?"

Gocri's jaws snapped closed.

Skellig looked up. "I'm sorry, I didn't catch that. Did you say something?"

"No," Gocri grumped.

"Yet, you should have," Skellig scolded. "Would you like to try again?"

Gocri sighed and faced Zeira. "Thank you for locating me. If you hadn't, I don't know how much longer I would have been a prisoner on this dreadful island."

"You're welcome," Zeira said. "You're with friends, Gocri. Will you join us?"

"Until such time as I find a suitable kai, I accept."

"That's how we started out," Skellig admitted, as he moved away from the others so that his wings wouldn't make contact with any of theirs when they were extended.

"Except me," Nuri announced, as she slowly walked back to the water. "But now I can carry a kai just like everyone else."

"You're a valthan, aren't you? The warrior caste of the water dragons, am I right?"

Nuri nodded. "That's right. I'm impressed you knew that. Not many do."

"Try being older than the stars," Gocri chuckled. "When you've been around as long as I have, you start to pick up things."

"How old are you?" Jerica wanted to know.

Gocri eyed the tiny human and shrugged. "I really don't know. I haven't found anyone older than me for many years. You. Valthan. Will you be able to keep us with us? I'd hate for you to be left behind."

"Please," Zeira scoffed. "She can swim faster than we can fly."

"Impossible," Gocri breathed.

Skellig was nodding. "That's what I said, too. As you will soon be, I was proved wrong."

"Hmmph. We'll see about that."

"Does anyone know where we're going?" Zeira asked.

"You're the leader," Skellig reminded her. "Pick a direction. North, south, it doesn't matter."

"If you don't mind," Gocri interjected, "I would like to head north, just for a day or two."

"Danger of Fading getting close?" Skellig guessed.

Gocri nodded. "That's right. You three aren't worried?"

Zeira, Skellig, and Nuri all shook their heads no, and then—as one—they turned to look down at Jerica, who was sitting complacently on a nearby rock.

"Not as long as she's nearby," Zeira said.

"What does her presence have to do with anything?" Gocri wanted to know.

"You heard us tell you she's a kairie, right?" Skellig asked.

Gocri nodded.

"Apparently, one of the effects of bonding with a kairie is that it wards off fading," Skellig said. "I was in danger of fading, especially after being imprisoned in the ice for nearly a week. Then, Jerica here happens along and just like that, I'm fine."

Gocri was silent as he studied the lone biped. About ready to launch into the air, Zeira refolded her wings and appeared at Jerica's side.

"Gocri, do you need Jerica to bond with you, too? How long has it been since you returned to the ice?"

"A while," Gocri admitted.

Jerica approached the huge Ice dragon and stared up at Gocri's distant head. "Would you like me to try? I've never witnessed anyone fading, but I certainly don't want that to happen to you."

Surprised, Gocri eyed Zeira, and then Skellig, who both nodded their encouragement. Shrugging, Gocri lowered his head until it was resting on the soft grass. He made eye contact with the human and finally nodded.

"If you would work your magic, I would be grateful. I have no plans to fade. If you can prevent me from returning to the north, I would be in your debt. Again."

Jerica dropped into a cross-legged sitting position and leaned up against Gocri's nearest leg. Her eyes closed and, taking deep breaths, she nodded her readiness.

"I can sense the other three," Jerica began, "but not you, Gocri. At least, not yet."

Gocri snorted once, closed his eyes, and opened his senses. Almost immediately, his eyes snapped back open and he stared, disbelieving, at Jerica.

"It's been many years since I've spoken with my mother about the kais, and what I can remember is that it took her hours before she and her rider were able to share senses. With you, it was instantaneous. I can hear your thoughts, and presumably, you can hear mine. How is that possible?"

All three dragons adopted smug expressions and moved behind Jerica, as if to say a line had been drawn and they clearly had chosen which side they wanted to join.

"Still need to go north?" Skellig nonchalantly asked.

Gocri's great white head swung left and right as he shook his head.

"Believe us now when we say we travel with a kairie?"

Gocri's head slowly nodded.

Nuri's face lit up. "Oh! Try your ability. I think you might be surprised."

"Why?" Gocri suspiciously asked.

"Just humor us," Skellig implored.

Gocri turned to the closest tree and blew what looked like a white cloud in its direction. When the mists cleared, the tree was perfectly coated in a thin layer of ice.

"Is that what you normally can do?" Nuri asked, impressed. "I like it."

Gocri was silent as he stared at the tree.

"What was supposed to happen?" Zeira asked quietly.

"I've always been able to breathe out a cloud of mist, which would typically coat anything it encounters with a fine layer of frost, freezing it solid."

"Looks like the mist melted, but rapidly froze again," Skellig decided. The Spark dragon then pointed at Jerica. "You can thank her for that. We've been having interesting results when we mix and match her power with our own."

"Mix and match?" Gocri repeated, confused. "You're telling me that, with her, you can mix your breaths together and form something completely new?"

"That's how you were freed," Zeira announced. "Nuri was the only one small enough to venture down into the tunnel. Jerica held the tip of her tail, and then laid an appendage on Skellig's wing talon. He then shot out a bolt of lightning, which traveled through Jerica …"

"… without killing her," Nuri hastily added.

"… without killing her," Skellig amended, offering Jerica a grin, "and then up Nuri's, er, *tail* and that, added to her existing echolocation skills, broke the crystal."

"Two dragons," Gocri mused, "bonding with a single human."

"At the same time," Skellig added.

"Very impressive. Yes, I will accompany you. It seems to

me I'd be a fool not to add my resources to your own, and I'm not a fool."

Zeira, Skellig, and Gocri separated as much as they were able on the island. Each spread their wings and prepared to lift off. Zeira turned to look at the sea, where Nuri was floating, waiting to depart. There, on Nuri's back, was Jerica, who still preferred to travel by sea instead of by air.

"Where are we headed?" Skellig asked. "Where's this Thunder King located?"

"Gilt."

"Guilt?" Zeira repeated, frowning. "I didn't know there was an actual region by that name."

Gocri's neck curved and brought his head around. "What, Gilt? Of course there is. But, that's not yet our destination. We are not prepared. As much as I'd like to think four dragons — and one human — would be more than adequate to challenge any foe, this particular villain wields weapons we cannot defeat."

"Yet," Skellig added, as he leapt into the sky.

"Yet," Gocri agreed.

Together, the three dragons lifted off the small island and headed west, toward the setting sun. Far below, but easily keeping pace with their aerial companions, valthan and human jetted along the surface of the water. For the first time, Zeira was filled with hope. There were not one, nor two, but three additional dragons accompanying her. On top of all of that, she had found a kai! Yes, the human could bond with any of them, but this, at least, gave them a fighting chance at defeating their enemy. Now, more than ever, they had to find the missing fragments of the seeing stone.

Confident they were heading in the right direction, both literally and figuratively, Zeira smiled and hurried to catch up to her new friends.

Chapter 8 — Ambush

Go on, take your pick. Surely, you have a preference. If you're not a fan, it's all right. You can say so. Otherwise, I can only assume Nuri has cast some type of enchantment over you."

"I heard that," Nuri's voice said, from within Zeira's head. "And I did no such thing. Jerica prefers the water over the air. There's nothing wrong with that."

"There isn't," Zeira confirmed. "However, before she passes judgment, I just feel she should give flying a fair shot."

"Jerica," Nuri called. "Do you want to come down?"

"She can't hear you," Zeira said. "She isn't telepathic."

"I am when I'm connected to one of you," Jerica's wry thought came.

"Oh, that's right. Sorry."

Zeira felt the human's mirth and knew she was being teased. For one of the first times ever, she wasn't offended by it.

"Were you teased often?" Jerica asked, picking up Zeira's thought.

"You've seen how I produce fire. Teasing occurred on a daily basis."

"I thought only humans were that cruel," Jerica softly muttered. "How old were you when they finally stopped?"

Zeira shook her head. "Who says they have stopped? It's the main reason I'm on this journey. I know I shouldn't care so much about what others think of me, but I can't help it. I just want to prove to everyone that I can be a useful member of my Gathering."

"Gathering?" Jerica repeated, curious.

"It's what we call ourselves," Zeira explained. "It can be an extended family, or an entire community."

"How many are in your Gathering?" Skellig wanted to know.

"Let me think. Nine families are Phoenix. Less than fifteen are Magma. Spurt has over twenty, and I think Scorch—the most prolific, by the way—have at least fifty. All told, I think we number around five hundred."

"I had no idea," Skellig breathed, amazed.

"How many of you are there?" Jerica asked. "As many as Zeira?"

"No. Gale is much smaller. Our *Gathering*, if you will, is less than a quarter of that number. Myself? I'm Plasma. There are, perhaps, ten other individuals like myself."

"I thought you called yourself a Spark?" Nuri recalled.

"*Spark* is the name we call ourselves," Skellig explained. "Zeira calls the dragons from her Gathering *Fire*, whereas someone who has no knowledge of Gale might call us *Lightning*. We prefer the term *Spark*."

"Are there other types of Spark dragons?" Zeira asked. "You say you're Plasma? What else is there?"

Skellig shrugged. "Well, there's Sonic, Storm, Current, and fairly recently, we created a fifth: Spectre."

"Sounds ominous," Gocri rumbled.

"We didn't know what else to call her," Skellig admitted. "She is smaller than any other Spark and faster than anyone I've ever seen in the air, making herself look like an apparition.

Hence the name of her new classification: spectre."

"What about you, Gocri?" Nuri wanted to know. "Would you care to tell us about your species?"

"We are the oldest," the Ice dragon's grating voice began. "We have been around long before the other species developed."

"How is that even verifiable?" Nuri asked, exasperation evident in her voice. "Unless you're suggesting you have been around since the beginning of time, then you wouldn't be able to … you haven't, have you?"

When Gocri neither confirmed nor denied the accusation, Nuri fell silent, impressed.

"He must be one of his Gathering's … ancients?" Skellig asked, doing a remarkable job of keeping a neutral expression on his face.

"It's probably different for every species," Zeira guessed. "In ours, the founders are known as … wait. What did you call your founders, Gocri?"

"They were simply known as *Frostfire*. And no, I am not one of them, in case you're wondering."

"Frostfire?" Zeira repeated, as she looked over at the large white form flying in formation off to her right. "You're sure?"

Gocri's great head shifted until he was staring at her. "Aye, why do you ask?"

"Frostfires were the name of my region's founders, too."

Two slitted, gray eyes stared at her. "Not possible."

Skellig grunted once.

"What?" Gocri inquired.

Skellig shook his head, which caused him to gently bank left. A quick dip in the opposite direction corrected the minor course deviation.

"You clearly have something to say, Spark. Out with it."

"It's plasma, if you want to get technical about it," Skellig corrected, "and no, I don't. Well, it's nothing that needs to be said here."

"You unsealed this cave," Gocri told him. "Kindly have the decency to fly through it."

"Fine. You and Zeira are distantly related."

"Am not," Gocri declared.

"No, we're not," Zeira added, at the same time.

"Common elements. I'd be willing to wager that if either of you were ... what did you call them? Frosties?"

"Frostfire," Gocri sternly corrected.

"Right. Frostfires. If either of you were Frostfires, then I'll bet you would be able to exist either on Blaze or ... I'm sorry. What was the name of your home region again?"

"Bliss."

"Right. Anyway, Bliss or Blaze, I think you two would be fine on either one."

"Nonsense," Gocri said, shaking his head. "I'm Ice, she's Fire. Our regions are not suited for one another."

"I couldn't survive on the ice!" Zeira exclaimed, horrified. "There's a reason my home is called Blaze!"

Skellig sighed and scratched the side of his head with one of his claws.

"Look, I'm not suggesting you should. I'm just saying that, since both of you happen to have an ancestor in common, it would suggest the two of you have a common element. Don't you recall what I said earlier about finding parts of Gale here and there? It's how I've been able to survive away from home for so long."

Interested, Gocri drifted close. "I'd like to hear more of your thoughts about this common elemental theory of yours."

While Skellig relayed his thoughts and theories to their large glacial friend, and since she had already heard what Skellig had to say about the ancient elements buried deep within the earth, she allowed herself to give the two of them some privacy. Content to ride the backs of the high-altitude air currents, Zeira settled herself in for the flight to ... to ... well, wherever she would be led, she supposed. The atmosphere was chilly, but her rider assured her she was fine. She could only assume it had something to do with her newfound kairie status.

"I'm still getting used to that," Jerica quietly admitted.

"Being a rider?" Zeira asked.

"Having magic. I don't understand how this happened."

"You're referring to your mark, aren't you?" Zeira gently inquired.

"Yes. I mean ... look at me! I'm a blacksmith's daughter. The only exciting thing I've ever done is to help my father in his shop. I can make a mean dirk, if you ask me, but I don't know how that's relevant now."

Unsure if she was expected to offer an opinion, especially since she hadn't been asked, Zeira elected to stay quiet.

"And now?" Jerica continued. "Apparently, I can take multiple powers and splice them together to create something new. How? How in the world can I do that?"

"I would say it has something to do with ..."

"Don't you *dare* reference that blasted mark again," Jerica groaned.

"It really is a good thing," Zeira told her, using as gentle a tone as she could muster. "Thanks to you, we've been able to rescue Gocri. Your powers are formidable. I'm sure your mother and father would be proud."

"I miss them, Zeira. My parents must be worried sick about me, and I have no way to tell them that I'm all right."

"How long has it been since you've seen them?" Zeira wanted to know.

"Several days now."

"Do they know you were supposed to be a sacrifice?"

Jerica let out another groan. "Yes. Hallis, my father, tried everything he could to take my place. I felt so bad."

"What a horrible thing to do," Zeira decided. "Making a family give up their offspring, and for what?"

"Tell me about it," Jerica glumly agreed.

"No, I'm serious. Who made the decision to offer a tribesm... er, a human, as a sacrifice?"

"That would be Doolan," Jerica sighed.

"And Doolan would be ...?"

"Oh, sorry. Doolan is Cael's mage. He's responsible for making sure the villagers are protected at night by keeping our powder horns full."

"Powder?" Zeira repeated, confused.

"Magic-infused dust," Jerica explained. "You see, what you do is take powder and sprinkle it around your house. You have to make certain you make a complete circle, otherwise they will find a way inside."

"Who is the *they* you are referring to?" Zeira curiously asked.

"Monsters," Jerica answered, frowning. "All the horrors of the night come out after the sun sets."

"That's terrible," Zeira decided.

"It really is," Jerica agreed.

"Is this what your parents must think has happened to you?"

"I don't know. Probably. I just want to let them know that I'm alive and presently safe. I don't think I've ever felt so safe in my entire life."

"Because you travel with four dragons?" Zeira wryly asked.

"Yes. There are no monsters large enough to pose a threat to you dragons. You're the perfect protection."

Just tell her, Z

Rizzen? Is that you?

Aye. Were you expecting someone else?

You're talking about Jerica? What do you want me to tell her?

"What's going on?" Jerica asked. "You went quiet."

"Open your senses," Zeira told the girl. "Open your senses and find out."

Open my senses and do what, exactly? Jerica's voice timidly asked.

Is this the tribesman you keep telling me about?

Human, Zeira corrected, *and aye, she's the one.*

Who else is here? Jerica wanted to know. *This voice is female. It's not Nuri, so are you talking to someone else?*

Jerica, this is Rizzen, my closest friend. Rizzen, this is Jerica, the kairie.

You are one lucky tri … human, do you know that?

W-why do you say that? Jerica's shy thought came. *You don't know me, and I really don't know you.*

You travel with four dragons while bearing the mark of the omnificent kairie.

Omnificent? Jerica repeated, confused.

I'll let Ziera fill you in. Before she does, though, I would ask her to initiate contact with your sire. Unlike Ziera, I know a few things about humans. You, for example, are underage.

I am not! I'm fifteen! I'm not a child!

You are in our eyes, youngling.

My father has already begun to search for a suitable husband for me. Not that I wish to be married and settle down, but there you go. See? I told you I'm not a child.

My mistake. Whatever was I thinking?

Zeira, this may be a telepathic connection, but somehow, I can tell she just rolled her eyes at me.

Perhaps. She is right, though. You are but a child in human terms. No, do not be cross. You cannot change what you are. However, in this case, it doesn't make any difference. You bear the mark. So, your destiny and mine, along with the rest of us, are intertwined. I think we should let your parents know.

You can do that? Jerica's incredulous thought came. *How?*

By now, I'm familiar with you, and am familiar with your … essence. It has a very distinct signature. I will simply search until I find a matching signature.

How will you know if you've found my parents? Jerica wanted to know.

Let's find out, shall we? I believe I have found your father.

What? Already?

I have found a male presence, whose essence is identical to yours.

You keep saying essence. I don't know what that means.

Zeira was silent as she considered her answer.

Soul?

Jerica was nodding. *All right. I understand soul. So, what do I have to do?*

I must've had a bad piece o' mutton. Now I be hearin' things in me own head? That can't be good.

Zeira immediately felt her rider perk up.

Father?

Oh, that's just great. Now I be talkin' to myself. Or … that's it. I have it now. I'm bein' haunted, which be no improvement.

Father? It's me, Jerica! It's really me! Can you hear me?

What manner of trickery be this? Doolan, if ye cast some type o' spell on me, it ain't funny. Mage or not, I'll thump some common sense into ye, I will.

Zeira, do I not sound like my normal self?

You do. Give him some time. Hearing voices in your head for the first time can be …

… unsettling, I know. Father? Please tell me you can hear me!

Jerica? Be that really you, girl?

Father? It's really me!

And ye be … yer not … are ye alive, girl? Yer not some ghost, are ye?

It's really me! Now, listen to me. I'm alive and well. Yes, I was supposed to be sacrificed, but …

I swear to any god who be listenin' … I will make Doolan pay for offerin' ye up as nothing more than an appetizer. He still thinks that turnin' ye into a sacrifice appeased the Terrans and that's why they've left us alone. In fact, he claims to have seen ye whisked away by a dragon. What happened? I thought I had lost ye forever!

Did he describe the dragon? Was it yellow or red?

He said it was red.

You don't need to worry, Father. I was saved. Zeira happened along and rescued me.

Who be this Zeira person? I want to offer my thanks!

I'm here. And you're welcome.

Eh? What's this? Another voice in me head? Perhaps it be time to swear off ale once and for all.

Not only did Zeira rescue me, so did Skellig. Zeira is the one who's allowing me to talk to you like this. Trust me when I say that I'm perfectly safe.

Ye cannot guarantee that, girl. And Zeira, I be indebted to ye. Be it possible to take my girl someplace safe?

As your offspring has indicated, she is quite safe with us. No harm will befall her.

Offspring? Ye called my daughter offspring? Yer not human, are ye?

I am not.

What are ye?

Zeira, I'd better answer this. Father, you're right. Zeira isn't human. She is … all right, this is harder than I thought. Zeira is a dragon.

Ye have fallen into the clutches o' a dragon? Oh, woe is me! How did this happen?

Dragons. Plural. I travel with four of them. This is Zeira. She's a Fire dragon. With us is Skellig, from Gale. He's a Spark dragon. Then we have Nuri, a valthan, which is their way of describing water dragons. I've ridden on her back, and let me just say that it's exhilarating! And finally, we have Gocri, whom we just rescued. He lives in the ice.

What the bloody hell are ye doin' with the likes of four dragons, girl? Are ye tryin' to get eaten?

Oh, it gets better, I'm afraid. Listen, before I answer that, can I ask you something? Is there anyone in our family who has been able to perform magic?

Wha'? Like a Mage? No, child. Why do ye ask?

Well, it would seem I can.

Not possible. Ye must be mistaken, girl.

Jerica, what's your father's name?

Hallis.

Hallis, believe me when I say your offspring has magic. How do I know this? Because she has bonded with all four of us. Several of us at the same time, in fact. That was how we were able to free Gocri, if you must know.

Yer name be Zeira? And yer a dragon?

I am. I am a Fire dragon of the Phoenix caste.

For the next twenty minutes, Jerica and Zeira regaled Hallis on their exploits, their theories as to what is currently happening to their world, and what they intend to do about it. It was only when the subject of the seeking stone arose did Hallis finally accept what he was hearing as truth.

A seein' stone? Ye search for an oron, do ye not?

Father, you know what they are?

Only that I know Doolan wants to get his hands on one and would stop at nothin' to get it. This is what ye seek now? All of ye?

It is, Zeira confirmed. *Or, more specifically, an oron fragment. We have one and are using it to hopefully locate other pieces.*

Father, once we can get our hands on three pieces, then we can form an oron stone and then use it to find something to use against … against … Zeira? What was it, again?

The Rastan Spear. One of your human kings wields it.

Izzat so? Which one? Tell me!

The information I have comes from Gocri. He refers to the wielder of the spear as Thunder King.

Thunder King? That makes no sense, dragon. The Thunder King I be thinkin' of is weak, gullible, and avoids confrontations like centaurs avoiding you dragons.

For the record, there are some things I tend to avoid.

Ye be a dragon! Ye mus' tower over all yer foes! How could anything strike fear in the heart o' a scaly beastie such as yerself?

I never said I feared anything, Zeira clarified. *I was simply saying there are some creatures so vile that I will do everything I can to avoid them. Take mud worms. Blech. Grompers have more honor than those filthy pests.*

Worms, dragons, it makes no difference. Ye be protectin' my girl, and that makes ye all right in my book. Ye have my thanks. I don't believe I be sayin' this, but pass along my thanks to yer dragon friends. Keep her safe, ye hear me?

We will, rest assured.

Good bye, Father! I love you!

Ah, er, ye know I do, too.

It would mean more if you said it back to me.

Wha'? In front of the dragons?

If it makes you feel any better, the only one who can hear you is Zeira.

I can bring the others into the discussion, if you'd like, Zeira idly suggested.

No! That won't be necessary. Fine, ye want me to say it? I love you, too, girl. Stay safe, that's an order.

"He's gone," Zeira reported. "I severed the connection."

"I had no idea dragons were telepathic. You were able to connect me to my parents. That means the world to me."

"You're welcome. Now, observe. I think we are arriving at our destination."

"We are?" Skellig's voice interrupted. "Where?"

"We have been following the coastline, but now we need to veer south," Zeira said. "Nuri, get as close as you can and wait for us. I'm thinking this shouldn't be too long."

Zeira felt the valthan's ire at not being included when the aerial dragons touched down.

"At least I can still see you from here. You'll only be a few hundred feet away."

"I'm closest, so I'll land first," Zeira told the two much larger dragons. "I know I shouldn't say anything without confirming it first, but I just *know* an oron fragment is down there."

"How can you tell?" Skellig asked.

"The fragment I'm currently carrying. For the first time, I can feel it growing warm. It must be reacting to the presence of another fragment."

"Exercise extreme caution," Nuri's voice ordered. "I don't trust this."

"Nor do I," Gocri agreed.

"You two are only moments behind me, so I'm not too concerned. There, see? There's nothing to ... Jerica, look out!"

Zeira snatched Jerica up and returned the human to her back. Concealed behind the many rocks and boulders were scores of humans, fully armed, and dressed in red chainmail. With a cry, the tiny bipeds pulled their weapons and advanced on the two of them.

Zeira puffed out her chest to look as menacing as possible. She leapt forward and roared a challenge, but the sudden movement dislodged Jerica. Within moments, the soldiers surrounded her rider and were dragging her away, toward the sea.

Zeira, unaware her rider was in danger, heard a loud commotion behind her. Another group of these humans were now advancing on her from the water, weapons drawn. Before she could form a plan, Skellig and Gocri had landed beside her and added their roars to her own.

Skellig pointed toward the sea. "Look to your rider. She's in trouble!"

Zeira's head whipped around, seeing Jerica in danger. Zeira leapt high into the air, flapping her wings and positioning herself between the sea and the group of soldiers. The leader of the gang ducked behind his hostage.

Zeira's anger focused and she locked eyes with the person threatening Jerica's life with a knife at her throat. She took a menacing step forward. The soldier took a step backward, pulling Jerica with him. Movement from the water caught

Zeira's eye.

"Keep them coming," Nuri's voice said, using the mind-speech they shared. "Once they're close enough, I'll handle the rest. Jerica, if you can hear me, fear not. I won't let them harm you."

Zeira kept moving forward. The group of humans shied away from the advancing dragon. Nuri slipped beneath the surface and the soldiers began to disappear, one after the other. When the soldier restraining Jerica arrived at the water's edge, he realized he alone stood against the towering dragon.

His smirk vanished, replaced by alarm. Then, just like that, he was gone. Moments later, Nuri's head reappeared above the frothing waves.

"Jerica, are you well?"

"Yes! Thank you." Jerica pointed east. "But there's more. Do you think that's too big to handle by yourself?"

There, about three hundred feet to the east, rising above the neighboring trees were three masts. A ship!

Nuri nodded once and disappeared into the waves. Seconds later, she was back.

"It's much larger than the fishing boats I've seen."

"It's a galleon," Jerica said. "They are so big, and so expensive, that only kings and queens can afford them."

"Whoever it belongs to, it clearly is responsible for bringing these humans here," Nuri observed. "I'll sink it unless you have another suggestion?"

"Oh, I don't mind you sinking the ship," Jerica said. "I just don't want anyone to lose their life over it. They're only following orders."

Nuri considered. "Very well. I'll encourage them to abandon ship, shall I?" She disappeared once more.

Zeira felt a surge of alarm, emanating from Skellig and Gocri. She spun, to discover a barrage of huge boulders, easily several times the size of a normal human, streak toward her two friends. Gocri swatted them aside using a recently felled tree. Skellig, being smaller, had resorted to seeking cover.

Zeira flew to the closest stone-throwing contraption and immediately brought up the mental picture of the hagfish. Right on cue, her stomach churned its displeasure. Without giving her embarrassment a second's thought, she lifted her tail and torched the trebuchet. The wooden device became engulfed in flames and was reduced to ash in a matter of minutes. Stones were still coming and she rushed toward the next device.

Back at the water's edge, Jerica saw the plight of the two dragons under assault. She rushed to their sides, to the spot where the tips of both of the dragons' tails were within reach. She reached out and grabbed a tail in each hand.

Skellig spotted her. "What are you doing down there? Do you want to get stepped on?"

"Tell Gocri to blast those people with his ice breath," she shouted. "If those people were frozen solid, maybe it would stop the shooting?"

Skellig nudged Gocri's shoulder to get his attention, and the larger dragon immediately understood and fired off an icy breath.

The power that manifested shocked them all.

Large blocks of ice materialized from Gocri's expelled breath and streaked toward the humans and their contraptions. The first block of ice shattered, as though it had been made of the most delicate crystal, but sparks of blue lightning arced in all directions, shocking every human they touched into unconsciousness.

In less than ten seconds, it was all over. There was simply no one left to man the trebuchets.

Gocri and Skellig both turned to Jerica and gave her incredulous looks.

"I've never been able to do that before. Ice and lightning? Clearly a hybrid of our two powers. That could only come from you, Miss Jerica."

Before Jerica could respond, the very air shimmered, as if heat waves were rising from the ground. More soldiers, clad in the same red chainmail. They halted, shocked at the sight of their unconscious comrades.

Zeira hurried to Gocri and Skellig's side and added her growl to theirs.

"Uh, General?" Zeira heard one of the red soldiers say. "I didn't sign up to be eaten, sir."

"They're nothing but overgrown lizards," the leader snapped. "Don't be intimidated by the likes of them. Battle formation! We attack on three! One! Two! Thr- aarrggghh!"

Gocri stretched a foreleg out and flicked away the 'general' human, whatever that was, as easily as an insect on his arm. The foolish biped tumbled end over end and crashed in a heap, face-first on the ground.

In shocked silence, the soldiers glanced nervously about. Zeira snorted with laughter. When none of the soldiers moved, Gocri growled menacingly before lazily picking his teeth with one of his talons.

"Look. Let's be honest. I could eat all of you, although I really don't want to."

More than half of the soldiers, Zeira noted with glee, seemed on the verge of fainting.

Gocri was now picking at one of his long, lower fangs. "And the reason is that humans taste bad and you've got a lot of teeny, tiny bones. I've spent hours picking all those bones out of my teeth. It's tedious, monotonous, and boring."

It was so still that Zeira could hear the scuttling of insects in the faraway trees.

Gocri raised himself up and sat on his haunches. "Very well, suit yourself. Don't say I didn't warn you. Now, I think I'll start with the plump one on the right. He looks juicy, so … ah. There they go."

Every soldier dropped his weapon and ran—screaming—away from the dragons. As one, they made for the sea, but slid to a halt as Nuri's head rose above the surface and roared her own warning.

Zeira watched the leader reach inside his pocket, pull something out, and start waving his arms in the air. Bright, colorful lines and symbols appeared, floating in mid-air. The symbols bobbed and danced before suddenly rushing together to form a large, pulsating ring of yellow energy.

The ring expanded and dropped to the ground. The human soldiers surged forward, diving head-first, in twos and threes, through the open circle, vanishing as they did. When the last one disappeared, the glowing circle rapidly shrunk until it was gone.

"What was that yellow glowing ring?" Skellig asked, once it became clear it was just the five of them once more.

"I saw it, too," Nuri reported, as she slowly pulled herself out of the water.

"It was a portal," Jerica glumly answered. "Doolan has conjured a few before. He did so again for Cael's last Haeger's Day Festival."

"And what is that?" Zeira wanted to know.

Jerica shrugged. "Just a celebration honoring our village's founder."

"The portal, girl. This is bad news?" Skellig asked.

"It means a mage is involved," Jerica explained. "However you want to look at it, that can't be a good thing."

"Did you see how those humans rushed us the moment I landed?" Zeira asked. "The instant I touched down, they were there. Someone knew we were coming."

Skellig pointed at Zeira's chest. "Well, is this where we're supposed to be? We might not be the only ones looking for an oron fragment."

Zeira nodded. "Good point. Let's see." She gently pried her loose chest scale up and caught the fragment as it fell to the ground. Clutching the piece of stone tightly in her claw, Zeira closed her eyes and nodded even before both eyelids had shut. "Yes, it's here. I mean, *something* is here. I can feel it."

"Where?" Skellig wanted to know.

With her eyes closed, Zeira started to move east but almost immediately paused. The gentle pull from the fragment grew faint. This wasn't the way to go. She looked left and headed south, but stopped after only taking a few steps. It wasn't the way, either. Grunting with annoyance, Zeira looked left again, this time looking east.

The pull was back, and for the first time, the fragment started emitting its own heat. She motioned Skellig over and placed the fragment in his open claw. She then pointed south.

"Go that way. Do you feel the pull?"

"No."

"Now, come back this way, to the east. What do you feel?"

"Warmth. This has to be the right place. Another oron fragment is nearby, but what do we have to do to find it?"

Skellig returned the piece of stone to Zeira, who started walking east when all of a sudden, she stopped again. Holding the fragment out in front of her, she swung her arm to the left, then the right, and then finally, dropped it low, so that it was pointing at the ground.

"There's our answer. We have to dig for it."

Chapter 9 — Second Task

Use your eyes," Skellig implored. "Look around you, Zeira. There's nothing here! Certainly nothing that will convince me to willingly get my talons dirty. What do you think I am, a gromper?"

"Remind me where I found you?" Zeira idly asked, as she paced around the open field of grass. She then turned to Gocri. "And you? Were you, or were you not, buried in the earth?"

Gocri's great head fell, like a dragonlet getting a thorough scolding from a parent.

"Have I not proven myself by now?" Zeira continued, raising her voice. "I found Skellig. I was able to follow Nuri, when she was swimming underwater. Gocri was next. Now this."

"You've made your point, young one," Skellig said, bemused.

"I have, aye," Zeira returned. "And, unless you'd like me to start referring to you as Decrepit One, please use my name."

Grinning, Gocri sat back on his haunches. "Ooo, I like her. I'm really starting to enjoy this expedition."

"Are you willing to dig?" Skellig asked.

"What do you have against it?" Gocri returned.

Skellig held up one of his claws and stared at it. "I have weak talons. They chip so easily."

Gocri snorted with laughter. "Oh, I'm sorry, Princess. I didn't see you there at first. If Her Royal Highness would care to step aside, we regular dragons will be more than happy to dig the much-needed hole."

Jerica burst out in laughter, which earned her a surprising grin from the Ice dragon.

"Fine," Skellig sighed. "Zeira, how big and how deep do we have to go?"

Zeira held the stone above the ground and gently let her claw wave back and forth.

"I can't tell. I just know it's somewhere around here. Who's the best digger? Gocri? Nuri? Oh, let me guess. Skellig?"

Grumbling to himself more than anyone, the Spark dragon eyed the gently swaying grass, raised his forearm, and then lashed out. A huge chunk of grass, with nearly two feet of soil still clinging to the roots, went flying over their heads. Warming up to the task, Skellig swiped again, and again. Chunks of dirt and greenery practically exploded in all directions. Whether the Spark dragon was a gifted digger, or he was simply taking his aggressions out on the grass, Zeira couldn't say. What she *could* say was that a large hole had appeared in no time at all. While Zeira watched with awe, and a little envy, the hole was enlarged, the depth extended, and soon, all they could see of Skellig were the tips of his wings as he threw the recently loosened earth over his shoulder and out of the hole.

"Have you found anything?" Nuri's anxious voice asked. "I can't see from back here."

The two-winged dragons turned to look at their valthan counterpart. Nuri had just raised her head out of the water and was looking in their direction.

"I know it's a fair distance," Skellig began, as he poked his head up and out of the hole, "but you're more than welcome to join us over here."

"No harm will befall you," Gocri rumbled. "Not as long as we three have your back."

They watched as Nuri carefully pulled herself out of the water and slowly made her way over to them. Once she was there, Skellig stepped out of the way and indicated the tunnel. "What do you think? You might be the only one here who's a better digger than I am. Care to give it a try?"

"Thanks, but no, if it's all the same to you. If you think I'm slow on dry land, then you should see me try to *dig* on dry land."

Zeira turned to Nuri. "Is that how you dug so fast? There was water under that island?"

Nuri nodded. "You didn't have to dig far to encounter water. Once I saw that, I realized I could probably dig my way over."

Zeira shrugged. "Skellig, would you do the honors?"

The large Spark dragon returned to his hole and bits of gravel, an occasional root, and sometimes a large boulder flew in all directions. Jerica scooted next to Zeira and made sure she was not in the direct line of fire. Not caring for the awkward silence that had befallen them, Zeira moved closer to Gocri and looked up at his imposing figure.

"What's life like, out on the ice?" Zeira asked, once the huge Ice dragon had glanced her way.

"Under," Gocri corrected. "And it's peaceful."

"Does your species interact with others or are they all sedimentary?"

Gocri snorted with amusement as he returned Zeira's frank stare. "I think you might mean solitary, unless you're suggesting I resemble a stone?"

"Oh, that's right. I'm sorry."

Gocri tapped the side of his head. "I think you'll find most dragons will choose to live a solitary life, but fear not. That doesn't mean we aren't in contact with others. All Gatherings have the ability to connect our minds together, when we so choose. I may live hundreds of feet beneath the ice, and I may not see another dragon for centuries, but that doesn't mean I haven't talked with one during that time."

"How long do you go?" Nuri asked.

"Between talking to others of my kind?" Gocri asked. "I typically will check in with my sister once every month or so."

Zeira offered the much larger dragon a smile. "You have a sister? Does she live near you?"

"I have no idea where she lives," Gocri admitted. "I would imagine that, if she wanted me to know where her den is, then she'd let me know."

"So, she doesn't know where you live, either, is that it?" Nuri asked.

Gocri nodded. "Correct. Is it not the same for you?"

Nuri blinked with surprise as she quickly shared a look with Zeira. "Are you asking me?"

"I am."

"It's your own personal preference, I suppose. Some of us prefer to be on our own. There are quite a few extended families who live within sight of one another. That's not to say that we would see each other every day, only that a friendly face is nearby, if the situation called for it."

"Called for what?" Zeira curiously asked. "If you encountered trouble?"

Nuri nodded. "Precisely. Gocri, is there an Ice King?"

"You're asking who I have allegiance to, is that it?" Gocri rumbled. An errant rock came out of the deepening hole and bounced harmlessly off of the Ice dragon's chest. Gocri picked himself up and moved a dozen feet away. Nuri and Zeira followed. "I serve my queen."

"An Ice Queen," Zeira said, as she shared a look with Nuri. "There isn't any king? Wouldn't the mate of the queen be considered the king?"

Gocri, anticipating the question, was already shaking his head no. "The king is defined as a male descendant of the royal blood. If there was a king, there wouldn't be a queen. Do you understand?"

"I think so."

"We have a problem," Skellig called out, as he slowly reversed out of the hole he had been digging.

Alarmed, everyone rushed to the rim and watched as

Skellig slowly emerged.

"What is it?" Zeira wanted to know. "Are you all right?"

"I'm fine, but the hole isn't," Skellig reported. "It's filling faster than I can dig."

"You've hit water," Zeira guessed.

"Er, no." Skellig reluctantly pointed at the hole. "Go see for yourself. This is very peculiar."

Zeira ascended the slight incline around the mouth of the hole and looked down. Skellig was right. The hole was filling in, but not with water. It was filling in with dirt! The hole was seemingly intent on filling itself back up and returning to its grassy state.

Bemused, she watched the level of soil rise, as though it was being fed from underneath, until it reached ground level. Then, right before her eyes, grass sprouted, and less than ten seconds later, they were looking at a patch of unbroken ground. Turning, Zeira looked at her companions. They, like her, had looks of surprise on their faces.

"It's another obstacle," Nuri observed. "Wouldn't this mean we're on the correct path?"

"It would, aye," Gocri decided. "The second piece of oron *must* be buried somewhere down there. The only problem is, I have no idea how to get down there to get it."

"Skellig was the fastest digger, and he couldn't do it," Nuri said. "That must mean there's some other way we can clear that dirt away."

"I'm listening," Gocri said.

Nuri turned to Zeira, who shrugged. Then, the valthan looked down at Jerica, who was scuffing a toe in the grass, as though the simple act would be able to defeat the strange hole.

"Jerica, do you think you could do it?"

"What, dig a hole? Sure, with the right tools. However, there's absolutely no way I'd be able to dig faster than Skellig."

"Blast," Nuri cursed. "What do we do now?"

Jerica motioned for everyone to huddle around her. Looking like a tiny speck standing next to the four dragons, the human began to pace.

"Whenever we have a problem like this at home, my

father always suggests we try a brainstorm session."

"I must confess I do not know what that means," Gocri admitted.

None of the dragons did.

"It means that we toss out ideas, regardless of how they sound, whether viable or impossible. Tell you what, I'll start. I say we find a mage and have him use his magic to remove all the dirt between us and the fragment."

None of the dragons said anything.

"And if someone had actually suggested that," Jerica continued, "then I would have said, it's impossible. Every mage I have ever known cannot be trusted."

"Meaning what?" Skellig wanted to know.

"Meaning he'd steal the fragment for himself," Jerica said, nodding.

"So, it was a waste of time," Gocri decided.

Zeira was shaking her head. "No, I see where she's going with this. We're looking for ideas, *any* ideas, which might have the desired effect."

Gocri was silent as he thought. "Make someone *else* come dig this hole."

Zeira sighed. "Well, that'd be one way to do it. However, we don't want to force anyone to do something they don't want to do."

"You just forced me to do something I didn't want to do," Skellig pointed out.

"Not helping," Zeira and Jerica both said, at the same time. "Anyone else?"

Jerica shrugged. "This has got to be about me. I'm the one who can bond with you dragons, and somehow—and I've yet to figure out how—I'm able to fuse powers together and come up with something new. So, logic would suggest there's something the five of us can do to defeat the obstacle. We just have to figure out what that is."

"Would you like us to just use our abilities on it?" Skellig asked.

Zeira nodded. "Sure, that'd be a great place to …"

A brilliant bolt of lightning arced back and forth between Skellig's two wingtips until, in seconds, it was almost too bright to look at. It streaked high into the air before curving down and slamming into the ground where the hole used to be. A large crater appeared, wider than the previous hole. Skellig grunted with satisfaction as he observed the results of his work. However, it was short-lived. The hole immediately began filling in and soon the field of grass was whole once more.

Jerica tapped Nuri's claw to get her attention.

"Would you mind if I watched from your back? I can't see anything from here. You four are too big."

"Of course."

"I really thought you had it," Zeira whispered to the much larger Spark dragon. "Oh, to have a power like that. I could fire a, er, blast of fire at it, but Skellig's attack was way more powerful. I'd say I'm out. Gocri, would you care to try your luck?"

The Ice dragon moved over to the unbroken patch of grass and took in several deep gulps of air. Seeing the huge dragon's chest slowly expand, the others vacated the area. Taking a moment to prepare himself, Gocri released his icy breath as fast as he could, aimed directly at the ground.

The blades of grass frosted over. A large section of the pristine green countryside turned white. But, as Gocri stepped back to view his handiwork, everyone could see the grass rapidly thawing and returning to normal.

Nuri observed, "It thawed much faster than it should have."

"It's the same process when I was digging," Skellig pointed out. "The faster I dug, the quicker it filled back in. In this case, the grass is thawing faster than Gocri can freeze it."

Zeira turned to the valthan. "Nuri, would you like to try?"

"I'm not sure what I can do that hasn't already been done, but sure, I'll give it a go. Jerica, do you need to jump down?"

"Are you planning on getting wet?" Jerica asked.

"No."

"Then I'm all right if you're all right."

"Very well. I'll try not to dislodge you."

The valthan approached the grass and gave an experimental swipe with one of her thin forelegs. As expected, nothing much happened. Moving into position so she could begin digging, Nuri rested her two front claws on the dirt and leaned forward. Seconds later, she was digging. But she only lasted about five seconds. From Zeira's vantage point, it looked as though either the valthan had broken a claw, or else something had become lodged under her talon. Something wasn't right, of that Zeira was certain.

"What is it?"

"Hmm, I'm not sure. Let me try that again."

The water dragon resumed her digging, but, as before, she stopped after a few seconds. What was going on? What was bothering her?

"Nuri, are you injured?" Skellig asked, concerned.

"No. I, er, think you all need to see this."

"What are we looking at?" Zeira wanted to know. "I see nothing but grass."

"Watch what happens when I dig."

The instant the valthan's talons dug into the soft grass, a transformation happened right in front of their eyes. The green grass turned blue, and moments later, became a liquid. The grass had turned into water!

"And if I stop, it will eventually revert back to grass."

As one, all four dragons, including Nuri, turned to look at Jerica, currently sitting on the valthan's back.

"What? I'm not doing anything."

"You're in physical contact with her," Skellig pointed out. "You're clearly doing *something* to her. No, I don't say that to be rude or cross. I'm simply saying in much the same way you allowed one of my lightning bolts to travel through you and into Nuri, something in you is allowing her to turn the dirt into water. The question is, can we use this to our advantage?"

"You're saying I'm the one turning dirt into water?" Jerica asked. "That's a bit far-fetched, even for you, isn't it?"

"There's an easy way to address this," Zeira said, shrugging. "Nuri, you've dug through dirt before, haven't you?"

Nuri's head nodded. "I have, aye."

"And has *that* ever happened?" Skellig wanted to know.

"No."

Triumphant, Skellig turned to Zeira and shared a look.

Then, together, they looked down at the human on Nuri's back.

"Fine. If I did it, can you tell me how?"

"I think I have an answer," Gocri announced, surprising everyone.

"I'm all ears," Jerica said.

Gocri chuckled. "A strange saying, if you ask me. You, Jerica. Do you remember what your power did to me? How I was spitting out chunks of ice? They exploded and lightning appeared."

"This was when we were fighting those nasty humans," Skellig reminded her. "Oh, er, not you specifically."

Jerica waved off the insult. "No offense was taken. And yes, I do remember that."

"Have you ever tried to use your own abilities?" Gocri wanted to know.

"I've never had abilities to try," Jerica argued.

"Humor us," Skellig said, as he appeared next to Gocri. "Try something, would you?"

Jerica held up her hands in frustration. "Like what?"

Twin boulders, each of which were half the size of Zeira, plunked silently down on either side of her. Jerica squealed with fright and ran straight for the closest dragon, which was Gocri.

"Are we being attacked again?"

Gocri, on the other hand, was studying the small human. Slowly, he turned to eye the boulders that had fallen from the sky. A smile formed.

"You did that, Miss Jerica. You conjured those stones into existence."

"There's no way," Jerica protested. "You're saying I can just wish for a boulder to appear, and one will?"

One boulder obligingly appeared, landing directly on Gocri's head. Everyone heard a resounding *THWACK* before the stone split into two. Each piece then fell to the ground on either side of the glacier dragon's body.

"Gocri, did I do that? I am so sorry! I had no idea I could summon that big rock."

A second boulder appeared and landed in the exact

same spot. After the second impact, which did not result in a broken stone this time, the boulder rolled off Gocri's head and fell harmlessly to the ground, landing beside half of the previous boulder.

"I'm getting a headache," Gocri said, as he lowered his neck so he could rub the top of his head. "I think I've proven my point, wouldn't you agree?"

"Are you injured?" Skellig asked, without taking his eyes off the sky. "Will there be more of those falling down on us?"

Gocri pointed at Jerica. "That's a question best answered by her. I knew it. I knew she had some type of ability."

"I may have one now," Jerica said, "but I didn't before. I didn't have one growing up. What's changed?"

"You summoned water before," Zeira recalled. "Now, it's rocks. Something has changed. What happened?"

Gocri grunted once. "I have an idea. You, Miss Jerica, are a *borrower*."

"What's that supposed to mean?" Jerica curiously asked.

"It would appear you're borrowing other abilities," Gocri explained.

"And how am I doing that?" Jerica demanded. "How can I be doing something when I have no idea what I'm doing?"

"Physical touch," Nuri murmured. "During the fighting, wasn't there a human soldier who came into contact with you?"

"Well, yeah, but …"

"And before?" Gocri continued. "Have you come into contact with any others of your kind?"

"Well, yes, but …"

"I think he's right," Skellig decided. "That's why our shared abilities keep changing. You, Jerica, are the conduit. Not only are *our* abilities fusing together, but you're adding whatever ability you happen to have at the moment."

"If this is true, why did it wait so long before I could use it?"

Skellig helplessly spread out his arms. "I cannot say, I'm sorry."

"I'd like to test this," Gocri said, breaking the silence.

"Miss Jerica, would you be amenable to trying out this theory with, say, Zeira?"

"Oh, it had to be me, didn't it?" Zeira moaned. "Fine. I'll do it."

Jerica shrugged. "Sure. What do you need me to do?"

Skellig approached and held out an open claw. "May I place you on Zeira's back?"

"Oh. Go ahead."

Gocri was nodding. "Now, Zeira, you're in physical contact with Miss Jerica. Try using your powers."

Zeira groaned again. "For that, I'd have to imagine that …"

"… oh so wonderful, aromatic, delicious hagfish is flopping around the insides of your stomach," Nuri finished, throwing a smile in Jerica's direction.

"Ooo, that did it. Oh, I don't feel so good."

"Turn around and face the other way," Skellig ordered. "If Gocri is right, then that means …"

There was a series of loud explosions. Flaming boulders, resembling huge chunks of burning lava, sped away, leaving trails of smoke against the blue sky. Skellig, Nuri, and Gocri looked appreciatively at Zeira.

"*That* was an impressive demonstration," Skellig said. "Zeira, what do you think?"

"That's the strongest example of a fire-based ability I think I have ever seen!" Zeira exclaimed. "And that's all thanks to you, Jerica. How can I properly thank you?"

"Well, from the sounds of it, you can't," Jerica dryly quipped, from her place on Zeira's back. "If what you say is right, and I end up touching someone else, it means your flaming poo boulders will be gone and something else will take its place."

"Flaming poo boulders," Gocri chuckled. "I love it."

"What about the rest of us?" Nuri asked. "Shouldn't we know what we're capable of doing?"

"You're just curious," Skellig accused. After a few moments, he was nodding. "But, so am I. Jerica, may we try?"

"Fine. Why not? This is actually kind of fun. Could someone move me over to Skellig's back?"

Skellig held out a claw. "Or, I could simply hold you in my

hand. Do you trust me?"

Jerica hopped onto the Spark dragon's open claw and nodded. "I do, yes."

Moments later, large stones were hurtling through the air once more, only this time, they were crackling with energy. In fact, everyone could see tiny blue arcs of lightning dancing along the surface of the rock as it sailed through the air. Skellig deliberately shifted his aim to a nearby island. Together, they watched one of the lightning-infused stones slam onto the beach. The resulting explosion sent up huge plumes of dust and debris. Once the smoke had cleared, they could see a giant crater on the beach, which was rapidly filling with water.

Curious, Zeira leaned forward and laid a hand on Skellig's foreleg. Surprised, the Spark dragon turned to see what Zeira was doing. Once he saw her claw resting on his arm, he nodded. This was just another test. How would their shared ability be affected this time?

Electrified magma shot out of Skellig's surprised mouth. Snapping it closed, he looked over at Zeira before turning his gaze on the lone human present. Jerica pointed at Zeira.

"You try it next."

"Me? Why? Wouldn't it be the same?"

Skellig was nodding. "That's a good point. It'd be interesting to see if all three of us exhibit the same mixed ability."

Zeira shrugged. She brought up the unpleasant memory of the hagfish and waited for her digestive system to recoil with disgust. Thankfully, it didn't take that long.

A fine red spray erupted from Zeira's hind end. It landed on the ground and immediately crackled and burned. Surprised, Zeira turned to Jerica.

"How did you know it'd be different for me?"

"It was just a guess," Jerica said, shrugging.

"Well, what about you?" Nuri said. "What happens when you activate the shared power?"

Surprised, the human shook her head. She clearly didn't know. Making certain she was pointed safely facing away from everyone in the group, Jerica climbed onto Nuri's back, closed her eyes, and braced herself.

A shadow cast over Jerica and Nuri. Looking up, Jerica

shrieked with surprise and immediately hunched over, hugging Nuri's scaled back as tightly as she could. A huge dollop of wet, squishy mud landed with a resounding *SPLAT*, completely enveloping Jerica before it followed the course of gravity and flowed over Nuri and down to the ground.

Skellig appeared next to the valthan and did his best to clear as much mud from Nuri's back as he could. The small mound of wet earth grew a pair of eyeballs and glared angrily at Skellig. Jerica's head appeared next, as the small human sat back up.

"I hate being dirty," Jerica exclaimed. She leaned as far over to the right as she could and ended up spitting a mouthful of dirt. "That was unpleasant."

"Stones," Gocri said. "Rocks. Earth. Nuri is valthan, so if you mix water and earth, what do you get?"

Skellig flicked a speck of mud off his talons. "You get this. Mud. It would appear Jerica's power is the ability to summon earth."

"For now," Gocri reminded him. "We all know what to expect right now, but should Miss Jerica come into physical contact with another human, then everything will change."

"Then, we can't let that happen," Nuri decided. "A moment, if you please. I am going to rinse myself off. Jerica, stay where you are. We could both use a good dunking."

"Fine by me," Jerica laughed, as she noticed the dirt on her clothes was rapidly drying. "I'll never complain about getting dirt on my hands ever again!"

Once Nuri and Jerica were back, the five of them gathered at the grassy clearing and stared at the area which had been, thus far, successful in rebuking their efforts. Zeira perked up. She turned to Nuri and pointed at the grass.

"When you were digging, and the earth became water, how fast did it revert back to earth?"

Nuri shrugged. "I'm not sure. Would you like me to try again?"

Zeira stepped away from the grass. "Yes, please. The answer is here, we just need to find it."

The dragons moved away, allowing Nuri the freedom to dig. However, after the valthan made the first swipe with her claw, everyone knew something was up. But, before Nuri could say anything, Skellig began laughing. He pointed at Jerica, who was standing next to Gocri's leg.

"Nuri, I do believe you're missing your rider."

Surprised, Nuri turned to look at Jerica. "Oh. I didn't know you had left."

"I'm sorry," Jerica apologized. "I needed to stretch my legs. It's not that comfortable, you know."

"What is?" the valthan returned.

Jerica pointed at her. "Riding you, Nuri. There's no comfortable place to sit. I've been straddling your back, but that forces my legs in opposite directions. I was talking with Gocri in an attempt to find a solution."

Nuri turned to the Ice dragon. "Any ideas?"

Gocri nodded. "Sure. A saddle?"

Skellig and Zeira both snorted with laughter.

"Don't laugh," Gocri scolded. "I recommend the same for you two. Think of your rider. Do you want harm to befall her?"

"I don't want to be falling anywhere," Jerica said.

"Befall," Gocri corrected. "In this case, I was asking if your companions would want you to come to harm. As for *befalling*, I think you might've blended two perfectly acceptable words together."

Zeira sidled close. "So, Jerica, alone, can conjure mud. Does this help us or hinder us?"

"I'd say hinder," Jerica answered, "seeing how we have to dunk ourselves in the sea in order to clean ourselves off."

"You didn't try with Zeira touching you," Gocri recalled. "Wasn't that the point of the test?"

Nuri and Jerica sighed, in unison. Skellig and Gocri grinned at each other and moved away.

"What do you think they'll get?" Skellig quietly asked Gocri. "Fiery mud?"

"I say it'll be something to that effect," Gocri decided.

The three experimenters readied themselves for Jerica's test. Zeira watched the small human take several deep breaths, close her eyes, and then nod her readiness. After a few moments, Jerica opened her eyes and looked nervously about.

"Did anything happen? Perhaps we needed to … agghh!"

A huge dollop of mud, even larger than the first, dropped on top of her, completely obscuring the three of them. Zeira nodded. It looked as though Skellig had been right: steam rose from the newly summoned mound of mud.

"You realize what that looks like, right?" Skellig chuckled.

Gocri nodded. "Like a huge pile of steaming dung. How warm is it?"

Skellig stared at the Ice dragon with mock horror on his face. "And you think I'm sticking a claw in that? Guess again."

Gocri moved close and held an open claw, palm facing down, over the mound. "Detectable, but not fatal. Come. Help me clear some of this away. Remember, there's a human in there."

Skellig groaned, but didn't resist. A few moments later, they had uncovered Jerica's head.

"Well, that was something," the human admitted.

"Was it bad or good?" Zeira wanted to know.

"Good, I guess. I know that mud is warm, but to me? It still felt cool to the touch."

"I suspected as much," Gocri said. "However, I didn't want to take any chances." The largest of the dragons turned to look back at the grass floor. "Nuri, would you try again? No, Jerica, stay as you are. I want to see something."

"We've already done this," Nuri pointed out, as she returned to the grass-covered ground. "It turns to water for me, eventually going back to grass."

Gocri nodded. "That's true, but you said something that bears investigation."

"I did? What'd I say?"

"That the water will *eventually* return to grass."

"I do remember saying that," Nuri said, nodding. "What about it?"

"Why did you say *eventually*?" Gocri pressed. "Does the hole fill up slower than it did when Skellig was digging?"

Nuri was silent as she considered.

"I think it did," Zeira recalled. "Could that be the key?"

"So it takes a little longer to return to grass," Skellig said, shrugging. "So what? How does that help us?"

Zeira's eyes widened. "If enough dirt is turned into water, and the water is removed from the hole before it can return to dirt, what does that leave us?"

"An empty hole," Gocri breathed, nodding.

Skellig held up a foreleg. "Umm, excuse me? How are we supposed to get the water out of the hole? What are you planning on doing, sucking it up and spitting it elsewhere?"

Zeira shared a look with the much larger Ice dragon. Clearly, Gocri was thinking the same thing she was. Skellig had come up with the winning solution! Zeira turned to their valthan companion and motioned her over.

"Let's try this again. Be prepared to dig. Dig just as fast as you can. As soon as you get a large pool of water, move out of the way. Skellig will come in and suck all the water out."

"I will *what*?" Skellig sputtered.

"Your idea, of course," Zeira told the Spark dragon. "It has merit. It *must* be the solution to digging on this particular island. Let's give it a try, shall we?"

Skellig grumbled something, but kept it soft enough where no one else could understand him.

For nearly five minutes, Nuri furiously dug into the soft earth. It wasn't until she was deep enough to threaten Jerica with getting wet when she hurriedly backed out of the hole. Skellig brushed by her, leaned down, and sucked in a huge mouthful of water. With drips falling off his fangs, he looked at Zeira and gave her a questioning look.

Zeira pointed south. "We need the water out of the way. Just spit it over there."

Skellig nodded, and spat the mouthful of water onto a section of grass further away. He repeated the process a few times until there was nothing but a tiny puddle of water at the bottom of the hole. With bated breath, the four dragons—and one human—waited to see if the hole would fill back up.

"It's staying empty!" Jerica exclaimed. "Way to go, Zeira! You figured it out!"

"We're not there yet," Skellig said, frowning. "How much deeper does Nuri have to make that hole?"

"Until we find something, I would imagine," Gocri said.

Nodding, Nuri moved back to the hole and resumed

digging. Another five minutes passed as she hurriedly dug deeper into the earth. Satisfied at the amount of water that had accumulated in the hole, she quickly retreated and waited for Skellig to remove the water.

Skellig had to empty the hole several more times, but just as she readied herself for her fifth round of digging, everyone heard a metallic clang the moment Nuri struck the ground. Surprised, the valthan dragon carefully dug around the object, working to clear as much earth from around whatever she had found as possible. Once more, she retreated, and waited for Skellig to remove the water.

"It's a metal cube," Nuri announced, surprised, as she carefully lifted the small object out of the hole. "This must be what we're looking for, right?"

"It's a metal cube?" Jerica repeated, confused. "What are we supposed to do with that?"

"Find a way to open it?" Gocri suggested.

Before anyone could respond, they all heard a loud gagging noise. Turning, they saw Skellig, with a look of abject disgust on his face.

"What is it?" Zeira wanted to know.

Skellig opened his jaws in response. Clods of dirt tumbled to the ground. Evidently, the Spark dragon had become curious, and stopped to watch Nuri pull the object from the ground. In the time he had hesitated, the water had reverted back to dirt.

Skellig spat chunks of dirt as he immediately looked for a way to rinse his mouth. However, they were on an island in the middle of the sea. There was no freshwater to be found.

Skellig's long, forked tongue appeared, caked in mud. He looked imploringly at his companions before turning to look at the nearby coast.

"It's saltwater," Zeira sadly told him. "We ... wait! Nuri, I hate to ask it, but could you dig another hole? Jerica, please return to Nuri's back. You two can give him some fresh water. Well, temporarily, that is. The poor fellow needs to rinse his mouth."

With his mouth properly rinsed, Skellig rose to his full height and shuddered.

"That had to be my worst nightmare," he confided.

"You're afraid of dirt?" Gocri asked, snorting with laughter.

"Being unable to breathe."

That sobered everyone.

"I'm so sorry," Nuri began.

"Can't you breathe through your nose?" Jerica asked. "I mean, I can see you have nostrils. I'm sorry, I don't mean any disrespect."

"My nose is plugged," Skellig admitted.

"I didn't know dragons get colds," Jerica giggled.

"Cold? I'm not cold."

Jerica shook her head. "No, I mean … forget it. What about that cube? How do we open it?"

The metal cube was passed from dragon to dragon. No one, it seemed, knew how to open it. That is, until it was given to Gocri, who simply crushed it in his enormous hand. Brushing away the scraps of metal, he held out a sliver of stone. And … the blue stone was glowing!

"We've found our second piece!" Zeira proudly announced. "We were able to work together to …"

Zeira trailed off after noticing a sudden absence of sunlight. The sky was growing dark! What was going on?

Gocri bared his fangs and moved close. He spread his great wings to shield the three other dragons from sight.

"Show yourself," the Ice dragon snarled.

"What is it?" Zeira nervously asked. "What's going on?"

"I *am* showing myself," a cool, calculating voice responded. "You landed on *my* island, and are trying to take something which does not belong to you."

Swirling mists coalesced into a form easily three times the size of Gocri. Zeira paled. Looking down at them was a pair of reptilian eyes! This was a dragon, but unlike any she had ever seen before.

"Drop the stone. I won't ask again."

Chapter 10 — Sifula

D oes anyone know *who* or *what* that is?" Zeira nervously whispered. The only thing she knew for certain was that it was a dragon, but one made up of mists and swirls? As she stared at it, the more substantial it became. "Uh, er, are you friendly?"

Those two gray reptilian eyes shifted, and fixated on Zeira's. She felt as though those two silvery orbs were peering into her very soul. A few moments of uncomfortable silence passed.

"You are not the trespassers I believed would come," the voice said.

"Who's there?" Skellig's voice demanded. "Gocri, lower your wings. We can't see a blasted thing back here."

The huge white wings slowly folded and tucked away. Five sets of eyes, four of them wyverian in nature, looked up at the distant head of their aggressor. Zeira couldn't keep herself from staring. She previously thought Gocri was far and away the largest dragon she had ever laid eyes on. But this one? The top of its head had to be sitting on a neck longer than her full body length! And the wings? Wow. Just one of those gigantic wings could sweep all five of them back to the sea.

"We will be leaving this place," Gocri growled, "and we will be taking that fragment with us."

"Methinks not, Ice," the smoke dragon said.

Gocri's nostrils pinged shut as he took in great gulps of air. Moments later, he fired off a huge white, icy cloud, which coated the grass and rocks. What *was* in its path, but remained unaffected, was the strange dragon.

Bright blue arcs of electricity crackled between Skellig's wing talons. Building up its intensity, the arcs jumped back and forth a few times until it was launched directly at the imposing smoky figure. As with the ice cloud, the bolts of electricity passed harmlessly through their assailant.

"I could try and hit him with a blast of fire," Zeira began, "but if he's unaffected by ice *and* lightning, I don't think I'd have much effect. Does anyone know what kind of dragon this is?"

"Smoke," Gocri announced. "We are facing a smoke dragon."

"You will cease this frivolous activity," the strange dragon ordered, ignoring Gocri's correct identification of the species.

"Or else what?" Gocri challenged.

Their adversary leaned down, opened its jaws, and allowed a single puff of black smoke to descend to the ground. The grass it touched immediately withered and died. Nearby stones crumbled into gravel. Catching the barest whiff of the noxious cloud caused their small group to break out coughing. Thinking fast, Gocri extended his wings, and then snapped them closed, which had the force of a thunderclap, shoving the toxic black cloud far out to sea. As for the smoke dragon itself, the blast of wind from Gocri's wings quite literally blew it away. However, before anyone could rejoice at their good fortune, the silvery swirls of smoke were back.

"That didn't seem to work," Zeira lamented.

"You've never encountered my kind before, have you,

young one?"

"I don't think any of us has," Zeira returned. "And is there something about me that comes off as being young? I'm not that young!"

Wisps of smoke trailed off this new dragon's long, sinewy neck as the head lowered to the ground. Once they were at eye-level, a few things became apparent. Gocri had been right. This was nothing more than another species of dragon.

The strange dragon brought its nose to within inches of her own. Then, the head swung around until it did the same with the remaining three dragons. Finally, just as the head was preparing to return to the great heights it had been at before, the nostrils flared. It hesitated as it sniffed the air.

"I recognize Fire, Spark, Ice, and Water," the powerful voice said. "But, there's one among you I have *not* smelled before. You. You are a human, are you not?"

Zeira turned to watch Jerica stare fearlessly up at the large dragon.

"That's correct. My name is Jerica. What's yours? What kind of dragon are you? Are you really a smoke dragon?"

"I am Sifula. You may call me Sif. As for my species, I am a drifter. I assume I am the first you have encountered? Would I be correct?"

Wordlessly, all four dragons—and one human—nodded.

Sifula pointed at the glowing blue stone Zeira was holding. "I apologize for the theatrics, but I found that fragment several years ago, and have been guarding it ever since."

"Can I ask why?" Skellig demanded. "Does it belong to you?"

Sifula fell silent. Zeira blinked as she gazed up at the mysterious smoke dragon. Was it her imagination, or did Sifula appear to be solidifying? The amount of smoke emanating from her body had decreased considerably, and less than ten seconds later, they could make out scales on Sif's upper chest and arms. Also, if Zeira didn't know any better, it looked as though their new friend was shrinking!

"You are intimidated by my physical presence," Sifula explained. "To ease your fears, I am reducing my mass."

"You can do that?" Gocri exclaimed, incredulous. "And I most certainly am not."

"Are you, or are you not, currently shielding your companions?" Sifula asked, as her body continued to slowly shrink.

"I ..."

"Hold that thought," Skellig said, as he stepped around Gocri's body. He looked up at the much larger figure. "Let's focus on the issue at hand. We recovered a second piece of oron stone. You seem to think that it belongs to you. Well, finders keepers, as they say."

"By that logic," Sifula argued, "the fragment would have become mine the instant I found it, would it not?"

Zeira tensed, unsure what the newcomer wanted. Surely, it wasn't the same piece of stone they had worked so hard to locate. Nervously eyeing her companions, she braced for the worst.

"You have misinterpreted the situation," Sifula said, as she sighed and turned back to Zeira. "Have I kept watch over that useless sliver of stone? Aye, I have. I will withdraw my objections to your possession of it ..."

"Thank you," Zeira said, after the smoke had trailed off.

"... provided you can prove to me your cause is noble."

Nuri nodded. "That's easy enough to prove. The four of us have banded together to address the growing unrest in our world. You've felt it, too, have you not?"

Much to their surprise, Sif nodded. "I have, aye. And *that* is why I am still on this island, after waiting four years. I knew someone would come looking for that tiny piece of rock. Why else would I devise such devious obstacles around it?"

"That was *you*?" Jerica demanded. "We almost didn't figure it out. I think we were close to just giving up. You wouldn't have wanted that to happen, would you?"

"For one so small, you certainly don't have problems being heard, do you?" Sifula said. For the first time, the impossibly huge dragon smiled. "I wish to join your group."

"You wish to *what*?" Zeira asked, shocked. "You want to join us? Why? You're so much bigger, you clearly can handle yourself better than we can, and yet you want to tag along?"

Sifula nodded. "Correct."

Zeira turned to her companions and motioned them closer. Huddled close together, she looked at each of her friends. "What do you think? Should we let him join? Do you think we can trust him?"

The smoke dragon's snout jerked upwards, as though someone had just struck it a blow. "Him? Did you say *him*? What's the matter? Didn't think a drakkaina could be considered dangerous?"

Jerica tapped Zeira's foreleg. "What is a drakkaina?"

Zeira shrugged. "I'm really not sure."

Sifula stared at Zeira with a look of pity on her face.

"A drakkaina is a female dragon. That means *you* are a drakkaina, young one. By the gods, you all must have led sheltered lives."

"Sheltered?" Skellig returned. "Aye, that's one way of putting it. Then again, living on a world like this, and only allowed to visit certain places, then we wouldn't have any other choice, would we?"

"What are you talking about?" Sifula argued. "Has someone prevented you from exploring the world? Has your mother forbid you leaving the nest?"

Skellig bristled with anger. "I do *not* live in my mother's nest. Besides, I've spent the better part of two years flying all over Andela."

"Two whole years, eh? What sights you must've seen in such a short amount of time."

Skellig turned to Gocri. "She's mocking me, isn't she?"

"Sure sounds like it," the Ice dragon rumbled, chuckling.

"Are you saying you've been able to go where you want and do what you want?" Zeira asked.

By now, just about all of Sifula's gaseous form had solidified into a smaller winged dragon. Zeira looked over at Gocri and shook her head. Sif might've been shooting for a body smaller than her regular form, but she was still nearly twice the size of the Ice dragon.

"Can you make yourself smaller?" Zeira curiously asked.

Sifula studied the much smaller dragon and went still. Her body reverted from solid back to vapor and condensed itself even further. After a few minutes, an exact mirror image of Zeira, herself, was looking back at her. The other dragons crowded close.

"Oh, you do impressions?" Nuri exclaimed, delighted.

"I'd give myself away as soon as I start talking," Sif explained, shrugging.

"How long can you stay like that?" Skellig asked.

"My natural state is vaporous, but I can hold a physical form for a little while. The larger the form, the shorter amount of time I can hold it. Conversely, the smaller the form, the longer I can keep it."

"Can you clone their abilities, too?" Gocri wanted to know.

Sifula shook her head. "I'm afraid not. I can mimic the appearance only."

Jerica stepped forward and looked at the second Phoenix dragon. "Can you adopt a form other than your own? Meaning, could you become me?"

The phony Zeira turned vaporous once more and continued to shrink. Right before their eyes, Zeira and her companions watched the strange form stand up on its rear appendages. Her body shifted, condensed, and shifted some more. Her torso thinned, and Zeira's long, serpentine tail withdrew into itself. A few moments later, a second biped had joined the group, and it was an exact duplicate of Jerica.

Zeira turned to the others. "All right, I'll say it. I'm impressed."

"That makes two of us," Skellig agreed.

"Oh, to be able to change your form," Nuri sighed. "I'd be able to adopt the form of a land dragon and move about with ease."

"Is this an ability you're born with?" Zeira asked. A few moments later, she blushed. "I'm sorry. I don't mean to pry."

Jerica's twin turned vaporous and quickly expanded, allowing Sifula to resume her natural form.

"Yes and no. We know how to change our mass from the moment we hatch. Being able to adopt the form of another, well, that's an acquired skill. As such, I'm proud to say that I excel at that skill."

"You most certainly do," Nuri agreed. "Having never encountered anyone like you, if you're willing, I'd love to hear more. Where does your kind live? I mean, how do you live? If a wind appears, will it threaten to blow you away?"

Sifula laughed and settled to the ground.

"This. This is what I missed. It's why I decided to change my living situation."

Zeira studied their new friend for a few moments. "Companionship. You're lonely."

Sifula shrugged. "Guilty as charged. I've been on my own for too long. I guess I'm just tired of traveling."

"Where is your home region?" Zeira wanted to know. "How far is it from here?"

Sifula was silent as she considered. Her form went vaporous and she changed herself into a small dragon half the size of Zeira. Her new form had two sets of wings, one regular-sized, and one much smaller, and could walk around on her hind legs. Dropping down, so that all four of her legs were in the sand, she scratched out a drawing.

"I'm assuming you're familiar with the three main land masses, correct? We are currently on the farthest one to the east. If we ... what? What'd I say?"

"Three?" Skellig repeated. "I was only aware of two."

"Three land masses?" Zeira echoed. "I never knew there was more than one!"

Sif looked at Nuri. "What about you? Which ones do you know about?"

"This one and the one to the west," the water dragon said. "This continent, it stretches all the way to the ice fields up north. The only way to swim past is to dive deep, below the ice. But, once you pass the ice, you'll discover a narrow inlet separating this continent from the next. I've explored those waters, but only the one time. As far as I know, I'm the only valthan who ever has. Gocri, you're nodding. Do you know the area of which I speak?"

"I do," Gocri rumbled. He studied Sif's drawing for a few moments before adding a few scratches of his own. "You're right. The land meets the ice about here. The two regions remain mixed for several hours' worth of flying. Nuri, you say you've been under the ice sheet here? Most impressive. I know they can run very thick."

Sif added more detail to the second land mass. The others were silent as they watched her add an elongated peninsula reaching southwest, and another straight down. Near the top, a smaller chunk of land was added, reaching west. She then pointed at the peninsula stretching southwest.

"You, Spark dragon. Skellig, is it? Is this where you're from?"

Skellig nodded and tapped the drawing. "Here, on the extreme tip of this chersonese, you'll find Gale."

There was a commotion by Zeira's right front foreleg. Jerica was there and she looked confused.

"Excuse me? Skellig, did you say chersonese? What is that? I'm not familiar with the word."

"Neither am I," Zeira admitted.

"It's another way to describe a body of land almost completely surrounded by water. This, here? To the east of Gale? It's all Terra."

Zeira perked up. She pointed at the first, and largest, of the two land masses. "It is? But ... but I thought it was over here!"

"That's what I've been trying to tell you," Skellig sighed. "Traces of our home elements can be found in more than one place. It's how I've been able to travel as extensively as I have. Sif, is this what you have done, too?"

"Finally! Someone who understands that we're not as geographically isolated as we've been led to believe! To answer your question, Skellig, yes, that is precisely what I've done. I have identified my home elements and have learned how to locate them without even touching down on the land below."

Skellig perked up. "Oh? I can only tell the area will work when I come into physical contact."

Sif tapped the side of her head. "If you ever want to learn, you have but to ask. You can tell everything you need to know by exploring your senses up here."

"Consider me interested," Skellig announced. "Gocri, Nuri, Zeira ... I say we take her up on her offer."

Jerica wandered over to the crude rendering of two of

Andela's continents and fell silent. Catching sight of their secret weapon, Zeira sidled up close to Sif and cleared her throat.

"There is something you ought to know about us."

Interested, Sif turned her attention on the youngest member of their group. "Oh? I'm listening."

Zeira indicated the small biped. "She's a kairie."

A blank look fell over Sif's face.

"A kairie. You know what a kai is, I'm sure."

Sif continued to say nothing.

"A rider?" Skellig translated. "You know, someone who gets up on your back and treats you like a horse?"

"I do not treat anyone like a horse," Jerica insisted.

"Very true, Miss Jerica," Skellig hastily said. "I apologize. Sif, you obviously are familiar with your abilities, aren't you?"

"Obviously," the smoke dragon returned.

"I am a Spark dragon. This is the extent of my abilities."

Twin bolts of lightning snaked out from Skellig's two wing talons and raked across the grass-covered ground. Two jagged lines of singed grass appeared. Surprisingly, the burnt grass remained just that: burned. Surprised, Skellig turned to Zeira.

"Now it decides to stay burned?"

"Of course it'll stay burned," Sif scoffed. "I'm no longer laying on the ground, am I?"

There was a collective gasp as the four dragons—and one human—turned to Sif and gaped at her.

"That was you?" Zeira asked, dumbfounded. "You kept filling the hole? What …? Why …? All right, I'll ask. How?"

"She admitted she can change her form," Jerica said, coming to Sif's defense. "Why couldn't she make herself look like grass and water? After all, if what she says is true, then she's been on this island for over four years."

"I was digging *into* you?" Skellig repeated, horrified. "I am so sorry. I, uh, did not know. Did it, er, hurt?"

"I was perfectly safe."

"You were serious about protecting that fragment, weren't you?" Zeira said.

Sif shrugged. "If you want to know the truth, I had fallen

asleep. I awoke to the sounds of digging."

"I think I'm going to be sick," Skellig groaned. "I sucked up mouthfuls of *you* and spit you out in a different location. That didn't hurt you at all?"

"Why should it?" Sif asked. "Your hesitation confuses me. There was no harm intended, nor was any done. I have been waiting for someone like you to come along. Now that you're here, I would like to formally ask to accompany you all as you make your way west."

"How do you know we're going west?" Nuri asked.

"That's the direction of the third continent. Didn't you know? I'm sorry, I assumed you did."

"Know what?" Gocri suspiciously asked.

"That the third and final piece of the oron stone is on the third continent, of course."

"And how do you know this?" Skellig demanded.

"I thought you knew all about those glowing rocks," Sif said, amazed. "If you are holding one of the three elemental pieces of an oron stone, then it'll undoubtedly lead you to another piece, and then another. I happened upon the earth fragment quite by accident. It ... before I go any further, do you all know about the oron stones and what happens if one of them is ever broken apart?"

"Pretend we don't," Gocri said, as he lowered himself to the ground and made himself comfortable. "What can you tell us about them?"

"An oron stone has also been called a seeing stone," Sif began. "Did you know that?"

Everyone nodded.

"Excellent. Now, if an oron stone should ever become separated into its base elements, then three fragments will form, one for each element: earth, water, and fire."

"What about air?" Jerica wanted to know. "Isn't that an element, too?"

"Don't mumble," Sif scolded. "I have a hard enough time hearing you as it is. Now, as I was saying, the stone will separate into three pieces. Hold the three back together and, just like that, you have yourself an intact stone. Now, we're all caught up. Does anyone have any questions?"

All four dragons nodded, and Jerica politely raised a hand.

Sif groaned. "What were you lot doing on a mission to recover and assemble an oron stone if you don't even know how the blasted thing works? Fine. We'll get to everyone. You, biped. You're first. What's your question?"

"Why would someone want to break an oron stone apart in the first place?" Jerica asked. "That would be counter-productive, wouldn't it?"

The vaporous dragon shrugged. "You would think, and I would think, but clearly not. Being able to see what you want most is not always a good thing." Zeira watched as Sif turned to stare directly into her eyes. "It can be very dangerous. Fire, you're next."

"My name is Zeira," she clarified. "Do you want us to call you *Gas*?"

Skellig snickered and looked away.

"Your point is taken," Sifula admitted. "What's your question, Zeira?"

"You are clearly more traveled than any of us. You managed to stumble across one of the oron stone fragments. How many have you come across in your travels?"

"Just the one. Gocri, you're up."

Skellig looked over at the large Ice dragon and shook his head. "I see what she's doing. Before you ask your question, I'd think about it long and hard. Make sure you phrase it in such a way that the answer would be more than one- or two-word sentences."

Gocri was nodding. "Understood. I noticed that, too. Tell us, Sifula, how many oron stones are left?"

"Just the one. Nuri, what would you like to know?"

"Wait a moment," the valthan implored. "There's only one oron stone left? I thought they numbered more than that?"

"They were once plentiful," Sif explained. "Now, however, they're being hoarded and aren't being replenished."

"Who is responsible for replenishing them?" Nuri wanted to know.

"You've asked your question. Who's next? Jerica, I believe it's your turn."

Giving a conspiratorial wink at Nuri, Jerica faced the vapor dragon and nodded. "Who is responsible for replenishing the oron stones?"

"The Master of Prophecies. All right, everyone has asked a question, so perhaps we can now ..."

"Oh, no you don't," Zeira interrupted. "You're only giving us teasers. You may be answering questions, sure, but you aren't giving us the information we need."

Sifula grinned. "You sound like my sire. Very well. I take it you'd like me to expand on those subjects. Well, what do you want to know?"

Jerica stepped forward. "Me first. Sifula, I asked you how many oron stones you have discovered in your travels, and you said just the one. I'm assuming it's the one Zeira is currently carrying? Am I correct?"

"She currently carries two," Sifula corrected. "And yes, that's the one I'm talking about. Zeira, do you need clarification?"

"I do, yes. What did you mean when you said that being able to see what you desire most could be dangerous?"

"Knowing not only what your heart desires most, but also where to acquire it, can lead to obsession," the vapor dragon explained, as though she was lecturing a nest of dragonlets. "Obsession leads to fixation, which can descend into desperation."

"I don't know if that helps me or not," Zeira decided. Shrugging, she shook her head. "Whatever. Skellig, I believe you're next."

Nodding, Skellig turned to look up at Sif, but was startled to see that their new friend was shrinking down to the same size as he was. Within moments, her form solidified into a female Spark dragon.

"Sorry. I'm just trying it out. I do not wish to offend."

"No offense is taken," Skellig assured her. "Have you encountered many female Spark dragons?"

"Only from a distance. Gocri, you're up."

"W-wait!" Skellig stammered. "I didn't get to ask a question."

"Yes, you did," Jerica giggled. "You asked her if she had

met many female Spark dragons. For the record, she answered you."

"Oh. All right. That's one point to you, Sif."

The vapor dragon bowed her head in acknowledgment. "Thank you. Anyone else? What about you?"

Startled, Gocri looked up. "Does the reason the oron stones are becoming rare have something to do with the reason why Andela is becoming more hostile? Is it responsible for the imbalance?"

Sifula smiled and gave the Ice dragon a curt bow. "Well done. That's the first intelligent question I've heard today. The answer is, the shortage is not directly responsible, but it is contributing. I hope that makes sense."

"Where is it?" Zeira suddenly asked. "I'm sorry, I know I'm probably out of turn, but I need to ask before I forget. Sif, you said the fragment is on the third continent. Where, exactly?"

Sif pointed at the crude map still visible in the sand.

"Everyone, gather round. Now, we are here, near the northern tip of Terra, where the ice floes are connected. Which direction have you been traveling? Where did you start, Zeira?"

Zeira pointed at a mountain range starting in the southwestern portion of the continent and ran in a diagonal line, ending in the northeast. At a point near the halfway mark in the mountain range, where the mountains dipped slightly south before resuming its trek northeast, Zeira tapped the sand.

"There's a large lake here. Game is plentiful, and we Fire dragons frequent it often. The majority of our nests are nearby, on the northern side of these mountains. That's where I started my journey."

"You've come a long way, young one," Gocri murmured, impressed. "All this for a kai?"

Zeira nodded. "Yes. I wanted to know what I could do to help. My king, er, Darazok Aeogan, instructed all able-bodied flyers to determine their eligibility for the bond. The only way I knew to do that was to locate a tribesman and see for myself if I could take on a rider."

Sif eyed Jerica. "You are the rider that was mentioned before. Human, you carry that title? You are Zeira's rider?"

Jerica nodded. "And Skellig's, and Gocri's, and Nuri's, and probably yours, too, if I could ride you."

"A rider is called a kai," Skellig patiently explained. "The rider bonds with the dragon, which causes their abilities to fuse together. Not all dragons can bond with a tribesman, er, human, and not all humans can bond with a dragon."

"Sounds like it's more trouble than it's worth," Sif decided.

"How do you not know this?" Skellig wondered. "I would think you'd be able to tell us all about how our abilities are spliced together, to form something completely different."

Interested, Sif perked up. "Spliced together? Are you suggesting your abilities are mixing with that of the human's?"

Gocri nodded. "Not only is it so, but it turns out Jerica is a *borrower*. She has taken the amalgamation of anyone in physical contact with her and returns something so unique that it defies explanation."

Sif lowered herself to the ground and solidified her form. "Indeed? I will confess to being extremely curious. What were some of the results?"

"Electrified rocks," Skellig answered. "Shooting a blast of my power through a human and into Nuri, all without causing any damage."

"Is that relevant?" Sif asked.

Skellig nodded. "I'm the only one who has ever been immune to my own power. To have it channeled through two others, and have them both walk away? Unscathed? Unheard of."

"And that's because of your human?"

All four dragons nodded and, as one, looked down at Jerica. Zeira studied their newest friend and saw Sifula's eyes were bright with curiosity. Would the vapor dragon allow someone to ride her?

"She doesn't have to ride her," Skellig softly pointed out. "Physical contact is all it takes."

Zeira nodded. "That's right. I forgot. Sif, what do you say?"

"I'll try it," Sif announced. "What do I have to do?"

"We need to establish what your abilities are now," Skellig said, "so we have an idea what might happen to them once you and Jerica are in contact with one another."

"I saw her spit out some really dark smoke," Nuri said, from her place at the water's edge. "Maybe being able to produce toxic smoke?"

Sif nodded. "A very astute observation. It's the defense mechanism all vapor dragons employ. At no point have any of us ever demonstrated anything else. What? Why are you all looking at me like that?"

"Prepare to be amazed," Skellig grinned. "Jerica, would you do the honors?"

The lone human curtsied. "Of course. Sif, could you make yourself solid for me?"

Sif nodded. Moments later, Jerica gasped with shock as she stared at the mirror image of herself. The remaining four dragons crowded close as they all stared down at the form Sif had decided to transform into.

"That's impressive," Gocri decided.

The gray-colored form Sif had become looked up at Gocri and nodded. "Thanks."

"How long can you hold a form that small?" Skellig wanted to know.

"I can hold smaller forms longer than the larger ones," Sif answered. The dragon's human form was only moving her lips. The eyes weren't blinking, and the body remained stiff. "Adopting a human form is harder than it looks."

"Can you walk like me?" Jerica asked.

"Not without practice," Sif admitted. "If I try taking a step now, I'd end up face-first on the ground. I'm used to either flying or using all four of my legs to move around. Your ... *bipedal locomotion* is quite difficult to master."

Jerica frowned. "My bipedal locomotion? You mean you have trouble just walking around? On two legs? *That* is what you consider difficult? Sif, you just shrank yourself down to my size, and look just like me! Sure, I am not a gray color, but it's still very impressive! Now, can you take my hand or should I take yours?"

Sif's form tried to extend one of her human arms, but ended up taking a step forward instead. She looked down at her own leg, as though it was acting with a mind of its own. With the leg finally down, she tried again. This time, her left arm lifted, but it was shaking so badly that it took several attempts before Jerica could grab it.

"What are you going to do?" Zeira asked. "In human form, are you still going to produce smoke?"

"Every form I take has a mouth," Sif explained. "Open the mouth and voila, instant smoke. I'm assuming that's what'll happen here."

Sif's human form opened her mouth, but what came out was a far cry from toxic smoke. Instead, a blast of something like a light brown aerosol, erupted from Sif's mouth. Surprised, the mouth remained open, which maintained the blast of the unknown substance. After a few moments, Sif finally composed herself and was able to close her human form's mouth.

"What is it?" Skellig wanted to know. He reached past Jerica and scooped a handful of the powdery substance from the ground, where Sif's *breath* had collected. He let the substance fall through his fingers before looking appreciatively at Sif. "It's sand!"

"Sand?" Gocri asked, intrigued. He scooped up a handful of the granular material and watched it trickle through his claws. He looked over at Sif and held out his claw so that she could watch the sand trickle away, too. "May I assume you've never done that before?"

"That came out of me?" Sif exclaimed, shocked. "But … but … that's impossible! What kind of an ability is that?"

"A unique one," Skellig decided.

"It's just not possible," Sif reiterated.

"Not with our kairie," Zeira proudly proclaimed. "Isn't she amazing? No, wait! Stay there, Jerica. Let's see what else Sif can do!"

"Now, wait a minute," Sif began.

Zeira held her tail next to Jerica's hand. Once the human was in physical contact with both of them, Zeira then gave Sif an expectant look.

"Well? Try something."

"I must confess I'm somewhat concerned," Sif said.

At least, that's what she intended to say. However, once her mouth opened, a cloud of smoke appeared, jet black with tinges of red interspersed throughout. The small cloud immediately sank to the ground and expanded outward, in the opposite direction. Anything it came into contact with was burned to a crisp.

"It's a pyroclastic cloud!" Zeira exclaimed.

"It's a *what*?" Skellig asked.

"I haven't heard of it, either," Gocri admitted.

"I have," Nuri reported. "Very powerful, and very dangerous."

"Would you tell us what it is?" Skellig asked.

Nuri nodded. "I've encountered several, but thankfully, I was always able to get away. Skellig, those clouds are generated by volcanoes. They're a mix of hot ash and gas, and will generally destroy everything that gets in its way. If you see one of those clouds coming, then you'd best be headed in the opposite direction."

Skellig nodded. "Got it, thank you. All right, important safety note. If Jerica and Zeira happen to touch Sif, then bad things will happen."

"What happens if *you* touch her?" Nuri wanted to know.

Skellig shrugged. "I have no idea. The number of possibilities are endless. We could all check to see what mixes Jerica could make for us, but let's face it, it wouldn't last. Because sooner or later, Jerica will come into contact with another human, which will change what her power is."

Sif nodded. "Understood. I do think it's important we understand what everyone can do."

The addition of Skellig caused Sif's ability to change to a dark, thundercloud-looking smoke, complete with internal flashes of lightning. When Nuri took Skellig's place, and Zeira wasn't in contact, Sif's breath became a dense fog. With Zeira attached, the fog became the thickest steam cloud anyone had ever seen.

In this manner, the six of them spent the next several hours learning which combinations were the most useful, and which were to be avoided at all costs. Consequently, the favorite combination, winning with an unanimous vote, was when Gocri and Skellig combined their abilities with Sif's. If Sif was the one using the ability, she could generate white, puffy clouds of smoke, but anything they touched would instantly freeze solid. It looked safe, but anyone touching the ice, presumably to break it, would receive a powerful shock.

"An electrified, ice-generating cloud," Gocri had said. "I'm enjoying this more and more."

"What have we decided is the most dangerous?" Zeira wanted to know. "That way, we'll know who to avoid mixing together."

"You, me, and Sif," Skellig said. "We haven't come across anything as destructive as that pyroclastic cloud."

"It could be incredibly useful," Gocri said.

"But only under the right circumstances," Nuri added.

The glacier dragon nodded. "True. So, Sif, what are your intentions? Will you be joining us after all?"

Sif reverted to her much larger, vaporous self. She sat companionably next to Skellig and Gocri and fell silent. Zeira had to smile. Since when did a dragon, whose body was comprised of nothing but swirling mists, need to sit down?

"You all are intent on confronting whatever it is that's making us fight among ourselves?"

Zeira sighed. "Yes, that's our intent. Speaking for myself and the others, we have all been tasked with finding something that will help us defeat the Thunder King."

"Which is why you seek an oron stone," Sif said, nodding. "Very well, I accept."

"We're glad to have you join our ranks," Zeira said, nodding. If only her parents could see her now! What would they say, knowing she was leading four other dragons, and a human, in a desperate attempt to restore the balance of their world? "Are we all prepared to make this journey?"

"Did I miss something?" Skellig asked. "Where are we going?"

Zeira pointed at Sif. "She told us where the third fragment is. That's where we have to go."

A look of incredulity appeared on the Spark dragon's

face. He turned to stare at Sif. "We have to go to the third continent? Do you have any idea how far away that is?"

Sif nodded. "As a matter of fact, I do."

"How far is it?" Zeira asked, growing concerned. "Sif, do you think we can all make it?"

"The only other oron fragment I have ever encountered is literally on the other side of the planet," Sif confirmed. "Since we know there's only one oron stone left—that we know of—then that's where we have to go."

"And, er, how long do you think it'll take us to get there?" Gocri hesitantly asked. "I'm not sure a trek around the world is what I signed up for."

"That goes for me, too," Skellig reluctantly admitted.

Sif pointed up at the thin, wispy clouds far above their heads. "Using the right currents, we can be there, with minimal effort, in less than two weeks."

"Two weeks?" Skellig repeated, dismayed. "That's an awfully long time."

"It's an awfully long way to go," Sif reminded him.

"What about Nuri?" Zeira asked. "We can't leave her behind."

"Don't worry about me," Nuri said. "In fact, I'll probably beat all of you there."

Sif was shaking her head. "I know you're a fast swimmer, valthan, but against these currents? Even *you* wouldn't stand a chance."

"Who says I won't be using a current?" Nuri challenged. "You have your air currents; I have my water currents. You just have to know where to look. There are a series of maelstroms, which will propel me from one to the other. In this manner, I'll make it to the third continent. You just have to tell me where."

After Sif had redrawn her map, and added as much detail as she could, she pointed at a bay in the southern hemisphere.

"This is where I was when I saw a glowing rock, similar to the two you carry, Zeira."

"Do we know which one?" Skellig asked.

Zeira retrieved the two fragments she was holding. Both were glowing—one blue, and the other green. "Water and earth. If this third one is the missing fragment, then it should be red."

"Which it was," Sif confirmed.

"Why didn't you take it when you saw it?" Gocri asked.

"It wasn't mine to take, of course," Sif informed him.

"Er, whose was it?" Zeira asked. She hadn't considered the possibility of the fragment being found by someone else. "Or, perhaps, is it guarded by something?"

"By some*one*," Sif corrected. "Didn't I mention this?"

"No, you haven't," Zeira groaned.

"Out with it," Skellig sighed. "Who has it?"

Zeira watched as an apologetic look appeared on Sif's face.

"I wish I knew. No one who has ever lain eyes on this foe has ever returned."

Chapter 11 — Devastation

Are we there yet? For the love of … it's been four days. Four days of solid flying! We haven't once spotted any piece of land large enough for us to step foot on. In fact, the last thing I've eaten was a bird so small that it doesn't qualify as a bite."

"Yes, Skellig," Zeira groaned, "we know you're hungry. We all know how angry you get when you're due a meal."

"Whoa, wait a minute. Who says I'm grouchy?"

"I do," Gocri said.

"And I," Sif added. "Nuri, what say you?"

Skellig, you do seem somewhat on edge when you hunger.

Silently, their entire airborne group looked down at the water, far below them. There, visible against the dark blue colors of the sea as a small white line of churning bubbles, was Nuri, who was effortlessly keeping up with the four flyers. Zeira twisted her neck around to check on Jerica, who had selected her to ride for this particular leg of their journey.

Being careful to fly as steady as she could, and keeping an eye on their valthan companion down below, Zeira found her thoughts kept lingering on the bizarre set of circumstances which led to her present situation. Had there ever been a time when a Fire dragon could be found calmly flying next to a Spark dragon, a glacier dragon, and even an ultra-rare vapor dragon? And, she couldn't forget the amazing valthan, keeping pace with them down on the surface of the sea.

"It's not that amazing, is it?" Sif asked.

Zeira glanced left. Her newest friend was flying side-by-side with her. If only her mother could see her now!

"You really *do* think too loud," Sif quietly told her. "Your youth and your eagerness are contagious, young Zeira."

"Young?" Zeira complained. "Not you, too. I'm not that young, am I?"

"How many years can you count?" Sif wanted to know.

"Fifty-seven. What about you?"

"My age is a bit higher than that," Sif admitted.

"Can you tell me?" Zeira asked.

Sif shrugged. "Very well. I don't want this information to change anything, is that understood?"

"What could possibly change?" Zeira curiously asked. "My attitude toward you? Not likely. After all, I think everyone here is older than me."

"Except the human," Sif recalled.

"True. So, how old are you?"

"I am over four thousand nine hundred years old."

Zeira stared at her companion, mouth agape. "I had no idea we dragons could live so long."

"My species is blessed with long life," Sif cheerfully explained. "I don't think others are nearly that long."

"How old *can* you get?" Zeira wanted to know.

Sif shrugged. "Who can say? How would you be able to confirm that? It's not as if my species has an unlucky member who must keep meticulous records on how old he is, so that once he's gone, we'll know how many years he attained. We can only go by our memories."

Zeira looked at Sif and shook her head. "I don't follow."

Sif tapped the side of her head. "Everything we vapor

dragons have ever learned is up here. Many of us, when we know our time has come, will share our entire consciousness with our gathering, so that what we are, and what we've become, will not be lost forever. Is this not the way with your species?"

Zeira scratched the side of her head. "Well, not to that extent. We'll remember the best places to hunt, or where we were when we spotted a ... what? Not the same thing?"

"How do you store your memories?" Sif asked. "You're a dragon, obviously, so there must be a way your elders manage it. Do you have a repository for your favorites? Do you have a records keeper?"

"Umm ..."

"You don't know, do you? Well, no worries, Zeira. I'm sure someone in Blaze handles it. If not, well, what happens if you forget something?"

"I forget things all the time," Zeira admitted. "I'd be interested to know what ... what ..." Sif's eyes widened and she pointed a claw. When Zeira looked, she felt her blood run cold.

"We see it, too," Skellig said, flying close. "I just don't believe it."

This is horrible, Nuri's thought came. *It extends into the water.*

"We're landing," Zeira decided. "I think this bears investigation."

Ten minutes later, the six of them were standing, together, at the edge of a crater, roughly a mile across. Zeira gasped as she took in the devastation before her. She had witnessed craters before, where she had watched glowing stones fall from the sky and smash into the ground at a ferocious speed. This, however, was completely different. This was artificial. Someone—or some*thing*—had created this ... this hole.

Stretching out below was a barren ring of concentric circles, with each subsequent ring sunk nearly twenty feet deeper than the last. Everywhere they looked, they could only see the raw, jagged scar cut deep into the earth. There was no trace of vegetation or animals.

"What could have done this?" Zeira whispered.

"I'm thinking it's more of a *who* than a *what*," Skellig said.

Zeira shook her head. "There are no giants on Andela. In fact, *we* are the apex predator. I don't know of anyone who could've done this."

"I wonder what they were looking for?" Nuri said, as she pulled herself nearly halfway out of the water. "Either they couldn't find it, or … or …"

"They found it in greater quantities than they had ever hoped," Gocri finished.

"But what?" Zeira asked. "You're suggesting that there was something in the ground here? There was something that somebody wanted so badly that they went to such lengths to get it?"

"Look how precise it is," Skellig said, as he sat back on his haunches and studied the many rings. "Each layer is just as detailed as the one above and below it."

"It's a pit mine," someone whispered.

The five dragons turned to the lone human present.

"What did you say, Jerica?" Zeira wanted to know.

Their kai pointed at the huge hole in the earth. "That right there? It's a pit mine. Somebody was looking for something, and used mechanics to dig it up."

"You've seen this before?" Skellig asked.

Jerica sadly nodded. "Not to this scale, but yes, I've seen the mechanics that are responsible for digging. The pits that it dug are very similar to this, only on a smaller scale, obviously."

"I can't even begin to picture a mechanic that would be responsible for that," Gocri said, shaking his head. "Describe it, would you?"

Jerica held her arms up, creating a large O.

"The one I saw had this big round base, with a long arm," Jerica explained. "The arm swung around in a circle as it dug, which explains why this hole is circular, too. Now, there was a belt on the arm, with metal scoops. As the belt rotated, like a pulley, it scooped up bits of dirt to carry it back to the central part, where it was dumped into a basin."

Zeira looked back at the enormous pit mine and shook her head. "I'm having a hard time imagining what this … device must have looked like. The size alone would have to be … that is, it'd have to be … I give up. I can't do it."

Jerica made a swirling motion with her finger. "Well, small or large, the mechanics to dig a mine like this will sit on a circular base and spin around as it digs, which is why the mine is a perfect circle. As it digs lower and lower, it slowly rotates. I had no idea there were mechanics as large as this."

"What did they do with all the earth that was dug up?" Skellig asked.

"It's usually carted out and processed at a different facility," Jerica explained. "Workers will then start feeding all the removed dirt into a sifter. That's the only way they would be able to determine if they've found what they're looking for. Let's say they are looking for a specific type of mineral. The stones, which have bits of precious metal laced throughout them, are then melted down and extracted from the ore. The process is repeated until it is as pure as it can be made."

Zeira sighed. "I wish we knew what they were looking for."

"How would that help us?" Skellig wanted to know.

"It might tell us where they would be headed next," Sif suggested.

"We don't even know what we're supposed to be looking for," Zeira complained. "And, if so, put a stop to it. Hey, I have a question. Do you think they could be looking for another fragment?"

About to ask his own question, Zeira watched Skellig snap his jaws closed. The Spark dragon considered for a few moments before shrugging. "You would be the best one to answer that. After all, you're carrying two of the fragments."

Zeira retrieved one of the fragments and stared deep into the heart of the glowing piece of rock. She was in the process of lifting her loose chest scale up to replace the oron fragment when she hesitated. Unless she was very much mistaken, she just felt the tiniest of pulls. Was there something nearby? She eyed the massive scar the pit mine presented and then suddenly understood what she was looking at: someone's attempt to retrieve one of the oron fragments. Worried, Zeira turned to look up at Sif, who at present, was nearly three times the size she was.

"Sif?

"Yes?"

"Didn't you say we were headed to the third continent? That the last fragment we're searching for is somewhere on the other side of the planet?"

The vapor dragon nodded. "I did, indeed. Why? Oh! Are you suggesting this might have been a resting place for an oron fragment?"

"Is it possible?" Gocri wanted to know. "That fragment is tiny when compared to *that*."

"Well, what if someone knew it was here, but didn't know exactly where?" Skellig pondered. "Isn't it just like a human? To be given a piece of an oron stone, uncertain where it was located, and to keep digging until it is found? Oh, my apologies, Jerica. I seem to keep placing my tail in my mouth, which is unlike me. Please know no offense was meant."

"It's all right," Jerica assured her much larger companion. She pointed at Zeira. "So, is it true? Are those fragments trying to tell you something?"

Holding the two glowing shards in her open claw, she passed one to Skellig and waited to see what he thought. The Spark dragon held his claw aloft, then dropped it low, and then spun to face a few different directions. Closing his eyes, holding his claw out in front of him, Skellig rotated for a few moments and then stopped. "I feel a faint pull from this way." His eyes opened. He was facing away from the pit mine. "Well, that answers that."

Zeira hurried to his side. "I want to try that. Let's see. Eyes closed, claw out, and let's see where I ... hmm, I end up facing the other way, too."

"Does anyone know what lies in that direction?" Jerica asked.

"That would be the third continent," Sif reported, wearing a smug expression on her face. "The third fragment awaits us there."

Zeira slid the first fragment back under her scale and took the second from Skellig. Just as she was preparing to slide the second shard into place next to the first, she hesitated.

"Still feel something, don't you?" Skellig quietly asked.

Zeira nodded. "I do. Do you have any idea what it is?"

Skellig pointed a claw at the mine. "I can only assume it has something to do with *that*. I ..."

"What is it?" Zeira asked, after noticing Skellig had trailed off.

"Who among us has the best nose?" Skellig suddenly asked.

The dragons curiously eyed each other before Gocri finally shrugged. "I guess that'd be me. Why?"

Skellig motioned the glacier dragon over. "Come. Sit here. Face south and tell me what you smell."

Gocri complied. As soon as he sniffed the air, his eyes flew open. "Kriew. The scent grows stronger, so they are inbound. Skellig, Zeira, and Nuri—protect Jerica."

"And me?" Sif asked.

Gocri turned to the vapor dragon and grinned. "I have a special task for you."

Sif nodded. "I'm listening."

Ten minutes later, the sky darkened as thousands of jet-black birds massed together. The writhing, pulsating flock of birds twisted this way and that as it seemingly decided what to do. Then, without warning, the cloud of birds streaked downward. A thunderous cacophony of screeches and squawks ripped through the air as the hurtling forms rushed toward them.

"I do believe lunch has been served," Gocri dryly announced. He positioned himself directly below the plummeting horde, folded his wings to make himself look as small as possible, and opened his jaws as wide as he could get them.

"What is it?" Nuri's voice suddenly asked, from within her mind.

"Who are you talking to?" Zeira inquired, speaking aloud.

"You. You are feeling unease. It leads me to believe you think something is wrong. With the swirling flock of birds? I would have to agree."

"You do?" Zeira sputtered. "Why? Have you dealt with many birds out on the water?"

"I'm currently out, *on* the water," Nuri reminded her. "And yes, occasionally. Like now, for instance. A number of them have broken off and appeared to be headed my way."

"There's definitely something wrong," Zeira said, nodding. "Nuri, can you avoid them?"

"Easily. I'll duck below the surface."

"Good. Skellig, Gocri, do me a favor. Don't hurt these birds."

Gocri's massive jaws slowly closed. "Whatever for? You're asking me to give up an easy meal."

"What do you think their chances are?" Zeira challenged. "Look at the five of us. What bird would be able to stand up to us?"

"Go on," Gocri urged.

"Maybe they're in a trance?" Jerica suggested.

Zeira looked up, at the dropping mass of flapping birds. "Trance? Hmm. Okay, everyone. New plan. Try to capture one. I think we need to see for ourselves what might be wrong with these creatures."

Zeira felt Gocri's disappointment. "Alive? How disappointing. Very well. I will procure you a live specimen."

It was easier said than done. The black birds became streaks of color moving so fast that they were almost invisible to the eye. In fact, as soon as Zeira had located one of the birds off by itself, she'd blink, and the bird would be gone. The only way she could grab one of these birds was if she did just that, *grab* it.

Zeira eyed her companions. They were having no more luck at trying to snare a live specimen. Waiting and watching, Zeira snapped her left wing out the instant she saw a few streaks headed her way.

Three objects slammed into her wing, and Zeira immediately rounded on them. She scooped up the birds and studied them closely. Each bird was just dazed, thankfully, although they seemed oblivious to the danger of being eaten.

"What's wrong with them?" Skellig wanted to know. "I saw them hit your wing. That had to smart, by the way. Perhaps the blow knocked them senseless?"

"I'd say they didn't even notice they were captured."

"What are you going to do with them?" Gocri asked, trying to sound nonchalant.

"No, you're not going to eat them," Zeira exclaimed, as she yanked her claw away from the Ice dragon. "These three won't do. We need to find one that hasn't been injured."

Zeira released the birds and watched them hesitantly take to the air and disappear into the flock still flying in circles above their heads.

"I have one!" Nuri shouted. "I'm holding it now."

"Come to shore, would you?" Zeira requested.

"I'm already here. Ah, there you are. Look. Does the behavior of this one match what the others were doing?"

Zeira watched the black bird squawk with irritation as it tried to fly. It, too, was completely ignoring the fact it was being held by a dragon.

"Do you suppose they are under some type of spell?"

Jerica arrived by Zeira's foot and signaled for her to bring the bird down to her level. "I kept a bird as a pet once. I know a little something about them. Maybe I can help?"

Nuri passed the tiny bird to Zeira, who then lowered it down to the ground. Jerica gently took the bird off of Zeira's claw and dropped into a sitting position near Zeira's front left leg. She began to carefully examine the bird, but found no signs of broken bones or discomfort. Nor did the bird track her movements.

"There's definitely something wrong with this bird," Jerica reported. "It's as if the poor thing is dizzy; confused. Could something have messed with its sense of direction?"

Zeira turned to look at the pit mine. "Something like that?"

"I'll wager some type of spell has been cast on them," Gocri said. "And, for the record, if it's bothering you in any way, I'll be more than happy to take it off your hands."

"You're not eating it, Gocri," Zeira reiterated. "They're helpless animals. In fact, we should see if we can find a way to snap them out of it."

"How?" Jerica wanted to know.

Zeira considered the question. How, indeed? She was a Fire dragon. The most she could do would be to blast some flames at it. If she was going to do that, then she may as well let Gocri eat the thing. It'd be way more humane. Then there was Skellig.

"What about me?" the Spark dragon inquired.

"Don't mind me," Zeira told her friend. "I'm thinking. Don't respond to my thoughts, either. I'm trying to determine our next course of action."

While she pondered, the remaining four dragons — and one human — decided to sink down to the ground and rest. Jerica, leaning up against one of Skellig's front forelegs, started to whistle. A few moments later, Nuri was softly humming notes, which flawlessly blended together, as though each had been practicing for months. Enjoying the impromptu concert, Gocri grunted his approval. Seeing how he had timed it to fall on the down beat, he waited a few moments before grunting again. In this manner, a light, airy ditty was heard by all as they waited for Zeira to come to a decision.

"I think I have it. Oh, what's this? I didn't realize you were all so musically inclined."

"I don't think any of us did, either" Jerica said, rising to her feet. "Nuri, you have a lovely voice."

"What have you deduced?" Gocri wanted to know.

Zeira pointed at the glacier dragon. "I think you may be the key here. I know you can freeze things solid with your breath, but can you partially freeze an object? In this case, can you apply enough of your breath to shock the bird? Without freezing it, that is."

Gocri shrugged. He looked at the bird, still looking this way and that, and let out the tiniest huff. Jerica ended up dropping the bird and whipping her hands out of the way.

"I'm sorry. I should have asked if you were ready to try." Gocri lowered his head to inspect the humans' hands. "Are you injured?"

Jerica nodded. "It's all right. I'm fine. Hey, look at the bird!"

The dragons turned to look at the small creature, now cowering on the ground. The bird was nervously eyeing them, as though it finally realized it was facing massive predators. It chirped worriedly.

"You're free to go," Jerica told the bird. "You'd better fly away now."

The bird didn't waste any time. It spread its wings, leapt into the air, and furiously flapped away. Jerica pointed up at the rest of the swirling cloud.

"What can you do for them? Will you be able to help them?"

Gocri nodded, and began taking huge gulps of air.

"Remember," Jerica cautioned, "we're not going to hurt them. We only want them to snap out of their trance."

"By the time my breath reaches all the way up there, then the strength would have dissipated."

"So, they won't freeze solid," Jerica said, nodding. "I like it."

"So do I," Zeira added. "Gocri, go ahead."

They waited in nervous silence as Gocri created a large cloud of ice particles and the first wave of birds flew through it. Zeira heard outraged squawks and trills, and saw that the first to encounter the cloud had stiffened with surprise and dropped. As she extended her wings to catch them, she discovered it wasn't needed. Almost immediately, the birds recovered and were madly flapping away. The six of them eyed each other before bursting out with laughter and applause.

"Great job, everyone," Zeira praised. "I think we saved them all."

"You owe me lunch," Gocri complained. When Zeira turned to the enormous Ice dragon, she was relieved to find a smile on his face. "But I do concede that there was something wrong with them and it's best not to eat them until you know what's wrong."

"I, for one, would like to know what happened to them," Nuri said.

"Have you noticed anything unusual?" Skellig asked, as he turned his attention on their valthan companion.

Nuri nodded. "As a matter of fact, several fish have approached me and appeared unaffected by my presence. In the water, I am the predator to avoid. Besides, these fish usually belong in schools."

A disturbance began near Sif's left hind leg. A mound of earth pushed upwards. The vapor dragon automatically moved a few steps away, lowering her head to inspect the swelling of the earth. A few moments later, the dome broke and a large, fuzzy creature appeared. Shaking off the dirt clumped to its fur revealed a rodent about the same size and mass of a human. It let out a series of trills before climbing out of the hole and shuffling off. Five others of various sizes soon followed the first out of the hole and headed after it.

"Grompers," Zeira stated. "I wonder what they're doing here?"

"Not fleeing from us," Skellig observed. He leaned forward to pluck one of the smaller ones from the ground. The small creature wandered aimlessly around his open palm, almost stepping into open air. He set it back on the ground and watched as it scampered off.

"First, those birds. Then, the fish. And now, grompers."

"I want to know what is going on," Zeira announced. "Whatever it is, it's affecting more than just one species. In their right mind, there's no way they'd come this close to us."

"Agreed," Skellig said. He turned to look back at the giant blemish on the countryside and pointed. "I'm thinking *that* has something to do with it."

"How?" Nuri wanted to know.

Zeira shrugged. "I wish I knew. I think Skellig is right. Somehow, that huge hole has affected the creatures living in this area."

"Or passing over," Gocri added.

Zeira nodded. "True. Maybe there was something in the ground, as was suggested earlier, and it was causing these problems?"

"Or," Sif said, adopting a thoughtful stance, "perhaps it's the *absence* of this material causing this … this …" The vapor dragon trailed off and held up her claws in a helpless manner.

"Imbalance," Zeira whispered. "This is just another example of the imbalance that's been plaguing us in Blaze! It must be what's causing us to war with our Terran brethren!"

"They're feeling the effects all the way over here?" Jerica asked.

"It would indicate there are more of these holes than just this one," Gocri decided. "I think that's what we have to do.

Find whatever is responsible for creating this destruction and bring it to an end."

"Agreed," Zeira said. "This is what my king would want."

"And mine," Skellig said.

"My queen as well," Gocri added.

Nuri nodded. "I don't know how I can help, but I promise you now, if I can do it, I will."

Everyone turned to Sif. Her vaporous body shrank to a third of its original size and solidified into a very reasonable facsimile of Gocri. She faced Zeira and nodded.

"I will do what I can to rectify this atrocity."

Zeira bowed her head in thanks. "I appreciate that, Sif. In fact, I appreciate you all pledging your support. And Sif, no one talks like that anymore."

Sif shrugged. "Maybe they should start again?"

"Perhaps." Zeira looked down at their human kai and lowered herself to the ground. "Jerica, thanks to you, we all have abilities we could never have dreamed of. You're just as much a part of this group as anyone else. What do you say?"

Jerica nodded. "Of course I'm in. What affects you dragons also affects us. We want to see it end just as much as you. I ... what is that? Can anyone hear that sound, besides me?"

All five dragons lifted their heads high. Sif immediately returned to her much larger smoky form. With five dragon heads all pointed in the same direction, everyone fell silent.

"Are you asking about the bell?" Nuri asked, as she turned to look southwest.

Jerica nodded. "Yes. It reminds me of my old school master, who would ring a bell to signal the beginning of lessons."

"I hear it," Gocri said. "I can tell it's coming this way."

"Maybe it's a *who*," Jerica suggested.

"If it is," Skellig said, as he turned his body south, "there's a strong chance that it's responsible for this mess. I say we face it, head on."

Gocri appeared at his side. "I agree. We'll take it, together."

"We all will," Sif added. For the first time, the vapor dragon's form actually *increased* to twice her normal size.

This time, she was heavily muscled, displaying two sets of wings — a primary and smaller secondary — and two sets of spiraled horns. Sif, noticing the abrupt silence, turned to look at her friends. "What is it?"

"What form is that?" Zeira asked. "You're huge!"

"This is the form of the horde dragon I encountered many years ago."

"Horde?" Nuri repeated, puzzled. "I don't think I've heard of that region."

"Nor have I," Zeira admitted.

"Not surprising," Sif said, as she turned to face the south. "Gilt is one of the smallest regions, and the horde dragons are the rarest of them all."

Zeira looked at Skellig. "Gilt? Didn't you say …?"

"Treasure dragons!" Skellig eagerly interrupted. "You're saying that's the form of a treasure dragon?"

Sif nodded. "Aye. Silver. Behold, whatever is making the noise is nearing."

"How long can you hold a form that size?" Gocri quietly asked.

"About ten minutes," Sif answered. She spread both sets of wings and adopted a fearsome stance. "I'll revert back when we either dispatch, or scare off, whatever is coming our way."

As the clanging of the bell grew steadily louder, all five dragons braced themselves for the worst. However, when the source of the bell finally rounded the ridge of boulders, all five of them relaxed, with Sif immediately shrinking back to her normal size.

"Humans!" Jerica exclaimed. "It looks like a whole family of them! How exciting!"

"They don't look happy," Zeira quietly observed. "May I suggest we hide?"

"Haven't they seen us by now?" Jerica asked, confused.

"Look at them," Skellig instructed. "They're humans. Tell me, would you keep heading this way had you noticed five dragons staring directly at you?"

"No, probably not," Jerica admitted. "Since when are you worried about what a human family thinks about you?"

"I don't," Skellig clarified. "but *you* do, Jerica. I make the suggestion in deference to you. They look distraught. Perhaps, you may be able to help them?"

"I didn't think of that. Perhaps I could."

"Therefore, it'd be best if we were not here to ... *distract* the meeting. I say we should all hide."

"Where are you going to hide?" Jerica asked, confused. "There's nowhere for something your size to ..." She trailed off as she noticed she was now standing by herself. "Huh. You learn something new each day. Hello, there!"

The family came to a stop a dozen feet away. There were two adults, and five children, ranging in age from three to fifteen years. Every single one of them, Jerica noted, had packs and bags strapped to their backs. The father figure stared at her for a few moments before dropping the small, metal gong he had been holding.

"What are you doing out here on your own, you foolish girl? Do you want to get caught? You must flee!"

Chapter 12 — Illumination

"What are you talking about?" Jerica shakily asked. The fear emanating from this family was palpable. The father had a wild look in his eye, while the mother refused to lift her gaze from the ground. "If they catch you, then they will make you work. Trust me when I say that you'd be better off feeding yourself to a dragon."

I beg your pardon, Zeira's voice mentally chided. *I have never eaten a human.*

Speak for yourself, Skellig mentally added.

I don't want to hear about this, Jerica proclaimed, as she fought to suppress a shudder. Hoping to put the family at ease, she offered the young father her friendliest smile.

"Who are you? Are you from these parts?"

The strange man eyed her a few moments more before finally relaxing his stance. Somewhat.

"We are the Draig family. I am Brenin. This is my wife, Akainu. As for what we're doing here, well, we are leaving. I will not put any of my remaining five children in harm's way again."

"Oh, I'm sorry. You lost one of your children?"

Brenin stooped to pick up the small, metal gong, holding it up , as though that one act alone would offer all the explanation necessary, and struck the surface with a wooden mallet.

He lost one of his offspring and he's making that racket? Skellig said, groaning. *It's giving me such a headache.*

I can't very well tell him to stop, can I? They're in mourning, Skellig. He should be allowed to honor his child in whatever way he chooses.

So be it.

"So, ah, Mr. Draig, you say you're leaving? Where are you coming from? Is there a village nearby?"

Brenin stopping hammering his gong long enough to point southwest. "Half a day's journey that way will lead you to Ponatoa."

"Ponatoa," Jerica repeated. "It sounds nice."

"It isn't. Stay away from there."

"But ... didn't you say that's where your family is from?"

"I did, aye, and that doesn't mean it's a nice place."

Why doesn't he like it? Skellig mentally asked.

"Why doesn't he like it?" Jerica relayed. "Um, I mean, why don't *you* like it?"

"Which rock did you crawl out from?" Brenin demanded. "Everyone knows to stay away from Ponatoa. They're nothing but slavers, all of 'em."

"They are no such thing," Akainu whispered.

Brenin angrily thrust the small gong in his wife's face. "I don't need to remind you about Miks. I won't ever forget what that blasted town did to our son, nor should *you.*"

"It was an accident," Akainu insisted.

"It most certainly was not!" Brenin shouted. "Risked his neck for that imbecile, he did, and for what? Have they acknowledged his death? Have they admitted fault? Of course not. You know, just as well as I, that they do not care. No one does. They only care about coal."

"Coal?" Jerica repeated. "No one uses coal any more.

There are more effective ways to …"

"Seriously, where are you from?" Brenin asked, as he turned his attention back on Jerica. "You know damn well I'm not talkin' about coal. Go on, admit it."

"I admit I haven't a clue what you're talking about," Jerica insisted, as she nervously took a step away from the angry man.

There's no need to show fear, Zeira assured her. *We five are near, and we have, as you humans would say, your spine.*

Jerica's mouth curved upwards in a smile.

Back. I think you mean, you have my back.

Isn't that what I said? Zeira asked, confused.

Close enough. Thanks.

"What are you smilin' for?" Brenin angrily demanded. "The loss of my firstborn is a laughing matter to you?"

"On the contrary," Jerica began, "I can't tell you how sorry I am upon hearing about your loss. I wish there was something I could do about it."

There is something you can do about it, Skellig said. *Whether or not you'd want to reveal yourself, and your status as a kairie, is the issue.*

What could I do to help these people out? Jerica wondered.

Think about it, Skellig urged. *You have five dragon companions. It'd only take one of us to confront the head.*

The head of what?

The biped in charge, Gocri translated. *Each village of tribesmen will have one person in command. Cut off the head, and the rest of the body will fail.*

Well, that's … morbid. Thanks for that.

Your fellow human is saying something else, Nuri pointed out.

"Just leave it be," Brenin was saying. "Leave them be, and they should leave you be. Don't accept anything from them, and maybe you just might find yourself staying *out* of trouble."

"I never look for trouble," Jerica said, frowning. "I can guarantee you I won't be a problem for anyone."

"You will be," Akainu announced, as she finally looked up from the ground. "You're a girl. They like fresh, young girls like yourself."

I don't understand, Zeira said. *They like girls? For what, supper?*

Are they cannibals?

Umm, not exactly, Jerica answered. *I think she's warning me off, because the males there aren't to be trusted. Whatever the reason, I think I'm going to avoid Ponatoa.*

Good, Zeira decided.

"You're suggesting that, even if I go to Ponatoa and mind my own business, I'll still be in trouble?"

"That's what happened to Miks," Akainu sighed, dejected. "I asked him to find the baker and to purchase a fresh loaf of bread. Next thing I know, my son is being arrested. They claim he tried to steal the bread, but I know he didn't. He was sentenced to work for the Guild, and that is the last we ever saw of him."

"What is the Guild?" Jerica whispered, certain she was going to hate the answer.

"It's a new faction of men, led—and founded—by the Marquis of Chete," Brenin said, unable to keep the bitterness from his voice.

Is this marquis person another name for the Thunder King? Skellig wanted to know.

"The Marquis of Chete," Jerica began, "is that another name for Thunder King?"

"Don't even say his name!" Brenin hissed. He stared suspiciously at the nearby shrubs and trees, as though there could be spies hiding on the other side. "He may live on the other side of the world, but he has eyes and ears *everywhere!* Don't say anything bad about him and, for that matter, don't even *think* about going against him."

"He's a mage?" Jerica asked, looking nervously around the area. "I didn't know that."

"Does it matter?" Akainu asked, growing more animated. "He rules this world with an iron fist."

No, he doesn't, Skellig argued.

He doesn't rule us, Gocri agreed.

I've never heard of him, Nuri admitted.

"What about the dragons?" Jerica quietly asked. "Couldn't they, you know, band together and take him down?"

"Why would those scaly beasts care about what happens to us?" Brenin wanted to know.

"He must be afraid of the dragons, so it would stand to reason …"

"He is *not*," Brenin insisted. "I've heard even dragons will do his bidding."

Not bloody likely, Gocri growled.

Agreed, Sif added.

Ask this fool if he knows anything about the hole, Skellig prompted.

A very good point, Zeira agreed. *See if he knows anything about the giant mine, Jerica.*

"Listen, do you know anything about what they were searching for with that mine? And, if so, did they find it?"

Ooo, good question, Zeira praised.

Thanks!

Brenin turned and spat on the ground. "Just scraps."

"Scraps?" Jerica repeated, confused. "Scraps of what?"

"Some new-fangled metal. No one knows what it's called, so we just call it *scrap*."

"I have never heard of it."

See if he'll expand on this metal, Sif suggested. *Perhaps it's something we haven't encountered?*

Jerica held up her hands in a helpless manner. Brenin caught sight and nodded.

"Scrap is some new precious metal Thunder King wants."

"He craves it," Akainu added.

Craves? Zeira said. *His desire is to consume it? I didn't know humans ingested metal.*

"We don't," Jerica confirmed.

"You don't *what*?" Brenin wanted to know.

"Oh, uh, crave … scrap?"

There was a pause as Brenin studied her.

We might need to intervene, Zeira said.

No harm must befall her, Gocri insisted.

And none will, Sif promised.

Thanks, everyone, Jerica sent, to her dragon friends.

"Good," Brenin snapped, after a few more moments of silence had passed. "Nothing good can come from that blasted metal."

"What can you tell us about it?" Jerica wanted to know.

"I've never heard of it."

"The only thing I can tell you is that it's a gray-colored metal," Brenin answered. "If you melt enough down, and burn off the impurities, the metal will darken. The darker it is, the stronger it is …"

Jerica nodded. "Oh, all right. A dark blade is a strong blade. I guess that makes sense."

"… in magic."

Jerica blinked and looked up. "What was that?"

What was that? five dragons echoed.

"This metal—scrap? It's infused with magic. Weapons made from scrap are said to be blessed by the Guild of Mages himself."

Has he seen one of these … weapons … in use?

"How do you know they're making weapons from this stuff?" Jerica asked.

"The thun… er, *he*," Brenin hastily corrected, "wields a dark sword. Some say the blade is blacker than a moonless night. It *must* be made from scrap."

"A black sword," Jerica thoughtfully repeated.

Brenin nodded. "A black sword. People say that there's nothing it can't cut through."

"I've heard it can cut through the very air itself," Akainu said.

"Nonsense," Brenin argued.

"Then why, when the sword was thrust into sky, did the blade disappear from sight? Would that not suggest the blade cut through the air?"

"You saw no such thing," Brenin argued. "We haven't been to Chete in over two years. You're misremembering."

"I told you I didn't see it, didn't I?" Akainu exclaimed, growing agitated. "You never listen to me, Brenin. I said I heard of the sword being used in the way I described."

"And the blade disappeared? I don't believe it."

Nor do I, Skellig admitted.

What if she's right? Zeira asked. *What would it mean?*

It would mean that this weapon, this dark sword, Sif began, *is able to cut through the very fabric of our reality.*

Huh? Jerica thought.

I have no idea what that means, either, Zeira said.

It is a discussion best left for another time, Sif pointed out. *For now, we need to focus on this scrap metal. If this substance has magical properties, then we can safely assume that's what they were digging for, at that huge pit mine. I wonder how much of it they found.*

"Brenin, can I ask you something?"

The harassed father nodded.

"Did they find what they were looking for? That is, after all, the biggest hole in the ground I have ever seen."

For the first time, Brenin smiled. "All that man-power, all those mechanics … what a waste."

"They didn't find anything?" Jerica asked, amazed.

Brenin shook his head. "That's not what I said. I said it was a wasted effort. The only bit of scrap they found was a lump of ore no larger than … well, your head, I suppose."

"If it's as precious as you say it is, that'd be a lot, wouldn't it?"

"No. You don't know anything about mining, do you?"

Jerica shrugged helplessly. "Guilty. I come from a fishing village."

"When you mine metal, it appears naturally as ore. It takes many pounds of ore to produce a single pound of the metal. The same goes for scrap. That pitifully small mound of ore they found last week? I'll wager it'll produce no more than half an ounce of the quality of scrap they're looking for."

"Are there other mines?" Jerica asked.

Ooo, that's a great question! Skellig praised.

Brenin held up a hand, with three fingers extended. "Three. There have been three other mines that I know about. Most have produced a few pounds of scrap, but the last two were just like this one: less than an ounce each."

"You've seen the mechanics used to dig the hole?"

"I, along with every other able-bodied person, was hired to assemble and maintain the mechanics."

"At least you were paid," Jerica said. Her smile quickly melted into a frown once she saw Brenin's scowl. "You were, weren't you?"

"I was, aye, only it was naught but a pittance. A few coins for days upon days of back-breaking work."

"Couldn't you have told them no?"

Akainu scoffed angrily. "You cannot. You're beaten if you refuse …"

"… or incarcerated for some phony crime," Brenin sighed.

Akainu agreed, with a heavy sigh. "And once you agree, you're doomed if you fall behind at your station, or show up late, or any of a long list of offenses, then you're punished and your earnings are taken from you."

"You'd think your king would be more concerned about his people," Jerica said, amazed.

Brenin had uncorked a water bottle and was taking a drink when he choked. "The king? He doesn't care about us. No one does. I just wish … I wish …"

"What?" Jerica quietly asked.

"I just wish that he would …"

"No," Akainu interrupted. "I know what you're going to say, Brenin. Leave it unspoken. There's no need to risk his ire."

"You're talking about …"

"Don't say his name!" husband and wife cried.

"All right, I won't. Let's call him … *apple*."

"Apple?" Brenin repeated, confused. He looked at his wife, who returned his confused stare.

"Yes, apple. What I want to know is, if apple is such a *bad* apple, and let's be honest, no one likes bad apples, can't we just … I don't know, *squash* the bad apple?"

Brenin was silent as he considered. "Fine. Using your analogy, I can tell you this bad apple would be on a tree at the top of an unsurmountable mountaintop, with a thousand guards …"

Not entirely impossible, Zeira said.

"… who just so happen to be trolls …"

"I've heard of them, but have never seen one," Jerica admitted.

"… at a palace no one can find," Brenin finished. "I think that about sums it up."

"Count your blessings that you've never seen one," Akainu said, unable to hide the bitterness in her voice. "They haunt my dreams."

"I'm sure if I ever saw one, they'd haunt mine, too."

"So," Brenin continued, "this apple you want to squash? Locate the castle you cannot find. Approach the mountain guarded by trolls. If you're not ripped limb from limb, then you have to climb that which cannot be climbed. Only there will you find the orchard full of apple trees, only now you must choose which one is the real apple."

The paranoid fool has decoys in place?

"He, uh, er, the apple hides among other, er, apples?" Jerica asked.

Brenin nodded. "Wouldn't you? When you have that much power, and are hated by that many people, then personal security *must* become your first priority."

We have a long way to go, Zeira thought, letting out a quiet groan.

Don't be intimidated, Skellig warned. *This was just an analogy this human gave in order to convey how difficult it would be for someone to simply* squash *this apple. Strange analogy, but one that I can understand.*

As do I, Zeira added. *That's why we need something to counter the … wait. Jerica?*

Yes?

Would you ask your bipedal companion whether or not he knows anything about the Rastan Spear?

I will.

"Brenin? Can I ask you a question?"

The head of the family had just hoisted his youngest child onto his shoulders when he turned to give her an irritable look.

"Yes?"

"Have you ever heard of something called the Rastan Spear?"

"Of course I have. Everyone has. What about it?"

"Um, could you tell me about it? I don't know anything about it and I, am, er, eager to learn more."

"You need a scholar, not someone such as I."

"Where can I find one?" Jerica asked.

"Go find Zebulon," Akainu told her. She took the hands

of the other children and led them away.

"Zebulon?" Jerica repeated, as she looked at Brenin for assistance.

"Ponatoa's seer. He's the closest thing you'll find to a scholar."

"Ponatoa? Didn't you say I shouldn't go anywhere near there?"

"I did, aye," Brenin said, nodding. "Why do you want to know about the spear? It's no longer lost."

We can take a guess as to who found it, Zeira said.

"I'm just curious. I've heard so much about it. I want to know how it works."

"I wouldn't be telling too many people you're searching for information about that spear. That's the type of thing that will see you clapped in irons."

"Understood. Thank you, Brenin, for your assistance."

"Good journeys to you," Brenin returned, before hurrying after his wife.

"He wants me to go to Ponatoa!" Jerica exclaimed to the open air, and when she turned to look behind her, four of her five dragon companions were already there. "How did you do that? Where were you hiding?"

"I say we avoid the human settlement," Skellig announced. "We can find the information we seek elsewhere."

I'd like to know what a 'seer' is, Nuri said.

"Where are you, Nuri?" Jerica asked.

Two dozen feet below you. I smelled water nearby, and was able to dig my way to concealment.

"How do you feel about visiting this human settlement?" Zeira asked.

"Not well," Jerica answered. "You heard what Brenin said, right? I could be detained on the spot, without doing anything. What would my father say?"

"I am not your father," Gocri rumbled, "but if I was, then I would say that you are not going there by yourself."

Zeira turned to the glacier dragon. "Agreed, but if we want to learn more about this unique weapon, a meeting with the tribesman known as the seer becomes necessary."

Gocri nodded. "I agree. One of us should accompany

you." He turned to stare at Sif.

Catching on to what Gocri had in mind, Zeira gaped at the vapor dragon.

"Is this something you can do?"

"I … I think so."

Just then, the ground swelled upward at their feet and Nuri's head broke through. She turned to look at Sif, as well. "You keep her safe, is that understood?"

Sif nodded. "No harm will befall her, you have my word."

* * *

"This is the weirdest thing I have ever done, moving about on two appendages."

"Try swinging your arms as you walk. It'll help you keep your balance as you move."

"That's actually working. Thank you."

"You've shrunk yourself down to a human, and a male human at that. Isn't that Brenin? You made yourself look like the one person we just met?"

"Your tone suggests I should have chosen differently."

"Brenin and his family just left Ponatoa. What happens if we encounter someone who knows him? If you want to pass yourself off as human, you need to look and sound like one."

"But I don't look like one."

"Granted, you're currently all gray, but we can get you clothes and just say you crossed a mage and he turned you gray."

"And your people will believe that?"

"We're humans. We'll believe anything we're told. Now, give it a try. Try talking like a human."

"Fine. Are you happy now?"

"I am, Sif, I really am. However …"

"What?" Sif prompted, after Jerica had trailed off.

"You're not moving your mouth."

"So?"

"You're going to freak people out if you don't move your mouth in time with your words."

Amused, Jerica watched Sif's human form slowly open

her mouth, and then close it. After a few more tries, Jerica burst out laughing.

"What is it?" Sif asked. "Am I doing something wrong?"

"You look like a fish out of water, gasping for breath."

"I most certainly do not."

"Look at my mouth, Sif. Do you see that I don't quite open it all the way when I'm talking? In order to make certain sounds, I have to move my mouth, tongue, and lips in the right manner. Do you understand?"

"I understand that I'm never going to get this."

It doesn't have to be perfect, Sif, Skellig told her. *You're not there to blend in, but to protect Jerica, that's all.*

"Good," Sif growled, "because that's all I think I'm going to be able to do."

Is it hard to hold that form? Nuri asked.

"No. Any form that's this much smaller than my own is quite easy to hold in place. However, moving in that form, well, it's a different story. It's complicated."

Jerica patted her arm. "You're doing an admirable job of passing as a human. Plus, I know you're doing this for me, so you have my thanks, Sif."

Taken aback, Sif blinked her form's eyes a few times. "You're welcome. Now, how far until we reach the settlement?"

As soon as you crest that ridge, you're there, Skellig reported.

Jerica and Sif looked upward.

"I don't see Skellig anywhere," Jerica admitted.

Sif studied the sky, her humanoid face becoming blurry.

"What just happened? Your human face became blurred."

The blurriness faded and Brenin's face returned. "Oh, sorry. I was looking at the sky. If I happened to be flying overhead, and didn't want to be spotted, I would fly as high as I could go. I had to blink a few times to get my eyes to focus that high, but I spotted them."

"You must have been trying to focus your dragon eyes on a point that falls outside of a human's typical range."

"And that caused my face to blur? Very well. Thank you for that information, I now know what *not* to do."

Thirty minutes later, with Sif walking reasonably well, the two of them wandered into the town of Ponatoa. Almost immediately, Jerica could sense that the vast majority of the people made their living on the water. Row after row of piers sat, nearly empty, as fishermen cast their nets on their boats out on the sea. Large cargo ships were loaded, and even bigger ships were unloaded. Sacks of flour, open crates laden with fresh produce, and stores of fish, packed in salt, were placed into the hands of a steady stream of dock workers, which were then delivered to a variety of locations.

"What's that smell?" Jerica whispered, as she covered her nose with her hand.

Sif's nose twitched, presumably as the transformed dragon sampled the air.

"Brine. Seawater."

"I know what brine and seawater smells like," Jerica scoffed. "Cael is located on a peninsula, so I'm very used to smelling it. In this case, I'm talking about that other one. It smells like ..."

"... excrement," Sif finished.

Jerica's face brightened. "That's it! Only, why are we smelling that? Do these people *not* use latrines? Is there no indoor plumbing?"

"I don't know what that means," Sif confessed.

"It's, uh, well, it's for ... you know what? It's not important. Perhaps someone's sewer line is stopped up? I don't think I've ever been to a village with such a powerful stench."

"Have you been to many villages?"

"A few. As I said, my home village is Cael. Less than two days to the east is another village, and a two-and-a-half day journey south will bring you to yet another. They aren't big, mind you, but they are large enough to provide everything we humans need to survive, I guess."

Do human villages often move?

Jerica shook her head. "Not unless there's a problem, or there's a newly discovered danger nearby. Why do you ask, Zeira?"

"Well, it's only because it took a long time for us to find you the first time. I was told that the tribesmen ... sorry, the humans were notoriously difficult to find, due to the constant moving around of your settlements."

Jerica faced Sif, knowing the rest of her dragon companions were looking through Sif's eyes, and held up her hands in surrender.

"I have no idea where you are getting your information about us, but rest assured, it's wrong."

I'm starting to see that, Zeira said.

"Me, too," Sif added, moving her humanoid form's mouth at the same time. "Any better?"

Jerica giggled. "Your mouth is still opening and closing, like a fish gasping for breath, but you're getting better. The one thing you haven't perfected yet is the subtle movements of the mouth that are necessary for certain sounds."

"I don't think I'll ever master that," Sif groaned.

"You don't have to. What you're doing is fine."

"You're sure?"

"I am. Now, stick with me. Let's go see if we can find this Zebulon figure together."

"Where do we start?"

Jerica pointed at a few children kicking around a hollowed-out gourd. "I say we ask for directions. Hello? Excuse me, could you possibly help me?"

The four kids stopped their game and stared curiously at the two of them.

"We're looking for Zebulon. Is he around here somewhere?"

The children all stared at her, unblinking.

"Perhaps they don't speak human?" Sif quietly suggested.

"I'm sure they do. They've probably been raised to not talk to strangers. That's what my parents drilled into me at an early age."

One boy, wearing a blue tattered shirt and brown trousers that had patches on both knees, approached. After staring at the two of them for a few moments, he held out a dirty hand.

"What does he want?" Sif asked.

Jerica nodded. "He wants something in exchange for the information. That's right, isn't it?"

The child, who looked like he could have been nine or ten years old, nodded eagerly. After a few moments, his playmates were crowding next to him, also with their hands out. Sighing,

Jerica turned to her companion.

"We have nothing to barter with. What can we give him?"

How many are there? Nuri suddenly asked.

"There are four of you," Jerica announced, raising her voice. "Such nice children. Let me think for a moment. I'm sure I can come up with something."

Four? Perfect. I just feasted on a large shellfish. It had several pearls inside. If you go to the nearest water, I'll get these to you. Would that suffice?

Jerica nodded. "That's perfect. All right, kids, I have a proposition for you. How would each of you like a nice, shiny pearl?"

All four of the cherubic faces lit up. They nodded eagerly.

"Come on. I need to rinse my hands off first. Then, you tell me where I can find Zebulon, and I'll give each of you a pearl. How does that sound?"

"Let's see the pearls first," the lead boy said, sounding skeptical.

"Not until I get the grime off my hands," Jerica said, thinking fast. "Follow me. We'll go down to that pier there."

I'm in the area. When you're ready, dunk your hands in the water. I'll give the pearls to you then.

"You're amazing," Jerica softly told the valthan. "Thank you so much."

"You're welcome, provided you have those pearls you promised," the boy said, thinking she was talking to him.

Kneeling on the wooden pier, Jerica stretched her hand down to the water and gently pushed it in. Stifling a gasp, as the water was ice cold, she almost immediately felt something. Nuri! The water dragon deftly placed four spherical objects in her hand. Standing, Jerica saw four shiny pearls nestled within.

"As promised, here are the four pearls," she said, showing the four kids the contents of her hand. "Now, before I give one to each of you, I need you to tell me where I can find Zebulon."

The ringleader of the group eyed his friends, as if to verify that they were okay with him divulging the location. The oldest girl nodded. Grunting, the boy turned back around, shrugged, and pointed at an alley running between two rows of buildings.

"You want the seer. See that alley? He's at the end of it. Look for the red door."

Jerica and Sif both turned to study the narrow street between two rows of single-story wood buildings.

"A red door," Jerica repeated. "Down there. Thank you! Oh, you want payment. Here you go. I have a pearl for each of you. Have a nice day!"

What are you doing? Skellig asked. Zeira thought he sounded angry. *That's because I* am *angry. You're putting yourself in danger, Jerica.*

"What? I am not! What's the problem?"

You're too nice. Look around you. No one in this village is as polite as you. You're drawing attention to yourself, and trust me when I say that's a bad thing.

"Oh, that's nonsense. I believe in seeing the good in people. My mother taught me that. Are you saying I shouldn't have listened to her after all these years?"

All I'm saying, Skellig insisted, *is to be careful. I trust this not.*

Seconded, Gocri added.

"Look, we're already halfway down the alley. Sif is right here with me, and she's doing an outstanding job of moving and talking.

That's because I'm afraid that, should I start talking, then I'm liable to fall flat on my face if I take my concentration away from my legs.

I feel an I-told-you-so moment is approaching.

Jerica stopped to look behind her, prompting Sif to do the same. "What was that? I don't see anything."

"Well, well," a voice sneered. "Lookee what we got here, fellas."

Jerica's head whipped around in time to see three men, dressed just as shabbily as the children playing in the street, step out from the shadows and quickly surround them.

"Hand over your valuables," the mugger ordered. "You and your pale friend will now hand over everything to us, including that piece of leather armor of yours, girlie."

Jerica glanced at the leather bracer, a gift from her mother, and instinctively placed a hand over it.

"I'm sorry, I can't. My mother gave me this. Is there something else you'd …?"

"Give us the ruddy thing or else we'll take *it* and your hand along with it," a second mugger snarled, as he unsheathed a long, curved dagger hanging from his belt. "Like it? It's my favorite. It has never failed me, so do as we say or it'll be tasting blood, get it?"

Jerica took a step back, but surprisingly, Sif did the opposite. The transformed dragon placed herself directly in front of their assailants, shook her head as if she was expressing her disappointment, and then pointed back the way they had come.

"You had better be on your way. It'd be a shame to see you three healthy boys hurt."

Cackles and guffaws echoed in the confines of the narrow alleyway. The gang's leader stepped forward and produced a coil of rope from somewhere within the folds of his clothes. He took two steps toward Jerica when he came to a sudden stop. Sif had yet to move a muscle. In fact, her hands were clasped behind her back and her eyes were closed!

"You won't be touching her," Sif announced, as her eyes opened and she let out a very inhuman-like growl.

What had stopped the muggers in their tracks, however, wasn't Sif's boldness, nor was it her growl. Suddenly, behind her a huge gray scorpion tail, tipped with a foot-long stinger, quivered, as if it had a mind of its own and was preparing to strike.

"What in the name of Jerod the Usurper is *that*?" the first thug cried.

Sif finally stirred. She brought her hands out from behind her back, hands that were now oversized pincers. Sif snapped them closed a few times for effect.

Two of the muggers, including the leader of the gang, screamed and fled. The third, however, gripped his sword tightly and was now advancing on Sif. Jerica paled. What was she supposed to do?

Where are you guys? Sif's in trouble! We could use your help!

We're here, came Skellig's immediate reply. *But, I believe your assessment is wrong. Sif does not need our help. Behold. She can take care of herself.*

Jerica spun in time to see the sword-wielding thug rush toward Sif, intent on slicing her in two. However, Sif caught the sword on its downward thrust with her right hand, er, *claw*, and held it tight.

"I will not give it back," Sif told the mugger. "You're a bad human, and you deserve to be punished."

The scorpion tail slammed downward, driving the stinger deep into the cobblestone road, shattering the round stones. The thug tried to pull his dirk free of her pincer, but after noticing his weapon hadn't budged an inch, he let out a string of curses and promptly fled, leaving his prized dagger behind. Shrugging, Sif held the knife out to Jerica, who tucked it into her belt.

"If you two are done showing off," a new voice suddenly announced, "then perhaps you'd like to get down to business? Jerica, of Cael, tell your dragon friend to follow me. We can't stay out in the open like this."

Jerica and Sif stared—open-mouthed—at a wrinkled old man, as he turned on his heel and quickly ducked through a nearby open door, which, Jerica noted, was a bright red color.

Chapter 13 — Seer

You will have to forgive me, my dear. It's not often that I can say that I've entertained a dragon at my humble abode. Well, let's be honest. I have never had the pleasure, but I'd like to think that, well, I wouldn't become a bumbling idiot. Oh, look. I seem to be doing that very thing, don't I? I am so sorry. Please accept my humblest of apologies. It's just that ... well, I've been looking forward to your arrival for so long that I ... yes, dear? What is it?"

"You knew Sif was a dragon disguised as a human," Jerica said. "How? Yes, she's currently gray, but that can be explained. How did you know?"

Zebulon faced Sif in her human form and bowed low. "Sifula, of the Reza Gathering, oldest offspring of Konungr the Wise. It is truly an honor to make your acquaintance."

Jerica turned to Sif and smiled. "He knows more about you than I do. How is that possible?"

"You know of my father?" Sif said, ignoring Jerica's

observation. "How? Do you know where he is? Have you heard any news?"

Jerica held up her hands in a time-out gesture. "Wait a moment. Your father is missing? When were you going to tell us about that?"

"His disappearance is always on my mind," Sif answered, as she managed to make her human form's head stiffly turn to face Jerica's direction. "You know nothing about it because that's the way I have always kept it: secret. He vanished without a trace more than ten years ago, and I have been searching for him ever since. In this case, my search is on hold until we deal with this power-hungry human."

Sif's sire is missing, Skellig said. *I did not know that. I pledge my assistance when all of this is said and done, my friend.*

"Your help is greatly appreciated," Sif said.

"You have mine, too," Jerica told the vapor dragon.

And mine, Nuri added.

That goes for us, too, Zeira announced. Jerica felt, rather than heard, Gocri's grunt of approval.

"Are you finished conversing with your other dragon friends?" Zebulon asked, as he pulled out one of the chairs at a heavily scarred table. "Tell Skellig I've always admired Spark dragons. I would love to meet him someday."

I heard what he said. How does he know my name? It was never spoken aloud.

"I wouldn't be much of a seer if I didn't have some secrets now, would I?" Zebulon said, offering Jerica a smile. He looked deep in her eyes and nodded. "Fear not, Master Spark Dragon. I will not reveal your involvement with this excursion."

Why would he say that? Zeira wanted to know. *Skellig, are you not supposed to be here?*

My presence is supposed to be a secret, Skellig finally confessed. *How this blasted human knew that is beyond me.*

A lucky guess? Gocri suggested.

"Of course not," Zebulon said, as he reached for a kettle and poured himself a cup of tea. Looking at the chipped white mug he was holding, he glanced up at his two guests and his face colored. "I beg your pardon. It's been a long time since I've had any guests. Let me fetch you both a cup."

A cup of what? Sif asked.

Tea, Jerica mentally answered.

What is 't'?

T-e-a. Tea. It's a beverage served hot. It helps warm you on a cold day.

I'm not cold, and it's quite warm outside, Sif pointed out.

He's being hospitable, Zeira said, coming to Jerica's aid. *Sif, just smile and accept the beverage when it's presented to you. Don't forget to thank your host.*

Zebulon appeared at Sif's side and placed a friendly hand on her shoulder. "Let me make this easy for you. I know you're not a human, obviously, my dear. You're a dragon. But, you're currently in human form. Do you see that? There are windows scattered throughout my shop, allowing someone from the *outside* to look *inside*. We must maintain the illusion that the two of you are both humans, wouldn't you agree?"

I would, Zeira said.

"And the others?" Zebulon prompted. "Skellig, Gocri, and Nuri?"

He knows about all of us! Nuri exclaimed. *I'm not sure I trust this.*

"It's nice to hear your voice, Nuri," Zebulon said, in a conversational manner, as he poured two additional cups of tea. Setting the kettle back on its holder over the fire, the seer placed the steaming cups of tea before his guests and sank back down into his chair. "I've never met a valthan before. I'm honored."

You certainly have the advantage, Nuri observed. *Whether good or bad, I haven't decided.*

"It's for the good, I assure you, my dear dragon," the old man crooned. "Now, before we proceed, I need to ask a question. Sifula, how well do you handle critique?"

Jerica had been helping Sif to grasp the delicate tea cup by its handle when both of them looked up.

"Critique?" Sif sputtered. "From a human? I guess it would depend upon what you wanted to critique."

"Your appearance, my fine vapor dragon."

Sif looked down at her humanoid form and frowned.

"What about it? I look like a human, do I not?"

"You look like an ash tray," the seer responded, with a chuckle. "If you really want to pass for a human, then you do need to get the coloring right. I've never seen a shade of human colored like that before. It makes you stand out, my dear girl."

"I'm a vapor dragon," Sif insisted. "This is the only color I have to work with."

Zebulon took a sip of his tea and then smiled patronizingly at the disguised dragon. "Is it, now? Would you try something with me?"

Sif nervously eyed Jerica.

"You're safe here," Jerica informed her dragon friend. "Besides, I think if he'd wanted to do something to us, then he would have done so by now."

"True," Zebulon admitted. "But, fear not. I would never hurt anyone in your party. Your mission is too important."

There are so many questions he now needs to answer because of that one statement, Skellig decided.

The seer nodded. "And answer them, I will. But first, let's fix your friend, here, shall we?"

What are you going to do?

"Fix me?" Sif repeated. "Dare I ask *how*, Zebulon?"

"Call me Zeb, it's easier. And to answer that, we'll take it one step at a time. Now, both of you, have a seat."

Jerica and Sif complied. At least, Sif tried. It took her a little longer to get her knees to bend at the right angle, while simultaneously lowering her rear. And then she fell—hard—onto the seat.

"Whoa ... ow!"

Jerica slapped a hand over her mouth. "Are you all right?"

"That didn't go so well. Well, nothing injured but my pride, I suppose."

"We have so much work to do," Zeb sighed.

For the next ten minutes, as they sipped their tea, Zeb coached Sif in the fine art of impersonating humans—wiggling her fingers, shaping her mouth to the words of the spoken language, and even applying realistic colors to the skin and clothing.

"And now," the seer said, turning to Jerica, "what can I do for you?"

"How to deal with the Thunder King, of course."

Ask him about the mine before he starts rambling again, Zeira said.

"And also … I believe you were about to tell us about the mine before you sorted out Sif."

"Are you sure that's what I was talking about?"

"I'm sure of it," Jerica said, as she flashed Zeb a smile.

"Now, let me see. There are six defunct jhorium mines and two active ones."

Jhorium? Zeira repeated.

Clarification requested, Skellig added.

I'll try.

"Oh, I'm pretty sure you were talking about the mine that's less than a day's walk from here? The one to the east?"

"Ah, the Daget Mine. What a disaster, dear girl, what a disaster."

"Why would you say that?" Jerica asked, throwing as much innocence as she could into the question. "Wasn't enough, er, jhorium found to make it worthwhile?"

An excellent question, Gocri praised.

Way to think on your feet! Skellig agreed.

"Not a chance, dear girl. There have been several low-yield mines, but that one was the worst of the lot. Never seen the baron angrier than that. He made one too many boasts about how much jhorium was buried in the hills, but did they find it? No. Instead, all they managed to find was a single lump of ore. What a waste! Is that really what you want to talk about, Miss Jerica?"

"We encountered the pit earlier today and figured it had something to do with why the world seems to be …"

"… going crazy?" Zebulon suggested, with a knowing smile. "You are correct, my dear. The two are directly related. But, as I said, I wouldn't think that would be the question foremost on your mind."

Jerica sat back in her chair and studied the seer.

"All right, what would be?"

"Your mark, of course. I'd like to see it and confirm my

suspicions."

"What mark?" Sif wanted to know.

Jerica automatically placed her left hand over the leather bracer on her right arm. "Er, what about it?"

"You and I know full well what I'm talking about," Zebulon scolded. "Wouldn't you like to be able to tell your dragon friends how you can control which ability is combined with any other ability?"

Sif turned to Jerica and placed a hand over hers.

"What is he talking about? You claimed you didn't know how you were able to create those combinations."

"And I still don't," Jerica insisted. "I just assumed it was based on whoever I was touching at the moment. The more dragons we travel with, the great number of variations that show up."

Zeb's eyebrows shot up. "You are able to use multiple dragons when combining abilities? O-ho! I don't need to see the mark now. I know full well what's under your armor."

"Excuse me?" Jerica sputtered.

Zebulon's face blushed bright red. "That's not what I meant."

"I'm just teasing you, Zeb. I know what you meant."

But I don't, Zeira said. *Jerica, is there a way to control how our abilities are combined?*

"I want to say I have no idea, Zeira, but after watching Zeb work with Sif, I think I'm starting to realize it's all in my head."

"Will you show the mark to us?" Zeb gently asked. "I do believe I already know what's there, but I strongly suspect your vaporous friend does not."

Sighing, Jerica nodded. She started unfastening the buckles holding her mother's bracer in place. Free from her arm, she placed the protective leather armor on the table before them and positioned her arm next to it. Sif leaned over and studied her bare arm.

"What are we looking at?"

"You know what it means?" Zeb asked, as he stared into Jerica's eyes.

"I do. Zeira's friend told us what it was and what it meant."

"And you know how coveted this particular symbol is?"

"Yes."

"Did your dragon friends tell you that you are now the envy of every human on this world, as well as coveted by every dragon you encounter?"

Jerica nodded. "They said something like that, yes."

Slowly, she rolled her arm on the table until the backside of her arm was exposed. Gently holding Jerica's wrist, the wizened seer studied the image before him. After a few moments, Zebulon looked up.

"Do you recognize the species of dragon?"

Jerica shook her head. "I don't, no. Do you?"

"Frostfire."

"The common ancestor between Zeira and Gocri," Jerica breathed.

We haven't established that as fact yet, Gocri was quick to point out.

Would it be such a bad thing? Zeira asked.

I suppose not.

"Frostfire is one of the ancient species," Zeb explained. "It's no wonder they chose its image as the symbol for the kairies. Frostfires are direct ancestors to well over eighty percent of all known dragons."

Told you, Zeira teased.

Shut up, Gocri returned.

Jerica smiled as she felt the friendly rivalry between her Fire and Ice dragon companions.

"What else can you tell me about this mark?" Jerica asked. "We know some, but I, for one, would love to hear more."

"Kairies can bond with any dragon, on any region," Zebulon answered. "The simple act of physical contact with you is the equivalent of stepping foot on your home region. For example, Skellig, I'm sure you've already bonded with her, haven't you?"

I have, aye.

"And when you did, it took care of your fading problem, did it not?"

As a matter of fact, it did. I will be eternally grateful.

"Any dragon, from any region. It means she's allowed to

travel to any region and will never have to worry about the Fade again. None of you will, provided you have all bonded with Jerica."

We all have, Zeira confirmed.

"Well, there you go," Zeb said. "Together, the six of you are a very formidable team. It's probably why the Thunder King has taken a sudden interest in you."

Jerica's head snapped up, as did Sif's. At last, the real reason for their visit!

"The Thunder King knows the only way that he could be defeated will be at the hands of a kairie. As of right now, I know of no other live kairies. You, dear girl, are Andela's one and only hope."

"No pressure there," Jerica grumped.

"Zeira," Zeb called. "Have you verified any of this yet?"

How did you know I was contacting my brethren? Zeira shakily asked.

"Let's move past that for now. Once you verify I'm telling the truth, then the six of you need to get as far away from here as you can."

"Why?" Sif wanted to know.

"Oh, didn't I say? The Thunder King has dispatched Dym. You'll want to be far from here when he arrives."

"Dim?" Jerica repeated.

Dym, Skellig groaned. *He's a Spark dragon, one of the fiercest I have ever met.*

That's just great, Zeira grumped. *How long before he'll arrive?*

"You've got some time," Zeb told them. "About three hours. It's more than enough time to get everyone to safety."

Properly scared, Jerica leapt to her feet and nervously eyed the door. "You're right. I think it's time we leave now."

"Not yet, dear girl, not yet. We still have a little time left. Let's make the best of it, shall we?"

Sighing, Jerica sank down on shaky legs, again seated at the table. Sif sat down next to her.

"I would love to hear all about the different variations of magical abilities you must have created by now," Zeb began, "but, sadly, we don't have *that* much time."

The image of flaming, molten rocks, arcing through the

air and slamming down, onto the grass-covered island flashed through Jerica's brain.

"An interesting image," Zeb admitted. "From one of your earlier exploits?"

"It's recent," Jerica admitted.

Flaming poo boulders, Skellig added, with a chuckle.

Don't tell him that! Zeira cried. *Yes, it's the most powerful manifestation of a fire ability I have ever had, but it isn't exactly the most flattering, is it?*

I'm sorry, Zeira.

It's all right. There are no secrets among us.

"And you, Sif," Zeb said, turning to the transformed vapor dragon. "May I make a recommendation?"

"You've been right about everything else, so I certainly won't say no to it," Sif said.

"Trust yourself. Even when changing to a form you've never heard of."

"What? I've never been able to do that. My mother warned me not to try, or disastrous results could befall me."

"Dear Sif, I don't know how to tell you this, but ... your mother was wrong. You vapor dragons have been given a tremendous gift. Use it! Master it! It might very well be the difference between life and death!"

Sif's human mouth fell open with surprise. "There's no way you're suggesting what I think you're suggesting."

"Oh yes, you have the ability to change into a form you've never heard of."

Sif shook her head. "Impossible. My mother has told me she's tried before. Many times."

"Would you humor me? I believe it can be done."

Sif stared at the seer with wide, unblinking eyes. "Very well. What do you want me to do?"

Zebulon was silent for a few moments, considering. After nearly thirty seconds had passed in awkward silence, the seer's eyes opened and he smiled at Sif.

"Change into a gyre dragon, if you please."

"Change into a *what?*" Sif asked, perplexed.

I've never heard of it, Zeira said.

Clever, Gocri said. *A gyre happens to be one of the smallest dragons in existence. Rare. It is also one of only a handful of dragons who only have two legs. This one can walk around on its hind legs and will fit on the palm of your hand—I mean, Jerica's hand.*

Jerica's eyes widened as she held out a hand and looked at her palm.

"I had no idea," Sif admitted. She looked at the seer. "What do I have to do?"

"Believe it or not, the same as before. Don't try to wonder what will happen. Allow the changes to come. Don't resist."

"A gyre dragon," Sif repeated, with exasperation. "I hope you're right. Here we go."

Jerica watched intently as her mirror image reverted to Sif's typical grey color and began shrinking, pulling itself inward until she was only a few inches high. However, her form was still humanoid. Then, a set of wings sprouted on her back. Scales erupted, and quickly spread across her body. Her neck became elongated and a long, serpentine tail sprouted in the back. After a few moments, the tiny dragon, now a mix of black and a very dark blue, was walking around the floor. No larger than a mouse now, Sif kept stumbling forward.

Damn, Sif swore, using the dragons' mind-speech. *I just can't seem to get the hang of bipedal locomotion.*

"I find that so hard to believe," Jerica said, letting out a small giggle. She stooped to gently pick Sif's tiny form up and place it on her hand. "Of all the things you dragons can do, the most difficult is simply walking around on two legs? You must be joking."

Sif's tiny gyre form stumbled again. This time, she wrapped her wings around two of Jerica's fingers and held tight. The lone human present cupped her hands together and gently set her back on the ground.

"Don't worry. I wouldn't let anything happen to you."

The gyre dragon turned to look up at Zebulon and growled, only what came out of Sif's mouth was— a high-pitched snarl, no more intimidating than a kitten.

"How is it he knows more about me than I do?" Sif complained. "He knew I could change the skin color of my different forms — something not even our esteemed leader knows, by the way — and he knew I could change into something I've never heard of before." The gyre dragon shimmered, became smoke, and quickly returned to human form. "So, can you tell me how you know so much?"

"I'm a seer," Zebulon said, shrugging. "It's what I do. I can look at something and automatically see its history. Let me give you an example. If you present to me a small stone, I can tell you where it broke off from the original, how far it's traveled, and so on. So, looking at the two of you, it's easy to determine who you are, where you've been, and what's in store for you."

"You know the future?" Jerica asked, amazed.

Zebulon waved a dismissive hand. "Forget I said that, all right? Let's focus on the present, shall we? Aren't there more pressing matters that need our attention?"

What can you tell us about jhorium? Zeira asked.

"An excellent question, young Zeira," Zeb praised.

Not you, too, Zeira groaned. *I'm much older than you people think.*

It's been established you're older than Jerica, Gocri chided, *but among us you are a hatchling. No, I mean no offense. You are probably the most intelligent, well-mannered dragon I have ever encountered.*

Umm, thanks?

"He's referring to every single dragon he's ever encountered," Zebulon helpfully translated, "and that includes his own species. Royalty included."

Aye, that is what I meant. And stop doing that.

"Doing what?"

Picking up my thoughts. Humans aren't supposed to be able to do that.

"Yet, your kairie is," Zeb pointed out.

Well, yes, but that's only because she has bonded with us. With all of us. It's expected. Your presence in my mind isn't.

Zebulon laughed. "Your concerns are duly noted. Now, Zeira, you inquired about jhorium. What would you like to know?"

Is that why the mine was dug?

"It's why *all* the mines were dug," Zeb clarified. "And, it's why there are an additional two being dug at this very minute, with plans for five more."

What is so special about this metal? Gocri wanted to know.

"Oh, it's nothing really," Zebulon said, as he poured himself a glass of water and held it up, inquiring whether Jerica or Sif would like a glass. Both declined. "It's only the source of all magic in Andela, so it's nothing to worry about."

"Wh-what?" Jerica stammered. "Jhorium is the source of magic?"

"It is," Zebulon confirmed. "That metal is *infused* with enough magic to make it the most valuable metal to have ever been discovered. Unfortunately, the Thunder King should really leave it alone."

It's the source of the imbalance! Zeira cried. *That's why everything has felt so … off. If the jhorium metal is removed, then … then …*

"Andela will suffer a catastrophe, the likes of which have never been seen before," Zebulon glumly answered. "That's why the six of you are on this quest. You must stop the Thunder King from pillaging all jhorium from the earth. If he remains unchecked, then our world — as we know it — will cease to exist."

Doesn't this foolish human know this? Skellig demanded. *Uh, no offense to you, Jerica.*

"None taken, I assure you," Jerica said.

"Oh, he knows everything that is happening is his doing," Zebulon said, shaking his head. "In his mind, he sees the absence of magic as a good thing because, wielding special weapons forged from the stolen jhorium, he has become nigh unstoppable."

"I'd say we have our work cut out for us," Jerica observed. "You say this metal is more valuable than gold?"

Zebulon nodded. "What would you rather have? A bag of gold coins, or suit of armor that will never fail? Or a sword which never loses its edge? What about a helmet which enables the wearer to read minds? When jhorium is involved, my dear child, the sky is the limit, unfortunately."

Skellig's thoughts came through. *How does this maniacal human know where to dig? How does he find these deposits of jhorium?*

"With a jhorium detector, of course," Zeb chuckled. "You cannot use magic to locate magic. Thunder King learned that lesson the hard way."

Zeira felt Skellig's exasperation. *Describe this jhorium detector,* she said. *Is it a special creature? Perhaps a human with an ability to locate this precious metal?*

"Neither," Zebulon scoffed. "No living creature can detect the presence of jhorium."

"Then what …?" Jerica started to ask.

"The Thunder King found what he was looking for," Zebulon sadly announced.

Trying to get information from this human is liking removing a bone stuck between two fangs, Skellig decided. *It's a pain, and it takes forever.*

"Oh, what's life without a little whimsy?" the seer laughed. "To answer your question, he found the Rastan Spear."

Zeira felt a thrill. *The name revealed by the centaurs!*

What's so special about this spear? Nuri wanted to know.

"Why, my dear valthan," Zeb tutted, "this spear is made of jhorium's opposite, of course. How else would they know jhorium is near?"

"Jhorium's opposite?" Sif said, shaking her head. "I think I'm getting a headache."

As am I, Gocri grumbled.

"Drininite," Zebulon proudly proclaimed. "It's almost as rare as jhorium itself. What you do is take some drininite and hold it above the ground. If jhorium is nearby, then drininite will be repelled away, as if given a mighty shove by an invisible hand."

We need to get that spear from Thunder King, Zeira declared.

"That'd be no easy feat, I assure you," the seer said, chuckling.

"That's why we're searching for an oron," Jerica said, drawing a nod from Sif. "We believe it will help us defeat the Thunder King."

Zebulon sat back in his chair and studied Jerica's pretty face. "You are aware of the difficulties with that course of action?"

"I think so," Jerica reluctantly admitted. "But, if there's something we don't know, then now would be the time to hear it."

Agreed, Skellig added.

"An oron is a very complex tool," Zeb began. "Only those with the most control over their minds should attempt to use the stone. And be warned! You may only use the stone once, like the ancient oracles of old."

"Only once?" Sif said, appalled. "That can't be good."

"And you must focus your mind," Zeb continued. "Be thinking very precise thoughts about what you're searching for, or else the stone will show you something you don't want to see."

"Like what?" Jerica asked.

"Like, perhaps, your own death?" the seer whispered. "Orons were deemed too powerful. The last complete stone was destroyed. I believe there is but one oron remaining, and it has been separated into its base elements."

We know, Zeira said. *We have located two of the pieces so far.*

"Indeed? Excellent, my dear dragons — and human girl. Tell me, how did you come by the fire fragment? It … the looks on your faces tell me that's the piece you're still searching for, isn't it?"

Yes, Skellig confirmed. *What can you tell us about it?*

"Its resting place is a very long way from here. It would take many days of flying."

We know, Zeira proudly announced. *We were told it's located on the third continent.*

"The third continent," Zebulon repeated, chuckling. "Well, that's one way to look at it. What's your plan? You're with dragons, so obviously you plan on flying all the way out there and back, is that it?"

Yes, Zeira confirmed.

"Your plan is doomed to failure," Zeb sadly announced.

What? Zeira sputtered. *Why would you say that?*

"I know you're all dragons, and the majority of you have wings, but it is simply too great a distance to travel. By the time you undergo that journey, the Thunder King will have long mined the last bit of jhorium from the land, thus dooming the inhabitants of Andela to a magic-free existence. Need I tell you how unpleasant *that* would be?"

Then … how are we supposed to make it in time? Zeira wanted to know.

Hush, young one, Skellig said. *If I'm not too mistaken, I do believe our friend has a suggestion.*

He said would, Nuri recalled. *That means he has another way for us to acquire the fragment quickly.*

"Excellent, Miss Nuri! Your powers of recall do you credit. Yes, there is but one way for you and your companions to travel that distance and make it back in time to stop your Thunder King."

Tell us, Zeira implored.

"First, I have to say that none of you are going to like it," Zebulon began. "Especially Nuri. You'll have to use the Ligeia Gateways."

Ligeia Gateways? Zeira repeated, as she frowned. *I've never heard of them. Nuri, have you any idea who — or what — that might be?* When she didn't get a response from her valthan companion, Zeira turned to look down at the water below her. Nuri was simply floating, motionless, on the surface of the sea. Zeira felt a wave of alarm pass over her aquatic friend.

Tell me there's another way, Nuri said. *There must be something besides ... besides ... that.*

"There isn't, I'm afraid," the seer admitted, shaking his head. "The Gateways, as I know you must be aware, are a series of interconnecting, underwater portals."

"There are more than one?" Jerica nervously asked. "How do we know which one to use?"

I believe he will let us know, Skellig said.

"I will, indeed," Zebulon agreed.

"Wait a minute," Sif implored, holding up a hand. "I don't get it. You want us to use portals found under the water? How are we supposed to get to them? Swim?"

And now you know why I think this course of action is foolhardy, Nuri groaned. *These portals were discovered centuries ago, by the greatest of valthan swimmers. The gateways are thousands of feet below the surface. I'm a valthan, and it's barely within my limits to reach those depths.*

"Now, would you like to hear the difficult part?" Zeb cheerfully asked.

Oh, by all means, do your worst, old man, Skellig sighed. *What could be worse than that?*

"Nuri, I know you can reach the depths necessary to find the first Void, but your companions will need help."

What, additional valthans? Nuri asked.

"Even your strongest swimmer would be unable to get a creature the size of Gocri, for example, to those depths. No, you need something larger. Much, much larger."

Like what? Skellig curiously asked.

But ... there's nothing large enough to get all of us down to that depth!

"Can you think of no one? Perhaps an insect of such gargantuan proportions ...?"

An archyx, Nuri moaned.

"An archyx," Zebulon said, at the same time.

A bug? Skellig scoffed. *I have lived many years, human. Never have I ever encountered an insect larger than me.*

Skellig, the archyxes exist, Nuri insisted.

Fine. Describe it for me.

"Nuri, would you care to answer this one?" Zeb asked.

It's a beetle, with huge pincers above its jaws, an outer carapace which changes color depending on the light, and a wingspan longer than ... than ... well, if each of us were to spread our wings, and stand wing-to-wing, we would still be shorter than one wing.

Wow, Zeira exclaimed. *I had no idea that such creatures exist. I can't wait to see one! I ... what? Why did everyone go so quiet?*

Hopping a ride on one of these mammoth bugs isn't going to be easy, Skellig grumped. *Something that large could easily crush us to death. No, this won't be an easy task. What else can you tell us about them?*

They could all hear the valthan sigh.

Well, they spend equal time in both the air and the sea. While in the sea, they can dive to depths which far exceed anything known. Why would an archyx be willing to help us?

"Because, it's a bug," Zebulon answered. "You won't find many lights on upstairs, if you catch my meaning. It follows its basic urges and ignores everything else."

I don't see how that helps us, Zeira said.

"The archyx is so large that it needs to feed every single day. In fact, whenever it's in the water, it'll be searching for food."

"What do huge bugs eat?" Jerica nervously asked. "And you better not tell me something I don't want to hear."

"Plankton, my dear girl," Zeb chuckled. "Archyx will feed on plankton. More specifically, those plankton that are attracted to bright lights."

Like from these Gateways? Skellig asked, catching on.

"Precisely, my dear Spark dragon. Precisely. Wherever you find an archyx, you'll find a gateway nearby. That is, far below the surface."

So, we find one of these giant bugs, we sneak aboard it, and catch a ride down? Zeira asked. *What about on the way back?*

"Each archyx will actually travel through the gateway," Zeb explained. "There, they will feed for a period of no more than twelve hours before returning through the gateway, back to their territory."

"How many gateways are there?" Jerica asked.

"I believe there are six of them. No, seven. Hmm, no more than eight. Do you know what? I really don't know, dear child. Besides, worrying about how to board an archyx and then depart would be the least of your worries," the seer said, hiding a smile.

Jerica nervously cleared her throat. "I, uh, am wondering what part we *should* be worrying about?"

Zebulon nodded. "Your powers of recollection do you credit, Miss Jerica. You are correct. That's not the worst part. You're looking for the final oron piece, the fire fragment, and it is guarded."

By what? Skellig sighed.

"A foe that's beyond any of you."

Hmmph, Skellig scoffed. *We'll decide who's beyond the likes of us.*

But, I am curious, Gocri admitted. *Seer, what guards the fragment? What foe would be beyond five dragons?*

"A djinn."

Chapter 14 — Archyx

"A djinn," Zeira explained, several hours later, as the dragons glided through the air, "is a spirit that can appear as an animal, or a human, and lives to … *influence* other beings."

"Influence?" Jerica repeated. "In what way?"

"I met one once," Sif reported.

"Well? Don't leave us in suspense. What happened?"

"This particular djinn was fond of granting wishes."

"Oh, that's good to hear," Jerica exclaimed. "Whew, I was starting to worry."

You should be worrying, Gocri argued. *The seer was right. Djinns are beyond dragons.*

"Well, maybe one, but five?" Jerica challenged.

Still no match, I'm afraid, Skellig said.

Zeira dipped her wing and followed the Spark dragon's yellow and black form as he flew through the air. Zebulon had provided instructions on where to find the gateway that would deposit them closest to the fire fragment, but that didn't mean it was nearby. It would take several solid hours of flying to reach the area before sunset.

Remembering that one of their number was a valthan, Zeira looked down at the roiling waves far below them and spotted the water dragon effortlessly shadowing them.

I see you, too, came Nuri's thought.

Sorry. I was just making sure you were all right.

Your concern for our well-being is what makes you a strong leader, Nuri returned. *I am honored to be one of your companions.*

You are one of my friends, Zeira corrected. *You all are.*

Don't get soft on us, Skellig teased. *Worry about that later. Right now, we have to find this huge bug.*

You don't believe the human? Sif inquired.

Honestly, I don't. Dragons are long-lived. I find it hard to believe that, should an insect of this size actually exist, no one has come across one of them yet. I've checked with my species. No one has any idea what I'm talking about.

Zeira looked back at Nuri, cruising steadily along on the surface of the sea.

Nuri, how fast can you really swim? Have we seen your maximum?

Zeira felt the valthan chuckle. "You've seen, perhaps, one-half of my full strength."

"One half?" Jerica sputtered, overhearing. "You're kidding!"

"I'm not. We valthans are unmatched in the water."

"Can you tell me again what 'brackish water' is? Is it dirty water? Untouchable water? Zebulon said we'd know we were near when we reached a patch of brackish water."

"Brackish water refers to the convergence of a source of freshwater spilling into seawater," Nuri explained. "It's the mix of the two."

"That should be easy enough," Zeira decided. "We just have to find a river, and then follow it until it drains into the sea."

"Perhaps. But not all rivers are above ground."

"But ... that's harder to see!"

"But not harder to taste," Nuri pointed out. "Above water, below water, it doesn't make any difference to me."

"You are sensitive enough to tell when you encounter

brackish water?"

"Have you ever smelled smoke in the air?" Nuri countered. "You may not be able to see the smoke, but you can smell it."

"Of course."

"It's much the same for me. Once I detect freshwater, in any variation, then I will investigate the source. In fact, I've already discovered over two dozen fresh water springs."

"You have? I've kept an eye on you. I haven't seen you swim below the surface."

"And that's how fast I am when properly motivated," Nuri informed her. "It doesn't take much to trace the bad water back, to the source."

"Freshwater isn't bad," Jerica insisted.

"It is if you live in seawater," Nuri countered. "Jerica, have you ever tasted seawater?"

"I have, yes."

"And? Can you substitute seawater for freshwater?"

"Absolutely not. My father says it's because of all the salt in it."

"Precisely. So, for a creature, such as myself, who thrives in salt water, the discovery of freshwater is very distinct, and easily traceable."

"I think I understand now. Thanks, Nuri!"

"My pleasure. Now, I want to investigate the latest freshwater spring … but it is tiny, dumping the equivalent of half a gallon of freshwater into the sea every hour. To keep this interesting, I'd like to propose something."

"What's that?" Zeira curiously asked.

"All you flyers have such difficulty believing we valthans can swim so fast, and thus far, I haven't shown you just how fast I am. So, I propose a challenge. Who thinks they can reach that island up ahead faster than me?"

"I do," Skellig immediately replied.

"Me," Gocri added.

Zeira looked at Sif, who was currently in her natural, vaporous form. "What about you, Sif? Are you going to try?"

Sif shook her head. "I've never had much of a competitive streak in me. I know I'm not the best flyer, so I will respectfully bow out. What about you, Zeira?"

"No races for me, thank you very much. I know I cannot beat her."

"Skellig and Gocri, you are hereby challenged to a race," Nuri boastfully began. "I say I can reach that island before you. What say you?"

"I say you're toast," Skellig said, grinning and flexing the muscles on his back. "There's no way you can beat me over there. Gocri?"

"I'll leave both of you in my dust," Gocri boasted.

Zeira reduced her speed and dropped to an altitude of five hundred feet. Gliding across the surface of the choppy sea, she could see Nuri, lazily doing the same, her long, serpentine body easily cutting through the waves, with her head held high. As if sensing her thoughts, Nuri turned to look up at her.

"Are you sure you don't want to try your luck, Z?"

"I'm good, thanks, Nuri. I already know you're faster than me, and I'm all right with it."

"Very well. Are you two ready?"

Why do I get the impression that she's about to hand our tails to us? Skellig quietly asked.

On a golden platter, Gocri agreed. *If that happens, you claim you had a sore wing. I'll blame it on age.*

Deal. Are you sure we should do this?

Aye. A challenge is a challenge. Come. Let's put this myth about being the fastest thing alive to rest. Aerial dragons hold that distinction, not the valthans.

"How far away would you say that island is?" Jerica asked, as she adjusted her seat on Zeira's back for a better look.

"At least ten miles," Sif answered.

"Perhaps we should pick something a little closer?" Jerica suggested. "We don't want anyone to hurt themselves."

"Are you three ready?" Sif loudly asked.

The three participants nodded. Gocri and Skellig sailed back, behind Nuri in the water.

"As soon as you reach Nuri, that'll be the start of the race," Sif decided. "And Nuri, I know it'll be like giving them a head-start, but I don't know what else to do."

"I could give them an actual head start," the valthan

began, as her long, sinewy body curled tightly together, like a spring. "They might have a chance then."

Jerica, Sif, and Zeira laughed out loud.

"Here they come!" the vapor dragon announced. "Get ready, Nuri!"

The instant both aerial dragons flew over Nuri, time seemed to slow to a standstill. Plumes of water rose high into the air as the very space where Nuri had been seemingly erupted. As the two dragons flew through the mist, they could see that the water dragon was no longer there. In fact, she was already several thousand feet ahead, and closing the distance to the island *fast*.

Zeira confided to Sif. "She's already halfway there!"

"Skellig and Gocri better get their tails moving," Sif agreed. "They have a long way to go to catch up. Look, Gocri is trying. He's pulling ahead of Skellig, and from the looks of it, Skellig doesn't like that one bit."

"What does it matter?" The distance between swimmer and flyers was growing steadily longer with each passing second. "Look at them. Nuri is going to reach the island in a matter of moments."

As predicted, the valthan touched the shore of the island less than twenty seconds later. She happily swam in large circles as she waited for Skellig and Gocri to arrive. Once they did, both flyers bowed their heads.

"We have been beaten," Gocri acknowledged.

"Thank you for admitting that," Nuri said, smiling.

"Should you repeat any of this, I will deny it under the most heinous of tortures," Gocri chuckled. "Outmaneuvered by a water dragon. What's this world coming to?"

"What are you complaining about?" Skellig grumbled. "I came in last. Do you think I can show my face back in Gale? Beaten by a water dragon, and outflown by an Ice dragon."

"Glacier," Gocri grunted.

"Whatever." Skellig eyed the direction they had come and chortled. "Care to try your luck again? I had the sun in my eyes earlier."

"Sure you did," Nuri laughed. "Well, come on, Sparkles. Let's see what you've got."

"Sparkles," Gocri grinned. "I love it."

"And you, IceChops? Care to try your luck again?"

"IceChops?" Gocri repeated. "And what should we call you? Something just as clever, wouldn't you agree, Skellig?"

"I do, IceChops, I really do."

Gocri fixed Skellig with a stare and shrugged. "Very well. If that's how we're playing, consider me a willing participant. Let's think of something good for Nuri, Sparkles."

"Hmm, I may not like this game after all," Skellig said, frowning.

"Sparkles," Zeira snorted. "I love it!"

Gocri announced. "From here on out, our valthan friend shall be ... wait for it ... Blue Streak, or Streak for short."

"Because of my speed," Nuri guessed. She nodded. "I have no objections. What about Zeira?"

"I suppose Ass-Blaster is out of the question?" Skellig innocently asked. "Too inappropriate?"

For the first time ever, Zeira actually chuckled at the thought of others teasing her for her method of using flames. Instead of feeling embarrassed, she was actually happy to be included with their teasing. After all, these were her friends, and they only wanted to give her some good-natured ribbing.

"I actually think that's funny," Zeira conceded.

"Only ... we're *not* calling her that," Sif vowed. "I say we call her Blaster."

Zeira nodded. "Blaster? Yes, I like it! Thank you, Sif! So, what about you?"

Sif turned to Zeira. "I don't know. Can you think of a nickname for me?"

"Uh, sure. Let me think. Hey, how about Misty?"

"That's not very teasing, is it?" Skellig complained.

"I'm not that type of a dragon," Zeira admitted. "She's my friend. I wouldn't want to cause her shame."

"I like it, Z. Or Blaster, whichever you prefer."

Nuri wriggled with excitement. "IceChops? Sparkles? You ready to try and win back some of your dignity?"

But before another race could begin, Nuri's expression turned serious. "I taste bad water," Nuri reported. "A lot of it. I'll investigate."

Five minutes later, Nuri's head resurfaced near the shore of a nearby island. The others flew to her side.

"I think we found it, Z! There's at least a thousand gallons of freshwater spilling into the ocean each minute directly below us. This has to be it!"

"How far down?" Skellig asked.

"Around five hundred feet. It looks like a tear in the ground to me, but whatever made it, I can tell you with one hundred percent certainty the water in that area is all brackish."

Gocri nodded. "Excellent. Now what? We wait for this giant insect to arrive?"

Zeira shrugged. "Remember what Zebulon said. 'Once the sun sets, and you all give thanks to Terra, that which you seek will reveal themselves.' I think that means once all of us are on land, then this giant insect appears?"

"We all give thanks to Terra," Zeira repeated, thinking hard. "We give thanks to the earth. That suggests we're all standing on the ground."

The group looked over at Nuri.

"What?" the valthan wanted to know. "I'm out of the water, aren't I?"

"Not all the way," Skellig pointed out.

"Fine. Look, here I am, all right? Wait. I won't fit. I need to walk in that direction. It's the only way I'll get all of myself on the shore. There, that's better. Now, we're all on Terra. What now?"

"When was sunset?" Jerica asked.

Sif looked west. "Judging by the sky, I'd say sunset was about twenty minutes ago. See? It's growing darker by the minute."

Jerica pointed at a spot on the water several hundred feet away, to the north.

"Look! There are lights in the water! Has that always been there?"

Wanting to investigate, Nuri headed to the water's edge, only to have her way blocked by Gocri.

"No, you don't. You need to stay out of the water, just like we need to stay on solid ground."

"For what purpose?" Nuri wanted to know. "I've never seen lights like that before. Maybe it's coming from the gateway?"

Right at that time, the ground trembled. Blades of grass swayed. Leaves rustled, and boulders rolled both downhill, and then *uphill*, when one side of the island suddenly sank low. Glancing fearfully around, it was Zeira who finally put all the pieces of the puzzle together.

"The island! The island is the bug! It's awakening!"

The six companions stared in disbelief as a deep crevasse appeared at their feet and rapidly deepened. The grassy floor of the island, now neatly split into two equal pieces, rose high into the air as the archyx lifted its hard, outer wings out of the way so that it could unfold its two sets of gossamer inner wings. Once extended, the dragons could only watch in awe as the scope of a single wing was revealed: over a thousand feet long and perhaps two hundred feet wide.

"It's not possible," Skellig breathed, as the archyx cast a strange, ethereal shadow over everything on the island, including themselves. "How are we supposed to use this to reach the gateway?"

The wings began a slow beat. The gentle breeze they had all been enjoying increased to a full-fledged hurricane as the archyx prepared for takeoff.

Zeira suddenly pointed at the grass-covered outer shell, used by the archyx to protect its wings and abdomen.

"That's our answer! Look at the ground we were just standing on. It's part of the bug's outer shell! With the wings out like this, the shell is open. But, when the archyx goes diving in the water, it'll close its shell back up. We have to be *under* that shell when that happens. That way, we'll have a free ride down, and *through*, this gateway."

"How are we supposed to do that?" Jerica asked.

The ground was shaking so badly by this time that all dragons had to resort to returning to the air. Skellig and Gocri were both holding Nuri as they hovered above what was now revealed to be the thorax of the archyx. From that vantage point, thankfully, they could see that there was more than enough room under the hard carapace for themselves *and* the archyx's folded inner wings. They just had to make sure they were in the right place when the huge bug decided to make its dive into the sea.

"Get down, onto the archyx's body," Sif instructed, coming to the same realization. "Hurry! It's flapping harder. We don't have long!"

The ground trembled again. The wings had increased speed to the point where they were almost impossible to see. The resulting downdraft was strong enough to knock any living thing off its feet. Fortunately, the dragons dug their talons into the thick skin of the archyx's thorax and crouched low. Worried about their valthan friend, Zeira fearfully scanned the area, but her mind was put at ease as she saw Nuri clutching the ground as best as she could. Gocri and Skellig had draped themselves over Nuri's body and were anchoring her in place as the massive bug became airborne.

Zeira spotted two objects rising out of the water and tried shouting a question to Skellig, but her words were ripped out of her mouth by the howling of the winds generated by the gigantic wings. Feeling silly, as she remembered she could switch her communication to the common mind-speech all dragons used, she sent her observation to Skellig, who immediately turned his head to stare at her. Zeira pointed west.

Look at the size of those pincers! One pincer alone is larger than all of us combined!

I am absolutely flabbergasted that something this size has gone unnoticed for so long, Skellig returned. *I'm sharing what I'm seeing with my Gathering. They claim I'm lucky. Seeing how I'm clinging to its back, about to be submerged into the sea, on a journey that will last for an unknown amount of time, I'd have to say I disagree.*

How far up do you think it will go? Sif asked.

Zeira glanced at their vaporous companion. Sifula had indicated that, for the duration of this excursion, she was going to reduce her form to something human-sized. As it turned out, Sif chose another dragon species Zeira hadn't heard of: a willow dragon. This one, Sif explained, was based on Terra, and resembled a tree with many low-hanging branches. In this manner, she could root herself in place on the archyx's thorax and wouldn't have to worry about being dislodged. In fact, she was currently helping Skellig and Gocri hold Nuri in place by wrapping several branches around their valthan friend and sending tendrils down, into the archyx's skin, wherever the branches made contact with the archyx.

You have a very useful ability, Sif. I am envious.

Don't be, Sif said, but she did give the Spark dragon a smile. *Your ability is formidable. I wish I could generate power at my wingtips like you can.*

We all have our strengths and weaknesses, Gocri said. *At the moment, I will say that I am experiencing one of my strongest weaknesses.*

And what would that be? Zeira wanted to know.

Loss of control. I don't like knowing my fate is in someone else's claws. Or … It's tipping over!

Not tipping over but tipping down! Zeira corrected. *This is it! We're headed for the water! Is everyone ready?*

As ready as we'll ever be. Jerica, where are you? Who's got you?

I do, Zeira confirmed. *I've got her in my right hand.*

Look out for her, Skellig warned. *Don't let anything happen to her.*

That's so sweet, Skellig! Jerica returned. *Thank you.*

If this doesn't go as planned, Gocri started, *then I'd like to say that it has been a real honor for me to accompany this team. I've never met nobler dragons than you. And Jerica, you will always have my eternal thanks.*

Don't get all sentimental on us, Skellig teased. *We are not dying on the back of some giant bug.*

Gocri grumbled. *Stay close. Deep breaths. We don't know if this thing is waterproof!*

The inner wings came to an abrupt stop and were immediately folded. The last thing anyone saw was the outer carapace slamming shut, moments before the archyx dove into the water, plunging them into a darkness so black that Zeira couldn't see her own claw in front of her face. After the impact and sudden deceleration, all but Sif managed to stay on their feet. With the absence of light — and noise — they all heard Sif's cry of alarm. Nuri's tail immediately wrapped around her. Having her long body anchored in place by Gocri and Skellig, Nuri kept coiling her tail.

Sif, are you well?

I am now, Gocri. Thank you, Nuri, for that swift intervention.

My pleasure. Now, could you change forms? Can you find something that generates its own light?

How about a vendiger, the larval form of a vantry moth, Gocri suggested. *It is often found in ice caverns. The light they can generate from their abdomens are quite bright.*

As was the case with most dragons, Zeira could say she had nocturnal vision. What it really meant was she, like most other dragons, had a parietal eye, commonly called a third eye. In situations where there was an absence of light, she could close her normal eyes and switch to her parietal eye, which would then allow her to pick up the tiniest flecks of light, illuminating far more than she would have thought possible. Back in her home of Blaze, she had never had to use her third eye before, but here, sitting among four other dragons—and one human—on the back of a titanic bug, with no light whatsoever, she decided to open her third eye for the first time. However, by the time she had made the decision to do just that, Sif had completed her transformation, and the bioluminescent properties of the vendiger went active.

She was seeing spots.

In the soft blue glow Sif's form was emitting, Zeira could see Skellig turn to her and cock his head.

"You've never used your nocturnal vision before?"

Zeira shrugged. "Never had a need for it, if you must know." A drop of water struck her face. Alarmed, she looked up at the archyx's sealed outer wings. "Well, that answers the question of whether it's waterproof."

"It's only a couple of drops," Gocri said, refusing to relinquish his hold on Nuri's upper half of her body. "It would seem our bug friend doesn't want to get his wings wet."

"Well, would you?" Skellig teased.

The coils holding Sif's form in place loosened. "Sif?" Nuri called.

The glowing head of the vendiger turned in the valthan's direction.

"I was all right holding you in dragon form, and even though I know it's still you, I find myself recoiling at the notion I'm holding on to a giant caterpillar. Do you need me to continue holding you?"

No, Sif's voice laughed. *What's the matter? Don't like bugs?*

"Not particularly," Nuri admitted.

Our present circumstances must render you catatonic, Gocri snorted.

"Ha, ha. Now, what are we going to do when the archyx encounters the gateway?"

"Nothing, I would imagine," Skellig answered.

"It already has," Nuri reported.

"Are you sure?" Zeira asked.

"I guess it's part of my echolocation. I have a highly refined sense of hearing, as well as touch. Besides, I felt the archyx jerk, as though it tripped over something. Since we're in the water, I can only assume it was just teleported several thousand miles away."

"We need to be ready," Gocri said. He turned to Skellig. "As soon as the wings open, we are leaping out. We'll continue to hold Nuri until we can verify we're still over water."

"Does anyone know how long we've been down here?" Jerica asked.

"Five, maybe ten minutes," Skellig answered.

"Ooo, it feels longer."

"Does it?" Zeira asked. She turned to the human. "Is everything all right? Are you well?"

"I, er, have to … you know."

"No, I don't," Zeira said.

"I have to visit the, er, water closet."

"What's a water closet?" Zeira asked, raising her voice.

"Don't go telling everyone!" Jerica squeaked. "It's embarrassing!"

"What is?" Zeira asked, completely confused. "I don't even know what we're talking about."

"She needs to pee," Skellig translated.

Zeira nodded. "Oh. You want to urinate?"

"Yes!"

"Personal ablutions are nothing to be embarrassed about."

"Stop talking about it, would you?"

"Why?"

"Because … it makes me want to go that much more!"

"Go? Where do you want to … oh. You're referring to this water closet place, aren't you? I don't think I'll ever understand humans. At any rate, I …I think you have your wish, Jerica. It feels as though we are rising."

Gocri grunted once. When Skellig turned to look, they both signaled their readiness. The trembling grew in intensity until it felt like the archyx knew they were there and was trying to dislodge them. Finally, after several minutes of shaking had passed, a crack of light appeared as the outer wings prepared to separate.

"Sif!" Zeira called. "Change to something with wings! Hurry!"

I'm on it!

The archyx's outer shell separated, revealing a bright blue sky peppered with small fluffy clouds. The delicate inner wings unfolded and slowly started to beat.

"That's our cue," Zeira decided. "Abandon bug! We need to clear out of here before the downdraft from those wings makes it impossible to fly!"

Gocri and Skellig, holding Nuri, took off first, followed by Zeira and Jerica, and then Sif, looking like a second Phoenix dragon. Striving to put as much distance as possible between themselves and the giant beetle, the group of six angled for the closest island and touched down, minutes later. They watched in silence as the archyx lifted itself from the surface of the water and flew away.

"We do know that thing is coming back, right?" Skellig asked, as he turned to Zeira.

"According to Zebulon, it will return here to feed in less than twelve hours."

"That should be enough time," Skellig decided. "Zeira, you have the pieces. Lead the way, would you?"

Zeira placed her claw over her chest and felt the two oron fragments tingle. Yes, the third piece was nearby! They just had to find it! Emboldened with their good fortune, Zeira flew in a lazy circle as she attempted to determine where the fire fragment was. As soon as her nose was pointing south, her chest grew warm.

"It's in that direction," she announced, pointing the way.

"Can you tell how far?" Sif asked.

"I'm sorry, no. I won't know we've gone far enough until we literally fly right past it."

"Has any of you ever been out here?" Jerica asked, from Zeira's back. "Skellig, didn't you say you've been everywhere?"

Skellig held up a claw. "I may have overembellished my travels a teensy bit. I do not recall ever seeing these sights before."

"Gocri," Jerica prompted. "How about you?"

"I have not, Miss Jerica."

"If you want to set me down now, I'll explore the sea," Nuri said.

Nodding, the two strongest flyers swooped low, over the sea, and at Nuri's signal, dropped her in. A few moments later, her head broke the surface of the water and immediately dipped down, vanishing from sight. Several seconds later, Nuri's head resurfaced, only it was nearly a mile away. In this manner, their water dragon friend mapped out the surrounding environment.

"Lots of brackish water here," Nuri reported. "Not surprising, as this is where the archyx appeared. Where the gateway is, or how deep it is, I don't know. Other than that, I don't see anything else out of the ordinary. Zeira, which direction are we going?"

"To the south."

"Next you'll tell me that we're looking for the volcano."

"Hmm? Why do you say that?"

"You don't smell the smoke?"

Zeira sniffed the air. "No, do you?"

"No, but I can taste the ash in the water."

That brought Zeira up short. There was supposed to be a djinn guarding the fire fragment. And, according to the seer, this was a foe beyond any of them. How, then, were they supposed to proceed?

Carefully, Skellig quietly told her, using mind-speech. *By being very careful. We will have to approach in stealth. If this demon senses our presence, then we are in for a very difficult time.*

With Nuri following her tastebuds, and Zeira following the pull from the other two oron pieces, they guided their group past islands, through channels, and into a large bay. Zeira knew, with a sinking feeling in her gut, that they were in the right place because there, in the distance, was a large plume of smoke. The column of ash rose thousands of feet into the sky before falling like snow to coat the surrounding landscape with a fine layer of soot.

The volcano itself towered over the bay, at over a mile and a half high. It had rivulets of lava streaming down all sides, to either collect and harden on land, creating misshapen formations as it pooled, or to send up additional lines of smoke as it met the sea.

What caught her attention wasn't the lava, or the smoke, or even the ash. Instead, her eyes had locked onto the huge, fiery figure leaning out of a jagged vent on the side of the mountain, as if it were an open castle window. The djinn was roughly humanoid in shape, but would not be mistaken for a human. The creature's arms were grossly misshapen, allowing the elbows to bend in obscene ways. The torso was elongated and heavily muscled, and it had two sets of curved horns protruding from its skull, one set much larger than the other, but all pointing straight up. All things considered, the djinn's appearance wasn't the worst part. What was?

It was wide awake and staring straight at them.

Chapter 15 — Third Task

"Why isn't it sleeping?" Jerica whispered, from Zeira's back. "I thought we were going to sneak right by it and find this oron piece without it even knowing!"

Zeira and the others were circling high over the bay, well out of range of the djinn, who would throw an occasional fireball at them if any of them ventured too close. Thankfully, Zeira got the impression that they were no more of a nuisance than an irritating fly attracted to a sweaty brow. She checked on her companions. No one was using mind-speech. No one was laughing, or joking. All of them, herself included, were watching the djinn as they passed overhead, wondering the same thing: how were they supposed to sneak by the djinn when it not only knew they were there, but was defending its place with fireballs?

Nuri had been instructed to keep her presence a secret, in case they could use that to their advantage. The volcano, it would seem, was directly linked to the djinn, seeing that whenever a fireball was thrown, the rivulets of lava pouring down the volcano would triple in size. Could they use that to their advantage?

"Any ideas?" Zeira softly asked. "He's not supposed to be awake."

Nor are you supposed to be here, Drakkaina. Be gone, while I'm still in a good mood.

Steeling herself, Zeira turned to look at the djinn, who had fixed its unsettling gaze upon her. Flaming red sockets, devoid of any eyes, glared evilly at her as the djinn waited to see what she would do. Perhaps she should tell the creature why they were there? Maybe it'd surprise them by being generous?

"We need the oron fragment," Zeira told the djinn. "I could explain what it is, but something tells me you're well aware of its existence."

I am, and no, you may not have it.

"Well, do *you* want it?" Zeira continued.

No.

"Do you need it for some reason?" Jerica wanted to know.

I thought I smelled humans. No, I do not.

"Can we negotiate?" Zeira asked, hopeful for a positive answer.

No.

"No?" Zeira said, growing desperate. "Why not?"

Because you want it.

"That's not an answer," Zeira insisted. "There must be something we can do in exchange for it. Please, it's important to us."

No. You're boring me.

"We can't leave until we get what we came for," Zeira insisted.

Then stay.

"Really?"

Stay and die.

"Such a sweet offer," Skellig said, coming to Zeira's aid, "but we'll have to decline your more than generous proposal."

The djinn finally stirred. It pulled itself out of the gaping hole on the side of the volcano, causing fresh streams of magma to trickle down the mountainside, which grew dark after only a few moments. Using its front arms, the djinn pulled itself up the mountain, pausing only when it reached the top. The djinn's entire body became visible, revealing that its lower half was represented by a tapering point from the waist down.

"It's not what I was expecting," Gocri admitted.

"That makes two of us," Skellig said, nodding.

You've been asked to leave, the djinn said, as it propped itself up on its two huge arms. *Stay and perish*.

With that, the djinn held out his right hand and a huge fireball flared to life. Testing the weight of the flaming orb, the djinn sighted Gocri just as he flew by and threw the fireball at him. This time, Zeira could tell the djinn was truly angry, because unlike before, this one covered the distance to its target with breathtaking speed. Gocri had to tuck his left wing and execute a very tight barrel roll in order to avoid being struck.

Roaring with anger as it realized the dragon hadn't been struck down, the djinn conjured two more fireballs and launched them directly afterwards.

"Separate!" Zeira told her companions. "Skellig, Gocri, we need to figure out what its weakness is. Sif, you're with me. Any ideas how to keep it distracted?"

Sif's form turned vaporous as she shifted into a different species.

"What are you now?" Zeira wanted to know. "I've never seen a dragon with three horns before."

"Two on the top of the skull, and one on the nose," Sif explained, as she spread her enlarged wings. "This is one of the few winged Terran dragons. It's heavily armored."

"Are you sure that's wise?" Zeira asked, as she took off after Sif. "I would think you'd want a form that's easy maneuverable, not …"

Sif deftly avoided two fireballs. Clearly, the vapor dragon had used that particular form before. Sticking close beside her, Zeira added her own aerial stunts in order to avoid the djinn's fireballs. The four of them zipped past their fiery adversary, creating the distractions needed to avoid being hit.

"Keep it up!" Skellig shouted.

His wing talons glowed and bolts of lightning lanced out to strike the djinn square on its chest, blowing it off balance. The volcano rumbled angrily as the djinn pulled itself upright once more. A series of fireballs sped after the Spark dragon, but couldn't match Skellig's twists and turns. The fireballs splashed down harmlessly into the sea.

The djinn roared angrily. Zeira could see that although they were staying safe, they were making no headway. Besides, did they even know where the third and final fragment had been hidden? Perhaps the djinn carried the piece with it at all times?

Just then, movement caught Zeira's attention. Far below her, skimming through the water, was their valthan companion, carrying Jerica. Zeira turned to watch as Gocri blasted the djinn with a powerful icy breath just moments after Sif zipped by. Her eyes dropped back to Nuri and Jerica. A notion had occurred, and it was one that could very well work.

Listen up, everyone! I … I know what we need to do.

* * *

"Are you sure this is a good idea?" Jerica asked, as she crouched low on Nuri's back.

"The plan is solid," Nuri said, nodding. She skirted a chain of small, heavily forested islands in her path and continued on her heading, throwing up huge waves in her wake. "Time is of the essence. We *must* find it."

"What if we don't?" Jerica asked, concerned.

"There are tribesmen aplenty. I saw them when I was investigating the area. It's one of their larger villages. It can't have simply walked away. Where is it …? I was cruising through this channel, when I … there it is! Jerica, there! Do you see them?"

Jerica rose to her feet and watched as they approached the shore. Dozens of fishing boats, of varying sizes, had been pulled up onto the beach. Fisherman were sorting their catch, manning stalls, and doing their best to entice the passing public to purchase a fish or two. It was a familiar scene to Jerica.

Screams and shouts assailed her ears as the two of them arrived on shore. Parents snatched up their children and fled. The fishermen, unwilling to abandon their catches, crouched fearfully behind their stalls. Within mere moments, activity on the beach came to a complete standstill.

"No, come back!" Jerica implored. "We need your help! This is an emergency."

"It's me," Nuri whispered. "I am the epitome of every sea-faring villager's worst nightmare. Perhaps I should return to the sea? Maybe then you could entice a villager to come out of hiding."

The yelling grew louder, as the occupants of the village marched their way to the shore. A dozen heavily armed soldiers, with drawn swords, appeared. They quickly surrounded Jerica, giving Nuri as wide a berth as they could.

A lone man, dressed in leather armor, rode up on horseback. One of the soldiers broke away from the others and approached. He bowed once before turning to point at Jerica.

"We caught them, sire. They were stopped before any carnage could befall us. What would you have us do with them? Dispatch them now?"

You couldn't, even if you tried, Nuri angrily said.

Jerica patted Nuri's foreleg before turning to the soldiers.

"Umm, hello. My name is Jerica, and this is Nuri. I ..."

"You introduce that monster as though it's your pet!" one soldier exclaimed.

Jerica placed a restraining hand on Nuri's abdomen and felt the growl emanating from within.

"As I said, this is Nuri, whom you can see is a valthan. She's ... that is to say, *I* am her kai."

Several soldiers gasped with surprise. The man with the leather armor dismounted and approached the two of them. Reverently, he dropped to one knee; the rest did the same.

"Honored kai, we had no idea you were here. Please forgive the rude welcome. I am Baron Hamish Zatek. Allow me to be the first to welcome you to our fair village of ...

Commander! There will not be any fighting here. Please have your men stand down."

Swords were sheathed as the soldiers were led away. Many cast furtive looks back at Nuri, as though she was the first dragon any of them had ever seen. What Jerica now took for granted would surely be the talk of the town for weeks to come. She turned to the head of the village and gave her best effort at a curtsy.

"Baron, please. We need your help."

"You have it," the baron instantly responded. "What can I do?"

Jerica held up her hands, as though she was looking at them for the first time. "I don't have a lot of time to explain this, so I'll give you the condensed version. It would seem I have a magical ability."

The baron nodded, encouraging her to continue. Jerica mentally rolled her eyes. Yes, she was a kai, and yes, she traveled with a dragon. Apparently, the idea of her having a magical ability was not that hard to believe.

"I can … *borrow* other abilities. My companions are back at the volcano, battling the djinn."

The baron's face became grim. "I have no love for that creature. Tell me what I can do."

"I need to physically touch one of your villagers and borrow their ability. The problem is, this talent would need to incorporate some type of throwing ability. Does that make sense?"

"So," the baron slowly began, "if we have a villager who could fling mud at someone, this would help you?"

"Yes! Do you have someone like that?"

"I'm sorry, I don't know. But, I will shortly. Come with me. Um, Nuri, is it? Will you be safe where you are? I'm sorry, I don't think we have the room for you to parade through town."

"I will be fine here. Listen to me, human. She is Jerica, and she is my kai. Should any harm befall her, I will personally sink every single one of the vessels you have here, and will pledge to destroy anything I see floating on the surface. Do we understand one another?"

The baron dropped to one knee. "You have my personal guarantee. No harm shall befall your rider, noble valthan. I promise."

Satisfied, Nuri turned to Jerica.

Watch yourself. I don't think this human will cause you any harm, but then again, I cannot speak for the villagers. Call if you need help.

I will. Thank you, Nuri.

Jerica hurried to catch up to the young baron, who was purposefully striding away from the beach and toward the many houses. All the residences here, Jerica could see, were single story lodgings, and almost perfectly round. The roofs were thatch, and many of them were in disrepair. In fact, she and the baron passed five different teams of people who were in the process of replacing the thatch and making repairs.

"What happened here?" Jerica quietly asked. "That is, if you don't mind me asking."

"A very uncharacteristic storm blew through last night," the baron answered, pausing only long enough to inspect one of the teams. "Usually, we don't see winds that high, but last night—I'm just thankful no one was hurt."

"What's the name of this village?"

The baron looked at her, surprised.

"You don't know?"

"My home village is very far away," Jerica admitted. "Cael. Have you heard of it?"

The baron shook his head. "I haven't, I'm sorry. But now I won't forget the name."

"It's a seaside village much the same as this one," Jerica continued, as she followed Baron Hamish up the steps of a large, two-story building. This one was square.

"Why isn't this building round?"

The baron turned to look at her with his hand on the doorknob. "That's easy. No one lives here. Well, I will admit there are times when it feels as though I do. Here we are. I will call for my Assemblors. By the way, you are in the village of Praen."

The baron pushed open the door and headed down the hallway on the left. Faced with two doors, he chose the one with the swordfish carved into the surface. Settling in behind his desk, he turned to an unobtrusive lever on the wall behind him and pulled it down. Almost immediately, they heard a single bell ring.

"Assemblors?" Jerica asked, as she sat in the closest chair.

"There are four, and each govern their own section of the village. North, south, east, west. Is this not the way with your village?"

Jerica shook her head. "There is a baron, but he doesn't have anyone he trusts. He does everything himself."

Baron Hamish snorted. "Sounds tedious. You said your village is named Cael?"

"Yes."

"How many people live there?"

"Oh, it's smaller than this. I'd say about five thousand."

"Ah. I'd still have at least two Assemblors."

"I will pass on your advice to our baron the next time I see him."

There was a knock on the door. Turning, Jerica saw three older men, and one young man with a bright red beard, standing in the hallway. One of the older men, clean-shaven, and holding a gray bowler hat in his hand, bowed low.

"You called for us, sire? How may we serve?"

"This is a visitor from Cael," Baron Hamish began. "She needs to …"

"From where, sire?" a second elderly gentleman asked.

The baron let out an exasperated sigh. "As I was saying, our new friend here has arrived with a valthan."

Two of the assemblors, including the younger fellow with the red beard, gasped with surprise.

"Oh, it gets better," the baron said, with a chuckle. "There are other dragons traveling with her. At the moment, they are engaging the djinn."

"Will that work?" Jerica heard one of the assemblors whisper to another. "Would a group of dragons be strong enough to successfully take on that djinn?"

"I wish I knew," the baron proclaimed. "Our new friend, the esteemed kai Jerica, has asked for our assistance."

"What can we do against a djinn?" one of the assemblors asked.

"What we can do is find an ability suitable for our kai," Baron Hamish answered.

Four blank faces stared back at the two of them.

"I'm a borrower," Jerica explained. "I can temporarily use the ability of whomever I touch. I need to find someone with the ability to throw."

"And that'll help you?" the bearded assemblor dubiously asked.

"It will. My dragon friends are engaging the djinn as we speak. The sooner we find someone with a suitable magical ability, the better."

"You heard her," the baron snapped. "Assemble the people. Everyone who has an ability will be asked. Go, now!"

The four assemblors nodded and hurried off.

"Thank you so much for your help," Jerica said. "Do you think we can find someone?"

"If that person exists, we'll find them," the baron vowed. "Besides, this is the perfect excuse to document the abilities we find. I've been trying to find an excuse to do just that for years. This is perfect, so you have my thanks for that."

"How long will it take?" Jerica nervously asked.

"The call for everyone to document their abilities will take a while to answer. But, what we *can* do is gather everyone in town. The majority of the population live within the city walls, so we should have some information for you very soon."

It took less than ten minutes for the village folk to be rounded up and questioned. One after the other, the townspeople stepped forward, described what they could do, and then waited while one of several scribes notated what was being reported. And sadly, one after the other, the villagers were all dismissed, having what the baron described as a low-power ability. When, after every villager had been interviewed, and it was apparent that no one had an ability that could be construed as useful, Jerica let out a heavy sigh and felt her hopes fall.

"I am so sorry," the baron apologized, for what had to be the fifth time. "I truly thought we could find someone that would be able to help you. Perhaps I could ... hmm."

Interested, Jerica looked up. "What is it? What do you see?"

Baron Hamish held up the latest list to be deposited on his desk. He flipped a few pages and then tapped an entry near the top. "This woman. Do you see what it says here? It says her occupation is to care for sick animals."

"How does that help us? The djinn isn't sick. It's perfectly healthy, I'm sorry to say."

The baron leaned forward at his desk, eager to share the information. "True, but look what was written for the description of her magic. It says here she generates a lullaby, which puts the animal to sleep."

That might work, Nuri said.

Jerica eagerly nodded. "I think that would work."

Baron Hamish pulled another lever. A different, lower-pitched bell rang twice. A young boy appeared at the baron's door. The town's leader reached for a piece of paper and hastily scribbled a note.

"Give this to Assemblor Devin from the North District. Tell him to fetch this woman and make haste here, to my office. Is that understood?"

The boy nodded and hurried off.

Baron Hamish sat back in his chair and fixed Jerica with a concerned gaze. "Can you tell me how your friends are holding up?"

Jerica closed her eyes. *Nuri, how is everyone doing?*

We're at a stalemate. The djinn has been unable to land a hit with any of its fireballs ...

Oh, that's such a relief!

... but, nothing anyone does seem to have any effect on the djinn. The djinn is only getting angrier and angrier.

I'm hurrying. They're locating the woman with the lullaby magic, and as soon as I touch her, I'll head back to shore.

Do hurry. I know our friends can handle themselves, but I don't want to risk anyone's safety by dallying too long.

The woman in question, a young housekeeper at a nearby inn, fidgeted nervously in front of the baron. She caught sight of Jerica and her gaze immediately dropped to the floor.

"There's no need to be afraid," the baron told her. "We

need an explanation of how your magic works."

"My magic?" the girl asked, in a voice so soft they almost couldn't hear her. "It's nothing, really."

"You tend sick animals, yet you work in an inn?" Jerica asked.

"I mostly care for the horses of the travelers who stay at the inn," the young woman answered.

"Tell me how it works," Jerica implored. "What can you do? Do you put the animals to sleep?"

"Most of the time," the girl admitted. "Some don't, but they do become more docile, making them easier to handle."

Baron Hamish looked at Jerica. "Will that do?"

Jerica nodded. "It will." She held out a hand. "I'm Jerica. What's your name?"

The girl hesitantly took the proffered hand. "Nardeen."

"Well, Nardeen, if this works as well as I think it will, I think you are going to need a raise."

The baron smiled. "Leave that to me. Now, how long does it take for you to borrow an ability? Does that mean Nardeen will be unable to use her magic?"

Jerica shook her head. "As far as I know, the person I borrow it from retains their magic."

Baron Hamish shook his head. "Then, you aren't a borrower, my dear kai. You are a *mimic*!"

"A mimic. Hmm, I'll have to think about that. A glancing touch is all I need to change my magic, so I know I have it now. Thank you both so much for your help. I won't ever forget it. Nuri, meet me at the piers."

Hear the screams? I'm already here, waiting for you.

Yelling and shouting *could* be heard. With the baron personally escorting her back to the water, he bowed in front of Nuri, who inclined her head, and then watched enviously as Jerica clambered onto the valthan's back. She waved at the awestruck spectators on the beach before Nuri turned around and sped off.

"Do you think this will work?" Nuri anxiously asked.

"It's not the magic I had hoped for, but something tells me that, if we all work together, this will still work."

"I've told Zeira about the lullaby to lure animals to sleep."

"Oh? What did she think?"

"She likes it just as much as her original plan, if not more," Nuri reported. The valthan sped around several small islands and veered east, toward the distant plume of smoke. "She and the others are hopeful that, along with you, we'll be able to put this foul creature back to sleep."

"And if we can't?" Jerica asked.

"Then … we'll find something else that will work. We're a formidable team, Jerica. We'll find a way."

Valthan and rider cruised into the bay and came to a halt. There was the volcano, still oozing lava, and there was the djinn, still sitting inside the crater at the top. A streak of yellow flew by, followed immediately by a bolt of lightning striking down, inside the volcano. The djinn roared with anger, but aside from being annoyed, showed no signs of being injured. Gocri followed next, flying in from the opposite direction. The djinn, about to unleash a barrage of fireballs at Skellig, paused as a thick layer of frost suddenly blanketed the side of the volcano.

The frost didn't actually touch the djinn, but from the way it was screeching, it was none too happy with the volcano receiving the brunt of Gocri's blast. Zeira suddenly flew by, overhead.

"You've noticed the relationship between the djinn and the volcano?"

"We have," Nuri confirmed. "Only, I don't know how that helps us."

"I think if we can put the djinn to sleep, then the volcano will more than likely go to sleep, too."

"And does anyone have any idea how to do that?" Skellig asked, as he zipped by overhead.

Jerica nodded. "As a matter of fact, I do. Here's what I think we should do."

Ten minutes later, after the plan had been explained to each of their group's six members, two of them eyed each other and then turned to give Jerica a withering glare.

"Now I *know* you're joking," Skellig said, bewildered.

"I fly alone," Gocri reiterated. "With the exception of you, Miss Jerica."

"Thanks, guys, I appreciate that, but not this time. You heard why it has to happen. I need the two of you to fly together."

"In physical contact with each other?" Gocri asked, appalled. "How are we supposed to do that? Our wings would interfere with each other. There's no way we could fly that close to one another."

Jerica smiled up at the two growling dragons towering over her. "Well, we're going to find out, aren't we? You are two of the most gifted, resourceful dragons I have ever met. If anyone could figure out how to pull this off, you are the ones to do it."

"She damns us with faint praise," Gocri scoffed. "Blast. Very well. Skellig, keep your left wing partially tucked, and I'll do the same for my right. Jerica, where will you sit?"

"Who's the better flyer?" Jerica asked.

"I am," Gocri declared.

"Me," Skellig said, at the same time.

Sif appeared before them. This time, her reptilian body was long, sinewy, and the wings were easily three times the size of the rest of her. Her coloring was dark brown, and her wings were so dark they almost looked black. Sif stretched her wings before folding them against her back.

"What form is that one?" Skellig wanted to know.

"Tangle. It's a type of plant dragon."

"Plant dragon?" Gocri snorted. "There are no such things."

Sif looked down at her. "This is the form I usually use when speed is of essence. Tangles are some of the speediest flyers. I use this form with permission."

Very well, Sif, Zeira's thought came. *You're backup. You are to watch Skellig and Gocri closely. If something happens, and Jerica is dislodged, then it'll be up to you to swoop in and save the day.*

Sif nodded. "It'll be my pleasure. So, what's the plan?"

Jerica motioned for Gocri to lift her to Skellig's neck. Gripping his scales tightly, she turned to Sif. "I'll show you. Gocri, grab Skellig's wings. Now, we have lightning and ice. I'm thinking we'll get a frozen lightning bolt."

Didn't you change your ability, too? Zeira asked. *What will your magic do to theirs?*

"I'll try to keep myself out of it. I've got a pretty good idea how to do it. All right, Skellig. Fire a blast of lightning at … that large rock over there."

Skellig shrugged, sighted the rock, and raised a wing talon. Moments later, a *white* bolt of lightning arced out and slammed into the rock, freezing it solid and blowing it up at the same time. Cold bits of gravel rained down on them as the rest of the group turned to give Skellig and Gocri an appreciative look.

"Nicely done!" Sif exclaimed.

"That wasn't what I was hoping it'd be," Jerica admitted. "Wait. Gocri, it's your turn. Let's see what happens."

The glacier dragon nodded, figuring he was going to be asked this sooner or later. He sighted what was left of the same rock and huffed out a cloud of his icy breath. However, what came out of him was not a white cloud but a yellow one.

"What's that going to do?" Jerica quietly asked.

Gocri stared at the cloud and shrugged. "I have no idea. It's a rather unsettling shade of yellow, isn't it?"

The cloud drifted over to the rock and everyone watched, mesmerized, as the stone frosted over, as though it now had a thin coating of snow. Moments later, electrical sparks flared into existence, showing the boulder was now electrified.

"So, it freezes first," Sif said, "then Skellig's electricity comes into play. Zeira, you're right! We can use that."

Skellig? Gocri? Are you ready?

Gocri growled. "Whatever happens here, *stays* here, is that understood?"

"What's the problem?" Jerica asked.

Gocri held up his own wing talon, which was now hooked through Skellig's. "Word of this must never reach anyone else."

"Agreed," Skellig glumly added.

The linked pair took off. They shuffled positions as they circled the bay, each trying to determine the best position for flying in such close proximity.

Watch out! Zeira warned. *The djinn knows something is up. It's holding a fireball in each hand and is ready to throw.*

I think it's time we tried this out, Gocri returned. *Skellig, we're going to make our first pass. Ready?*

Do it. I've got your back.

And I've got your front. Wait. That didn't come out right.

Zeira watched the pair flying in tandem, circling close, as close as they dared, to the djinn. As the first fireball was launched, both dragons deftly spun out of the way, but not before Gocri took a deep breath and exhaled at the exact moment they passed the djinn. The yellow cloud started to lazily drift about, until Sif flew close and snapped her wings together. As expected, the cloud flew straight toward the djinn, who saw it at the last moment and tried to clear it away. The cloud slammed into the djinn, who howled in indignation.

A split second later, everyone heard the distinctive crackle of electricity as the sparks formed and flared bright enough to be seen from hundreds of feet away. The djinn's mouth twisted into an O of sheer outrage as it shook its head.

It's stunned! Jerica happily reported. *Now, we have a great way to distract him.*

They hit the djinn with a few more electrified ice clouds. It screeched even louder, but took longer to shake off the shock each time.

Now is our chance! Fly close! Hurry! I'm going to try and put it to sleep!

Both dragons nodded and immediately swung around, readying themselves for another run. Jerica hurried across Skellig's wing and then up Gocri's. Nestling herself at the junction point of the great glacier dragon's wings, Jerica braced herself for this final onslaught.

The linked dragons angled straight for the djinn, who was shrugging off the effects of the last electrified frost cloud. It saw the three of them approaching and roared a defiant challenge.

This will not end the way you think it will. I will not give up my good luck Talisman. Ever!

Look! Zeira cried. *Look at the monster's right wrist!*

He's wearing the fire fragment on his arm! Jerica added. *At least we know where it is now!*

Be careful up there! Nuri cautioned. *I know you plan to knock the djinn out and make him sleep, but he's not like that yet. Watch out!*

Spark and Ice dragons increased their speed, until the winds were howling. Right at the last possible moment, Skellig fired off several blasts of his lightning power and then waited to see what would happen.

Two white bolts of pure energy snaked out from Skellig's wing talons and raced toward the djinn. The fire demon's glazed expression watched as the bolts careened by him and slammed into the side of the volcano.

"You missed," Gocri grunted, annoyed.

Skellig was taken aback. "I missed? I've never missed a shot in my life! Gocri, you had to have done something. You … you pulled me off course, didn't you?"

"I most certainly did not. Can I help it if your aim is subpar?"

"I'll show you subpar. Turn around. We're going for another shot."

"Is this wise?" Gocri asked. "The djinn is not only awake, but is watching us! He's going to know something is up."

Focus! Zeira announced. *Get a shot down his throat.*

Gocri nodded. *Freeze him solid from the inside out. I like it.*

What about my side of it? Skellig inquired. *What if my ability is responsible for waking it back up?*

That's why I'm going first, Jerica declared. *I'm going to try and put him to sleep. Then we can freeze him solid. Let's give this a try before I come to my senses.*

I say we make several passes as close as we can, Skellig said. *We'll distract it. Let it fire off shots at us. Then Jerica takes her turn.*

Zeira nodded. *Agreed.*

As soon as the djinn took the two blasts from the frost dragon's icy breath, and then got shocked senseless as the frost became electrified, Zeira and Sif took off. Leaning into the wind, the two unlikely companions flew — as one — directly to the top of the volcano, toward the smoking crater. Closing her eyes, Jerica imagined a calm and soothing melody. Would it work?

A melancholy tune started up, each note clear and powerful as the music grew in strength. This had to work!

Jerica noticed the djinn. Did it look like the fragment's guardian was teetering to the left? One of the djinn's hands slipped, and it crashed — hard — to the ground. After a few moments, it shakily lifted itself back to the rim of the volcano and angrily glared about.

It's working, Jerica! Skellig cried. *Keep it up! It's making him drowsy!*

How much longer? Jerica wanted to know. *I'm worried about you. I don't want anyone to get hurt.*

Tell that to Skellig, Gocri said, using his gravelly voice. *Perhaps I could give him a few pointers on actually hitting the target?*

Don't even insinuate you're a better shot than me, Skellig angrily began.

Unlike some of us, Gocri continued, *I've actually hit what I've been shooting at.*

Zeira, never one to enjoy an argument, was about to intervene when she sensed the mirth coming from their glacier friend. Gocri was teasing Skellig, even in the midst of a situation as serious and dire as this!

Hang on to my talon, Skellig instructed. *We're making another pass. You'll see just how good a shot I truly am.*

Go ahead, Gocri urged. *Impress me, Sparkles.*

Keep it up, IceChops. There. The djinn is facing us.

It's now or never, Gocri agreed.

Zeira watched as Skellig's right wing talon glowed blue. Energy crackled, and tiny strings of blue electricity were visible jumping around on his right wing. The two of them flew as close as they dared, just as the djinn spotted them and let out a deafening challenge. As the djinn's mouth opened, the two attacking dragons got the perfect opportunity to fire off a shot, and what a shot it was! A pure white bolt of lightning shot out of Skellig's talon and nailed the djinn directly in its mouth.

"You did it!" Jerica cried.

They heard the explosion, as the bolt detonated inside the djinn. Sadly, it didn't do any harm to the fragment's protector, only this time, it *did* render it unconscious. Then, in front of everyone's eyes, the djinn froze solid.

Skellig let out a victorious roar. "Nicely done, my friend."

"You made the shot," Gocri returned. "Excellent work."

Glacier and Spark dragon unhooked their wing talons. Skellig had a thought. "Wait. Zeira, you're immune to fire. Can you get in there and get the fragment?"

Zeira nodded. She approached the rim of the volcano and looked at the djinn, who was still gripping the side of the crater. Its eyes were closed, its head was down, and it looked like it was asleep. There, on its right wrist, was the fragment, now covered in a layer of white frost.

Any time now, Zeira, Skellig teased. *The sooner you get that fragment, the sooner Gocri can hit it with his breath. We'd like to see him frozen solid for the next several centuries, if you don't mind.*

The fragment looks like it's tied to the djinn's wrist.

Then untie it, Sif suggested. *Hurry!*

Zeira flew close and reached out with her left claw to grip the side of the crater, holding herself steady. With her free claw, she hooked a talon under the leather strap holding the fragment in place and gave it a quick jerk. The fragment went flying straight up and would have fallen into the crater, if Zeira hadn't caught it. Free of the djinn's cold body, the fragment quickly defrosted and began to emit a deep red glow. She held it up to show her friends.

I've got it!

That's great! Now, let's put that djinn to bed for a very long time!

Chapter 16 — Oron

"That wasn't too bad," Zeira decided, as they hurriedly flew off the archyx on the return trip. "What a strange life. Your food source is so far down into the sea that you have to fly to great heights, and then drop like a stone to get deep enough to feed."

"Don't forget about going through the portal," Jerica added.

"Right. All of that, and then go through the portal? Whatever. I'm just glad we're back."

"I'm just glad we're away from that djinn," Nuri said. "I don't like watching my friends do battle with a creature, and not being able to help."

"You did help," Skellig argued. "You kept Jerica safe until it was time to act. For that, you have my thanks."

"And mine," Gocri said. "Now, we have all three pieces of the oron stone. What now? How do we reassemble it?"

Zeira retrieved the two pieces she was holding. The green

earth fragment, along with the blue water fragment, glowed brightly as she reverently set them on the beach. Reaching under a second loose scale, she retrieved the prized fire fragment and placed it next to the other two pieces.

"Now what?" Jerica wanted to know. "What's the completed stone supposed to look like?"

"You have the smallest hands," Zeira pointed out, as she turned to Jerica. "Perhaps you'd like to try and reassemble it?"

"Me? I don't have any idea what it's supposed to look like."

"Then, that'd make two of us," Zeira informed her. She looked around the group. "Does anyone have any ideas?"

Sif nodded. "I enjoy puzzles. I can give it a try."

"You're too big," Skellig pointed out.

Sif's sleek willow dragon form turned smoky and shrunk down. Moments later, Jerica's twin was back and was studying the stones. After a few moments of scrutinizing the earth fragment this way and that, and then doing the same for the water piece, she started pressing the two pieces together. Unsatisfied with how they looked, she'd reverse one piece and try again, only to have the same luck. Try as she might, though, no matter how the two stones were held together, she couldn't find an exact match.

"Of all the things I *thought* we'd have a problem with," Zeira sighed, "this was nowhere on the list."

"There's only three pieces," Jerica pointed out. "How hard could it be?"

Sif slid the three fragments over to her. "Be my guest. I will admit that I am stymied. None of the three look as though they belong together. Could we have, perhaps, picked up the wrong set?"

"What do you mean?" Skellig wanted to know. He then pointed at the fragments. "Look. There are three different colors, which means we have all three: earth, water, and fire. How could we have messed that up?"

"What if …" Nuri began, "what if each oron stone generates its own unique set of fragments? What if the water fragment, for example, came off a completely separate oron stone than the earth and fire pieces?"

Gocri groaned. "I see where she's going with this. I hadn't even considered that option."

Jerica approached and dropped into a sitting position. "I thought there was only one of these stones left. Isn't that what we were told? So, if that's true, and I'm inclined to believe it, then that means these three are from the same stone. Therefore, they should fit together. One last obstacle, I suppose."

"And you're doing great," Zeira praised, taking several steps backward, as did the other dragons.

Jerica looked up. "Oh, sure. Why not? I guess it's up to me now, is it?"

The dragons fell silent as they watched her work. She selected two at random, the water and fire pieces, and studied their shapes. Nothing was recognizable, and no matter how she held the stones next to each other, there were no indications she was on the right path. Growing frustrated, she returned the two fragments to the sand and picked up the green earth piece and turned the fragment over and over in her hands. Without realizing it, her eyes closed and she pictured her home village of Cael. Visions of her father, and her two older sisters flashed through her mind, causing her to smile. She let out a sigh and hefted the stone. There was no indication of how this piece was supposed to attach to one of the other fragments. It was almost as if … as if … Jerica's eyes widened. It was almost as if the fragments weren't showing their true shapes!

"What is it?" Zeira wanted to know. "You've figured something out?"

Jerica held up the earth fragment. "I think there might be some type of enchantment on this piece. Somehow, and I don't know how, it's masking the true shape of the oron fragment."

Zeira settled on the beach, next to Jerica. "An interesting notion. How do we test it? If you're right, how do we nullify it?"

Jerica shrugged. "I was hoping by getting all three pieces together that the enchantment would be broken. I don't see anything different, so … wait. Did you see that?"

All five dragons crowded as close as they could.

"What did you see?" Nuri asked.

Jerica was on her feet, waving the pieces around. "Look! Look what happens when I hold this blue piece next to the green piece, like this."

Zeira blinked as she watched the glow fade from the stones. "It's no longer glowing. That's significant, isn't it?"

"Perhaps it means you're holding the stones in exactly the formation it needs to be in?" Gocri suggested.

"Try the third," Sif encouraged. "Here, hand me those two. I'll keep them from moving while you try placing the third."

Jerica nodded, and passed the two stones over to Sif. The glow briefly returned, but faded as the stones were returned to the correct orientation. Jerica leaned around Sif's body and held the fire fragment in a variety of different poses. Growing exasperated, she held the smallest side, what she thought of as the tail end, next to a depression in the fire piece, and just like that, the red glow faded. After a few moments, the stones fused together and with a bright flash of light, Jerica was suddenly holding what looked like a glass ball filled with swirling smoke. It was shiny, dense, and about the size of her head. Realizing her arms were tiring, she lowered the sphere to the ground and gazed at it.

"There you go. That must be the oron stone."

Skellig lowered his head for a cursory sniff. "Excellent. Well, how do we use it? Better yet, *who* is going to be the first to use it?"

"Remember what the old human said," Gocri said. "We're only allowed to use the stone once."

"That means," Zeira slowly began, "we need to be extremely certain we're asking the right question. There can be no room for mistakes, so it has to be phrased *just right*."

Gocri nodded. "Agreed. After you, Zeira. This is your quest."

Zeira took a deep breath and, before she could talk herself out of it, plucked the sphere from the ground. Holding the mystical stone on the palm of her hand, Zeira took several calming breaths and then decided she didn't know what else to do but address the stone as though it was capable of listening.

"I am Zeira, of the Phoenix caste of Fire, from Blaze. I seek a way to victoriously confront the Thunder King and his Rastan Spear and defeat him, so as to prevent the mineral jhorium from being depleted. If there's something we need to do, or to acquire, then I ask that you reveal it to me now."

The stone grew warm in her hand. She looked at the orb and saw that it was glowing. Then, inexplicably, it felt like her gaze was drawn *into* the sphere. Bright lights and swirling colors danced before her vision. Unsure of where she was, or what she was supposed to do, Zeira decided to turn around and fly away, only she was shocked to discover that she didn't seem to have a body. All she could do was sit back and watch the scene unfold in front of her.

The swirling colors lessened. An image materialized and began playing out in front of her. It was of a human male, and he was holding a long, metal lance (the spear?). The human muttered something and angrily began pacing around the room he was in. Not watching what, or where, he was doing or going, he clipped the side of a desk. Zeira watched the human dance about, holding his knee, before he pulled his sword and angrily hacked the desk into tiny pieces. Mollified, the human returned to pacing.

"I have no idea what I'm looking at," Zeira confessed, unsure if anyone could hear her. "If I were to guess, I'd say I'm looking at the Thunder King. Yes, I can see the spear. That's the Rastan Spear?"

The image remained. Apparently, she had not yet guessed whatever the oron stone was trying to show her.

"Let's try it this way. I'm fairly certain *that* is the Thunder King, and he has the Rastan Spear, which we already knew about. Obviously, this weapon has special abilities, one of which will lead him to jhorium? So, if that's what he wants, then why does he look so angry? I would have thought he'd be in a great mood. After all, isn't he winning? This scene … it makes me think something isn't right, and he's furious about it. Or frustrated, I guess. I just wish I knew why.

"You're not going to tell me, are you? Fine. If you wanted me to see that the Thunder King has the spear and he's not happy about something, what am I supposed to do about it? How do we fight him? What can we use to counter this spear? Whatever it is, please show me. We need the help."

The swirling colors returned, and completely blotted out the image. After a few moments, the whirls faded away, revealing a second scene. This time, the image settled on an empty stone chamber, except for a single dais set in the center of the room. Sitting on the pedestal was a gray goblet with a ring of runes etched around the base. On the stem of the goblet was a knop, similar to those found on chalices, embedded with a single emerald.

"It's a cup," Zeira said to the open room.

Unsurprisingly, there was no response.

"So, you're showing me this cup, I have to assume it can negate the effects of the spear? Or perhaps generate its own magic so that we're on even ground? This is good. I can work with this. Show me where to find this cup."

The scene remained locked on the image of the goblet.

"You don't know where it is? Then why show it to me?"

This time, the scene changed. Slightly. Two men became visible. One reached for the cup and took a sip from it. The first man then looked at the second man and gave him an order. The second man promptly sat on the ground. The first man then pointed to a different corner. The sitting man rose to his feet and immediately moved to where he had been ordered. Then, both men left the room, leaving it exactly how it had started, with the single cup sitting alone, on the dais.

"The cup ... it allows the person who drinks from it to command others?"

Several swirls of color appeared, and just as quickly, disappeared.

"I'll take that as a yes. All right, we're making progress. This cup, how do I find it?"

The image remained unchanged.

"Wait. You're unable to show me because ... well, because it hasn't been made yet, is that it? What's it made of?"

For the first time since closing her eyes, Zeira felt another ... presence. The oron stone? Was it capable of thought? Why would she now feel like it was laughing at her?

And then the answer came to her. She knew exactly what the cup had to be made of. That's why it was gray. She groaned. This wasn't going to be easy.

The image fuzzed out, leaving Zeira in pitch darkness. Then, after a few minutes had passed and nothing else appeared, she hesitantly opened her eyes. There were her friends and companions, looking worriedly at her.

"Well?" Skellig demanded. "Did you see anything? Although, I don't know how, since you barely had your eyes closed."

"Barely had my eyes closed?" Zeira repeated, surprised. "I had them closed for at least ten minutes."

"No, you didn't," Gocri argued. "I can confirm what Skellig said: you took the stone, your eyes closed, and then a few seconds later, they opened."

"I don't know how to explain it," Zeira said, shrugging. "Time must pass at different speeds there. That's the only thing I can suggest."

Sif nodded eagerly. "So, something happened? Did you see anything?"

Zeira nodded. "I saw two images, two visions. First, I saw a human male, pacing angrily around a room. He was holding what I'm guessing was the Rastan Spear."

"You saw the Thunder King?" Jerica exclaimed, impressed. "How did he look?"

"Angry," Zeira answered. "He may have had the spear, and he may be winning this war, but there's something going on that is making him unhappy."

"And the second vision?" Jerica prompted. "What did it show you?"

"A cup."

That got the attention of everyone present. Being the only person to ever use one, Jerica cleared her throat.

"What did it look like? Can you describe it?"

Zeira shrugged. "The top part flared open, to hold a liquid of some sort. The bottom was wider still, so that it didn't tip over once it was set down."

Jerica giggled. "That doesn't help much. What I meant was, what was it made of? Were there any markings on it? Do we know what it does?"

Zeira nodded. "I thought the cup might have been made from iron, or maybe silver, but the longer I looked at it, the more I realized that it was neither of those metals." She then held up a claw and made a circular motion. "I should also mention, before I forget, that around the base part I saw some markings. Runes, I think, only I couldn't understand them."

"This is encouraging," Skellig decided. "What did you ask it? For a way to defeat this Thunder King?"

"That's *exactly* what I wanted to know. I figured that, if this was my only chance to ask a question, then I was going to get it right. I specifically said I wanted to be able to confront the Thunder King, with that spear, and be able to defeat him, to stop the theft of jhorium from Andela."

"Nice question," Gocri praised. "I think you may have saved us all from having to ask the stone for advice. Wait, do you know what this cup will do?"

"I wondered that very thing. The stone expanded the second vision, and two humans appeared. One drank from the cup, and then appeared to be able to command the other to do his bidding."

The dragons fell silent as they considered this news.

"That would be perfect," Skellig said. "If we get in front of this Thunder King, with that cup, we can make him put all the jhorium back and rescind his ways."

"I wonder if the effects are permanent or if they'll wear off over time?" Nuri said.

Sif nodded. "When we get the cup, we'll have to make sure we do some experimenting, so that we understand everything it can do."

Gocri nodded. "Seconded. Zeira, where do we find this cup?"

Zeira's face fell. "That's the problem, everyone. The cup doesn't exist."

"It doesn't exist?" Skellig scoffed, as he growled with anger. "Why show us the blasted thing if we cannot … wait. It doesn't exist? But, clearly it can. We have to make it, don't we?"

"Or else find someone who can," Zeira said.

Nuri pointed at the oron stone, sitting on the ground next to Zeira. "If you hand me that, I'll personally find out who can make it."

Surprised, Zeira looked down at the seeing stone and almost burst out laughing. Of course! Why hadn't she thought of that? The oron indicated what had to be used against the Thunder King. Someone else could then ask who was capable of making it.

Zeira gently plucked the stone from the ground and passed it to Nuri, who took it in one of her small hands. Hefting the thing as though it was a weapon to be thrown, Nuri looked at Zeira and gave her a questioning glance.

"Is there anything I should know before I do this?"

Zeira nodded. "You'll immediately get the sensation of feeling like your body is missing. Don't panic. Make sure you are as concise as possible when you formulate your question. Once you do, you'll be presented with an image. Allow the vision to play out. It should show you what you want to know. Now, I don't know if it'll do it in one vision, or maybe two. Possibly more. It's up to you to determine what you're looking at. Does that make sense?"

"You've come a long way since we first met," Nuri said, as she smiled at Zeira. She gazed at the seeing stone and lowered herself so that she was resting her entire body on the ground. "Here we go."

Zeira watched the valthan's eyes close and started to wonder what vision the stone would show her when, inexplicably, Nuri's eyes opened and she rose from the ground.

"That was exhilarating!"

Zeira turned to Gocri. "That's what you meant, wasn't it? That's why you thought nothing could have happened, since our eyes were only closed for a few seconds?"

Gocri nodded. "Correct. Nuri, have you an answer?"

Nuri nodded. "I do. I know where we need to go, but I have no idea how to find it."

"Are we looking for someone?" Zeira hopefully asked.

The valthan nodded. "Aye, a human. A human male."

The dragons turned to Jerica, who shrugged. "It's probably a mage. They're the ones who perform magic and can make enchanted weapons. It makes sense."

"How many mages are there?" Sif wanted to know.

Jerica sighed. "In my village, there's just the one: Doolan. He's old, creepy, and has an unhealthy fascination for young girls."

Zeira growled. "He eats them? Remind me to pay him a visit."

"No," Jerica laughed, "he doesn't eat them. He … you know what? Maybe it isn't such a bad idea if you pay him a visit."

"We all should," Skellig vowed. He turned to Nuri. "Describe what you saw. Maybe one of us has seen it before."

"Water," Nuri responded. "From the north. I saw the ice fields."

Gocri perked up. "Was the ice mostly white, or did it look light blue?"

"White," Nuri answered.

"East," Gocri said, nodding. "There's something in the water in the west which causes the ice to have a slight bluish hue to it."

"We're headed northeast," Skellig said, pleased. "We're making progress! Nuri, what else? What about this human?"

Nuri shook her head. "I don't have much experience with humans. Let me think. Older than Jerica. He was male, with white hair."

"Most mages are old," Jerica said, shaking her head. "That's not too surprising. Anything else?"

"He was coming out of a building. Other humans were there, but he paid them no heed."

"What about the building?" Zeira asked. "Perhaps one of us has flown over it at some point in our lives?"

Nuri traced a large triangle with her claw. "The top was golden, and came to a point. It …"

"Was the mage's hair stringy?" Jerica interrupted. "Was he wearing blue robes, with a dirty white hat?"

Nuri nodded. "The tip was bent over, like … you know who we seek?"

"Why, oh why, did it have to be *him*?" Jerica groaned.

Zeira lowered her head so that it was resting next to her human companion. "You're talking about your village's mage, aren't you? The one you aren't fond of?"

"Doolan," Jerica sighed. "Guys, we have to go to my home. We're going to Cael."

"Do you think we can find any jhorium there?" Zeira asked.

"Why would we need that?" Skellig wondered.

Zeira sighed. "Did I forget to mention that part? This cup … it needs to be made from jhorium."

TO BE CONTINUED

in

STRIKE THE SPARK
(DRAGONS OF ANDELA #2)

Author's Note

This one took way too long. LOL What was supposed to be a simple new fantasy series, which I should've been able to write in about two months, took twelve times longer. Two years. (sigh) There's more to creating a world than simply writing a story. At least, for me, it is. On top of which, I was a good 40,000 words in when I decided I didn't like the direction the story was going and, for the first time ever, scrapped what I had been working on and started fresh. But … I'm glad I did.

Next in the series is Strike the Spark. This story will be told from Skellig's point of view, whereas the previous was Zeira. So, now that the world has been created, and the characters all have their backstories in place, it should be a lot easier to write.

And finally, I'm going to be returning to Lentari, for ToL10. A villain from the past is threatening the future, and it's up to everyone's favorite husband and wife team, Steve and Sarah, to set things straight. Oh, I should also mention the Ancients are involved, and there may be a wager or two.

Finally, I'd like to say thanks. Thanks for giving one of my books a chance. I know there are many to choose from, so thank you from the bottom of my heart. Like the book? Didn't like it? Please don't hesitate to leave a (hopefully good) review wherever you purchased it. Those reviews make it easier for my books to be found by prospective readers!

Don't want to miss a new release? Want a chance to name a fictional character? You can sign up for my newsletter, located on my website: www.AuthorJMPoole.com. Until next time!

J.
July, 2021

Fan Submissions

Thanks to the help of some fans & readers, several characters in this book have some unique names! The following names were used:

Vanze — Vance Schollmeyer
Skellig — Kate Craven
Doolan — Elizabeth Davis
Gocri — Robert Allen Chalk
Zeira — Caryl Nantze
Akainu, Dym — Andrew Dyer
Sifula, Hamish — Carol Minot
Nuri — Nicki Jones
Myrdaynth — Justin Morgan
Darazok Aeogan — Kimberley Richardson
Brenin Draig — Claire Jones
Zebulon — Jennifer Salmon
Aldebrand — Mechelle Salyers
Konungr — Yuliya Mulvaney
Brakkis — Justin Morgan
Ligeia — Julie Granger

About The Author

Jeffrey M. Poole is a professional writer who writes in both the fantasy and mystery genres. His series are listed below. Jeffrey lives in picturesque Southern Oregon, with his wife, Giliane, and their Welsh Corgi, Kinsey. His interests include archery, astronomy, archaeology, scuba diving, collecting movies, collecting swords, and tinkering with any electronic gadget he can get his hands on.

He is a member of SFWA, the Science Fiction & Fantasy Writers of America, and Mystery Writers of America. Jeffrey encourages readers to connect with him on Facebook (facebook.com/bakkianchronicles). Fans can also follow him online at: www.AuthorJMPoole.com and sign up for his newsletter there.

BOOKS BY JEFFREY POOLE

Epic Fantasy
BAKKIAN CHRONICLES
The Prophecy
Insurrection
Amulet of Aria
Disneyland Debacle (short story)
Winter Wonderland (short story)

TALES OF LENTARI
Lost City
Something Wyverian This Way Comes
A Portal for Your Thoughts
Thoughts for A Portal
Wizard in the Woods
Close Encounters of the Magical Kind
The Hunt for Red Oskorlisk (short story)
May the Fang Be With You (Pirates trilogy #1)
The Hammer is Strong with This One (Pirates #2)
These are Not the Stones You're Looking For (Pirates #3)
Blast from the Past

DRAGONS OF ANDELA
Harness the Fire
Strike the Spark
Crash the Thunder

Mystery
CORGI CASE FILES
Case of the One-Eyed Tiger
Case of the Fleet-Footed Mummy
Case of the Holiday Hijinks
Case of the Pilfered Pooches
Case of the Muffin Murders
Case of the Chatty Roadrunner
Case of the Highland House Haunting
Case of the Ostentatious Otters
Case of the Dysfunctional Daredevils
Case of the Abandoned Bones
Case of the Great Cranberry Caper
Case of the Shady Shamrock
Case of the Ragin' Cajun
Case of the Missing Marine
Case of the Stuttering Parrot
Case of the Rusty Sword
Case of the Secret Staircase (short story)
Case of the Unlucky Emperor
Case of the Ice Cream Crime
Case of the Hobbit Heist